P9-DTP-875

THE SECOND SAINT OMNIBUS

BACK AGAIN in an exciting series of rousing adventures is Simon Templar, the Robin Hood of modern crime who also answers to the *nom de guerre,* the Saint. Pirate or philanthropist as the occasion demands, sportsman, master linguist, connoisseur of the best in food, drink, and women, Templar is at home in any situation, his mere presence usually signifying the imminence of murder, mayhem, or dangerous intrigue.

One of the best-known figures in detective fiction since Sherlock Holmes, but less often on the side of the law, this buccaneer in a dinner jacket meets all problems with ingenious cunning and a strong sense of humor, customarily managing to extricate himself unscathed and with some degree of personal profit.

For this volume, Leslie Charteris has hand-picked three novelettes and seven short stories from those hazardous diversions of the Saint which have been recorded since the publication of the first such collection in 1941, and he introduces each with colorfully appropriate comments. Herein, the debonaire Templar variously visits the High Sierras to fish for trout and New Orleans to steal pearls. He matches wits and prowess with bandits in Mexico, boxers in Manhattan, and a mad scientist in Miami. There are thrilling episodes involving saboteurs in Texas, and the Broadway theater crowd; a Hollywood philatelist, and a Palm Springs playboy; and, of course, a never-ending parade of sensationally beautiful women.

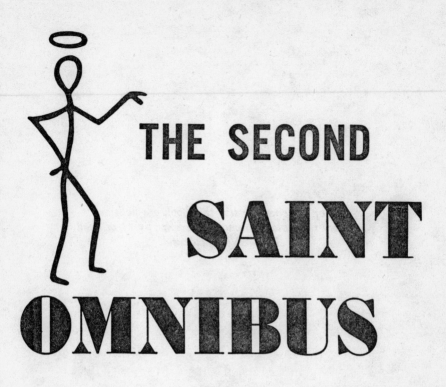

THE SECOND
SAINT
OMNIBUS

BY LESLIE CHARTERIS

DOUBLEDAY & COMPANY, INC.   GARDEN CITY, NEW YORK

*All of the characters in this book are fictitious
and any resemblance to actual persons, living or dead,
is purely coincidental.*

CONTENTS

FOREWORD

SOME TWELVE YEARS AGO my publishers, who even then had perceived the onset of that creeping laziness whose final perfection has filled my present life with so much magnificently unproductive spare time, suggested that if I had no immediate plans for a new book I might at least compile them an Omnibus, or sampler, of Saint stories, culled from the output of hungrier and more energetic years. It was their belief that this rehash, thus disguised, could be unloaded on an unsuspecting public almost as easily as a new dish. And just to show you how true the saying is that the wicked shall not prosper, they were perfectly right.

Whether the frustrated indignation of the deluded purchasers contributed materially to the outbreak of World War II, which followed almost immediately, is something which other historians will have to determine.

Anyway, being a man with a highly prehensile approach to any idea for making money without working, my major contribution to the scheme was to instantly change the proposed title from *The Saint Omnibus* to *The First Saint Omnibus*. This was a perfectly true title—it *was* the first Saint Omnibus—and it committed us to nothing; but, if this barefaced swindle paid off, it cagily left a highway paved to a repeat performance. We were all set, theoretically, not merely for *The Second*, but even for *The Twenty-Second Saint Omnibus*.

Well, at least that potential horror still remains far in the problematical future. This is only *The Second Saint Omnibus*; and it was hard enough to get to that.

One of the difficulties about doing an anthology of your own writings is that you have to have an adequate number of writings to compile the anthology from. This means that between omnibuses you still have to work—an operation to which, as I was saying, I am acutely allergic.

The last story in *The First Saint Omnibus* was taken from a book called *Follow the Saint*, which was published about a year earlier, and which completed about a score of volumes devoted to this character, which had provided me with a fair slice of bread and butter, and even jam, over the preceding decade. But in the twelve years since then, my bibliography shows only eight new Saint books added to the list.

It hardly takes an electronic computer to figure out that this reveals a shrinkage of more than 65% in the creative zeal of your favorite adventure writer.

Moreover, out of these mere eight books, three were full-length novels—a high percentage for me. And while a complete novel, slipped into a tombstone volume such as this, certainly contributes valuable weight to the satisfaction of those who buy their literature by the pound, it doesn't exactly provide the anthologist with a garden from which to pluck a few well-chosen flowers. It has to go in as a lump, or give nothing.

A meager five books, then, were all I was left with from which to winnow a representative cross-section of the Saint's progress since *The First Saint Omnibus* till now.

The only thing that made this possible was the fact that while my output was declining, the cost of all commodities and their fabrication was going up, so that the simple cost of the paper and printing and binding of a book like this, even ignoring the claims of the genius who supplies the words, obliges any publisher who wants to remain solvent to charge much more for much less. Just like it has happened to everything else you buy.

So this is a smaller, more modern, inflation-sized omnibus, for which you have certainly had to pay more than you did for the fat, antiquated, pre-World-War-II, prosperity omnibus—if you were ever honest enough to buy either of them, which I doubt. You probably got the last one from a lending library, and this one too, and even at those bargain prices you probably still haven't paid your bill.

I know you.

An English newspaper recently paid me the dubious compliment of surmising that the Saint must have made me a millionaire. The writer of the article, I imagine, was sheltered as a child from the brutal facts of income tax and the thriftiness of the reading public.

Don't get me wrong.

I am reading public myself. That is, I read a few books every year. Not so many as I should, I guess; but as many as I have time for. The business of living takes up too much of my time, and I enjoy it more than the vicarious thrills of fiction.

And when I read, I am just as callous about hungry writers as you are. I, too, rent books from libraries. Or borrow them from friends, if I can.

In spite of these reprehensible economies, quite a few writers have succeeded in making a fair living; and you have been kind enough to let me be one of them.

What the public never seems to have cared about is that, no matter how well he sells, a writer is stuck with one of the most underprivileged professions of modern times; and I am in a mood to take this opportunity of putting my gripe on record.

Let a man build up any other kind of business, and any stock, good will, or other interest pertaining to it that he does not sell, hypothecate, or give away is his perpetual property, which he may leave to his heirs and which they in turn may leave to their heirs, or which if they choose they may sell at a price commensurate with the fact that the buyer is acquiring a permanent asset. And since the idea of personal property was first conceived, this has always seemed an obviously right and just arrangement, except to Communists.

But let a man devote his life to the production of literature, and the laws of copyright give him no such lasting protection. The British law allows the private ownership of his creation to continue for fifty years after his death; the American law respects his ownership for only twenty-eight years, renewable for another fourteen years, after the date of copyrighting; other countries are even worse. But universally it appears to be thought entirely right that after a very limited time the fruit of a writer's brain should be taken from him or his heirs or assigns and thrown into a thing called the "public domain"—an almost Communistic concept in itself. This means, simply, that after the expiration of the copyright in a book, printers may still earn money for printing it, publishers may make money by publishing it, and booksellers may sell it for a profit; but there is held to be no further obligation upon anyone to pay a single penny for the use of the original intellectual material which they are dealing in.

For this fantastic discrimination I have to hold you, the public, responsible. Writers, themselves, will never be a sufficiently large class to attract the benevolent interest of a politician. And this politician, whom you elect, knows very well that he will never lose any of your votes for continuing to ignore such a well-established injustice against an insignificant minority of rogues and vagabonds, which everybody knows writers are, anyway.

Your apathy, and nothing else, permits this to continue. So you may understand why we are sometimes a little cynical about your applause. Of course your applause is music to us while it lasts, and we like the coins you toss us. We like eating, too. But we know also that when the lights go out we were only the clowns who entertained you for a few hours.

In the front of *The First Saint Omnibus* I wrote:

I have been trying to make a picture of a man. Changing, yes. Developing, I hope. Fantastic, improbable—perhaps. Quite worthless, quite irritating, if you feel that way. Or a slightly cockeyed ideal, if you feel

*differently. It doesn't matter so much, so long as you feel that you would
recognise him if you met him tomorrow.*

What has happened in the twelve years since then?

For more than half of them, there was a world at war. And since then
there has been little peace.

It may seem strange to say that such a turbulent character as the Saint
was a product of peace, or relative peace. But this is true. In approximate
peace, it may be that mankind stagnates. The daily round, the common task,
do not necessarily furnish all we need to ask. The daring and ebullience of
the spirit of man can only be exercised against conflict. A spring has no
power until it is compressed. Thus, in an era of dull peace and routine
normalcy, a man like the Saint must look for trouble; and the readers who
find their escape through him must feel the same need for stimulation.

For many years we have had too little of this need. The morning newspaper is more exciting and alarming than any fiction. A news broadcast can
scare you more than any radio drama. And even the dragons are mechanized.
Don Quijote could tilt at windmills: he can hardly tilt at tanks.

Man the individual can only enjoy satisfying combat with an individual
foe. The thief, the swindler, the usurer, the narcotic peddler, the corrupt
official, the tyrant—these were villains that everyone could visualize and
hate in a simple automatic way. Basically they could be personified as indi-
viduals, even though they might control henchmen or hatchet men or even
small gangs. They were human, and vulnerable, and the reader could enjoy
the satisfaction of smiting them down, through the Saint; and when they
were dead, or at least jailed, they were done for, and a racket had been disposed of, and something final had been accomplished, and everybody could
sit back with a sigh of relief and feel that the world was a better place.

But then along came a magnetic madman with a Charlie Chaplin mustache, and all that was changed. When the Nazi machine rolled, all individual robbers and murderers seemed insignificant. Then at once it became
ridiculous for such a highly publicized paladin as the Saint to be battling
rats, when a real full-grown dragon was ravaging Europe.

Yet he could not do the same things to the dragon that he used to do to
the rats. He could only nibble at it. Oh, yes, I could turn his attention to
spies and saboteurs, fifth columnists and traitors; but there was a very short
limit to the number of those stories I could write without seeming repetitive,
first of all to myself. And never could there be the complete catharsis of
the old formula—the villain defeated, the crime foiled or avenged, and the
sun shining again, all through the cleverness and courage of one crusader
with whom a reader might identify himself.

No personal St George slew that dragon. It cost the blood and agony of millions, and brought forth heroisms that made everything I ever wrote about the Saint seem childish. But it lacked the flamboyant personal drama that the Saint stood for, and that could give the sense of personal fulfillment by proxy which I think appealed most to the Saint's public.

It shows a fine social conscience to take your place as a cog in the machine, to be a bee in the hive, to be a good member of the team—and all the other platitudes. But Man the individual still sees the universe revolving around his own personal head; and when he dies, the world ends—for him. He can be as selfless as you like, but his instinct cries for the one triumphant moment that is his alone. To be one of the million ants that dragged down the dragon is a noble thing, you have been taught to think, and you accept it; but it is not the same as being St George in your own shining armor, with your foot on the dragon's neck, and your single sword in its heart.

That was the biggest problem I couldn't lick during those years of overt war. The Saint couldn't ignore what was going on, and he didn't; and yet, to retain any realism, his contribution ultimately had to be minuscule, and for that he had to lose some of the spurious greatness I had endowed him with when the going was easy, and there were not so many real heroes to compare him with.

Of course I wrote my war stories. But there is not much trace of them in this volume. I have tried to put this collection together mostly with less baldly dated bricks. But that alone makes me feel the need for this apology. During those years, when I had time from my own infinitesimal part of what we used to call the war effort, I did manage to write some things that were not war stories. But they frankly seemed quite trivial when I wrote them, and I still feel that this fundamental insincerity reflects in them.

You may not like the result, but few authors will ever be so honest with you, and that alone should be worth the price of admission.

Taking another look at the contents page, I realize that in my desire to get away from the synthetic product of the World War II years I have made many of my selections from stories that were actually written before then, although they were collected in volume form later, when my publishers were still demanding books and my own lack of productivity reduced me to digging back among magazine stories of happier days which had somehow never been made part of the permanent Saint record by being assembled between hard covers.

This, to confuse you more, results in the inclusion of stories which actually span a writing life which might be said to extend, in geological terms, from the pre-Hitlerian to the neo-Stalinolithic epochs.

This may not be a bad deal historically, but it does somehow fail to carry out the implied promise of the quotation I just made from *The First Saint Omnibus*.

If our boy has changed, it is not conspicuously for the better. If he has developed, the development may be largely negative. He may be less fantastic and improbable, but, if so, he may be just as worthless and irritating. If you feel that way.

Is he still a slightly cockeyed ideal, if you feel differently? I wouldn't know. The ideal is less sharp to me now than when I first outlined it. I am a lot older, and my sight has mellowed. The edge between black and white is not so crisp. The issues are not so simple. The hero that I dreamed up in my twenties is less conclusive now.

We are all different.

In twenty-two years, by the count, since the first Saint story was published, a whole lot of things have changed.

Not only the author, but the readers too. Many of you, just for one thing, were not even born when the first Saint book was published. And even when *The First Saint Omnibus* was published, many more of you were still too young to have noticed the planting of that milestone in literary history. A whole generation has grown up while I have been writing this stuff, who never even knew the world in which the Saint first lived.

Pretty soon those first books will practically rank as historical novels, and we shall be able to reprint them with pictures of busty women on the jackets, and probably sell a lot more copies.

Meanwhile, I must just ask you to forgive the slightly antique flavor which you may detect in some of these stories. I have not revised them or tried to bring them up to date, for I feel that that would be cheating. I only hope you will be tender with their olde-worlde charm.

Well, I can hope, can't I?

THE SECOND SAINT OMNIBUS

THE STAR PRODUCERS

From *The Happy Highwayman*

EVER SINCE I CAN REMEMBER, I have been feebly protesting against the criticism most commonly leveled at the Saint stories, which is that my plots are farfetched and implausible. It has done me little good to insist that in truth I have a rather poor imagination, and that therefore I find it much easier to steal plots from the newspapers than to dream them up. Obviously, I give them some artistic distortions and trimmings; but far more often than not the hard core of the story is something that intrigued me in real life.

I have even given my sources, sometimes, which is the kind of excuse that I don't think a writer really ought to make. But the brand is still on me, and I think my good friend "Ellery Queen" is the only critic who has ever acknowledged my defense.

And now I am going to take my protest a stage further.

I solemnly assert that even when I do write a story out of pure imagination, my mind works with such a faultless sense of realism that life itself will sometimes be constrained to make my story come true.

This story is one of those.

I will not spoil the story by giving away the surprise ending before you start it. But I have to tell you, and the fact can be verified by anyone who cares to take the trouble, that soon after I wrote this story a gentleman in London (who was, however, completely honest, and in no other way resembled my Star Producers) wrote and produced a play of similar caliber to the opus which I invented in my story, only it was called *Young England*, and the result was exactly the same as you will read of here.

THE STAR PRODUCERS

MR HOMER QUARTERSTONE was not, to be candid, a name to conjure with in the world of the Theatre. It must be admitted that his experience behind the footlights was not entirely confined to that immortal line: "Dinner is served." As a matter of fact, he had once said "The Baron is here" and "Will there be anything further, madam?" in the same act; and in another never-to-be-forgotten drama which had run for eighteen performances on Broadway, he had taken part in the following classic dialogue:

> NICK: Were you here?
> JENKINS (*Mr Homer Quarterstone*): No sir.
> NICK: Did you hear anything?
> JENKINS: No sir.
> NICK: A hell of a lot of use you are.
> JENKINS: Yes sir.
>
> (*Exit, carrying tray.*)

In the executive line, Mr Quarterstone's career had been marked by the same magnanimous emphasis on service rather than personal glory. He had not actually produced any spectacles of resounding success but he had contributed his modest quota to their triumph by helping to carry chairs and tables on to the stage and arrange them according to the orders of the scenic director. And although he had not actually given his personal guidance to any of the financial manœuvres associated with theatrical production, he had sat in the box office at more than one one-night stand, graciously controlling the passage over the counter of those fundamental monetary items without which the labours of more egotistical financiers would have been fruitless.

Nevertheless, while it is true that the name of Quarterstone had never appeared in any headlines, and that his funeral cortege would never have attracted any distinguished pallbearers, he had undoubtedly found the Theatre more profitable than many other men to whom it had given fame.

He was a man of florid complexion and majestic bearing, with a ripe convexity under his waistcoat and a forehead that arched glisteningly back to the scruff of his neck; and he had a taste for black homburgs and astrakhan-collared overcoats which gave an impression of great artistic prosperity. This prosperity was by no means illusory, for Mr Homer Quarterstone, in his business capacity, was now the principal, president, director, owner and twenty-five percent of the staff of the Supremax Academy of Dramatic Art, which according to its frequent advertisements had been the training ground, the histrionic hothouse, so to speak, of many stars whose names were now household words from the igloos of Greenland to the tents of the wandering Bedouin. And the fact that Mr Quarterstone had not become the principal, president, director, owner, etc., of the Supremax Academy until several years after the graduation of those illustrious personages, when in a period of unaccustomed affluence and unusually successful borrowing he had purchased the name and good will of an idealistic but moribund concern, neither deprived him of the legal right to make that claim in his advertising nor hampered the free flow of his imagination when he was expounding his own experience and abilities to prospective clients.

Simon Templar, who sooner or later made the acquaintance of practically everyone who was collecting too much money with too little reason, heard of him first from Rosalind Hale, who had been one of those clients; and she brought him her story for the same reason that many other people who had been foolish would often come to Simon Templar with their troubles, as if the words "The Saint" had some literally supernatural significance, instead of being merely the nickname with which he had once incongruously been christened.

"I thought it was only the sensible thing to do—to get some proper training—and his advertisements looked genuine. You wouldn't think those film stars would let him use their names for a fraud, would you? . . . I suppose I was a fool, but I'd played in some amateur things, and people who weren't trying to flatter me said I was good, and I really believed I'd got it in me, sort of instinctively. And *some* of the people who believe they've got it in them must be right, and they must do something about it, or else there wouldn't be any actors and actresses at all, would there? . . . And really I'm—I—well, I don't make you shudder when you look at me, do I?"

This at least was beyond argument, unless the looker was a crusted misogynist, which the Saint very firmly was not. She had an almost childishly heart-shaped face, with small features that were just far enough from perfection to be exciting, and her figure had just enough curves in just the right places.

The Saint smiled at her without any cynicism.

"And when you came into this money . . ."

"Well, it looked just like the chance I'd been dreaming about. But I still wanted to be intelligent about it and not go dashing off to Hollywood to turn into a waitress, or spend my time sitting in producers' waiting rooms hoping they'd notice me and just looking dumb when they asked if I had any experience, or anything like that. That's why I went to Quarterstone. And he said I'd got everything, and I only wanted a little schooling. I paid him five hundred dollars for a course of lessons, and then another five hundred for an advanced course, and then another five hundred for a movie course and by that time he'd been talking to me so that he'd found out all about that legacy, and that was when his friend came in and they got me to give them four thousand dollars to put that play on."

"In which you were to play the lead."

"Yes, and——"

"The play never did go on."

She nodded, and the moistness of her eyes made them shine like jewels. She might not have been outstandingly intelligent, she might or might not have had any dramatic talent, but her own drama was real. She was crushed, frightened, dazed, wounded in the deep and desperate way that a child is hurt when it has innocently done something disastrous, as if she was still too stunned to realize what she had done.

Some men might have laughed, but the Saint didn't laugh. He said in his quiet friendly way: "I suppose you checked up on your legal position?"

"Yes. I went to see a lawyer. He said there wasn't anything I could do. They'd been too clever. I couldn't *prove* that I'd been swindled. There really was a play and it could have been put on, only the expenses ran away with all the money before that, and I hadn't got any more, and apparently that often happens, and you couldn't prove it was a fraud. I just hadn't read the contracts and things properly when I signed them, and Urlaub—that's Quarterstone's friend—was entitled to spend all that money, and even if he was careless and stupid you couldn't prove it was criminal. . . . I suppose it was my own fault and I've no right to cry about it, but it was everything I had, and I'd given up my job as well, and—well, things have been pretty tough. You know."

He nodded, straightening a cigarette with his strong brown fingers.

All at once the consciousness of what she was doing now seemed to sweep over her, leaving her tongue-tied. She had to make an effort to get out the last words that everything else had inevitably been leading up to.

"I know I'm crazy and I've no right, but could you—could you think of anything to do about it?"

He went on looking at her thoughtfully for a moment, and then, incredulously, she suddenly realized that he was smiling, and that his smile was still without satire.

"I could try," he said.

He stood up, long immaculately tailored legs gathering themselves with the lazy grace of a tiger, and all at once she found something in his blue eyes that made all the legends about him impossible to question. It was as if he had lifted all the weight off her shoulders without another word when he stood up.

"One of the first things I should prescribe is a man-sized lunch," he said. "A diet of doughnuts and coffee never produced any great ideas."

When he left her it was still without any more promises, and yet with a queer sense of certainty that was more comforting than any number of promises.

The Saint himself was not quite so certain; but he was interested, which perhaps meant more. He had that impetuously human outlook which judged an adventure on its artistic quality rather than on the quantity of boodle which it might contribute to his unlawful income. He liked Rosa-lind Hale, and he disliked men such as Mr Homer Quarterstone and Com-rade Urlaub sounded as if they would be; more than that, perhaps, he disliked rackets that preyed on people to whom a loss of four thousand dollars was utter tragedy. He set out that same afternoon to interview Mr Quarterstone.

The Supremax Academy occupied the top floor and one room on the street level of a sedate old-fashioned building in the West Forties; but the entrance was so cunningly arranged and the other intervening tenants so modestly unheralded that any impressionable visitor who presented him-self first at the ground-floor room labelled "Inquiries," and who was thence whisked expertly into the elevator and upwards to the rooms above, might easily have been persuaded that the whole building was taken up with various departments of the Academy, a hive buzzing with ambitious Thes-pian bees. The brassy but once luscious blonde who presided in the Inquiry Office lent tone to this idea by saying that Mr Quarterstone was busy, very busy, and that it was customary to make appointments with him some days in advance; when she finally organized the interview it was with the regal generosity of a slightly flirtatious goddess performing a casual miracle for an especially favoured and deserving suitor—a beautifully polished rou-tine that was calculated to impress prospective clients from the start with a gratifying sense of their own importance.

Simon Templar was always glad of a chance to enjoy his own importance, but on this occasion he regretfully had to admit that so much flattery was undeserved, for instead of his own name he had cautiously given the less notorious name of Tombs. This funereal anonymity, however, cast no shadow over the warmth of Mr Quarterstone's welcome.

"My dear Mr Tombs! Come in. Sit down. Have a cigarette."

Mr Quarterstone grasped him with large warm hands, wrapped him up, transported him tenderly and installed him in an armchair like a collector enshrining a priceless piece of fragile glass. He fluttered anxiously round him, pressing a cigarette into the Saint's mouth and lighting it before he retired reluctantly to his own chair on the other side of the desk.

"And now, my dear Mr Tombs," said Mr Quarterstone at last, clasping his hands across his stomach, "how can I help you?"

Simon looked at his hands, his feet, the carpet, the wall and then at Mr Quarterstone.

"Well," he said bashfully, "I wanted to inquire about some dramatic lessons."

"Some—ah—oh yes. You mean a little advanced coaching. A little polish-ing of technique?"

"Oh no," said the Saint hastily. "I mean, you know your business, of course, but I'm only a beginner."

Mr Quarterstone sat up a little straighter and gazed at him.

"You're only a beginner?" he repeated incredulously.

"Yes."

"You mean to tell me you haven't any stage experience?"

"No. Only a couple of amateur shows."

"You're not joking?"

"Of course not."

"Well!"

Mr Quarterstone continued to stare at him as if he were something rare and strange. The Saint twisted his hatbrim uncomfortably. Mr Quarterstone sat back again, shaking his head.

"That's the most extraordinary thing I ever heard of," he declared.

"But why?" Simon asked, with not unreasonable surprise.

"My dear fellow, anyone would take you for a professional actor! I've been in the theatrical business all my life—I was on Broadway for ten years, played before the King of England, produced hundreds of shows —and I'd have bet anyone I could pick out a professional actor every time. The way you walked in, the way you sat down, the way you use your hands, even the way you're smoking that cigarette—it's amazing! Are you *sure* you're not having a little joke?"

"Absolutely."

"May I ask what is your present job?"

"Until a couple of days ago," said the Saint ingenuously, "I was working in a bank. But I'd always wanted to be an actor, so when my uncle died and left me twenty thousand dollars I thought it was a good time to start. I think I could play parts like William Powell," he added, looking sophisticated.

Mr Quarterstone beamed like a cat full of cream.

"Why not?" he demanded oratorically. "Why ever not? With that natural gift of yours . . ." He shook his head again, clicking his tongue in eloquent expression of his undiminished awe and admiration. "It's the most amazing thing! Of course, I sometimes see fellows who are nearly as good-looking as you are, but they haven't got your manner. Why, if you took a few lessons——"

Simon registered the exact amount of glowing satisfaction which he was supposed to register.

"That's what I came to you for, Mr Quarterstone. I've seen your advertisements——"

"Yes, yes!"

Mr Quarterstone got up and came round the desk again. He took the

Saint's face in his large warm hands and turned it this way and that, studying it from various angles with increasing astonishment. He made the Saint stand up and studied him from a distance, screwing up one eye and holding up a finger in front of the other to compare his proportions. He stalked up to him again, patted him here and there and felt his muscles. He stepped back again and posed in an attitude of rapture.

"Marvellous!" he said. "Astounding!"

Then, with an effort, he brought himself out of his trance.

"Mr Tombs," he said firmly, "there's only one thing for me to do. I must take you in charge myself. I have a wonderful staff here, the finest staff you could find in any dramatic academy in the world, past masters, every one of 'em—but they're not good enough. I wouldn't dare to offer you anything but the best that we have here. I offer you myself. And because I only look upon it as a privilege—nay, a sacred duty, to develop this God-given talent you have, I shall not try to make any money out of you. I shall only make a small charge to cover the actual value of my time. Charles Laughton paid me five thousand dollars for one hour's coaching in a difficult scene. John Barrymore took me to Hollywood and paid me fifteen thousand dollars to criticize him in four rehearsals. But I shall only ask you for enough to cover my out-of-pocket expenses—let us say, one thousand dollars—for a course of ten special, personal, private, exclusive lessons. . . . No," boomed Mr. Quarterstone, waving one hand in a magnificent gesture, "don't thank me! Were I to refuse to give you the benefit of all my experience, I should regard myself as a traitor to my calling, a very—ah—Ishmael!"

If there was one kind of acting in which Simon Templar had graduated from a more exacting academy than was dreamed of in Mr Quarterstone's philosophy, it was the art of depicting the virgin sucker yawning hungrily under the baited hook. His characterization was pointed with such wide-eyed and unsullied innocence, such eager and open-mouthed receptivity, such a succulently plastic amenability to suggestion, such a rich response to flattery—in a word, with such a sublime absorptiveness to the old oil—that men such as Mr Quarterstone, on becoming conscious of him for the first time, had been known to wipe away a furtive tear as they dug down into their pockets for first mortgages on the Golden Gate Bridge and formulae for extracting radium from old toothpaste tubes. He used all of that technique on Mr Homer Quarterstone, so effectively that his enrolment in the Supremax Academy proceeded with the effortless ease of a stratospherist returning to terra firma a short head in front of his punctured balloon. Mr Quarterstone did not actually brush away an unbidden tear, but he did bring out an enormous leather-bound ledger and enter up particulars of his newest student with a gratifying realization that Life, in spite of the pessimists, was not wholly without its moments of unshadowed joy.

"When can I start?" asked the Saint, when that had been done.

"Start?" repeated Mr Quarterstone, savouring the word. "Why, whenever you like. Each lesson lasts a full hour, and you can divide them up as you wish. You can start now if you want to. I had an appointment . . ."

"Oh."

"But it is of no importance, compared with this." Mr Quarterstone picked up the telephone. "Tell Mr Urlaub I shall be too busy to see him this afternoon," he told it. He hung up. "The producer," he explained, as he settled back again. "Of course you've heard of him. But he can wait. One day he'll be waiting on your doorstep, my boy." He dismissed Mr Urlaub, the producer, with a majestic *ademán*. "What shall we take first—elocution?"

"You know best, Mr Quarterstone," said the Saint eagerly.

Mr Quarterstone nodded. If there was anything that could have increased his contentment, it was a pupil who had no doubt that Mr Quarterstone knew best. He crossed his legs and hooked one thumb in the armhole of his waistcoat.

"Say 'Eee.'"

"Eee."

"Ah."

Simon went on looking at him expectantly.

"Ah," repeated Mr Quarterstone.

"I beg your pardon?"

"I said 'Ah.'"

"Oh."

"No, ah."

"Yes, I——"

"Say it after me, Mr Tombs. 'Aaaah.' Make it ring out. Hold your diaphragm in, open your mouth and bring it up from your chest. This is a little exercise in the essential vowels."

"Oh. *Aaaah.*"

"Oh."

"Oh."

"I."

"I."

"*Ooooo.*"

"*Ooooo.*"

"Wrong."

"I'm sorry . . ."

"Say 'Wrong,' Mr Tombs."

"Wrong."

"Right," said Mr Quarterstone.

"Right."

"Yes, yes," said Mr Quarterstone testily. "I——"

"Yes, yes, I."

Mr Quarterstone swallowed.

"I don't mean you to repeat *every* word I say," he said. "Just the examples. Now let's try the vowels again in a sentence. Say this: 'Faaar skiiies loooom O-ver meee.'"

"Faaar skiiies loooom O-ver meee."

"Daaark niiight draaaws neeear."

"The days are drawing in," Simon admitted politely.

Mr Quarterstone's smile became somewhat glassy, but whatever else he may have been he was no quitter.

"I'm afraid he is a fraud," Simon told Rosalind Hale when he saw her the next day. "But he has a beautiful line of sugar for the flies. I was the complete gawky goof, the perfect bank clerk with dramatic ambitions—you could just see me going home and leering at myself in the mirror and imagining myself making love to Greta Garbo—but he told me he just couldn't believe how anyone with my poise couldn't have had any experience."

The girl's white teeth showed on her lower lip.

"But that's just what he told me!"

"I could have guessed it, darling. And I don't suppose you were the first, either. . . . I had two lessons on the spot, and I've had another two today; and if he can teach anyone anything worth knowing about acting, then I can train ducks to write shorthand. I was so dumb that anyone with an ounce of artistic feeling would have thrown me out of the window, but when I left him this afternoon he almost hugged me and told me he could hardly wait to finish the course before he rushed out to show me to Gilbert Miller."

She moved her head a little, gazing at him with big sober eyes.

"He was just the same with me, too. Oh, I've been such a fool!"

"We're all fools in our own way," said the Saint consolingly. "Boys like Homer are my job, so they don't bother me. On the other hand, you've no idea what a fool I can be with soft lights and sweet music. Come on to dinner and I'll show you."

"But now you've given Quarterstone a thousand dollars, and what are you going to do about it?"

"Wait for the next act of the stirring drama."

The next act was not long in developing. Simon had two more of Mr Quarterstone's special, personal, private, exclusive lessons the next day, and two more the day after—Mr Homer Quarterstone was no apostle of the old-fashioned idea of making haste slowly, and by getting in two lessons daily he was able to double his temporary income, which then chalked up at the very pleasing figure of two hundred dollars per diem, minus the overhead, of which the brassy blonde was not the smallest item. But this method of gingering up the flow of revenue also meant that its duration was reduced from ten days to five, and during a lull in the next day's first hour (Diction, Gesture and Facial Expression) he took the opportunity of pointing out that Success, while already certain, could never be too certain or too great, and therefore that a supplementary series of lessons in the Art and Technique of the Motion Picture, while involving only a brief delay, could only add to the magnitude of Mr Tombs's ultimate inevitable triumph.

On this argument, for the first time, Mr Tombs disagreed.

"I want to see for myself whether I've mastered the first lessons," he said. "If I could get a small part in a play, just to try myself out . . ."

He was distressingly obstinate, and Mr Quarterstone, either because he convinced himself that it would only be a waste of time, or because another approach to his pupil's remaining nineteen thousand dollars seemed just as simple, finally yielded. He made an excuse to leave the studio for a few minutes, and Simon knew that the next development was on its way.

It arrived in the latter part of the last hour (Declamation with Gestures, Movement and Facial Expression—The Complete Classical Scene).

Mr Quarterstone was demonstrating.

"To be," trumpeted Mr Quarterstone, gazing ceilingwards with an ecstatic expression, the chest thrown out, the arms slightly spread, "or not to be." Mr Quarterstone ceased to be. He slumped, the head bowed, the arms hanging listlessly by the sides, the expression doleful. "That—is the question." Mr Quarterstone pondered it, shaking his head. The suspense was awful. He elaborated the idea. "Whether 'tis nobler"—Mr Quarterstone drew himself nobly up, the chin lifted, the right arm turned slightly across the body, the forearm parallel with the ground—"in the mind"—he clutched his brow, where he kept his mind—"to suffer"—he clutched his heart, where he did his suffering—"the slings"—he stretched out his left hand for the slings—"and arrows"—he flung out his right hand for the arrows—"of outrageous fortune"—Mr Quarterstone rolled the insult lusciously around his mouth and spat it out with defiance—"or to take arms"—he drew himself up again, the shoulders squared, rising slightly on tiptoe—"against a sea of troubles"—his right hand moved over a broad panorama, undulating symbolically—"and by opposing"—the arms rising slightly from the elbow, fists clenched, shoulders thrown back, chin drawn in—"end them!"—the forearms striking down again with a fierce chopping movement, expressive of finality and knocking a calendar off the table.

"Excuse me," said the brassy blonde, with her head poking round the door. "Mr Urlaub is here."

"Tchah!" said Mr Quarterstone, inspiration wounded in mid-flight. "Tell him to wait."

"He said——"

Mr Quarterstone's eyes dilated. His mouth opened. His hands lifted a little from his sides, the fingers tense and parted rather like plump claws, the body rising. He was staring at the Saint.

"Wait!" he cried. "Of course! The very thing! The very man you've got to meet! One of the greatest producers in the world today! Your chance!"

He leapt a short distance off the ground and whirled on the blonde, his arm flung out, pointing quiveringly.

"Send him in!"

Simon looked wildly breathless.

"But—but will he——"

"Of course he will! You've only got to remember what I've taught you. And sit down. We must be calm."

Mr Quarerstone sank into a chair, agitatedly looking calm, as Urlaub bustled in. Urlaub trotted quickly across the room.

"Ah, Homer."

"My dear Waldemar! How is everything?"

"Terrible! I came to ask for your advice . . ."

Mr Urlaub leaned across the desk. He was a smallish, thin, bouncy man with a big nose and sleek black hair. His suit fitted him as tightly as an extra skin, and the stones in his tiepin and in his rings looked enough like diamonds to look like diamonds. He moved as if he were hung on springs, and his voice was thin and spluttery like the exhaust of an anemic motor-cycle.

"Niementhal has quit. Let me down at the last minute. He wanted to put some goddam gigolo into the lead. Some ham that his wife's got hold of. I said to him, 'Aaron, your wife is your business and this play is my business.' I said, 'I don't care if it hurts your wife's feelings and I don't care if she gets mad at you, I can't afford to risk my reputation on Broadway and my investment in this play by putting that ham in the lead.' I said, 'Buy her a box of candy or a diamond bracelet or anything or send her to Paris or something, but don't ask me to make her happy by putting that gigolo in this play.' So he quit. And me with everything set, and the rest of the cast ready to start rehearsing next week, and he quits. He said, 'All right, then use your own money.' I said, 'You know I've got fifty thousand dollars in this production already, and all you were going to put in is fifteen thousand, and for that you want me to risk my money and my reputation by hiring that ham. I thought you said you'd got a good actor.' 'Well, you find yourself a good actor and fifteen thousand dollars,' he says, and he quits. Cold. And I can't raise another cent—you know how I just tied up half a million to save those aluminum shares."

"That's tough, Waldemar," said Mr Quarterstone anxiously. "Waldemar, that's tough! . . . Ah—by the way—pardon me—may I introduce a student of mine? Mr Tombs . . ."

Urlaub turned vaguely, apparently becoming aware of the Saint's presence for the first time. He started forward with a courteously extended hand as the Saint rose.

But their hands did not meet at once. Mr Urlaub's approaching movement died slowly away, as if paralysis had gradually overtaken him, so that he finally came to rest just before they met, like a clockwork toy that had run down. His eyes became fixed, staring. His mouth opened.

Then, very slowly, he revived himself. He pushed his hand onwards again and grasped the Saint's as if it were something precious, shaking it slowly and earnestly.

"A pupil of yours, did you say, Homer?" he asked in an awestruck voice.

"That's right. My star pupil, in fact. I might almost say . . ."

Mr Urlaub paid no attention to what Quarterstone might almost have said. With his eyes still staring, he darted suddenly closer, peered into the Saint's face, took hold of it, turned it from side to side, just as Quarterstone had once done. Then he stepped back and stared again, prowling round the Saint like a dog prowling round a tree. Then he stopped.

"Mr Tombs," he said vibrantly, "will you walk over to the door, and then walk back towards me?"

Looking dazed, the Saint did so.

Mr Urlaub looked at him and gulped. Then he hauled a wad of typescript out of an inside pocket, fumbled through it and thrust it out with one enamelled fingernail dabbing at a paragraph.

"Read that speech—read it as if you were acting it."

The Saint glanced over the paragraph, drew a deep breath and read with almost uncontrollable emotion:

"*No, do not lie to me. You have already given me the answer for which I have been waiting. I am not ungrateful for what you once did for me, but I see now that that kind act was only a part of your scheme to ensnare my better nature in the toils of your unhallowed passions, as though pure love were a thing that could be bought like merchandise. Ah, yes, I loved you, but I did not know that that pretty face was only a mask for the corruption beneath. How you must have laughed at me! Ha, ha. I brought you a rose, but you turned it into a nest of vipers in my bosom. They have stabbed my heart! (Sobs.)*"

Mr Urlaub clasped his hands together. His eyes bulged and rolled upwards.

"My God," he breathed hoarsely.

"What?" said the Saint.

"Why?" said Mr Quarterstone.

"But it's like a miracle!" squeaked Waldemar Urlaub. "He's the man! The type! The face! The figure! The voice! The manner! He is a genius! Homer, where did you find him? The women will storm the theatre." He grasped the Saint by the arm, leaning as far as he could over the desk and over Mr Quarterstone. "Listen. He must play that part. He must. He is the only man. I couldn't put anyone else in it now. Not after I've seen him. I'll show Aaron Niementhal where he gets off. Quit, did he? Okay. He'll be sorry. We'll have a hit that'll make history!"

"But, Waldemar . . ."

Mr Urlaub dried up. His clutching fingers uncoiled from Simon's arm. The fire died out of his eyes. He staggered blindly back and sank into a chair and buried his face in his hands.

"Yes," he whispered bitterly. "I'd forgotten. The play can't go on. I'm sunk, Homer—just for a miserable fifteen grand. And now, of all times, when I've just seen Mr Tombs!"

"You know I'd help you if I could, Waldemar," said Mr Quarterstone earnestly. "But I just bought my wife a fur coat, and she wants a new car, and that ranch we just bought in California set me back a hundred thousand."

Mr Urlaub shook his head.

"I know. It's not your fault. But isn't it just the toughest break?"

Quarterstone shook his head in sympathy. And then he looked at the Saint.

It was quite a performance, that look. It started casually, beheld inspiration, blazed with triumph, winked, glared significantly, poured out encouragement, pleaded, commanded and asked and answered several questions, all in a few seconds. Mr Quarterstone had not at any period in his career actually held down the job of prompter, but he more than made up with enthusiasm for any lack of experience. Only a man who had been blind from birth could have failed to grasp the idea that Mr Quarterstone was suggesting, and the Saint had not strung along so far in order to feign blindness at the signal for his entrance.

Simon cleared his throat.

"Er—did you say you only needed another fifteen thousand dollars to put on this play?" he asked diffidently, but with a clearly audible note of suppressed excitement.

After that he had to work no harder than he would have had to work to get himself eaten by a pair of hungry lions. Waldemar Urlaub, once the great light had dawned on him, skittered about like a pea on a drum in an orgy of exultant planning. Mr Tombs would have starred in the play anyhow, whenever the remainder of the necessary wind had been raised—Urlaub had already made up his mind to that—but if Mr Tombs had fifteen thousand dollars as well as his genius and beauty, he would be more than a star. He could be co-producer as well, a sharer in the profits, a friend and an equal, in every way the heir to the position which the great Aaron Niementhal would have occupied. His name would go on the billing with double force—Urlaub grabbed a piece of paper and a pencil to illustrate it:

SEBASTIAN TOMBS

and

WALDEMAR URLAUB

present

SEBASTIAN TOMBS

in

"LOVE—THE REDEEMER"

There would also be lights on the theatre, advertisements, photographs, newspaper articles, news items, gossip paragraphs, parties, movie rights, screen tests, Hollywood, London, beautiful and adoring women . . . Mr Urlaub built up a luminous picture of fame, success and fortune, while Mr Quarterstone nodded benignly and slapped everybody on the back and beamed at the Saint at intervals with a sublimely smug expression of "I told you so."

"And they did all that to me, too," said Rosalind Hale wryly. "I was practically Sarah Bernhardt when they'd finished. . . . But I told you just how they did it. Why do you have to let yourself in for the same mess that I got into?"

"The easiest way to rob a bank is from the inside," said the Saint cryptically. "I suppose you noticed that they really have got a play?"

"Yes. I read part of it—the same as you did."

"Did you like it?"

She made a little grimace.

"You've got a right to laugh at me. I suppose that ought to have been warning enough, but Urlaub was so keen about it, and Quarterstone had already made me think he was a great producer, so I couldn't say that I thought it was awful. And then I wondered if it was just because I didn't know enough about plays."

"I don't know much about plays myself," said the Saint. "But the fact remains that Comrade Urlaub has got a complete play, with three acts and everything, god-awful though it is. I took it away with me to read it over and the more I look at it the more I'm thinking that something might be done with it."

Rosalind was aghast.

"You don't mean to say you'd really put your money into producing it?"

"Stranger things have happened," said the Saint thoughtfully. "How bad can a play be before it becomes good? And how much sense of humour is there in the movie business? Haven't you seen those reprints of old two-reelers that they show sometimes for a joke, and haven't you heard the audience laughing itself sick? . . . Listen. I only wish I knew who wrote *Love—the Redeemer*. I've got an idea . . ."

Mr Homer Quarterstone could have answered his question for him, for the truth was that the author of *Love—the Redeemer* resided under the artistic black homburg of Mr Homer Quarterstone. It was a matter of considerable grief to Mr Quarterstone that no genuine producer had ever been induced to see eye to eye with him on the subject of the superlative merits of that amorous masterpiece, so that after he had grown weary of collecting rejections Mr Quarterstone had been reduced to the practical expedient of using his magnum opus as one of the props in the more profitable but by no means less artistic drama from which he and Mr Urlaub derived their precarious incomes; but his loyalty to the child of his brain had never been shaken.

It was therefore with a strange squirmy sensation in the pit of his stomach that Mr Quarterstone sat in his office a few mornings later and gazed at a card in the bottom left-hand corner of which were the magic words, "*Paragon Pictures, Inc., Hollywood, Calif.*" A feeling of fate was about him, as if he had been unexpectedly reminded of a still-cherished childhood dream.

"Show her in," he said with husky magnificence.

The order was hardly necessary, for she came in at once, shepherded by a beaming Waldemar Urlaub.

"Just thought I'd give you a surprise, Homer," he explained boisterously. "Did your heart jump when you saw that card? Well, so did mine. Still, it's real. I fixed it all up. Sold her the play. 'You can't go wrong,' I said, 'with one of the greatest drammers ever written.'"

Mrs Wohlbreit turned her back on him coldly and inspected Mr Quarterstone. She looked nothing like the average man's conception of a female from Hollywood, being gaunt and masculine with a sallow lined face and gold-rimmed glasses and mousey hair plastered back above her ears, but Mr Quarterstone had at least enough experience to know that women were used in Hollywood in executive positions which did not call for the decorative qualities of more publicized employees.

She said in her cold masculine voice: "Is this your agent?"

Mr Quarterstone swallowed.

"Ah——"

"Part owner," said Mr Urlaub eagerly. "That's right, isn't it, Homer? You know our agreement—fifty-fifty in everything. Eh? Well, I've been working on this deal——"

"I asked you," said Mrs Wohlbreit penetratingly, "because I understand that you're the owner of this play we're interested in. There are so many chisellers in this business that we make it our policy to approach the author first direct—if he wants to take any ten-percenters in afterwards, that's his affair. A Mr Tombs brought me the play first, and told me he had an interest in it. I found out that he got it from Mr Urlaub, so I went to him. Mr Urlaub told me that you were the original author. Now, who am I to talk business with?"

Mr Quarterstone saw his partner's mouth opening for another contribution.

"With—with us," he said weakly.

It was not what he might have said if he had had time to think, but he was too excited to be particular.

"Very well," said Mrs Wohlbreit. "We've read this play, *Love—the Redeemer,* and we think it would make a grand picture. If you haven't done anything yet about the movie rights . . ."

Mr Quarterstone drew himself up. He felt as if he was in a daze from which he might be rudely awakened at any moment, but it was a beautiful daze. His heart was thumping, but his brain was calm and clear. It was, after all, only the moment with which he had always known that his genius must ultimately be rewarded.

"Ah—yes," he said with resonant calm. "The movie rights are, for the moment, open to—ah—negotiation. Naturally, with a drama of such quality, dealing as it does with a problem so close to the lives of every member of the thinking public, and appealing to the deepest emotions and beliefs of every intelligent man and woman——"

"We thought it would make an excellent farce," said Mrs Wohlbreit blandly. "It's just the thing we've been looking for for a long time." But before the stricken Mr Quarterstone could protest, she had added consolingly: "We could afford to give you thirty thousand dollars for the rights."

"Ah—quite," said Mr Quarterstone bravely.

By the time that Mrs Wohlbreit had departed, after making an appointment for the contract to be signed and the check paid over at the Paragon offices the following afternoon, his wound had healed sufficiently to let him take Mr Urlaub in his arms, as soon as the door closed, and embrace him fondly in an impromptu rumba.

"Didn't I always tell you that play was a knockout?" he crowed. "It's taken 'em years to see it, but they had to wake up in the end. Thirty thousand dollars! Why, with that money I can——" He sensed a certain stiffness in his dancing partner and hastily corrected himself: "I mean, we—we can——"

"Nuts," said Mr Urlaub coarsely. He disengaged himself and straightened the creases out of his natty suit. "What you've got to do now is sit down and figure out a way to crowbar that guy Tombs out of this."

Mr Quarterstone stopped dancing suddenly and his jaw dropped. "Tombs?"

"Yeah! *He* wasn't so dumb. He had the sense to see that that play of yours was the funniest thing ever written. When we were talking about it in here he must have thought we thought it was funny, too."

Mr Quarterstone was appalled as the idea of duplicity struck him.

"Waldemar—d'you think he was trying to——"

"No. I pumped the old battle-axe on the way here. He told her he only had a part interest, but he wanted to do something for the firm and give us a surprise—he thought he could play the lead in the picture, too."

"Has she told him——"

"Not yet. You heard what she said. She gets in touch with the author first. But we got to get him before he gets in touch with her. Don't you remember those contracts we signed yesterday? Fifty percent of the movie rights for him!"

Mr Quarterstone sank feebly on to the desk.

"Fifteen thousand dollars!" He groaned. Then he brightened tentatively. "But it's all right, Waldemar. He agreed to put fifteen thousand dollars into producing the play, so we just call it quits and we don't have to give him anything."

"You great fat lame-brained slob," yelped Mr Urlaub affectionately. "Quits! Like hell it's quits! D'you think I'm not going to put that play on, after this? It took that old battle-axe to see it, but she's right. They'll be rolling in the aisles!" He struck a Quarterstoneish attitude. " '*I brought you a rose,*' " he uttered tremulously, " '*but you turned it into a nest of vipers in my bosom. They have stabbed my heart!*' My God! It's a natural! I'm going to put it on Broadway whatever we have to do to raise the dough—but we aren't going to cut that mug Tombs in on it."

Mr Quarterstone winced.

"It's all signed up legal," he said dolefully. "We'll have to spend our own dough and buy him out."

"Get your hat," said Mr Urlaub shortly. "We'll cook up a story on the way."

When Rosalind Hale walked into the Saint's apartment at the Waldorf-Astoria that afternoon, Simon Templar was counting crisp new hundred-dollar bills into neat piles.

"What have you been doing?" she said. "Burgling a bank?"

The Saint grinned.

"The geetus came out of a bank, anyway," he murmured. "But Comrades Quarterstone and Urlaub provided the checks. I just went out and cashed them."

"You mean they bought you out?"

"After a certain amount of haggling and squealing—yes. Apparently Aaron Niementhal changed his mind about backing the show, and Urlaub didn't want to offend him on account of Aaron offered to cut him in on another and bigger and better proposition at the same time; so they gave me ten thousand dollars to tear up the contracts, and the idea is that I ought to play the lead in Niementhal's bigger and better show."

She pulled off her hat and collapsed into a chair. She was no longer gaunt and masculine and forbidding, for she had changed out of a badly fitting tweed suit and removed her sallow make-up and thrown away the gold-rimmed glasses and fluffed out her hair again so that it curled in its usual soft brown waves around her face, so that her last resemblance to anyone by the name of Wohlbreit was gone.

"Ten thousand dollars," she said limply. "It doesn't seem possible. But it's real. I can see it."

"You can touch it, if you like," said the Saint. "Here." He pushed one of the stacks over the table towards her. "Fifteen hundred that you paid Quarterstone for tuition." He pushed another. "Four thousand that you put into the play." He drew a smaller sheaf towards himself. "One thousand that I paid for my lessons. Leaving three thousand five hundred drops of gravy to be split two ways."

He straightened the remaining pile, cut it in two and slid half of it on to join the share that was accumulating in front of her. She stared at the money helplessly for a second or two, reached out and touched it with the tips of her fingers, and then suddenly she came round the table and flung herself into his arms. Her cheek was wet where it touched his face.

"I don't know how to say it," she said shakily. "But you know what I mean."

"There's only one thing bothering me," said the Saint some time later, "and that's whether you're really entitled to take back those tuition fees. After all, Homer made you a good enough actress to fool himself. Maybe he was entitled to a percentage, in spite of everything."

His doubts, however, were set at rest several months afterwards, when he had travelled a long way from New York and many other things had happened, when one day an advertisement in a New York paper caught his eye:

> *14th Week!*   *Sold out 3 months ahead!*
> The Farce Hit of the Season:
> LOVE—THE REDEEMER
> by HOMER QUARTERSTONE
> Imperial Theatre   A Waldemar Urlaub Production

Simon Templar was not often at a loss for words, but on this occasion he was tongue-tied for a long time. And then, at last, he lay back and laughed helplessly.

"Oh well," he said. "I guess they earned it."

THE WICKED COUSIN

From *The Happy Highwayman*

IN RECENT TIMES, the common courtesy of trying to avoid wantonly stepping on people's toes has developed into an editorial phobia of almost psychotic intensity.

This exaggerated concern for the tender toe has of course been vociferously encouraged by every sort of hypersensitive minority. The most frantic form of it is displayed by movie producers, who are more sensitive to the tinkle of the cash register than any other species of artistic entrepreneur, and who also know that they are catering to a more infantile audience than that of any other medium except television.

It is a fact that many of our most distinguished gangsters have been of Italian descent; but to portray a gangster with an Italian name on the screen is not only an automatic way to discover more pro-Italian clubs, societies, and protective associations than you would otherwise have known existed, but not so long ago would have seen the fist of Mussolini shaken at State Department level. A Latin-American heavy in a picture might strain the whole structure of Pan-American amity. Even on the domestic scene, Negroes, Chinese, Jews, Catholics, Baptists or Holy Rollers can only be depicted as lovable paragons. It has reached the point where the only villain who can be safely used today is a white American or British agnostic, preferably named Smith.

Only one step is lacking to achieve the final *reductio ad absurdum,* and that will be when a few more firebrands found the Society for the Preservation of the Caucasian Race, the International Association of Agnostics, and the League Against Libeling People Named Smith. After which the only villains at our disposal will be men from Mars—until the Committee for the Protection of Martians takes over. Then all the writers whose stories depend on the conflict between goodness and villainy can fold up their typewriters and silently steal away. Except that the Authors' League would certainly object to the mere suggestion that writers would steal anything.

To a lesser degree, there has grown up a similar tabu against combining moral turpitude with physical defects. If Robert Louis Stevenson had been writing *Treasure Island* today, he would probably be told that his picture of Long John Silver might give offense to a large body of unfortunate amputees. Sir James Barrie would probably have been urged to reconsider the anatomy of Captain Hook. And Victor Hugo would have been warned that the *Hunchback of Notre Dame* might be construed as an attack on all hunchbacks.

An extension of this thinking (or lack of it) has even begun to make it seem in bad taste to make even kindly fun of an infirmity. As soon as this movement has really taken hold, I expect clowns to be banned from circuses, on the grounds that their make-up is a direct affront to any man who is naturally afflicted with a bulbous nose, and that their oversized splayfooted shoes might wound the feelings of anyone suffering from fallen arches.

Well, it should be known by now that the Saint, and therefore presumably his creator, is not in the business of persecuting or deriding the underprivileged or the unfortunate. But I promise you here that any time a good story reason calls for me to produce a villain or a comic who is a Negro, an Eskimo, a Jew, a Catholic, a Christian Scientist, a diabetic, or a dwarf—I am going to do it, and let the squawks rise to heaven.

This story contains a character with an impediment in his speech, perhaps even a cleft palate. His misfortune is essential to the story. So if any of you readers are stutterers or honkers, I just hope you have a sense of humor.

THE WICKED COUSIN

WHEN SIMON TEMPLAR arrived in Los Angeles there was a leaden ceiling of cloud over the sky and a cool wind blowing. A few drops of unenthusiastic rain moistened the pavements and speckled the shoulders of his coat. The porter who was loading his bags into a taxi assured him that it was most unusual weather, and he felt instantly at home.

Later on, comfortably stretched out on a divan in the sitting room of his suite at the hotel in Hollywood upon which he had chosen to confer the somewhat debatable honour of his tenancy, with a highball at his elbow and a freshly lighted cigarette smouldering contentedly between his lips, he turned the pages of the address book on his knee and considered what his next steps should be to improve that first feeling of a welcome return.

He was not there on business. To be quite accurate, none of the stages of the last few months of carefree wandering which had just completed their vague object of leading him across America from coast to coast had been undertaken with a view to business. If business had materialized on more than one occasion, it was because there was something about Simon Templar which attracted adventure by the same kind of mysterious but inescapable cosmic law which compels a magnet to attract steel or a politician to attract attention; and if much of that business was not looked upon favourably by the Law—or would not have been favourably looked upon if the Law had known all that there was to know about it—this was because Simon Templar's business had an unfortunate habit of falling into categories which gave many people good reason to wonder what right he had to the nickname of the Saint by which he was far more widely known than he was by his baptismal titles. It is true that these buccaneering raids of his which had earned him the subtitle of "The Robin Hood of Modern Crime" were invariably undertaken against the property, and occasionally the persons, of citizens who by no stretch of the imagination could have been called desirable; but the Law took no official cognizance of such small details. The Law, in the Saint's opinion, was a stodgy and elephantine institution which was chiefly justified in its existence by the pleasantly musical explosive noises which it made when he broke it.

Certainly he was not thinking of business. In Hollywood he had many genuine friends, few of whom gave much consideration to the sensational legends that were associated with his name in less unsophisticated circles, and his only immediate problem was to which one of them he should first break the dazzling news of his arrival. He paused at one name after another, recalling its personality: movie executives, directors, writers, actors and actresses both great and small and a certain number of ordinary human beings. He wanted—what did he want? A touch of excitement, preferably feminine, beauty, a little of the glamour and gay unreality with which the very name of Hollywood is inseparably linked in imagination if not in fact. He wanted some of these things very much. His last stop had been made in the state of Utah.

There was a girl called Jacqueline Laine whom Simon remembered suddenly, as one does sometimes remember people, with a sense of startling familiarity and a kind of guilty amazement that he should have allowed her to slip out of his mind for so long. Once she was remembered, he had no more hesitation. No one else could have been so obviously the one person in the world whom he had to call up at that moment.

He picked up the telephone.

"Hello, Jacqueline," he said when she answered. "Do you know who this is?"

"I know," she said. "It's Franklin D. Roosevelt."

"You have a marvellous memory. Do you still eat?"

"Whenever I'm thirsty. Do you?"

"I nibble a crumb now and then. Come out with me tonight and see if we can still take it."

"Simon, I'd love to; but I'm in the most frantic muddle——"

"So is the rest of the world, darling. But it's two years since I've seen you, and that's about seven hundred and thirty days too long. Don't you realize that I've come halfway around the world, surviving all manner of perils and slaying large numbers of ferocious dragons, just to get here in time to take you out to dinner tonight?"

"I know, but—— Oh well. It would be so thrilling to see you. Come around about seven and I'll try to get a bit straightened out before then."

"I'll be there," said the Saint.

He spent some of the intervening time in making himself the owner of a car, and shortly after half-past six he turned it westwards into the stream of studio traffic homing towards Beverly Hills. Somewhere along Sunset Boulevard he turned off to the right and began to climb one of the winding roads that led up into the hills. The street lights were just beginning to trace their twinkling geometrical network over the vast panorama of cities spread out beneath him, as the car soared smoothly higher into the luminous blue-grey twilight.

He found his way with the certainty of vivid remembrance; and he was fully ten minutes early when he pulled the car into a bay by the roadside before the gate of Jacqueline Laine's house. He climbed out and started towards the gate, lighting a cigarette as he went, and as he approached it he perceived that somebody else was approaching the same gate from the opposite side. Changing his course a little to the left so that the departing guest would have room to pass him, the Saint observed that he was a small and elderly gent arrayed in clothes so shapeless and ill fitting that they gave his figure a comical air of having been loosely and inaccurately strung together from a selection of stuffed bags of cloth. He wore a discolored Panama hat of weird and wonderful architecture, and carried an incongruous green umbrella furled, but still flapping in a bedraggled and forlorn sort of way, under his left arm; his face was rubicund and bulbous like his body, looking as if it had been carelessly slapped together out of a few odd lumps of pink plasticine.

As Simon moved to the left, the elderly gent duplicated the manœuvre. Simon turned his feet and swerved politely to the right. The elderly gent did exactly the same, as if he were Simon's own reflection in a distorting mirror. Simon stopped altogether and decided to economize energy by letting the elderly gent make the next move in the ballet on his own.

Whereupon he discovered that the game of undignified dodging in which he had just prepared to surrender his part was caused by some dimly discernible ambition of the elderly gent's to hold converse with him. Standing in front of him and blinking shortsightedly upwards from his lower altitude to the Saint's six foot two, with his mouth hanging vacantly open like an inverted "U" and three long yellow teeth hanging down like stalactites from the top, the elderly gent tapped him on the chest and said, very earnestly and distinctly: "Hig fwmgn glugl phnihklu hgrm skhlglgl?"

"I beg your pardon?" said the Saint vaguely.

"Hig fwmgn," repeated the elderly gent, "glugl phnihklu hgrm skhlglgl?"

Simon considered the point.

"If you ask me," he replied at length, "I should say sixteen."

The elderly gent's knobbly face seemed to take on a brighter shade of pink. He clutched the lapels of the Saint's coat, shaking him slightly in a positive passion of anguish.

"Flogh ghoglu sk," he pleaded, "klngnt hu ughlgstghnd?"

Simon shook his head.

"No," he said judiciously, "you're thinking of weevils."

The little man bounced about like a rubber doll. His eyes squinted with a kind of frantic despair.

"Ogmighogho," he almost screamed, "klngt hu ughglstghnd? Ik ghln ngmnpp sktlghko! Klugt hu hgr? *Ik wgnt hlg phnihkln hgrm skhlglgl!*"

The Saint sighed. He was by nature a kindly man to those whom the Gods had afflicted, but time was passing and he was thinking of Jacqueline Laine.

"I'm afraid not, dear old bird," he murmured regretfully. "There used to be one, but it died. Sorry, I'm sure."

He patted the elderly gent apologetically upon the shoulder, steered his way around him, and passed on out of earshot of the frenzied sputtering noises that continued to honk despairingly through the dusk behind him. Two minutes later he was with Jacqueline.

Jacqueline Laine was twenty-three; she was tall and slender; she had grey eyes that twinkled and a demoralizing mouth. Both of these temptations were in play as she came towards him; but he was still slightly shaken by his recent encounter.

"Have you got any more village idiots hidden around?" he asked warily, as he took her hands; and she was puzzled.

"We used to have several, but they've all got into Congress. Did you want one to take home?"

"My God, no," said the Saint fervently. "The one I met at the gate was bad enough. Is he your latest boy friend?"

Her brow cleared.

"Oh, you mean the old boy with the cleft palate? Isn't he marvellous? I think he's got a screw loose or something. He's been hanging around all day—he keeps ringing the bell and bleating at me. I'd just sent him away for the third time. Did he try to talk to you?"

"He did sort of wag his adenoids at me," Simon admitted, "but I don't think we actually got on to common ground. I felt quite jealous of him for a bit, until I realized that he couldn't possibly kiss you nearly as well as I can, with that set of teeth."

He proceeded to demonstrate this.

"I'm still in a hopeless muddle," she said presently. "But I'll be ready in five minutes. You can be fixing a cocktail while I finish myself off."

In the living room there was an open trunk in one corner and a half-filled packing case in the middle of the floor. There were scattered heaps of paper around it, and a few partially wrapped and unidentifiable objects on the table. The room had that curiously naked and inhospitable look which a room has when it has been stripped of all those intimately personal odds and ends of junk which make it a home, and only the bare furniture is left.

The Saint raised his eyebrows.

"Hullo," he said. "Are you moving?"

"Sort of." She shrugged. "Moving out, anyway."

"Where to?"

"I don't know."

He realized then that there should have been someone else there, in that room.

"Isn't your grandmother here any more?"

"She died four weeks ago."

"I'm sorry."

"She was a good soul. But she was terribly old. Do you know she was just ninety-seven?" She held his hand for a moment. "I'll tell you all about it when I come down. Do you remember where to find the bottles?"

"Templars and elephants never forget."

He blended bourbon, applejack, vermouth and bitters, skilfully and with the zeal of an artist, while he waited for her, remembering the old lady whom he had seen so often in that room. Also, he remembered the affectionate service that Jacqueline had always lavished on her, cheerfully limiting her own enjoyment of life to meet the demands of an unconscious tyrant who would allow no one else to look after her, and wondered if there was any realistic reason to regret the ending of such a long life. She had, he knew, looked after Jacqueline herself in her time, and had brought her up as her own child since she was left an orphan at the age of three; but life must always belong to the young. . . . He thought that for Jacqueline it must be a supreme escape, but he knew that she would never say so.

She came down punctually in the five minutes which she had promised. She had changed her dress and put a comb through her hair, and with that seemed to have achieved more than any other woman could have shown for an hour's fiddling in front of a mirror.

"You should have been in pictures," said the Saint, and he meant it.

"Maybe I shall," she said. "I'll have to do something to earn a living now."

"Is it as bad as that?"

She nodded.

"But I can't complain. I never had to work for anything before. Why shouldn't I start? Other people have to."

"Is that why you're moving out?"

"The house isn't mine."

"But didn't the old girl leave you anything?"

"She left me some letters."

The Saint almost spilt his drink. He sat down heavily on the edge of the table.

"She left you some *letters*? After you'd practically been a slave to her ever since you came out of finishing school? What did she do with the rest of her property—leave it to a home for stray cats?"

"No, she left it to Harry."

"Who?"

"Her grandson."

"I didn't know you had any brothers."

"I haven't. Harry Westler is my cousin. He's—well, as a matter of fact he's a sort of black sheep. He's a gambler, and he was in prison once for forging a check. Nobody else in the family would have anything to do with him, and if you believe what they used to say about him they were probably quite right; but Granny always had a soft spot for him. She never believed he could do anything wrong—he was just a mischievous boy to her. Well, you know how old she was . . ."

"And she left everything to him?"

"Practically everything. I'll show you."

She went to a drawer of the writing table and brought him a typewritten sheet. He saw that it was a copy of a will, and turned to the details of the bequests.

To my dear granddaughter Jacqueline Laine, who has taken care of me so thoughtfully and unselfishly for four years, One Hundred Dollars and my letters from Sidney Farlance, knowing that she will find them of more value than anything else I could leave her.

To my cook, Eliza Jefferson, and my chauffeur, Albert Gordon, One Hundred Dollars each, for their loyal service.

The remainder of my estate, after these deductions, including my house and other personal belongings, to my dear grandson Harry Westler, hoping it will help him to make the success of life of which I have always believed him capable.

Simon folded the sheet and dropped it on the table from his finger tips as if it were infected.

"Suffering Judas," he said helplessly. "After all you did for her—to pension you off on the same scale as the cook and the chauffeur! And what about Harry—doesn't he propose to do anything about it?"

"Why should he? The will's perfectly clear."

"Why shouldn't he? Just because the old crow went off her rocker in the last days of senile decay is no reason why he shouldn't do something to put it right. There must have been enough for both of you."

"Not so much. They found that Granny had been living on her capital for years. There was only about twenty thousand dollars left—and the house."

"What of it? He could spare half."

Jacqueline smiled—a rather tired little smile.

"You haven't met Harry. He's—difficult . . . He's been here, of course. The agents already have his instructions to sell the house and the furniture. He gave me a week to get out, and the week is up the day after tomorrow. . . . I couldn't possibly ask him for anything."

Simon lighted a cigarette as if it tasted of bad eggs and scowled malevolently about the room.

"The skunk! And so you get chucked out into the wide world with nothing but a hundred dollars."

"And the letters," she added ruefully.

"What the hell are these letters?"

"They're love letters," she said; and the Saint looked as if he would explode.

"*Love letters?*" he repeated in an awful voice.

"Yes. Granny had a great romance when she was a girl. Her parents wouldn't let her get any further with it because the boy hadn't any money and his family wasn't good enough. He went abroad with one of these heroic young ideas of making a fortune in South America and coming back in a gold-plated carriage to claim her. He died of fever somewhere in Brazil very soon after, but he wrote her three letters—two from British Guiana and one from Colombia. Oh, I know them by heart—I used to have to read them aloud to Granny almost every night, after her eyes got too bad for her to be able to read them herself. They're just the ordinary simple sort of thing that you'd expect in the circumstances, but to Granny they were the most precious thing she had. I suppose she had some funny old idea in her head that they'd be just as precious to me."

"She must have been screwy," said the Saint.

Jacqueline came up and put a hand over his mouth.

"She was very good to me when I was a kid," she said.

"I know, but——" Simon flung up his arms hopelessly. And then, almost reluctantly, he began to laugh. "But it does mean that I've just come back in time. And we'll have so much fun tonight that you won't even think about it for a minute."

Probably he made good his boast, for Simon Templar brought to the solemn business of enjoying himself the same gay zest and inspired impetuosity which he brought to his battles with the technicalities of the law. But if he made her forget, he himself remembered; and when he followed her into the living room of the house again much later, for a goodnight drink, the desolate scene of interrupted packing, and the copy of the will still lying on the table where he had put it down, brought the thoughts with which he had been subconsciously playing throughout the evening back into the forefront of his mind.

"Are you going to let Harry get away with it?" he asked her, with a sudden characteristic directness.

The girl shrugged.

"What else can I do?"

"I have an idea," said the Saint; and his blue eyes danced with an unholy delight which she had never seen in them before.

Mr Westler was not a man whose contacts with the Law had conspired to make him particularly happy about any of its workings; and therefore when he saw that the card which was brought to him in his hotel bore in its bottom left-hand corner the name of a firm with the words "Attorneys at Law" underneath it, he suffered an immediate hollow twinge in the base of his stomach for which he could scarcely be blamed. A moment's reflection, however, reminded him that another card with a similar inscription had recently been the forerunner of an extremely welcome windfall, and with this reassuring thought he told the bellboy to bring the visitor into his presence.

Mr Tombs, of Tombs, Tombs, and Tombs, as the card introduced him, was a tall lean man with neatly brushed white hair, bushy white eyebrows, a pair of gold-rimmed and drooping pince-nez on the end of a broad black ribbon and an engagingly avuncular manner which rapidly completed the task of restoring Harry Westler's momentarily shaken confidence. He came to the point with professional efficiency combined with professional pomposity.

"I have come to see you in connection with the estate of the—ah—late Mrs Laine. I understand that you are her heir."

"That's right," said Mr Westler.

He was a dark, flashily dressed man with small greedy eyes and a face rather reminiscent of that of a sick horse.

"Splendid." The lawyer placed his finger tips on his knees and leant forward peering benevolently over the rims of his glasses. "Now I for my part am representing the Sesame Mining Development Corporation."

He said this more or less as if he were announcing himself as the personal herald of Jehovah, but Mr Westler's mind ran in practical channels.

"Did my grandmother have shares in the company?" he asked quickly.

"Ah—ah—no. That is—ah—no. Not exactly. But I understand that she was in possession of a letter or document which my clients regard as extremely valuable."

"A letter?"

"Exactly. But perhaps I had better give you an outline of the situation. Your grandmother was in her youth greatly—ah—enamoured of a certain Sidney Farlance. Perhaps at some time or other you have heard her speak of him."

"Yes."

"For various reasons her parents refused to give their consent to the alliance; but the young people for their part refused to take no for an answer, and Farlance went abroad with the intention of making his fortune in foreign parts and returning in due course to claim his bride. In this ambition he was unhappily frustrated by his—ah—premature decease in Brazil. But it appears that during his travels in British Guiana he did become the owner of a mining concession in a certain very inaccessible area of territory. British Guiana, as you are doubtless aware," continued Mr Tombs in his dry pedagogic voice, "is traditionally reputed to be the source of the legend of El Dorado, the Gilded King, who was said to cover himself with pure gold and to wash it from him in the waters of a sacred lake called Manoa——"

"Never mind all that baloney," said Harry Westler, who was not interested in history or mythology. "Tell me about this concession."

Mr Tombs pressed his lips with a pained expression but he went on.

"At the time it did not appear that gold could be profitably obtained from this district and the claim was abandoned and forgotten. Modern engineering methods, however, have recently revealed deposits of almost fabulous value in the district, and my clients have obtained a concession to work it over a very large area of ground. Subsequent investigations into their title, meanwhile, have brought out the existence of this small—ah—prior concession granted to Sidney Farlance, which is situated almost in the centre of my client's territory and in a position which—ah—exploratory drillings have shown to be one of the richest areas in the district."

Mr Westler digested the information, and in place of the first sinking vacuum which had afflicted his stomach when he saw the word Law on his visitor's card, a sudden and ecstatic awe localized itself in the same place and began to cramp his lungs as if he had accidentally swallowed a rubber balloon with his breakfast and it was being rapidly inflated by some supernatural agency.

"You mean my grandmother owned this concession?"

"That is what—ah—my clients are endeavouring to discover. Farlance himself, of course, left no heirs, and we have been unable to trace any surviving members of his family. In the course of our inquiries, however, we did learn of his—ah—romantic interest in your grandmother, and we have every reason to believe that in the circumstances he would naturally have made her the beneficiary of any such asset, however problematical its value may have seemed at the time."

"And you want to buy it out—is that it?"

"Ah—yes. That is—ah—provided that our deductions are correct and the title can be established. I may say that my clients would be prepared to pay very liberally——"

"They'd have to," said Mr Westler briskly. "How much are they good for?"

The lawyer raised his hands deprecatingly.

"You need have no alarm, my dear Mr Westler. The actual figure would, of course, be a matter for negotiation but it would doubtless run into a number of millions. But first of all, you understand, we must trace the actual concession papers which will be sufficient to establish your right to negotiate. Now it seems that in view of the relationship between Farlance and your grandmother, she would probably have treasured his letters as women do even though she later married someone else, particularly if there was a document of that sort among them. People don't usually throw things like that away. In that case you will doubtless have inherited these letters along with her other personal property. Possibly you have not yet had an occasion to peruse them, but if you would do so as soon as possible——"

One of Harry Westler's few Napoleonic qualities was a remarkable capacity for quick and constructive thinking.

"Certainly I have the letters," he said, "but I haven't gone through them yet. My lawyer has them at present and he's in San Francisco today. He'll be back tomorrow morning, and I'll get hold of them at once. Come and see me again tomorrow afternoon and I expect I'll have some news for you."

"Tomorrow afternoon, Mr Westler? Certainly. I think that will be convenient. Ah—certainly." The lawyer stood up, took off his pince-nez, polished them and revolved them like a windmill on the end of their ribbon. "This has indeed been a most happy meeting, my dear sir. And may I say that I hope that tomorrow afternoon it will be even happier?"

"You can go on saying that right up till the time we start talking prices," said Harry.

The door had scarcely closed behind Mr Tombs when he was on the telephone to his cousin. He suppressed a sigh of relief when he heard her

voice and announced as casually as he could his intention of coming around
to see her.

"I think we ought to have another talk—I was terribly upset by the shock
of Granny's death when I saw you the other day and I'm afraid I wasn't quite
myself, but I'll make all the apologies you like when I get there," he said
in an unfamiliarly gentle voice which cost him a great effort to achieve,
and was grabbing his hat before the telephone was properly back on its
bracket.

He made a call at the bank on his way, and sat in the taxi which carried
him up into the hills as if its cushions had been upholstered with hot
spikes. The exact words of that portion of the will which referred to the
letters drummed through his memory with a staggering significance. *"My
letters from Sidney Farlance, knowing that she will find them of more
value than anything else I could leave her."* The visit of Mr Tombs had
made him understand them perfectly. His grandmother had known what
was in them; but did Jacqueline know? His heart almost stopped beating
with anxiety.

As he leapt out of the taxi and dashed towards the house he cannoned
into a small and weirdly apparelled elderly gent who was apparently emerg-
ing from the gate at the same time. Mr Westler checked himself involuntarily, and the elderly gent, sent flying by the impact, bounced off a gate-
post and tottered back at him. He clutched Harry by the sleeve and peered
up at him pathetically.

"Glhwf hngwglgl," he said pleadingly, "kngnduk glu bwtlhjp mnyihgli?"

"Oh, go climb a tree," snarled Mr Westler impatiently.

He pushed the little man roughly aside and went on.

Jacqueline opened the door to him, and Mr Westler steeled himself to
kiss her on the forehead with cousinly affection.

"I was an awful swine the other day, Jackie. I don't know what could
have been the matter with me. I've always been terribly selfish," he said
with an effort, "and at the time I didn't really see how badly Granny had
treated you. She didn't leave you anything except those letters, did she?"

"She left me a hundred dollars," said Jacqueline calmly.

"A hundred dollars!" said Harry indignantly. "After you'd given up everything else to take care of her. And she left me more than twenty thousand
dollars and the house and everything else in it. It's—disgusting! But I don't
have to take advantage of it, do I? I've been thinking a lot about it lately——"

Jacqueline lighted a cigarette and regarded him stonily.

"Thanks," she said briefly. "But I haven't asked you for any charity."

"It isn't charity," protested Mr Westler virtuously. "It's just a matter of
doing the decent thing. The lawyers have done their share—handed everything over to me and seen that the will was carried out. Now we can

start again. We could pool everything again and divide it the way we think it ought to be divided."

"As far as I'm concerned, that's been done already."

"But I'm not happy about it. I've got all the money, and you know what I'm like. I'll probably gamble it all away in a few months."

"That's your affair."

"Oh, don't be like that, Jackie. I've apologized, haven't I? Besides, what Granny left you is worth a lot more than money. I mean those letters of hers. I'd willingly give up five thousand dollars of my share if I could have had those. They're the one thing of the old lady's which really means a great deal to me."

"You're becoming very sentimental all of a sudden, aren't you?" asked the girl curiously.

"Maybe I am. I suppose you can't really believe that a rotter like me could feel that way about anything, but Granny was the only person in the world who ever really believed any good of me and liked me in spite of everything. If I gave you five thousand dollars for those letters, it wouldn't be charity—I'd be paying less than I think they're worth. Let's put it that way if you'd rather, Jackie. An ordinary business deal. If I had them," said Mr. Westler, with something like a sob in his voice, "they'd always be a reminder to me of the old lady and how good she was. They might help me to go straight . . ."

His emotion was so touching that even Jacqueline's cynical incredulity lost some of its assurance. Harry Westler was playing his part with every technical trick that he knew, and he had a mastery of these emotional devices which victims far more hard-boiled than Jacqueline had experienced to their cost.

"I'm thoroughly ashamed of myself and I want to put things right in any way I can. Don't make me feel any worse than I do already. Look here, I'll give you ten thousand dollars for the letters and I won't regret a penny of it. You won't regret it either, will you, if they help me to keep out of trouble in future?"

Jacqueline smiled in spite of herself. It was not in her nature to bear malice, and it was very hard for her to resist an appeal that was made in those terms. Also, with the practical side of her mind, she was honest enough to realize that her grandmother's letters had no sentimental value for her whatever, and that ten thousand dollars was a sum of money which she could not afford to refuse unless her pride was compelled to forbid it; her night out with the Saint had helped her to forget her problems for the moment, but she had awakened that morning with a very sober realization of the position in which she was going to find herself within the next forty-eight hours.

"If you put it like that I can't very well refuse, can I?" she said, and Harry jumped up and clasped her fervently by the hand.

"You'll really do it, Jackie? You don't know how much I appreciate it." She disengaged herself quietly.

"It doesn't do me any harm," she told him truthfully. "Would you like to have the letters now?"

"If they're anywhere handy. I brought some money along with me, so we can fix it all up right away."

She went upstairs and fetched the letters from the dressing table in her grandmother's room. Mr Westler took them and tore off the faded ribbon with which they were tied together with slightly trembling fingers which she attributed to an unexpected depth of emotion. One by one he took them out of their envelopes and read rapidly through them. The last sheet of the third letter was a different kind of paper from the rest. The paper was brown and discoloured and cracked in the folds, and the ink had the rust-brown hue of great age; but he saw the heavy official seal in one corner and strained his eyes to decipher the stiff old-fashioned script.

We, Philip Edmond Wodehouse, Commander of the Most Noble Order of the Bath, Governor in the name of His Britannic Majesty of the Colony of British Guiana, by virtue of the powers conferred upon us by His Majesty's Privy Council, do hereby proclaim and declare to all whom it may concern that we have this day granted to Sidney Farlance, a subject of His Majesty the King, and to his heirs and assigns being determined by the possession of this authority, the sole right to prospect and mine for minerals of any kind whatsoever in the territory indicated and described in the sketch map at the foot of this authority, for the term of nine hundred and ninety-nine years from the date of these presents.

Given under our hand and seal this third day of January Eighteen Hundred and Fifty-Six.

At the bottom of the sheet below the map and description was scrawled in a different hand: *"This is all for you. S.F."*

Harry Westler stuffed the letters into his pocket and took out his wallet. His heart was beating in a delirious rhythm of ecstasy and sending the blood roaring through his ears like the crashing crescendo of a symphony. The Gates of Paradise seemed to have opened up and deluged him with all their reservoirs of bliss. The whole world was his sweetheart. If the elderly gent whose strange nasal garglings he had dismissed so discourteously a short time ago had cannoned into him again at that moment, it is almost certain that Mr Westler would not have told him to go and climb a tree. He would probably have kissed him on both cheeks and given him a nickel.

For the first time in his life, Harry Westler counted out ten thousand-dollar bills as cheerfully as he would have counted them in.

"There you are, Jackie. And I'm not kidding—it takes a load off my mind. If you think of anything else I can do for you, just let me know."

"I think you've done more than anyone could have asked," she said generously. "Won't you stay and have a drink?"

Mr Westler declined the offer firmly. He had no moral prejudice against drinking, and in fact he wanted a drink very badly, but more particularly he wanted to have it in a place where he would not have to place any more restraint on the shouting rhapsodies that were seething through his system like bubbles through champagne.

Some two hours later, when Simon Templar drifted into the house, he found Jacqueline still looking slightly dazed. She flung her arms around his neck and kissed him.

"Simon!" she gasped. "You must be a mascot or something. You'll never guess what's happened."

"I'll tell you exactly what's happened," said the Saint calmly. "Cousin Harry has been here, told you that he'd rather have dear old Granny's love letters than all the money in the world and paid you a hell of a good price for them. At least I hope he paid you a hell of a good price."

Jacqueline gaped at him weakly.

"He paid me ten thousand dollars. But how on earth did you know? Why did he do it?"

"He did it because a lawyer called on him this morning and told him that Sidney Farlance had collared an absolutely priceless mining concession when he was in British Guiana, and that there was probably something about it in the letters which would be worth millions to whoever had them to prove his claim."

She looked at him aghast.

"A mining concession? I don't remember anything about it——"

"You wouldn't," said the Saint kindly. "It wasn't there until I slipped it in when I got you to show me the letters at breakfast time this morning. I sat up for the other half of the night faking the best imitation I could of what I thought a concession ought to look like, and apparently it was good enough for Harry. Of course I was the lawyer who told him all about it, and I think I fed him the oil pretty smoothly, so perhaps there was some excuse for him. I take it that he was quite excited about it—I see he didn't even bother to take the envelopes."

Jacqueline opened her mouth again, but what she was going to say with it remained a permanently unsolved question, for at that moment the unnecessarily vigorous ringing of a bell stopped her short. The Saint cocked his ears speculatively at the sound and a rather pleased and seraphic smile worked itself into his face.

"I expect this is Harry coming back," he said. "He wasn't supposed to see me again until tomorrow but I suppose he couldn't wait. He's probably tried to ring me up at the address I had printed on my card and discovered that there ain't no such lawyers as I was supposed to represent. It will be rather interesting to hear what he has to say."

For once, however, Simon's guess was wrong. Instead of the indignant equine features of Harry Westler, he confronted the pink imploring features of the small and shapeless elderly gent with whom he had danced prettily around the gateposts the day before. The little man's face lighted up and he bounced over the doorstep and seized the Saint joyfully by both lapels of his coat.

"Mnyng hlfwgl!" he crowed triumphantly. "Ahkgmp glglgl hndiuph-wmp!"

Simon recoiled slightly.

"Yes. I know," he said soothingly. "But it's five o'clock on Fridays. Two dollars every other yard."

"Ogh hmbals!" said the little man.

He let go the Saint's coat, ducked under his arms and scuttled on into the living room.

"Oi!" said the Saint feebly.

"May I explain, sir?"

Another voice spoke from the doorway, and Simon perceived that the little man had not come alone. Someone else had taken his place on the threshold—a thin and mournful-looking individual whom the Saint somewhat pardonably took to be the little man's keeper.

"Are you looking after that?" he inquired resignedly. "And why don't you keep it on a lead?"

The mournful-looking individual shook his head.

"That is Mr Horatio Ive, sir—he is a very rich man, but he suffers from an unfortunate impediment in his speech. Very few people can understand him. I go about with him as his interpreter, but I have been in bed for the last three days with a chill——"

A shrill war whoop from the other room interrupted the explanation.

"We'd better go and see how he's getting on," said the Saint.

"Mr Ive is very impulsive, sir," went on the sad-looking interpreter. "He was most anxious to see somebody here, and even though I was unable to accompany him he has called here several times alone. I understand that he found it impossible to make himself understood. He practically dragged me out of bed to come with him now."

"What's he so excited about?" asked the Saint, as they walked towards the living room.

"He's interested in some letters, sir, belonging to the late Mrs Laine.

She happened to show them to him when they met once several years ago, and he wanted to buy them. She refused to sell them for sentimental reasons, but as soon as he read of her death he decided to approach her heirs."

"Are you talking about her love letters from a bird called Sidney Farlance?" Simon asked hollowly.

"Yes sir. The gentleman who worked in British Guiana. Mr Ive is prepared to pay something like fifty thousand dollars—— Is anything the matter, sir?"

Simon Templar swallowed.

"Oh, nothing," he said faintly. "Nothing at all."

They entered the living room to interrupt a scene of considerable excitement. Backing towards the wall, with a blank expression of alarm widening her eyes, Jacqueline Laine was staring dumbly at the small elderly gent, who was capering about in front of her like a frenzied redskin, spluttering yard after yard of his incomprehensible adenoidal honks interspersed with wild piercing squeaks apparently expressive of intolerable joy. In each hand he held an envelope aloft like a banner.

As his interpreter came in, he turned and rushed towards him, loosing off a fresh stream of noises like those of a hysterical duck.

"Mr Ive is saying, sir," explained the interpreter, raising his voice harmoniously above the din, "that each of those envelopes bears a perfect example of the British Guiana one-cent magenta stamp of 1856, of which only one specimen was previously believed to exist. Mr Ive is an ardent philatelist, sir, and these envelopes——"

Simon Templar blinked hazily at the small crudely printed stamp in the corner of the envelope which the little man was waving under his nose.

"You mean," he said cautiously, "that Mr Ive is really only interested in the envelopes?"

"Yes sir."

"Not the letters themselves?"

"Not the letters."

"And he's been flapping around the house all this time trying to tell somebody about it?"

"Yes sir."

Simon Templar drew a deep breath. The foundations of the world were spinning giddily around his ears but his natural resilience was unconquerable. He took out a handkerchief and mopped his brow.

"In that case," he said contentedly, "I'm sure we can do business. What do you say, Jacqueline?"

Jacqueline clutched his arm and nodded breathlessly.

"Hlgagtsk sweghlemlgl," beamed Mr Ive.

THE MAN WHO LIKED ANTS

FROM *The Happy Highwayman*

IN THE SACRED CAUSE OF ACCURACY, and out of selfless devotion to what I grandiloquently call My Public, I have done many weird and laborious things in order to protect the readers of the Saint Saga, so far as possible, from anything misleading or synthetic.

I have traveled to distant and insanitary places, bored myself with a multitude of dull and dangerous characters, learned to fly airplanes, crawled around the bottom of the sea in diving suits, consumed large quantities of alcohol, and generally left no gallstone unturned to insure that my vicarious adventurers shall receive the greatest authenticity I can deliver.

In order to get the background for this short story I did nothing so glamorous. I merely browsed through some twenty volumes on the subject of Ants and kindred insects. And I am here obliged to admit that even that concentrated course of study was not enough.

Two or three important entomologists with alphabets after their names have taken the trouble to write and point out to me certain biological impossibilities in the background of this story.

I mention this merely in order to impress upon the amateur and professional entomologists in the audience that I am now thoroughly bored with the subject, and that I do not want any more heckling or quibbling from the bleachers.

Here is the story for what it is worth, and if you don't like it you can feed it to your termites.

I still like it as an experiment. In the course of a frightening number of Saint stories, I have tried to project him into as many established story styles as possible. This is my one attempt to put the Saint into a pure horror-science story; and those readers who like Frankenstein and Dracula may get a pleasant goose-pimple out of my ants.

THE MAN WHO LIKED ANTS

I WONDER what would have happened if you had gone into a respectable business, Saint," Ivar Nordsten remarked one afternoon.

Simon Templar smiled at him so innocently that for an instant his nickname might almost have seemed justified—if it had not been for the faint lazy twinkle of unsaintly mockery that stirred at the back of his blue eyes.

"The question is too farfetched, Ivar. You might as well speculate about what would have happened if I'd been a Martian or a horse."

They sat on the veranda of the house of Ivar Nordsten—whose name was not really Ivar Nordsten, but who was alive that day and the master of fabulous millions only because the course of one of the Saint's lawless escapades had once crossed his path at a time when death would have seemed a happy release. He of all living men should have had no wish to change the history of that twentieth-century Robin Hood, whose dark reckless face could be found photographed in half the police archives of the world, and whose gay impudence of outlawry had in its time set the underworlds of five continents buzzing like nests of infuriated wasps. But in that mood of idle fantasy which may well come with the after-lunch contentment of a warm Florida afternoon, Nordsten would have put forward almost any preposterous premise that might give him the pleasure of listening to his friend.

"It isn't as farfetched as that," he said. "You will never admit it, but you have many respectable instincts."

"But I have so many more disreputable ones to keep them under control," answered the Saint earnestly. "And it's always been so much more amusing to indulge the disreputable instincts. . . . No, Ivar, I mustn't let you make a paragon out of me. If I were quite cynically psychoanalyzing myself, I should probably say that the reason why I only soak the more obvious excrescences on the human race is because it makes everything okay with my respectable instincts and lets them go peacefully to sleep. Then I can turn all my disreputable impulses loose on the mechanical problem of soaking this obvious excrescence in some satisfyingly novel and juicy manner, and get all the fun of original sin out of it without any qualms of conscience."

"But you contradict yourself. The mere fact that you speak in terms of what you call 'an obvious excrescence on the human race' proves that you have some moral standards by which you judge him, and that you have some idealistic interest in the human race itself."

"The human race," said the Saint sombrely, "is a repulsive, dull, bloated, ill-conditioned and ill-favoured mass of dimly conscious meat, the chief justification for whose existence is that it provides a contrasting back-

ground against which my beauty and spiritual perfections can shine with a
lustre only exceeded by your own."

"You have a natural modesty which I had never suspected," Nordsten
observed gravely, and they both laughed. "But," he added, "I think you will
get on well with Dr Sardon. "

"Who is he?"

"A neighbour of mine. We are dining with him tonight."

Simon frowned.

"I warned you that I was travelling without any dress clothes," he began,
but Nordsten shook his head maliciously.

"Dr Sardon likes dress clothes even less than you do. And you never
warned me that you were coming here at all. So what could I do? I accepted
his invitation a week ago, so when you arrived I could only tell Sardon what
had happened. Of course he insisted that you must come with me. But I
think he will interest you."

The Saint sighed resignedly and swished the highball gently around in
his glass so that the ice clinked.

"Why should I be interested in any of your neighbours?" he protested. "I
didn't come here to commit any crimes; and I'm sure all these people are as
respectable as millionaires can be."

"Dr Sardon is not a millionaire. He is a very brilliant biologist."

"What else makes him interesting?"

"He is very fond of ants," said Nordsten seriously, and the Saint sat up.
Then he finished his drink deliberately and put down the glass.

"Now I know that this climate doesn't agree with you," he said. "Let's
get changed and go down to the tennis court. I'll put you in your place
before we start the evening."

Nevertheless he drove over to Dr Sardon's house that evening in a mood
of open-minded curiosity. Scientists he had known before, men who went
down thousands of feet into the sea to look at globigerina ooze and men who
devised complicated electrical gadgets in laboratories to manufacture gold;
but this was the first time that he had heard of a biologist who was fond of
ants. Everything that was out of the ordinary was prospective material for
the Saint. It must be admitted that in simplifying his own career to elementary equations by which obvious excrescences on the human race could be
soaked, he did himself less than justice.

But there was nothing about the square smooth-shaven man who was
introduced to him as Dr Sardon to take away the breath of any hardened
outlaw. He might perhaps have been an ordinary efficient doctor, possibly
with an exclusive and sophisticated practice; more probably he could have
been a successful stockbroker, or the manager of any profitable commercial
business. He shook hands with them briskly and almost mechanically, seem-

ing to summarize the Saint in one sweeping glance through his crisp-looking rimless pince-nez.

"No, you're not a bit late, Mr Nordsten. As a matter of fact I was working until twenty minutes ago. If you had come earlier I should have been quite embarrassed."

He introduced his niece, a dark slender girl with a quiet and rather aloof beauty which would have been chilling if it had not been relieved by the friendly humour of her brown eyes. About her, Simon admitted, there might certainly have been things to attract the attention of a modern buccaneer.

"Carmen has been assisting me. She has a very good degree from Columbia."

He made no other unprompted reference to his researches, and Simon recognized him as the modern type of scientist whose carefully cultivated pose of matter-of-fact worldliness is just as fashionable an affectation as the mystical and bearded eccentricity of his predecessors used to be. Dr Sardon talked about politics, about his golf handicap and about the art of Otto Soglow. He was an entertaining and effective conversationalist but he might never have heard of such a thing as biology until towards the close of dinner Ivar Nordsten skilfully turned a discussion of gardening to the subject of insect pests.

"Although, of course," he said, "you would not call them that."

It was strange to see the dark glow that came into Sardon's eyes.

"As a popular term," he said in his deep vibrant voice, "I suppose it is too well established for me to change it. But it would be much more reasonable for the insects to talk about human pests."

He turned to Simon.

"I expect Mr Nordsten has already warned you about the—bee in my bonnet," he said; but he used the phrase without smiling. "Do you by any chance know anything about the subject?"

"I had a flea once," said the Saint reminiscently. "I called him Goebbels. But he left me."

"Then you would be surprised to know how many of the most sensational achievements of man were surpassed by the insects hundreds of years ago without any artificial aids." The finger tips of his strong nervous hands played a tattoo against each other. "You talk about the Age of Speed and Man's Conquest of the Air; and yet the fly *Cephenomia*, the swiftest living creature, can outpace the fastest of your boasted aeroplanes. What is the greatest scientific marvel of the century? Probably you would say radio. But Count Arco, the German radio expert, has proved the existence of a kind of wireless telegraphy, or telepathy, between certain species of beetle, which makes nothing of a separation of miles. Lakhovsky claims to have demonstrated that this is common to several other insects. When the *Redemanni* termites build their twenty-five-foot conical towers topped with ten-foot chimneys they are performing much greater marvels of engineering than building an Empire State Building. To match them, in proportion to our size, we should have to put up skyscrapers four thousand feet high—and do it without tools."

"I knew the ants would come into it," said Nordsten sotto voce.

Sardon turned on him with his hot piercing gaze.

"Termites are not true ants—the term 'white ants' is a misnomer. Actually they are related to the cockroach. I merely mentioned them as one of the most remarkable of the lower insects. They have a superb social organization, and they may even be superior strategists to the true ants, but they were never destined to conquer the globe. The reason is that they cannot stand light and they cannot tolerate temperatures below twenty degrees centigrade. Therefore, their fields of expansion are for ever limited. They are one of Nature's false beginnings. They are a much older species than man, and they have evolved as far as they are likely to evolve. . . . It is not the same with the true ants."

He leaned forward over the table, with his face white and transfigured as if in a kind of trance.

"The true ant is the destined ruler of the earth. Can you imagine a state of society in which there was no idleness, no poverty, no unemployment, no unrest? We humans would say that it was an unattainable Utopia; and yet it was in existence among the ants when man was a hairy savage scarcely distinguishable from an ape. You may say that it is incompatible with progress—that it could only be achieved in the same way that it is achieved by domestic cattle. But the ant has the same instincts which have made man the tyrant of creation in his time. *Lasius fuliginosus* keeps and milks its own domestic cattle, in the form of plant lice. *Polyergus rufescens* and *Formica sanguinea* capture slaves and put them to work. *Messor barbarus,* the harvesting ant, collects and stores grain. The *Attiini* cultivate mushrooms in underground forcing houses. And all these things are done, not for private gain, but for the good of the whole community. Could man in any of his advances ever boast of that?"

"But if ants have so many advantages," said the Saint slowly, "and they've been civilized so much longer than man, why haven't they conquered the earth before this?"

"Because Nature cheated them. Having given them so much, she made them wait for the last essential—pure physical bulk."

"The brontosaurus had enough of that," said Nordsten, "and yet man took its place."

Sardon's thin lips curled.

"The difference in size between man and brontosaurus was nothing compared with the difference in size between man and ant. There are limits to the superiority of brain over brawn—even to the superiority of the brain of an ant, which in proportion to its size is twice as large as the brain of a man. But the time is coming . . ."

His voice sank almost to a whisper, and in the dim light of candles on the table the smouldering luminousness of his eyes seemed to leave the rest of his face in deep shadow.

"With the ant, Nature overreached herself. The ant was ready to take his place at the head of creation before creation was ready for him—before the solar system had progressed far enough to give him the conditions in which his body, and his brain with it, his brain which in all its intrinsic qualities is so much finer than the brain of man, could grow to the brute size at which all its potentialities could be developed. Nevertheless, when the solar system is older, and the sun is red because the white heat of its fire is exhausted, and the red light which will accelerate the growth of all living cells is stronger, the ant will be waiting for his turn. Unless Nature finds a swifter instrument than Time to put right her miscalculation . . ."

"Does it matter?" asked the Saint lightly, and Sardon's face seemed to flame at him.

"It matters. That is only another thing which we can learn from the ant—that individual profit and ambition should count for nothing beside more enduring good. Listen. When I was a boy I loved small creatures. Among them I kept a colony of ants. In a glass box. I watched them in their busy lives, I studied them as they built their nest, I saw how they divided their labour and how they lived and died so that their common life could go on. I loved them because they were so much better than everyone else I knew. But the other boys could not understand. They thought I was soft and stupid. They were always tormenting me. One day they found my glass box where the ants lived. I fought them, but there were so many of them. They were big and cruel. They made a fire and they put my box on it, while they held me. I saw the ants running, fighting, struggling insanely——" The hushed voice tightened as he spoke until it became thin and shrill like a suppressed scream. "I saw them curling up and shriveling, writhing, tortured. I could hear the hiss of their seething agony in the flames. I saw them going mad, twisting—sprawling—blackening—*burning alive before my eyes*——"

"Uncle!"

The quiet voice of the girl Carmen cut softly across the muted shriek in which the last words were spoken, so quietly and normally that it was only in the contrast that Simon realized that Sardon had not really raised his voice.

The wild fire died slowly out of Sardon's eyes. For a moment his face remained set and frozen, and then, as if he had only been recalled from a fleeting lapse of attention, he seemed to come awake again with a slight start.

"Where was I?" he said calmly. "Oh yes. I was speaking about the intelligence of ants. . . . It is even a mistake to assume, because they make no audible sounds, that they have not just as excellent means of communication as ourselves. Whether they share the telepathic gifts of other insects is a disputed point, but it is certain that in their antennae they possess an idiom which is adequate to all ordinary needs. By close study and observation it has even been possible for us to learn some of the elementary gestures. The work of Karl Escherich . . ."

He went into details, in the same detached incisive tone in which he had been speaking before his outburst.

Simon Templar's fingers stroked over the cloth, found a crumb of bread and massaged it gradually into a soft round pellet. He stole a casual glance at the girl. Her aloof oval face was pale, but that might have been its natural complexion; her composure was unaltered. Sardon's outburst might never have occurred, and she might never have had to interrupt it. Only the Saint thought that he saw a shadow of fear moving far down in her eyes.

Even after Carmen had left the table, and the room was richening with the comfortable aromas of coffee and liqueur, brandy and cigars, Sardon was still riding his hobbyhorse. It went on for nearly an hour, until at one of the rare lulls in the discussion Nordsten said: "All the same, Doctor, you are very mysterious about what this has to do with your own experiments."

Sardon's hands rested on the table, white and motionless, the fingers spread out.

"Because I was not ready. Even to my friends I should not like to show anything incomplete. But in the last few weeks I have disposed of my uncertainty. Tonight, if you like, I could show you a little."

"We should be honoured."

The flat pressure of Sardon's hands on the table increased as he pushed back his chair and stood up.

"My workshops are at the end of the garden," he said, and blew out the four candles.

As they rose and followed him from the room, Nordsten touched the Saint's arm and said in a low voice: "Are you sorry I dragged you out?"

"I don't know yet," answered the Saint soberly.

The girl Carmen rejoined them as they left the house. Simon found her walking beside him as they strolled through the warm moonlight. He dropped the remains of his cigar and offered his cigarette case; they stopped for a moment while he gave her a light. Neither of them spoke, but her arm slipped through his as they went on.

The blaze of lights which Sardon switched on in his laboratory wiped the dim silvery gloom out of their eyes in a crash of harsh glaring illumination.

In contrast with the tasteful furnishings of the house, the cold white walls and bare tiled floor struck the Saint's sensitive vision with the hygienic and inhuman chill which such places always gave him. But Sardon's laboratory was not like any other place of that kind in which he had ever been.

Ranged along the walls were rows of big glass-fronted boxes, in which apparently formless heaps of litter and rubble could be dimly made out. His eye was caught by a movement in one of the boxes, and he stepped up to look at it more closely. Almost in the same moment he stopped, and nearly recoiled from it, as he realized that he was looking at the largest ant that he had ever seen. It was fully six inches long; and, magnified in that proportion, he could see every joint in its shiny armour-plated surface and the curious bifurcated claws at the ends of its legs. It stood there with its antennae waving gently, watching him with its bulging beady eyes . . .

"*Tetramorium cespitum*," said Dr Sardon, standing beside him. "One of my early experiments. Its natural size is about three tenths of an inch, but it did not respond very well to treatment."

"I should say it had responded heroically," said the Saint. "You don't mean you can do better than that?"

Sardon smiled.

"It was one of my early experiments," he repeated. "I was then merely trying to improve on the work of Ludwig and Ries of Berne, who were breeding giant insects almost comparable with that one, many years ago, with the aid of red light. Subsequently I discovered another principle of growth which they had overlooked, and I also found that an artificial selective cross-breeding between different species not only improved the potential size but also increased the intelligence. For instance, here is one of my later results—a combination of *Oecophylla smaragdina* and *Prenolepsis imparis*."

He went to one of the longer and larger boxes at the end of the room. At first Simon could see nothing but a great mound of twigs and leaves piled high in one corner. There were two or three bones, stripped bare and white, lying on the sandy floor of the box. . . . Then Sardon tapped on the glass, and Simon saw with a sudden thrill of horror that what had been a dark hole in the mound of leaves was no longer black and empty. There was a head peering out of the shadow—dark bronze-green, iridescent, covered with short sparse bristly hairs. . . .

"*Oecophylla* is, of course, one of the more advanced species," Sardon was saying, in his calm precise manner. "It is the only known creature other than man to use a tool. The larvae secrete a substance similar to silk, with which the ants weave leaves together to make their nests, holding the larvae in their jaws and using them as shuttles. I don't yet know whether my hybrid has inherited that instinct."

"It looks as if it would make a charming pet, anyway," murmured the Saint thoughtfully. "Sort of improved lap dog, isn't it?"

The faint sly smile stayed fixed on Sardon's thin lips. He took two steps further, to a wide sliding door that took up most of the wall at the end of the laboratory, and looked back at them sidelong.

"Perhaps you would like to see the future ruler of the world," he said, so very softly that it seemed as if everyone else stopped breathing while he spoke.

Simon heard the girl beside him catch her breath, and Nordsten said quickly: "Surely we've troubled you enough already——"

"I should like to see it," said the Saint quietly.

Sardon's tongue slid once over his lips. He put his hand up and moved a couple of levers on the glittering panels of dials and switches beside the door. It was to the Saint that his gaze returned, with that rapt expression of strangely cunning and yet childish happiness.

"You will see it from where you stand. I will ask you to keep perfectly still, so as not to draw attention to yourselves—there is a strain of *Dorylina* in this one. *Dorylina* is one of the most intelligent and highly disciplined species, but it is also the most savage. I do not wish it to become angry——"

His arm stretched out to the handle of the door. He slid it aside in one movement, standing with his back to it, facing them.

The girl's cold hand touched the Saint's wrist. Her fingers slipped down over his hand and locked in with his own, clutching them in a sudden convulsive grip. He heard Ivar Nordsten's suppressed gasp as it caught in his throat, and an icy tingle ran up his spine and broke out in a clammy dew on his forehead.

The rich red light from the chamber beyond the door spilled out like liquid fire, so fierce and vivid that it seemed as if it could only be accompanied by the scorching heat of an open furnace; but it held only a slight appreciable warmth. It beat down from huge crimson arcs ranged along the cornices of the inner room among a maze of shining tubes and twisted wires; there was a great glass ball opposite in which a pale yellow streak of lightning forked and flickered with a faint humming sound. The light struck scarlet highlights from the gleaming bars of a great metal cage like a gigantic chicken coop which filled the centre of the room to within a yard of the walls. And within the cage something monstrous and incredible stood motionless, staring at them.

Simon would see it sometimes, years afterwards, in uneasy dreams. Something immense and frightful, glistening like burnished copper, balanced on angled legs like bars of plated metal. Only for a few seconds he saw it then, and for most of that time he was held fascinated by its eyes, understanding something that he would never have believed before. . . .

And then suddenly the thing moved, swiftly and horribly and without sound; and Sardon slammed the door shut, blotting out the eye-aching sea of red light and leaving only the austere cold whiteness of the laboratory.

"They are not all like lap dogs," Sardon said in a kind of whisper.

Simon took out a handkerchief and passed it across his brow. The last thing about that weird scene that fixed itself consciously in his memory was the girl's fingers relaxing their tense grip on his hand, and Sardon's eyes, bland and efficient and businesslike again, pinned steadily on them both in a sort of secret sneer. . . .

"What do you think of our friend?" Ivar Nordsten asked, as they drove home two hours later.

Simon stretched out a long arm for the lighter at the side of the car.

"He is a lunatic—but of course you knew that. I'm only wondering whether he is quite harmless."

"You ought to sympathize with his contempt for the human race."

The red glow of the Saint's cigarette end brightened so that for an instant the interior of the car was filled with something like a pale reflection of the unearthly crimson luminance which they had seen in Dr Sardon's forcing room.

"Did you sympathize with his affection for his pets?"

"Those great ants?" Nordsten shivered involuntarily. "No. That last one—it was the most frightful thing I have ever seen. I suppose it was really alive?"

"It was alive," said the Saint steadily. "That's why I'm wondering whether Dr Sardon is harmless. I don't know what you were looking at, Ivar, but I'll tell you what made my blood run cold. It wasn't the mere size of the thing—though any common or garden ant would be terrifying enough if you enlarged it to those dimensions. It was worse than that. It was the proof that Sardon was right. That ant was looking at me. Not like any other insect or even animal that I've ever seen, but like an insect with a man's brain might look. That was the most frightening thing to me. *It knew!*"

Nordsten stared at him.

"You mean that you believe what he was saying about it being the future ruler of the world?"

"By itself, no," answered Simon. "But if it were not by itself——"

He did not finish the sentence; and they were silent for the rest of the drive. Before they went to bed he asked one more question.

"Who else knows about these experiments?"

"No one, I believe. He told me the other day that he was not prepared to say anything about them until he could show complete success. As a matter of fact, I lent him some money to go on with his work, and that is the only reason he took me into his confidence. I was surprised when he showed us his laboratory tonight—even I had never seen it before."

"So he is convinced now that he can show a complete success," said the Saint quietly, and was still subdued and preoccupied the next morning.

In the afternoon he refused to swim or play tennis. He sat hunched up in a chair on the veranda, scowling into space and smoking innumerable cigarettes, except when he rose to pace restlessly up and down like a big nervous cat.

"What you are really worried about is the girl," Nordsten teased him.

"She's pretty enough to worry about," said the Saint shamelessly. "I think I'll go over and ask her for a cocktail."

Nordsten smiled.

"If it will make you a human being again, by all means do," he said. "If you don't come back to dinner I shall know that she is appreciating your anxiety. In any case, I shall probably be very late myself. I have to attend a committee meeting at the golf club and that always adjourns to the bar and goes on for hours."

But the brief tropical twilight had already given way to the dark before Simon made good his threat. He took out Ivar Nordsten's spare Rolls-Royce and drove slowly over the highway until he found the turning that led through the deep cypress groves to the doctor's house. He was prepared to feel foolish; and yet as his headlights circled through the iron gates he touched his hip pocket to reassure himself that if the need arose he might still feel wise.

The trees arching over the drive formed a ghostly tunnel down which the Rolls chased its own forerush of light. The smooth hiss of the engine accentuated rather than broke the silence, so that the mind even of a hardened and unimaginative man might cling to the comfort of that faint sound in the same way that the mind of a child might cling to the light of a candle as a comfort against the gathering terrors of the night. The Saint's lip curled cynically at the flight of his own thoughts. . . .

And then, as the car turned a bend in the drive, he saw the girl, and trod fiercely on the brakes.

The tires shrieked on the macadam and the engine stalled as the big car rocked to a standstill. It flashed through the Saint's mind at that instant, when all sound was abruptly wiped out, that the stillness which he had imagined before was too complete for accident. He felt the skin creep over his back, and had to call on an effort of will to force himself to open the door and get out of the car.

She lay face downwards, halfway across the drive, in the pool of illumination shed by the glaring headlights. Simon turned her over and raised her head on his arm. Her eyelids twitched as he did so; a kind of moan broke from her lips, and she fought away from him, in a dreadful wildness of panic, for the brief moment before her eyes opened and she recognized him.

"My dear," he said, "what has been happening?"

She had gone limp in his arms, the breath jerking pitifully through her lips, but she had not fainted again. And behind him, in that surround of stifling stillness, he heard quite clearly the rustle of something brushing stealthily over the grass beside the drive. He saw her eyes turning over his shoulder, saw the wide horror in them.

"*Look!*"

He spun round, whipping the gun from his pocket, and for more than a second he was paralyzed. For that eternity he saw the thing, deep in the far shadows, dimly illumined by the marginal reflections from the beam of the headlights—something gross and swollen, a dirty grey-white, shaped rather like a great bleached sausage, hideously bloated. Then the darkness swallowed it again, even as his shot smashed the silence into a hundred tiny echoes.

The girl was struggling to her feet. He snatched at her wrist.

"This way."

He got her into the car and slammed the door. Steel and glass closed round them to give an absurd relief, the weak unreasoning comfort to the naked flesh which men under a bombardment find in cowering behind canvas screens. She slumped against his shoulder, sobbing hysterically.

"Oh, my God. My God!"

"What was it?" he asked.

"It's escaped again. I knew it would. He can't handle it——"

"Has it got loose before?"

"Yes. Once."

He tapped a cigarette on his thumbnail, stroked his lighter. His face was a beaten mask of bronze and granite in the red glow as he drew the smoke down into the mainsprings of his leaping nerves.

"I never dreamed it had come to that," he said. "Even last night, I wouldn't have believed it."

"He wouldn't have shown you that. Even when he was boasting, he wouldn't have shown you. That was his secret . . . And I've helped him. Oh God," she said. "I can't go on!"

He gripped her shoulders.

"Carmen," he said quietly. "You must go away from here."

"He'd kill me."

"You must go away."

The headlamps threw back enough light for him to see her face, tear-streaked and desperate.

"He's mad," she said. "He must be. Those horrible things . . . I'm afraid. I wanted to go away but he wouldn't let me. I can't go on. Something terrible is going to happen. One day I saw it catch a dog . . . Oh, my God, if you hadn't come when you did——"

"Carmen." He still held her, speaking slowly and deliberately, putting every gift of sanity that he possessed into the level dominance of his voice. "You must not talk like this. You're safe now. Take hold of yourself."

She nodded.

"I know. I'm sorry. I'll be all right. But——"

"Can you drive?"

"Yes."

He started the engine and turned the car round. Then he pushed the gear lever into neutral and set the hand brake.

"Drive this car," he said. "Take it down to the gates and wait for me there. You'll be close to the highway, and there'll be plenty of other cars passing for company. Even if you do see anything, you needn't be frightened. Treat the car like a tank and run it over. Ivar won't mind—he's got plenty more. And if you hear anything, don't worry. Give me half an hour, and if I'm not back go to Ivar's and talk to him."

Her mouth opened incredulously.

"You're not getting out again?"

"I am. And I'm scared stiff." The ghost of a smile touched his lips, and then she saw that his face was stern and cold. "But I must talk to your uncle."

He gripped her arm for a moment, kissed her lightly and got out. Without a backward glance he walked quickly away from the car, up the drive towards the house. A flashlight in his left hand lanced the darkness ahead of him with its powerful beam, and he swung it from left to right as he walked, holding his gun in his right hand. His ears strained into the gloom which his eyes could not penetrate, probing the silence under the soft scuff of his own footsteps for any sound that would give him warning; but he forced himself not to look back. The palms of his hands were moist.

The house loomed up in front of him. He turned off to one side of the building, following the direction in which he remembered that Dr Sardon's laboratory lay. Almost at once he saw the squares of lighted windows through the trees. A dull clang of sound came to him, followed by a sort of furious thumping. He checked himself; and then as he walked on more quickly some of the lighted windows went black. The door of the laboratory opened as the last light went out, and his torch framed Dr Sardon and the doorway in its yellow circle.

Sardon was pale and dishevelled, his clothes awry. One of his sleeves was torn, and there was a scratch on his face from which blood ran. He flinched from the light as if it had burned him.

"Who is that?" he shouted.

"This is Simon Templar," said the Saint in a commonplace tone. "I just dropped in to say hullo."

Sardon turned the switch down again and went back into the laboratory. The Saint followed him.

"You just dropped in, eh? Of course. Good. Why not? Did you run into Carmen, by any chance?"

"I nearly ran over her," said the Saint evenly.

The doctor's wandering glance snapped to his face. Sardon's hands were shaking, and a tiny muscle at the side of his mouth twitched spasmodically.

"Of course," he said vacantly. "Is she all right?"

"She is quite safe." Simon had put away his gun before the other saw it. He laid a hand gently on the other's shoulder. "You've had trouble here," he said.

"She lost her nerve," Sardon retorted furiously. "She ran away. It was the worst thing she could do. They understand, these creatures. They are too much for me to control now. They disobey me. My commands must seem so stupid to their wonderful brains. If it had not been that this one is heavy and waiting for her time——"

He checked himself.

"I knew," said the Saint calmly.

The doctor peered up at him out of the corners of his eyes.

"You knew?" he repeated cunningly.

"Yes. I saw it."

"Just now?"

Simon nodded.

"You didn't tell us last night," he said. "But it's what I was afraid of. I have been thinking about it all day."

"You've been thinking, have you? That's funny." Sardon chuckled shrilly. "Well, you're quite right. I've done it. I've succeeded. I don't have to work any more. They can look after themselves now. That's funny, isn't it?"

"So it is true. I hoped I was wrong."

Sardon edged closer to him.

"You hoped you were wrong? You fool! But I would expect it of you. You are the egotistical human being who believes in his ridiculous conceit that the whole history of the world from its own birth, all the species and races that have come into being and been discarded, everything—everything has existed only to lead up to his own magnificent presence on the earth. Bah! Do you imagine that your miserable little life can stand in the way of the march of evolution? Your day is over! Finished! In there"—his arm stiffened and pointed—"in there you can find the matriarch of the new ruling race of the earth. At any moment she will begin to lay her eggs, thousands upon thousands of them, from which her sons and daughters will breed—

as big as she is, with her power and her brains." His voice dropped. "To me it is only wonderful that I should have been Nature's chosen instrument to give them their rightful place a million years before Time would have opened the door to them."

The flame in his eyes sank down as his voice sank and his features seemed to relax so that his square clean-cut efficient face became soft and beguiling like the face of an idiot child.

"I know what it feels like to be God," he breathed.

Simon held both his arms.

"Dr Sardon," he said, "you must not go on with this experiment."

The other's face twisted.

"The experiment is finished," he snarled. "Are you still blind? Look—I will show you."

He was broad-shouldered and powerfully built, and his strength was that of a maniac. He threw off the Saint's hands with a convulsive wrench of his body and ran to the sliding door at the end of the room. He turned with his back to it, grasping the handle, as the Saint started after him.

"You shall meet them yourself," he said hoarsely. "They are not in their cage any more. I will let them out here, and you shall see whether you can stand against them. Stay where you are!"

A revolver flashed in his hand; and the Saint stopped four paces from him.

"For your own sake, Dr Sardon," he said, "stand away from that door."

The doctor leered at him crookedly.

"You would like to burn my ants," he whispered.

He turned and fumbled with the spring catch, his revolver swinging carelessly wide from its aim; and the door had started to move when Simon shot him twice through the heart.

Simon was stretched out on the veranda, sipping a highball and sniping mosquitoes with a cigarette end, when Nordsten came up the steps from his car. The Saint looked up with a smile.

"My dear fellow," said Nordsten, "I thought you would be at the fire."

"Is there a fire?" Simon asked innocently.

"Didn't you know? Sardon's whole laboratory has gone up in flames. I heard about it at the club, and when I left I drove back that way thinking I should meet you. Sardon and his niece were not there, either. It will be a terrible shock for him when he hears of it. The place was absolutely gutted—I've never seen such a blaze. It might have been soaked in gasoline. It was still too hot to go near, but I suppose all his work has been destroyed. Did you miss Carmen?"

The Saint pointed over his shoulder.

"At the present moment she's sleeping in your best guest room," he said.

"I gave her enough of your sleeping tablets to keep her like that till breakfast time."

Nordsten looked at him.

"And where is Sardon?" he asked at length.

"He is in his laboratory."

Nordsten poured himself out a drink and sat down.

"Tell me," he said.

Simon told him the story. When he had finished, Nordsten was silent for a while. Then he said: "It's all right, of course. A fire like that must have destroyed all the evidence. It could all have been an accident. But what about the girl?"

"I told her that her uncle had locked the door and refused to let me in. Her evidence will be enough to show that Sardon was not in his right mind."

"Would you have done it anyhow, Simon?"

The Saint nodded.

"I think so. That's what I was worried about, ever since last night. It came to me at once that if any of these brutes could breed——" He shrugged a little wearily. "And when I saw that great queen ant, I knew that it had gone too far. I don't know quite how rapidly ants can breed, but I should imagine that they do it by thousands. If the thousands were all the same size as Sardon's specimens, with the same intelligence, who knows what might have been the end of it?"

"But I thought you disliked the human race," said Nordsten.

Simon got up and strolled across the veranda.

"Taken in the mass," he said soberly, "it will probably go on nauseating me. But it isn't my job to alter it. If Sardon was right, Nature will find her own remedy. But the world has millions of years left, and I think evolution can afford to wait."

His cigarette spun over the rail and vanished into the dark like a firefly as the butler came out to announce dinner; and they went into the dining room together.

PALM SPRINGS

From *The Saint Goes West*

PALM SPRINGS, if anybody doesn't know it by this time, is an oasis in the desert a little more than a hundred miles east of Los Angeles. When I first went there, the business district was about three blocks long and a block wide; there were about three hotels, much too big for the town, a reasonable number of homes, a few auto courts, and a dude ranch on the outskirts. Today the neon signs of the motels greet you miles out in the desert and escort you in unbroken procession to a main street as long as the whole village used to be when I first knew it, and the houses have spread way out where we used to ride after jackrabbits, and they have flowed all around the dude ranch on the other side, and then for about fifteen miles out on the highway beyond more villages or communities have sprung up in an almost uninterrupted chain to take advantage of the overflow that even this enlarged Palm Springs cannot swallow; and I seldom go there any more, because it is too different from the place I used to love.

But I spent six consecutive winters there in the good old days which ended at Munich, and it would have been strange if I had never set a story there.

The actual process of doing it, however, suffered some vicissitudes.

My first attempt was when RKO was making Saint movies. Thinking how pleasant it would be to work on a picture in my own favorite location, I cleverly suggested that we should make one called *The Saint in Palm Springs*. They liked the idea very much, and I went to work on the script. It turned out to be an excellent story; so naturally the producers (who always knew that they could have written much better Saint stories than I did, only they never got around to it) didn't like it much. They hired various wizards to improve it, and did such a thorough job that the final script contained absolutely nothing whatsoever of mine except the title. I have never been able to guess why they flinched from that ultimate alteration, unless it was because they feared they might obscure the genius of the inspired executive who decreed that this epic should be shot at Palmdale, which is only a hundred and fifty miles away from Palm Springs.

Then, early in 1941, Dan Longwell, chairman of the Editorial Board of

Life magazine, paid me a visit in California. I had known Dan many years before, when he was one of the editors of my New York publishers, a firm then known as Doubleday, Doran & Co. (Everything in this busy life keeps changing, as we reminiscent ancients are continually being reminded.) Dan, or somebody on his staff, had abruptly recalled that in 1841 Edgar Allan Poe had published *The Murders in the Rue Morgue,* that therefore in 1941 the world should theoretically be celebrating the centenary of the detective story, and that therefore *Life* should somehow be represented in the chorus of tribute.

Dan's idea was that *Life* should mark the occasion by publishing the first "mystery" story of the new era; and for reasons which I am far too bashful to speculate about, he wanted me to write it. It was, of course, to be done in a series of photographs with captions, rather like stills from an unmade movie.

Again I thought of Palm Springs, and what could be better than a trip there, in good company, at the expense of *Life?*

But RKO still owned (and for that matter still owns) the original Palm Springs story I had written, since they had paid me handsomely for it—even though to this day they have never used a line of it. (This is why it costs you so much to go to the movies.)

So I wrote another story, and was especially careful to include three beautiful girls in it. And since *Life* magazine, at that time anyway, had not discovered that it was as great a creative genius as the current crop of producers at RKO, they stupidly accepted it as I wrote it. We went to Palm Springs with three models and a photographer—and they not only left me to direct the shots but, God help me, made me play the part of the Saint as well.

This was my first and only appearance as a film star, even on static film, and I am not going to pretend I didn't enjoy it. A hell of a time was had by all.

The resultant million-dollar comic strip was duly published in eight pages of *Life* magazine in May 1941. And there again an immortal Palm Springs story might have been decently interred.

But I am a very persistent, or at least economical, writer. I still wanted a Palm Springs story; and even after a lapse of years I thought this was a good one. I went to work elaborating it. And the story you are about to read is what came out.

PALM SPRINGS

"LOOK," said Freddie Pellman belligerently. "Your name *is* Simon Templar, isn't it?"

"I think so," Simon told him.

"You *are* the feller they call the Saint?"

"So I'm told."

"The Robin Hood of modern crime?"

Simon was tolerant.

"That's a rather fancy way of putting it."

"Okay then." Pellman lurched slightly on his bar stool, and took hold of his highball glass more firmly for support. "You're the man I want. I've got a job for you."

The Saint sighed.

"Thanks. But I wasn't looking for a job. I came to Palm Springs to have fun."

"You'll have plenty of fun. But you've got to take this job."

"I don't want a job," said the Saint. "What is it?"

"I need a bodyguard," said Pellman.

He had a loud harsh voice that made Simon think of a rusty frog. Undoubtedly it derived some of this attractive quality from his consumption of alcohol, which was considerable. Simon didn't need to have seen him drinking to know this. The blemishes of long indulgence had worked deeply into the mottled puffiness of his complexion, the pinkish smeariness of his eyes, and the sagging lines under them. It was even more noticeable because he was not much over thirty, and could once have been quite good-looking in a very conventional way. But things like that frequently happen to spoiled young men whose only material accomplishment in life has been the by no means negligible one of arranging to be born into a family with more millions than most people hope to see thousands.

Simon Templar knew about him, of course—as did practically every member of the newspaper-reading public of the United States, not to mention a number of other countries. In a very different way, Freddie Pellman was just as notorious a public figure as the Saint. He had probably financed the swallowing of more champagne than any other individual in the twentieth century. He had certainly been thrown out of more night clubs, and paid more bills for damage to more hotels, than any other exponent of the art of uproar. And the number of complaisant show girls and models who were indebted to him for such souvenirs of a lovely friendship as mink coats, diamond bracelets, Packards, and other similar trinkets would have made the late King Solomon feel relatively sex-starved.

He travelled with a permanent entourage of three incredibly beautiful

young ladies—one blonde, one brunette, and one redhead. That is, the assortment of colorings was permanent. The personnel itself changed at various
intervals, as one faithful collaborator after another would retire to a well-
earned rest, to be replaced by another of even more dazzling perfections;
but the vacancy was always filled by another candidate of similar complexion, so that the harmonious balance of varieties was retained, and any type
of pulchritude could always be found at a glance. Freddie blandly referred
to them as his secretaries; and there is no doubt that they had given him
great assistance with his life work, which had left a memorable trail of
scandal in every playground and every capital city in Europe and the Americas.

This was the man who said he wanted a bodyguard; and the Saint
looked at him with cynical speculation.

"What's the matter?" he asked coolly. "Is somebody's husband gunning
for you?"

"No, I never mess about with married women—they're too much grief."
Pellman was delightfully insensitive and uninhibited. "This is serious.
Look."

He dragged a crumpled sheet of paper out of his pocket and unfolded it
clumsily. Simon took it and looked it over.

It was a piece of plain paper on which a cutting had been pasted. The
cutting was from *Life,* and from the heading it appeared to have formed
part of a layout reviewing the curtain calls in the careers of certain famous
public enemies. This particular picture showed a crumpled figure stretched
out on a sidewalk with two policemen standing over it in attitudes faintly
reminiscent of big-game hunters posing with their kill, surrounded by the
usual crowd of gaping blankfaced spectators. The caption said:

> *A village policeman's gun wrote finis to the career of
> "Smoke Johnny" Implicato, three times kidnapper and
> killer, after Freddie Pellman, millionaire playboy, recog-
> nised him in a Palm Springs restaurant last Christmas
> Day and held him in conversation until police arrived.*

Underneath it was pencilled in crude capitals:

> DID YOU EVER WONDER HOW JOHNNY
> FELT? WELL YOU'LL SOON FIND OUT.
> YOU GOT IT COMING MISTER.
>   A FRIEND OF JOHNNY.

Simon felt the paper, turned it over, and handed it back.

"A bit corny," he observed, "but it must be a thrill for you. How did
you get it?"

"It was pushed under the front door during the night. I've rented a house here, and that's where it was. Under the front door. The Filipino boy found it in the morning. The door was locked, of course, but the note had been pushed under."

When Freddie Pellman thought that anything he had to say was important, which was often, he was never satisfied to say it once. He said it several times over, trying it out in different phrasings, apparently in the belief that his audience was either deaf or imbecile but might accidentally grasp the point if it were presented often enough from a sufficient variety of angles.

"Have you talked to the police about it?" Simon asked.

"What, in a town like this? I'd just as soon tell the Boy Scouts. In a town like this, the police wouldn't know what to do with a murderer if he walked into the station and gave them a signed confession."

"They got Johnny," Simon pointed out.

"Listen, do you know who got Johnny? I got Johnny. Who recognised him? I did. I'd been reading one of those true detective magazines in a barber shop, and there was a story about him in it. In one of those true detective magazines. I recognised him from the picture. Did you read what it said in that clipping?"

"Yes," said the Saint; but Freddie was not so easily headed off.

He took the paper out of his pocket again.

"You see what it says? *'A village policeman's gun wrote finis to the career . . .'*"

He read the entire caption aloud, following the lines with his forefinger, with the most careful enunciation and dramatic emphasis, to make sure that the Saint had not been baffled by any of the longer words.

"All right," said the Saint patiently. "So you spotted him and put the finger on him. And now one of his pals is sore about it."

"And that's why I need a bodyguard."

"I can tell you a good agency in Los Angeles. You can call them up, and they'll have a first-class, guaranteed, bonded bodyguard here in three hours, armed to the teeth."

"But I don't want an ordinary agency bodyguard. I want the very best man there is. I want the Saint."

"Thanks," said the Saint. "But I don't want to guard a body."

"Look," said Pellman aggressively, "will you name your own salary? Anything you like. Just name it."

Simon looked around the bar. It was starting to fill up for the cocktail session with the strange assortment of types and costumes which give Palm Springs crowds an unearthly variety that no other resort in America can approach. Everything was represented—cowboys, dudes, tourists, trippers, travelling salesmen, local business men, winter residents, Hollywood; men and women of all shapes and sizes and ages, in levis, shorts, business suits, slack suits, sun suits, play suits, Magnin models, riding breeches, tennis outfits, swim suits, and practically nothing. This was vacation and flippancy and fun and irresponsibility for a while; and it was what the Saint had promised himself.

"If I took a job like that," he said, "it'd cost you a thousand dollars a day."

Freddie Pellman blinked at him for a moment with the intense concentration of the alcoholic.

Then he pulled a thick roll of green paper out of his pocket. He fumbled through it, and selected a piece, and pushed it into the Saint's hand. The Saint's blue eyes rested on it with a premonition of doom. Included in its decorative art work was a figure "1" followed by three zeros. Simon counted them.

"That's for today," said Freddie. "You're hired. Let's have a drink."

The Saint sighed.

"I think I will," he said.

CHAPTER TWO

ONE REASON why there were no gray hairs on the Saint's dark head was that he never wasted any energy on vain regrets. He even had a humorous fatalism about his errors. He had stuck his neck out, and the consequences were strictly at his invitation. He felt that way about his new employment. He had been very sweetly nailed with his own smartness, and the only thing to do was to take it with a grin and see if it might be fun. And it might. After all, murder and mayhem had been mentioned; and to Simon Templar any adventure was always worth at least a glance. It might not be so dull. . . .

"You'll have to move into the house, of course," Pellman said, and they drove to the Mirador Hotel to redeem the Saint's modest luggage, which had already run up a bill of some twenty dollars for the few hours it had occupied a room.

Pellman's house was a new edifice perched on the sheer hills that form the western wall of the town. Palm Springs itself lies on the flat floor of the valley that eases imperceptibly down to the sub-sea level of the Salton Sea; but on the western side it nestles tightly against the sharp surges of broken granite that soar up with precipitous swiftness to the eternal snows of San Jacinto. The private road to it curled precariously up the rugged

edges of brown leaping cliffs, and from the jealously stolen lawn in front
of the building you could look down and see Palm Springs spread out
beneath you like a map, and beyond it the floor of the desert mottled gray-
green with greasewood and weeds and cactus and smoke tree, spreading
through infinite clear distances across to the last spurs of the San Ber-
nardino mountains and widening southwards towards the broad baking
spreads that had once been the bed of a forgotten sea whose tide levels
were still graven on the parched rocks that bordered the plain.

The house itself looked more like an artist's conception of an oasis hide-
away than any artist would have believed. It was a sprawling bungalow in
the California Spanish style that meandered lazily among pools and patios
as a man might have dreamed it in an idle hour—a thing of white stucco
walls and bright red tile roofs, of deep cool verandahs and inconsequential
arches, of sheltering palm trees and crazy flagstones, of gay beds of petunias
and ramparts of oleanders and white columns dripping with the richness of
bougainvillea. It was a place where an illusion had been so skilfully created
that with hardly any imagination at all you could feel the gracious tempo
of a century that would never come again; where you might see courtly
hacendados bowing over slim white hands with the suppleness of velvet
and steel, and hear the tinkle of fountains and the shuffle of soft-footed
servants, and smell the flowers in the raven hair of laughing señoritas;
where at the turn of any corner you might even find a nymph——

Yes, you might always find a nymph, Simon agreed, as they turned a
corner by the swimming pool and there was a sudden squeal and he had
a lightning glimpse of long golden limbs uncurling and leaping up, and
rounded breasts vanishing almost instantaneously through the door of the
bath house, so swiftly and fleetingly that he could easily have been convinced that he had dreamed it.

"That's Esther," Freddie explained casually. "She likes taking her clothes
off."

Simon remembered the much-publicised peculiarities of the Pellman ménage, and took an even more philosophical attitude towards his new job

"One of your secretaries?" he murmured.

"That's right," Freddie said blandly. "Come in and meet the others."

The others were in the living-room, if such a baronial chamber could be
correctly designated by such an ordinary name. From the inside, it looked
like a Hollywood studio designer's idea of something between a Cordoban
mosque and the main hall of a medieval castle. It had a tiled floor and a
domed gold mosaic ceiling, with leopard and tiger skin rugs, Monterey
furniture, and fake suits of armor in between.

"This is Miss Starr," Freddie introduced. "Call her Ginny. Mr Templar."

Ginny had red hair like hot dark gold, and a creamy skin with freckles.

You could study all of it except about two square feet which were accidentally concealed by a green lastex swim suit that clung to her soft ripe figure—where it wasn't artistically cut away for better exposures—like emerald paint. She sat at a table by herself, playing solitaire. She looked up and gave the Saint a long disturbing smile, and said: "Hi."

"And this is Lissa O'Neill," Freddie said.

Lissa was the blonde. Her hair was the color of young Indiana corn, and her eyes were as blue as the sky, and there were dew-dipped roses in her cheeks that might easily have grown beside the Shannon. She lay stretched out on a couch with a book propped up on her flat stomach, and she wore an expensively simple white play suit against which her slim legs looked warmly gilded.

Simon glanced at the book. It had the lurid jacket of a Crime Club mystery.

"How is it?" he asked.

"Not bad," she said. "I thought I had it solved in the third chapter, but now I think I'm wrong. What did he say your name was?"

"She's always reading mysteries," Ginny put in. "She's our tame crime expert—Madam Hawkshaw. Every time anyone gets murdered in the papers she knows all about it."

"And why not?" Lissa insisted. "They're usually so stupid, anyone but a detective could see it."

"You must have been reading the right books," said the Saint.

"Did he say 'Templar'?" Lissa asked.

The door opened then, and Esther came in. Simon recognised her by her face, a perfect oval set with warm brown eyes and broken by a red mouth that always seemed to be whispering *"If we were alone . . ."* A softly waved mane the color of smoked chestnuts framed the face in a dark dreamy cloud. The rest of her was not quite so easily identifiable, for she had wrapped it in a loose blue robe that left a little scope for speculation. Not too much, for the lapels only managed to meet at her waist, and just a little below that the folds shrank away from the impudent obtrusion of a shapely thigh.

"A fine thing," she said. "Walking in on me when I didn't have a stitch on."

"I bet you loved it," Ginny said, cheating a black ten out of the bottom of the pack and slipping it on to a red jack.

"Do we get introduced?" said Esther.

"Meet Miss Swinburne," said Freddie. "Mr Templar. Now you know everybody. I want you to feel at home. My name's Freddie. We're going to call you Simon. All right?"

"All right," said the Saint.

"Then we're all at home," said Freddie, making his point. "We don't have to have any formality. If any of the girls go for you, that's all right too. We're all pals together."

"Me first," said Ginny.

"Why you?" objected Esther. "After all, if you'd been there to give him the first preview——"

The Saint took out his cigarette-case with as much poise as any man could have called on in the circumstances.

"The line forms on the right," he remarked. "Or you can see my agent. But don't let's be confused about this. I only work here. You ought to tell them, Freddie."

The Filipino boy wheeled in the portable bar, and Pellman threaded his way over to it and began to work.

"The girls know all about that threatening letter. I showed it to them this morning. Didn't I, Lissa? You remember that note I showed you?" Reassured by confirmation, Freddie picked up the cocktail shaker again and said: "Well, Simon Templar is going to take care of us. You know who he is, don't you? The Saint. That's who he is," said Freddie, leaving no room for misunderstanding.

"I thought so," said Lissa, with her cornflower eyes clinging to the Saint's face. "I've seen pictures of you." She put her book down and moved her long legs invitingly to make some room on the couch. "What do you think about that note?"

Simon accepted the invitation. He didn't think she was any less potentially dangerous than the other two, but she was a little more quiet and subtle about it. Besides, she at least had something else to talk about.

"Tell me what you think," he said. "You might have a good point of view."

"I thought it sounded rather like something out of a cheap magazine."

"There you are!" exclaimed Freddie triumphantly, from the middle distance. "Isn't that amazing? Eh, Simon? Listen to this, Ginny. That's what she reads detective stories for. You'll like this. D'you know what Simon said when I showed him that note? What did you say, Simon?"

"I said it sounded a bit corny."

"There!" said Freddie, personally vindicated. "That's the very word he used. He said it was corny. That's what he said as soon as he read it."

"That's what I thought too," said Esther, "only I didn't like to say so. Probably it's just some crackpot trying to be funny."

"On the other hand," Simon mentioned, "a lot of crackpots have killed people, and plenty of real murders have been pretty corny. And whether you're killed by a crackpot or the most rational person in the world, and whether the performance is corny or not, you end up just as dead."

"Don't a lot of criminals read detective stories?" Lissa asked.

The Saint nodded.

"Most of them. And they get good ideas from them, too. Most writers are pretty clever, in spite of the funny way they look, and when they go in for crime they put in a lot of research and invention that a practising thug doesn't have the time or the ability to do for himself. But he could pick up a lot of hints from reading the right authors."

"He could learn a lot of mistakes not to make, too."

"Maybe there's something in that," said the Saint. "Perhaps the stupid criminals you were talking about are only the ones who don't read books. Maybe the others get to be so clever that they never get caught, and so you never hear about them at all."

"Brrr," said Ginny. "You're giving me goose-pimples. Why don't you just call the cops?"

"Because the Saint's a lot smarter than the cops," said Freddie. "That's what I hired him for. He can run rings round the cops any day. He's been doing it for years. Lissa knows all about him, because she reads things. You tell them about him, Lissa."

He came over with clusters of Manhattans in his hands, poured out in goblets that would have been suitable for fruit punch.

"Let her off," said the Saint hastily. "If she really knows the whole story of my life she might shock somebody. Let's do some serious drinking instead."

"Okay," said Freddie amiably. "You're the boss. You go on being the mystery man. Let's all get stinking."

The fact that they did not all get stinking was certainly no fault of Freddie Pellman's. It could not be denied that he did his generous best to assist his guests to attain that state of ideal ossification. His failure could only be attributed to the superior discretion of the company, and the remarkably high level of resistance which they seemed to have in common.

It was quite a classic performance in its way. Freddie concocted two more Manhattans, built on the same scale as milk shakes. There was then a brief breathing spell while they went to their rooms to change. Then they went to the Doll House for dinner. They had two more normal-sized cocktails before the meal, and champagne with it. After that they had brandy. Then they proceeded to visit all the other bars up and down the main street, working from north to south and back again. They had Zombies at the Luau, Planter's Punches at the Cubana, highballs at the Chi Chi, and more highballs at Bil-Al's. Working back, they freshened up with some beer at Happy's, clamped it down with a Collins at the Del Tahquitz, topped it with Daiquiris at the Royal Palms, and discovered tequila at Claridge's. This brought them back to the Doll House for another bottle of champagne. They were all walking on their own feet and talking intelligibly, if not profoundly. People have received medals for less notable feats. It must be admitted nevertheless that there had been a certain amount of cheating. The girls, undoubtedly educated by past experiences, had contrived to leave a respectable number of drinks unfinished; and Simon Templar, who had also been around, had sundry legerdemains of his own for keeping control of the situation.

Freddie Pellman probably had an advantage over all of them in the insulating effect of past picklings, but Simon had to admit that the man was remarkable. He had been alcoholic when Simon met him, but he seemed to progress very little beyond that stage. Possibly he navigated with a little more difficulty, but he could still stand upright; possibly his speech became a little more slurred, but he could still be understood; certainly he became rather more glassy-eyed, but he could still see what was going on. It was as if there was a definite point beyond which his calloused tissues had no further power to assimilate liquid stimulus: being sodden already, the overflow washed over them without depositing any added exhilaration.

He sat and looked at his glass and said: "There must be some other joints we haven't been to yet."

Then he rolled gently over sideways and lay flat on the floor, snoring.

Ginny gazed down at him estimatingly and said: "That's only the third time I've seen him pass out. It must be catching up with him."

"Well, now we can relax," said Esther, and moved her chair closer to the Saint.

"I think we'd better get him home," Lissa said.

It seemed like a moderately sound idea, since the head waiter and the proprietor were advancing towards the scene with professional restraint.

Simon helped to hoist Freddie up, and they got him out to the car without waking him. The Saint drove them back to the house, and the lights went up as they stopped at the door. The Filipino boy came out and helped phlegmatically with the disembarcation. He didn't show either surprise or disapproval. Apparently such homecomings were perfectly normal events in his experience.

Between them they carried the sleeper to his room and laid him on the bed.

"Okay," said the boy. "I take care of him now."

He began to work Freddie expertly out of his coat.

"You seem to have the touch," said the Saint. "How long have you been in this job?"

" 'Bout six months. He's all right. You leave him to me, sir. I put him to bed."

"What's your name?"

"Angelo, sir. I take care of him. You want anything, you tell me."

"Thanks," said the Saint, and drifted back to the living-room.

He arrived in the course of a desultory argument which suggested that the threat which had been virtually ignored all evening had begun to seem a little less ludicrous with the arrival of bedtime.

"You can move in with me, Ginny," Lissa was saying.

"Nuts," said Ginny. "You'll sit up half the night reading, and I want some sleep."

"For a change," said Esther. "I'll move in with you, Lissa."

"You snore," said Lissa candidly.

"I don't!"

"And where does that leave me?" Ginny protested.

"I expect you'll find company," Esther said sulkily. "You've been working for it hard enough."

Simon coughed discreetly.

"Angelo is in charge," he said, "and I'm going to turn in."

"What, so soon?" pouted Esther. "Let's all have another drink first. I know, let's have a game of strip poker."

"I'm sorry," said the Saint. "I'm not so young as I was this afternoon. I'm going to get some sleep."

"I thought you were supposed to be a bodyguard," said Ginny.

The Saint smiled.

"I am, darling. I guard Freddie's body."

"Freddie's passed out. You ought to keep us company."

"It's all so silly," Lissa said. "I'm not scared. We haven't anything to be afraid of. Even if that note was serious, it's Freddie they're after. Nobody's going to do anything to us."

"How do you know they won't get into the wrong room?" Esther objected.

"You can hang a sign on your door," Simon suggested, "giving them directions. Goodnight, pretty maidens."

He made his exit before there could be any more discussion, and went to his bedroom.

The bedrooms trailed away from the house in a long L-shaped wing. Freddie's room was at the far end of the wing, and his door faced the broad screened verandah by which the rooms were reached. Simon had the room next to it, from which one of the girls had been moved: their rooms were now strung around the angle of the L towards the main building. There was a communicating door on both sides of his room. He tried the one which should have opened in to Freddie's room, but he found that there was a second door backing closely against it, and that one was locked. He went around by the verandah, and found Angelo preparing to turn out the lights.

"He sleep well now," said the Filipino with a grin. "You no worry."

Freddie was neatly tucked into bed, his clothes carefully folded over a chair. Simon went over and looked at him. He certainly wasn't dead at that point—his snoring was stertorously alive.

The Saint located the other side of the communicating door, and tried the handle. It still wouldn't move, and there was no key in the lock.

"D'you know how to open this, Angelo?" he asked.

The Filipino shook his head.

"Don't know. Is lock?"

"Is lock."

"I never see key. Maybe somewhere."

"Maybe," Simon agreed.

It didn't look like a profitable inquiry to pursue much further, and Simon figured that it probably didn't matter. He still hadn't developed any real conviction of danger overshadowing the house, and at that moment the idea seemed particularly farfetched. He went out of the room, and the Filipino switched off the light.

"Everything already lock up, sir. You no worry. I go to sleep now."

"Happy dreams," said the Saint.

He returned to his own room, and undressed and rolled into bed. He felt in pretty good shape, but he didn't want to start the next day with an unnecessary headache. He was likely to have enough other headaches without that. Aside from the drinking pace and the uninhibited feminine hazards, he felt that a day would come when Freddie Pellman's conversational style would cease to hold him with the same eager fascination that it created at the first encounter. Eventually, he felt, a thousand dollars a day would begin to seem like a relatively small salary for listening to Freddie talk. But that was something that could be faced when the time came. Maybe he would be able to explain it to Freddie and get a raise . . .

With that he fell asleep. He didn't know how long it lasted, but it was deep and relaxed. And it ended with an electrifying suddenness that was as devastating as the collapse of a tall tower of porcelain. But the sound was actually a little different. It was a shrill shattering scream that brought him wide awake in an instant and had him on his feet while the echo was still ringing in his ears.

CHAPTER THREE

THERE WAS ENOUGH starlight outside for the windows to be rectangles of silver, but inside the room he was only just able to find his dressing-gown without groping. His gun was already in his hand, for his fingers had closed on it instinctively where the butt lay just under the edge of the mattress at the natural length of his arm as he lay in bed. He threw the robe on and whipped a knot into the belt, and was on his way to the doors within two seconds of waking.

Then the scream came again, louder now that he wasn't hearing it through a haze of sleep, and in a way more deliberate. And it came, he was certain, not from the direction in which he had first automatically placed it, without thinking, but from the opposite quarter—the room on the opposite side of his own.

He stopped in mid-stride, and turned quickly back to the other communicating door. This one was not locked. It was a double door like the one to Freddie's room, but the second handle turned smoothly with his fingers. As he started to open it, the door outlined itself with light: he did the only possible thing, and threw it wide open quickly but without any noise, and stepped swiftly through and to one side, with his gun balanced for instant aiming in any direction.

He didn't see anything to aim at. He didn't see anyone there except Lissa.

She was something to see, if one had the time. She was sitting upright in bed, and she wore a filmy flesh-colored nightgown with white overtones. At least, that was the first impression. After a while, you realised that it was just a filmy white nightgown and the flesh color was Lissa. She had her mouth open, and she looked exactly as if she was going to scream again. Then she didn't look like that any more.

"Hello," she said, quite calmly. "I thought that'd fetch you."

"Wouldn't there have been a more subtle way of doing it?" Simon asked.

"But there was someone here, really. Look."

Then he saw it—the black wooden hilt of a knife that stood up starkly from the bedding close beside her. The resignation went out of his face again as if it had never been there.

"Where did he go?"

"I don't know—out of one of the doors. If he didn't go into your room, he must have gone out on to the porch or into Ginny's room."

Simon crossed to the other door and stepped out on to the verandah. Lights came on as he did so, and he saw Freddie Pellman swaying in the doorway at the dead end of the L.

"Whassamarrer?" Freddie demanded thickly. "What goes on?"

"We seem to have had a visitor," said the Saint succinctly. "Did anybody come through your room?"

"Anybody come through my room? I dunno. No. I didn't see anybody. Why should anybody come through my room?"

"To kiss you goodnight," said the Saint tersely, and headed in the other direction.

There was no other movement on the verandah. He knocked briefly on the next door down, and opened it and switched on the light. The bed was rumpled but empty, and a shaft of light came through the communicating door. All the bedrooms seemed to have communicating doors, which either had its advantages or it didn't. Simon went on into the next room. The bed in there had the covers pulled high up, and appeared to be occupied by a small quivering hippopotamus. He went up to it and tapped it on the most convenient bulge.

"Come on," he said. "I just saw a mouse crawl in with you."

There was a stifled squeal, and Esther's head and shoulders and a little more jumped into view in the region of the pillow.

"Go away!" she yelped inarticulately. "I haven't done anything——"

Then she recognised him, and stopped abruptly. She took a moment to straighten her dark hair. At the same time the other half of the baby hippopotamus struggled up beside her, revealing that it had a red-gold head and a snub nose.

"Oh, it's you," said Ginny. "Come on in. We'll make room for you."

"Well, make yourselves at home," said Esther. "This just happens to be my room——"

"Little children," said the Saint, with great patience, "I don't want to spoil anybody's fun, but I'm looking for a hairy thug who seems to be rushing around trying to stick knives into people."

They glanced at each other in a moment's silence.

"Wh-who did he stick a knife into?" Ginny asked.

"Nobody. He missed. But he was trying. Did you see him?"

She shook her head.

"Nobody's been in here," said Esther, "except Ginny. I heard a frightful scream, and I jumped up and put the light on, and the next minute Ginny came rushing in and got into my bed."

"It was Lissa," said Ginny. "I'm sure it was. The scream sounded like it was right next door. So I ran in here. But I didn't see anyone." She swallowed, and her eyes grew big. "Is Lissa——?"

"No," said the Saint bluntly. "Lissa's as well as you are. And so is Freddie. But somebody's been up to mischief tonight, and we're looking for him. Now will you please get out of bed and pull yourselves together, because we're going to search the house.

"I can't," said Esther. "I haven't got anything on."

"Don't let it bother you," said the Saint tiredly. "If a burglar sees you he'll probably swoon on the spot, and then the rest of us will jump on him and tie him up."

He took a cigarette from a package beside the bed, and went on his way. It seemed as if he had wasted a lot of time, but actually it had scarcely been a minute. Out on the verandah he saw that the door of Lissa's room was open, and through it he heard Freddie Pellman's obstructed croak repetitiously imploring her to tell him what had happened. As he went on towards the junction of the main building, lights went on in the living-room and a small mob of chattering figures burst out and almost swarmed over him as he opened the door into the arched alcove that the bedroom wing took off from. Simon spread out his arms and collected them in a sheaf.

"Were you going somewhere, boys?"

There were three of them, in various interesting costumes. Reading from left to right, they were: Angelo, in red, green, and purple striped pajamas, another Filipino in a pair of very natty bright blue trousers, and a large gentleman in a white nightshirt with spiked moustaches and a Vandyke.

Angelo said: "We hear some lady scream, so we come to see what's the matter."

Simon looked at him shrewdly.

"How long have you worked for Mr Pellman?"

"About six months, sir."

"And you never heard any screaming before?"

The boy looked at him sheepishly, without answering.

The stout gentleman in the nightshirt said with some dignity: "Ziss wass not ordinairy screaming. Ziss wass quite deefairent. It sounds like somebody iss in trobble. So we sink about ze note zat Meestair Pellman receive, and we come to help."

"Who are you?" asked the Saint.

"I am Louis, sir. I am ze chef."

"Enfin, quand nous aurons pris notre assassin, vous aurez le plaisir de nous servir ses rognons, légèrement grillés."

The man stared at him blankly for a second or two, and finally said: "I'm sorry, sir, I don't ondairstand."

"You don't speak French?"

"No, sir."

"Then what are you doing with that accent?"

"I am Italian, sir, but I lairn this accent because she iss good business."

Simon gave up for the time being.

"Well, let's get on with this and search the house. You didn't see any strangers on your way here?"

"No, sir," Angelo answered. "Did anyone get hurt?"

"No, but we seem to have had a visitor."

"I no understand," the Filipino insisted. "Everything lock up, sir. I see to it myself."

"Then somebody opened something," said the Saint curtly. "Go and look."

He went on his own way to the front door. It was locked and bolted. He opened it and went outside.

Although there seemed to have been a large variety of action and dialogue since Lissa's scream had awakened him, it had clicked through at such a speed that the elapsed time was actually surprisingly short. As he stood outside and gave his eyes a moment to adjust themselves to the darkness he tried to estimate how long it had been. Not long enough, he was sure, for anyone to travel very far . . . And then the night cleared from his eyes, and he could see almost as well as a cat could have seen there. He went to the edge of the terrace in front of the house, and looked down. He could see the private road which was the only vehicular approach to the place dropping and winding away to his left like a gray ribbon carelessly thrown down the mountainside, and there was no car or moving shadow on it. Most of the street plan at the foot of the hill was as clearly visible also as if he had been looking down on it from an airplane, but he could see nothing human or mechanical moving there either. And even with all his delays, it hardly seemed possible that anything or anyone could have travelled far enough to be out of sight by that time—at least without making a noise that he would have heard on his way through the house.

There were, of course, other ways than the road. The steep slopes both upwards and downwards could have been negotiated by an agile man. Simon walked very quietly around the building and the gardens, scanning every surface that he could see. Certainly no one climbing up or down could have covered a great distance: on the other hand, if the climber had gone only a little way and stopped moving he would have been very hard to pick out of the ragged patchwork of lights and shadows that the starlight made out of tumbles of broken rock and clumps of cactus and incenso and greasewood. By the same token, a man on foot would be impossibly dangerous game to hunt at night: he only had to keep still, whereas the hunter had to move, and thereby give his quarry the first timed deliberate shot at him.

The Saint could be reckless enough, but he had no suicidal inclinations. He stood motionless for several minutes in different bays of shadow, scanning the slopes with the unblinking patience of a headhunter. But nothing moved, and presently he went back in by the front door and found Angelo.

"Well?" he said.

"I no find anything, sir. Everything all lock up. You come see yourself."

Simon made the circuit with him. Where there were glass doors they were all metal framed, with sturdy locking handles and bolts in addition. All the windows were screened, and the screen frames fastened on the inside. None of them showed a sign of having been forced or tampered with in any way; and the Saint was a good enough burglar in his own right to know that doors and casements of that type could not have been fastened from outside without leaving a sign that any such thing had been done—particularly by a man who was trying to depart from the premises in a great hurry.

His tour ended back in Lissa's room, where the rest of the house party was now gathered. He paused in the doorway.

"All right, Angelo," he said. "You can go back to your beauty sleep . . . Oh, yes, you could bring me a drink first."

"I've got one for you already," Freddie called out.

Simon went on in.

"That's fine." He stood by the portable bar, which had already been set up for business, and watched Freddie manipulating a bottle. It was a feat which Freddie could apparently perform in any condition short of complete unconsciousness. All things considered, he had really staged quite a comeback. Of course, he had had some sleep. The Saint looked at his watch, and saw that it was a few minutes after four. He said: "I think it's so nice to get up early and catch the best part of the morning, don't you?"

"Did you find out anything?" Freddie demanded.

"Not a thing," said the Saint. "But that might add up to quite something."

He took the highball that Freddie handed him, and strolled over to the windows. They were the only ones in the house he had not yet examined. But they were exactly like the others—the screens latched and intact.

Lissa still sat up in the bed, the covers huddled up under her chin, staring now and again at the knife driven into the mattress, as if it were a snake that somebody was trying to frighten her with and she wasn't going to be frightened. Simon turned back and sat down beside her. He also looked at the knife.

"It looks like a kitchen knife," he remarked.

"I wouldn't let anyone touch it," she said, "on account of fingerprints."

Simon nodded and smiled, and took a handkerchief from the pocket of his robe. Using the cloth for insulation, he pulled the knife out and held it delicately while he inspected it. It was a kitchen knife—a cheap piece of steel with a riveted wooden handle, but sharp and pointed enough to have done all the lethal work of the most expensive blade.

"Probably there aren't any prints on it," he said, "but it doesn't cost anything to try. Even most amateurs have heard about fingerprints these days, and they all wear gloves. Still, we'll see if we have any luck."

He wrapped the knife carefully in the handkerchief and laid it on a Carter Dickson mystery on the bedside table.

"You're going to get tired of telling the story," he said, "but I haven't heard it yet. Would you like to tell me what happened?"

"I don't really know," she said. "I'd been asleep. And then suddenly for no reason at all I woke up. At least I thought I woke up, but maybe I didn't, anyway it was just like a nightmare. But I just knew there was somebody in my room, and I went cold all over, it was just as if a lot of spiders were crawling all over me, and I didn't feel as if I could move or scream or anything, and I just lay there hardly breathing and my heart was thumping away till I thought it would burst."

"Does that always happen when somebody comes into your room?" Ginny asked interestedly.

"Shut up," said the Saint.

"I was trying to listen," Lissa said, "to see if I couldn't hear something, I mean if he was really moving or if I'd just woken up with the frights and imagined it, and my ears were humming so that it didn't seem as if I could hear anything. But I did hear him. I could hear him breathing."

"Was that when you screamed?"

"No. Well, I don't know. It all happened at once. But suddenly I knew he was awful close, right beside the bed, and then I knew I was wide awake and it wasn't just a bad dream, and then I screamed the first time and tried to wriggle out of bed on the other side from where he was, to get away from him, and he actually touched my shoulder, and then there was a sort of thump right beside me—that must have been the knife— and then he ran away and I heard him rush through one of the doors, and I lay there and screamed again because I thought that would bring you or somebody, and besides if I made enough noise it would help to scare him and make him so busy trying to get away that he wouldn't wait to have another try at me."

"So you never actually saw him at all?"

She shook her head.

"I had the shades drawn, so it was quite dark. I couldn't see anything. That's what made it more like a nightmare. It was like being blind."

"But when he opened one of these doors to rush out—there might have been a little dim light on the other side——"

"Well, I could just barely see something, but it was so quick, it was just a blurred shadow and then he was gone. I don't think I've even got the vaguest idea how big he was."

"But you call him 'he,' " said the Saint easily, "so you saw that much, anyway."

She stared at him with big round blue eyes.

"I didn't," she said blankly. "No, I didn't. I just naturally thought it was 'he.' Of course it was 'he.' It had to be." She swallowed, and added almost pleadingly: "Didn't it?"

"I don't know," said the Saint, flatly and dispassionately.

"Now wait a minute," said Freddie Pellman, breaking one of the longest periods of plain listening that Simon had yet known him to maintain. "What is this?"

The Saint took a cigarette from a package on the bedside table and lighted it with care and deliberation. He knew that their eyes were all riveted on him now, but he figured that a few seconds' suspense would do them no harm.

"I've walked around outside," he said, "and I didn't see anyone making a getaway. That wasn't conclusive, of course, but it was an interesting start. Since then I've been through the whole house. I've checked every door and window in the place. Angelo did it first, but I did it again to make sure. Nothing's been touched. There isn't an opening anywhere where even a cat could have got in and got out again. And I looked in all the closets and under the beds too, and I didn't find any strangers hiding around."

"But somebody was here!" Freddie protested. "There's the knife. You can see it with your own eyes. That proves that Lissa wasn't dreaming."

Simon nodded, and his blue eyes were crisp and sardonic.

"Sure it does," he agreed conversationally. "So it's a comfort to know that we don't have to pick a prospective murderer out of a hundred and thirty million people outside. We know that this is strictly a family affair, and you're going to be killed by somebody who's living here now."

CHAPTER FOUR

IT WAS nearly nine o'clock when the Saint woke up again, and the sun, which had been bleaching the sky before he got back to bed, was slicing brilliantly through the Venetian blinds. He felt a lot better than he had expected to. In fact, he decided, after a few minutes of lazy rolling and stretching, he felt surprisingly good. He got up, sluiced himself under a cold shower, brushed his hair, pulled on a pair of swimming trunks and a bath robe, and went out in search of breakfast.

Through the french windows of the living-room he saw Ginny sitting alone at the long table in the patio beside the barbecue. He went out and stood over her.

"Hullo," she said.

"Hullo," he agreed. "You don't mind if I join you?"

"Not a bit," she said. "Why should I?"

"We could step right into a Van Druten play," he observed.

She looked at him rather vaguely. He sat down, and in a moment Angelo was at his elbow, immaculate and impassive now in a white jacket and a black bow tie.

"Yes, sir?"

"Tomato juice," said the Saint. "With Worcester sauce. Scrambled eggs, and ham. And coffee."

"Yes, sir."

The Filipino departed; and Simon lighted a cigarette and slipped the robe off his shoulders.

"Isn't this early for you to be up?"

"I didn't sleep so well." She pouted. "Esther does snore. You'll find out."

Before the party broke up for the second time, there had been some complex but uninhibited arguments about how the rest of the night should be organised with a view to mutual protection, which Simon did not want revived at that hour.

"I'll have to thank her," he said tactfully. "She's saved me from having to eat breakfast alone. Maybe she'll do it for us again."

"You could wake me up yourself just as well," said Ginny.

The Saint kept his face noncommittal and tried again.

"Aren't you eating?"

She was playing with a glass of orange juice as if it were a medicine that she didn't want to take.

"I don't know. I sort of don't have any appetite."

"Why?"

"Well . . . you *are* sure that it was someone in the house last night, aren't you?"

"Quite sure."

"I mean—one of us. Or the servants, or somebody."

"Yes."

"So why couldn't we just as well be poisoned?"

He thought for a moment, and chuckled.

"Poison isn't so easy. In the first place, you have to buy it. And there are problems about that. Then, you have to put it in something. And there aren't so many people handling food that you can do that just like blowing out a match. It's an awfully dangerous way of killing people. I think probably more poisoners get caught than any other kind of murderer. And any smart killer knows it."

"How do you know this one is smart?"

"It follows. You don't send warnings to your victims unless you think you're pretty smart—you have to be quite an egotist and a show-off to get that far—and anyone who thinks he's really smart usually has at least enough smartness to be able to kid himself. Besides, nobody threatened to kill you."

"Nobody threatened to kill Lissa."

"Nobody did kill her."

"But they tried."

"I don't think we know that they were trying for Lissa."

"Then if they were so halfway smart, how did they get in the wrong room?"

"They might have thought Freddie would be with her."

"Yeah?" she scoffed. "If they knew anything, they'd know he'd be in his own room. He doesn't visit. He has visitors."

Simon felt that he was at some disadvantage. He said with a grin: "You can tie me up, Ginny, but that doesn't alter anything. Freddie is the guy that the beef is about. The intended murderer has very kindly told us the motive. And that automatically establishes that there's no motive for killing anyone else. I'll admit that the attack on Lissa last night is pretty confusing, and I just haven't got any theories about it yet that I'd want to bet on; but I still know damn well that nobody except Freddie is going to be in much danger unless they accidentally find out who the murderer is, and personally I'm not going to starve myself until that happens."

He proved it by taking a healthy sip from the glass of tomato juice which Angelo set in front of him, and a couple of minutes later he was carving into his ham and eggs with healthy enthusiasm.

The girl watched him moodily.

"Anyway," she said, "I never can eat anything much for breakfast. I have to watch my figure."

"It looks very nice to me," he said, and was able to say it without the slightest effort.

"Yes, but it has to stay that way. There's always competition."

Simon could appreciate that. He was curious. He had been very casual all the time about the whole organisation and mechanics of the ménage, as casual as Pellman himself, but there just wasn't any way to stop wondering

about the details of a set-up like that. The Saint put it in the scientific
category of post-graduate education. Or he was trying to.

He said, leading her on with a touch so light and apparently disinterested that it could have been broken with a breath: "It must be quite a life."

"It is."

"If I hadn't seen it myself, I wouldn't have believed it was really possible."

"Why not?"

"It's just something out of this world."

"Sheiks and sultans do it."

"I know," he said delicately. "But their women are brought up differently.
They're brought up to look forward to a place in a harem as a perfectly
normal life. American girls aren't."

One of her eyebrows went up a little in a tired way.

"They are where I came from. And probably most everywhere else, if
you only knew. Nearly every man is a wandering wolf at heart, and if he's
got enough money there isn't much to stop him. Nearly every woman knows
it. Only they don't admit it. So what? You wouldn't think there was anything freakish about it if Freddie kept us all in different apartments and
visited around. What's the difference if he keeps us all together?"

The Saint shrugged.

"Nothing much," he conceded. "Except, I suppose, a certain amount of
conventional illusion."

"Phooey," she said. "What can you do with an illusion?"

He couldn't think of an answer to that.

"Well," he said, "it might save a certain amount of domestic strife."

"Oh, sure," she said. "We bicker and squabble a bit."

"I've heard you."

"But it doesn't often get too serious."

"That's the point. That's what fascinates me, in a way. Why doesn't
anybody ever break the rules? Why doesn't anybody try to ride the others
off and marry him, for instance?"

She laughed shortly.

"That's two questions. But I'll tell you. Nobody goes too far because
they wouldn't be here if they did. Or they'd only do it once. And then—
out. No guy wants to live in the middle of a mountain feud; and after all,
Freddie's the meal ticket. He's got a right to have some peace for his money.
So everybody behaves pretty well. As for marrying him—that's funny."

"Guys have been married before."

"Not Freddie Pellman. He can't afford to."

"One thing that we obviously have in common," said the Saint, "is a
sense of humor."

She shook her head.

"I'm not kidding. Didn't you know about him?"

"No. I didn't know about him."

"There's a will," she said. "All his money is in a trust fund. He just gets the income. I guess Papa Pellman knew Freddie pretty well, and so he didn't trust him. He sewed everything up tight. Freddie never will be able to touch most of the capital, but he gets two or three million to play with when he's thirty-five. On one condition. He mustn't marry before that. I guess Papa knew all about girls like me. If Freddie marries before he's thirty-five, he doesn't get another penny. Ever. Income or anything. It all goes to a fund to feed stray cats or something like that."

"So." The Saint poured himself some coffee. "I suppose Papa thought that Freddie would have attained a certain amount of discretion by that time. How long does that keep him safe for, by the way?"

"As a matter of fact," she said, "it's only a few more months."

"Well, cheer up," he said. "If you can last that long you may still have a chance."

"Maybe by that time I wouldn't want it," she said, with her disturbing eyes dwelling on him.

Simon lighted a cigarette and looked up across the patio as a door opened and Lissa and Esther came out. Lissa carried a book, with her forefinger marking a place: she put it down open on the table beside her, as if she was ready to go back to it at any moment. She looked very gay and fresh in a play suit that matched her eyes.

"Have you and Ginny solved it yet?" she asked.

"I'm afraid not," said the Saint. "As a matter of fact, we were mostly talking about other things."

"I'll take two guesses," said Esther.

"Why two?" snapped Ginny. "I thought there was only one thing you could think of."

The arrival of Angelo for their orders fortunately stopped that train of thought. And then, almost as soon as the Filipino had disappeared again and the cast were settling themselves and digging their toes in for another jump, Freddie Pellman made his entrance.

Like the Saint, he wore swimming trunks and a perfunctory terry-cloth robe. But the exposed portions of him were not built to stand the comparison. He had pale blotchy skin and the flesh under it looked spongy, as if it had softened up with inward fermentation. Which was not improbable. But he seemed totally unconscious of it. He was very definitely himself, even if he was nothing else.

"How do you feel?" Simon asked unnecessarily.

"Lousy," said Freddie Pellman, no less unnecessarily. He sank into a chair and squinted blearily over the table. Ginny still had some orange juice in her glass. Freddie drank it, and made a face. He said: "Simon, you should have let the murderer go on with the job. If he'd killed me last night, I'd have felt a lot better this morning."

"Would you have left me a thousand dollars a day in your will?" Simon inquired.

Freddie started to shake his head. The movement hurt him too much, so he clutched his skull in both hands to stop it.

"Look," he said. "Before I die and you have to bury me, who *is* behind all this?"

"I don't know," said the Saint patiently. "I'm only a bodyguard of sorts. I didn't sell myself to you as a detective."

"But you must have some idea."

"No more than I had last night."

A general quietness came down again, casting a definite shadow as if a cloud had slid over the sun. Even Freddie Pellman became still, holding his head carefully in the hands braced on either side of his jawbones.

"Last night," he said soggily, "you told us you were sure it was someone inside the house. Isn't that what he said, Esther? He said it was someone who was here already."

"That's right," said the Saint. "And it still goes."

"Then it could only be one of us—Esther or Lissa or Ginny."

"Or me. Or the servants."

"My God!" Freddie sat up. "It isn't even going to be safe to eat!" The Saint smiled slightly.

"I think it is. Ginny and I were talking about that. But I've eaten . . . Let's take it another way. You put the finger on Johnny Implicato last Christmas. That's nearly a year ago. So anybody who wanted to sneak in to get revenge for him must have sneaked in since then. Let's start by washing out anybody you've known more than a year. How about the servants?"

"I hired them all when I came here this season."

"I was afraid of that. However. What about anybody else?"

"I only met you yesterday."

"That's quite true," said the Saint calmly. "Let's include me. Now what about the girls?"

The three girls looked at each other and at Freddie and at the Saint. There was an awkward silence. Nobody seemed to want to speak first; until Freddie scratched his head painfully and said: "I think I've known you longer than anyone, Esther, haven't I?"

"Since last New Year's Eve," she said. "At the Dunes. You remember. Somebody had dared me to do a strip tease——"

"—never dreaming you'd take them up on it," said Ginny.

"All right," said the Saint. "Where did you come in?"

"In a phone booth in Miami," said Ginny. "In February. Freddie was passed out inside, and I had to make a phone call. So I lugged him out. Then he woke up, so we made a night of it."

"What about you, Lissa?"

"I was just reading a book in a drug store in New York last May. Freddie came in for some Bromo-Seltzer, and we just got talking."

"In other words," said the Saint, "any one of you could have been a girl friend of Johnny's, and promoted yourselves in here after he was killed."

Nobody said anything.

"Okay," Freddie said at last. "Well, we've got fingerprints, haven't we? How about the fingerprints on that knife."

"We can find out if there are any," said the Saint.

He took it out of the pocket of his robe, where he had kept it with him still wrapped in his handkerchief. He unwrapped it very carefully, without touching any of the surfaces, and laid it on the table. But he didn't look at it particularly. He was much more interested in watching the other faces that looked at it.

"Aren't you going to save it for the police?" asked Lissa.

"Not till I've finished with it," said the Saint. "I can make all the tests they'd use, and maybe I know one or two that they haven't heard of yet. I'll show you now, if you like."

Angelo made his impassive appearance with two glasses of orange juice for Lissa and Esther, and a third effervescent glass for Freddie. He stood stoically by while Freddie drained it with a shudder.

"Anything else, Mr Pellman?"

"Yes," Freddie said firmly. "Bring me a brandy and ginger ale. And some waffles."

"Yes, sir," said the Filipino; and paused, in the most natural and expressionless way, to gather up three or four plates, a couple of empty glasses, and, rather apologetically, as if he had no idea how it could have arrived there, the kitchen knife that lay in front of the Saint with everyone staring at it.

CHAPTER FIVE

AND THAT, Simon reflected, was as smooth and timely a bit of business as he had ever seen. He sat loose-limbed on his horse and went on enjoying it even when the impact was more than two hours old.

It had a superb simplicity of perfection which appealed to his sardonic
sense of humor. It was magnificent because it was so completely incalcula-
ble. You couldn't argue with it or estimate it. There was absolutely no percentage in claiming, as Freddie Pellman had done, in a loud voice and
at great length, that Angelo had done it on purpose. There wasn't a thing
that could be proved one way or the other. Nobody had told Angelo anything. Nobody had asked Angelo to leave the knife alone, or spoken to
him about fingerprints. So he had simply seen it on the table, and figured
that it had arrived there through some crude mistake, and he had discreetly
picked it up to take it away. The fact that by the time it had been rescued
from him, with all the attendant panic and excitement, any fingerprints
that might have been on the handle would have been completely obscured
or without significance was purely a sad coincidence. And that was the
literal and ineluctable truth. Angelo could have been as guilty as hell or as
innocent as a newborn babe: the possibilities were exactly that, and if
Sherlock Holmes had been resurrected to take part in the argument his
guess would have been worth no more than anyone else's.

So the Saint hooked one knee over the saddle horn and admired the
pluperfect uselessness of the whole thing, while he lighted a cigarette and
let his horse pick its own serpentine trail up the rocky slope towards Andreas
Canyon.

The ride had been Freddie's idea. After two more brandies and ginger
ale, an aspirin, and a waffle, Freddie Pellman had proclaimed that he
wasn't going to be scared into a cellar by any goddam gangster's friends.
He had hired the best goddam bodyguard in the world, and so he ought
to be able to do just what he wanted. And he wanted to ride. So they were
going to ride.

"Not me," Lissa had said. "I'd rather have a gangster than a horse, any
day. I'd rather lie out by the pool and read."

"All right," Freddie said sourly. "You lie by the pool and read. That
makes four of us, and that's just right. We'll take lunch and make a day
of it. You can stay home and read."

So there were four of them riding up towards the cleft where the
gray-green tops of tall palm trees painted the desert sign of water. Simon
was in the lead, because he had known the trail years before and it came
back to him as if he had only ridden it yesterday. Freddie was close behind
him. Suddenly they broke over the top of the ridge, and easing out on to
the dirt road that had been constructed since the Saint was last there to
make the canyon more accessible to pioneers in gasoline-powered arm-
chairs. But bordering the creek beyond the road stood the same tall palms,
skirted with the dry drooped fronds of many years, but with their heads
still rising proudly green and the same stream racing and gurgling around

their roots. To the Saint they were still ageless beauty, unchanged, a visual awakening that flashed him back with none of the clumsy encumbrances of time machines to other more leisured days and other people who had ridden the same trail with him; and he reined his horse and thought about them, and in particular about one straight slim girl whom he had taken there for one stolen hour, and they had never said a word that was not casual and unimportant, and they had never met again, and yet they had given all their minds into each other's hands, and he was utterly sure that if she ever came there again she would remember, exactly as he was remembering . .

So that it was like the shock of a cold plunge when Freddie Pellman spurred up beside him on the road and said noisily: "Well, how's the mystery coming along?"

The Saint sighed inaudibly and tightened up, and said : "What mystery?"

"Oh, go on," Freddie insisted boisterously. "You know what I'm talking about. The mystery."

"So I gathered," said the Saint. "But I'm not so psychic after a night like last night. And if you want to know, I'm just where I was last night. I just wish you were more careful about hiring servants."

"They had good references."

"So had everybody else who ever took that way in. But what else do you know about them?"

"What else do I know about them?" Freddie echoed, for the sake of greater clarity. "Nothing much. Except that Angelo is the best houseboy and valet I ever had. The other Filipino—Al he calls himself—is a pal of his. Angelo brought him."

"You didn't ask if they'd ever worked for Smoke Johnny?"

"No." Freddie was surprised. "Why should I?"

"He could have been nice to them," said the Saint. "And Filipinos can be fanatically loyal. Still, that threatening letter seems a little bit literate for Angelo. I don't know. Another way of looking at it is that Johnny's friends could have hired them for the job . . . And then, did you know that your chef was an Italian?"

"I never thought about it. He's an Italian, is he? Louis? That's interesting." Freddie looked anything but interested. "But what's that got to do with it?"

"So was Implicato," said the Saint. "He might have had some Italian friends. Some Italians do."

"Oh," said Freddie.

They turned over the bridge across the stream, and there was a flurry of hoofs behind them as Ginny caught up at a gallop. She rode well, and she knew it, and she wanted everyone else to know. She reined her pony up to a rearing sliding stop, and patted its damp neck.

"What are you two being so exclusive about?" she demanded.

"Just talking," said the Saint. "How are you doing?"

"Fine." She was fretting her pony with hands and heels, making it step nervously, showing off. "Esther isn't so happy, though. Her horse is a bit frisky for her."

"Don't worry about me," Esther said, coming up. "I'm doing all right. I'm awful hot, though."

"Fancy that," said Ginny.

"Never mind," said the Saint tactfully. "We'll call a halt soon and have lunch."

They were walking down towards a grove of great palms that rose like columns in the nave of a natural cathedral, their rich tufted heads arching over to meet above a cloister of deep whispering shade. They were the same palms that Simon had paused under once before, years ago; only now there were picnic tables at their feet, and at some of them a few hardy families who had driven out there in their automobiles were already grouped in strident fecundity, enjoying the unspoiled beauties of Nature from the midst of an enthusiastic litter of baskets, boxes, tin cans, and paper bags.

"Is this where you meant we could have lunch?" Freddie asked rather limply.

"No. I thought we'd ride on over to Murray Canyon—if they haven't built a road in there since I saw it last, there's a place there that I think we still might have to ourselves."

He led them down through the trees, and out on a narrow trail that clung for a while to the edge of a steep shoulder of hill. Then they were out on an open rise at the edge of the desert, and the Saint set his horse to an easy canter, threading his way unerringly along a trail that was nothing but a faint crinkling in the hard earth where other horses had followed it before.

It seemed strange to be out riding like that, so casually and inconsequentially, when only a few hours before there had been very tangible evidence that a threat of death to one of them had not been made idly. Yet perhaps they were safer out there than they would have been anywhere else. The Saint's eyes had never stopped wandering over the changing panoramas, behind as well as ahead; and although he knew how deceptive the apparently open desert could be, and how even a man on horseback, standing well above the tallest clump of scrub, could vanish altogether in a hundred yards, he was sure that no prospective sniper had come within sharpshooting range of them. Yet . . .

He stopped his horse abruptly, after a time, as the broad flat that they had been riding over ended suddenly at the brink of a sharp cliff. At the foot of the bluff, another long column of tall silent palms bordered a rustling stream. He lighted a cigarette, and wondered cynically how many of the spoiled playboys and playgirls who used Palm Springs for their wilder weekends, and saw nothing but the smooth hotels and the Racquet Club, ever realised that the name was not just a name, and that there really were Palm Springs, sparkling and crystal clear, racing down out of the over-shadowing mountains to make hidden nests of beauty before they washed out into the extinction of the barren plain. . . .

Freddie Pellman reined in beside him, looked the landscape over, and said, tolerantly, as if it were a production that had been offered for his approval: "This is pretty good. Is this where we eat?"

"If everybody can take it," said the Saint, "there's a pool further up that I'd like to look at again."

"I can take it," said Freddie, comprehensively settling the matter.

Simon put his horse down the steep zigzag, and stopped at the bottom to let it drink from the stream. Freddie drew up beside him again—he rode well enough, having probably been raised to it in the normal course of a millionaire's son's upbringing—and said, still laboring with the same subject: "Do you really think one of the girls could be in on it?"

"Of course," said the Saint calmly. "Gangsters have girl friends. Girl friends do things like that."

"But I've known all of them for some time at least."

"That may be part of the act. A smart girl wouldn't want to make it too obvious—meet you one day, and bump you off the next. Besides, she may have a nice streak of ham in her. Most women have. Maybe she thinks it would be cute to keep you in suspense for a while. Maybe she wants to make an anniversary of it, and pay off for Johnny this Christmas."

Freddie swallowed.

"That's going to make some things—a bit difficult."

"That's your problem," Simon said cheerfully.

Freddie sat his saddle unhappily and watched Ginny and Esther coming down the grade. Ginny came down it in a spectacular avalanche, like a mountain cavalry display, and swept off her Stetson to ruffle her hair back with a bored air while her pony dipped its nose thirstily in the water a few yards downstream. Esther, steering her horse down quietly, joined her a little later.

"But this is *Wunn*derful!" Ginny called out, looking at the Saint. "How do you find all these marvellous places?" Without waiting for an answer, she turned to Esther and said in a solicitous undertone which was per-fectly pitched to carry just far enough: "How are you feeling, darling? I hope you aren't getting too miserable."

Simon was naturally glancing towards them. He wasn't looking for anything in particular, and as far as he was concerned Esther was only one of the gang, but in those transient circumstances he felt sorry for her. So for that one moment he had the privilege of seeing one woman open her soul in utter stark sincerity to another woman. And what one woman said to another, clearly, carefully, deliberately, quietly, with serious pre-mediation and the intensest earnestness, was: "You bitch."

"Let's keep a-goin'," said the Saint hastily, in a flippant drawl, and lifted his reins to set his horse at the shallow bank on the other side of the stream.

He led them west towards the mountains with a quicker sureness now, as the sense of the trail came back to him. In a little while it was a track that only an Indian could have seen at all, but it seemed as if he could have found it at the dead of night. There was even a place where weeds and spindly clawed scrub had grown so tall and dense since he had last been there that anyone else would have sworn that there was no trail at all; but he set his horse boldly at the living wall and smashed easily through into a channel that could hardly have been trodden since he last opened it . . . so that presently they found the creek again at a sharp bend, and he led them over two deep fords through swift-running water, and they came out at last in a wide hollow ringed with palms where hundreds of spring floods had built a broad open sandbank and gouged out a deep sheltered pool beside it.

"This is lunch," said the Saint, and swung out of the saddle to moor his bridle to a fallen palm log where his horse could rest in the shade.

They spread out the contents of their saddlebags on the sandbank and ate cold chicken, celery, radishes, and hard-boiled eggs. There had been some difficulty when they set out over convincing Freddie Pellman that it would have been impractical as well as strictly illegal to take bottles of champagne on to the reservation, but the water in the brook was sweet and ice-cold.

Esther drank it from her cupped hands, and sat back on her heels and gazed meditatively at the pool.

"It's awful hot," she said, suggestively.

"Go on," Ginny said to Simon. "Dare her to take her clothes off and get in. That's what she's waiting for."

"I'll go in if you will," Esther said sullenly.

"Nuts," said Ginny. "I can have a good time without that."

She was leaning against the Saint's shoulder for a backrest, and she gave a little snuggling wriggle as she spoke which made her meaning completely clear.

Freddie Pellman locked his arms around his knees and scowled. It had been rather obvious for some time that all the current competition was being aimed at the Saint, even though Simon had done nothing to try and encourage it; and Freddie was not feeling so generous about it as he had when he first invited the girls to take Simon into the family.

"All right," Freddie said gracelessly. "I dare you."

Esther looked as if a load had been taken off her mind.

She pulled off her boots and socks. She stood up, with a slight faraway smile, and unbuttoned her shirt and took it off. She took off her frontier pants. That left her in a wisp of sheer close-fitting scantiness. She took that off, too.

She certainly had a beautiful body.

She turned and walked into the pool, and lowered herself into it until the water lapped her chin. It covered her as well as a sheet of glass. She rolled, and swam lazily up to the far end, and as the water shallowed she rose out again and strolled on up into the low cascade where the stream tumbled around the next curve. She waded on up through the falls, under the palms, the sunlight through the leaves making glancing patterns on her skin, and disappeared around the bend, very leisurely. It was quite an exit.

The rustle of the water seemed very loud suddenly, as if anyone would have had to shout to be heard over it. So that it was surprising when Ginny's voice sounded perfectly easy and normal.

"Well, folks," she said, "don't run away now, because there'll be another super-colossal floor show in just a short while." She nestled against the Saint again and said: "Hullo."

"Hullo," said the Saint restrainedly.

Freddie Pellman got to his feet.

"Well," he said huffily, "I know you won't miss me, so I think I'll take a walk."

He stalked off up the stream the way Esther had gone, stumbling and balancing awkwardly on his high-heeled boots over the slippery rounded boulders.

They watched him until he was out of sight also.

"Alone at last," said Ginny emotionally.

The Saint reached for a cigarette.

"Don't you ever worry about getting complicated?" he asked.

"I worry about not getting kissed," she said.

She looked up at him from under her long sweeping lashes, with bright impudent eyes and red lips tantalisingly parted. The Saint had been trying conscientiously not to look for trouble, but he was not made out of ice cream and bubble gum. He was making good progress against no resistance when the crash of a shot rattled down the canyon over the chattering of the water and brought him to his feet as if he had actually felt the bullet.

CHAPTER SIX

HE RAN up the side of the brook, fighting his way through clawing scrub and stumbling over boulders and loose gravel. Beyond the bend, the stream rose in a long twisting stairway of shallow cataracts posted with the same shapely palms that grew throughout its length. A couple of steps further up he found Freddie.

Freddie was not dead. He was standing up. He stood and looked at the Saint in a rather foolish way, with his mouth open.

"Come on," said the Saint encouragingly. "Give."

Freddie pointed stupidly to the rock behind him. There was a bright silver scar on it where a bullet had scraped off a layer of lead on the rough surface before it riccoed off into nowhere.

"It only just missed me," Freddie said.

"Where were you standing?"

"Just here."

Simon looked at the scar again. There was no way of reading from it the caliber or make of gun. The bullet itself might have come to rest anywhere within half a mile. He tried a rough sight from the mark on the rock, but within the most conservative limits it covered an area of at least two thousand square yards on the other slope of the canyon.

The Saint's spine tingled. It was a little like the helplessness of his trip around the house the night before—looking up at that raw muddle of shrubs and rocks, knowing that a dozen sharpshooters could lie hidden there, with no risk of being discovered before they had fired the one shot that might be all that was necessary. . . .

"Maybe we should go home, Freddie," he said.

"Now wait." Freddie was going to be obstinate and valiant after he had found company. "If there's someone up there——"

"He could drop you before we were six steps closer to him," said the Saint tersely. "You hired me as a bodyguard, not a pallbearer. Let's move."

Something else moved, upwards and a little to his left. His reflexes had tautened instinctively before he recognised the flash of movement as only a shifting of bare brown flesh.

From a precarious flat ledge of rock five or six yards up the slope, Esther called down: "What goes on?"

"We're going home," Simon called back.

"Wait for me."

She started to scramble down off the ledge. Suddenly she seemed much more undressed than she had before. He turned abruptly.

"Come along, then."

He went back, around the bend, past the pool, past Ginny, to where they had left the horses, hearing Freddie's footsteps behind him but not looking back. There were no more shots, but he worked quickly checking the saddles and tightening the cinches. The place was still just as picturesque and enchanting, but as an ambush it had the kind of topography where he felt that the defending team was at a great disadvantage.

"What's the hurry?" Ginny complained, coming up beside him; and he locked the buckle he was hauling on and gave the leather a couple of rapid loops through the three-quarter rig slots.

"You heard the shot, didn't you?"

"Yes."

"It just missed Freddie. So we're moving before they try again."

"Something's always happening," said Ginny resentfully, as if she had been shot at herself.

"Life is like that," said the Saint, untying her horse and handing the reins to her.

As he turned to the next horse Esther came up. She was fully dressed again, except that her shirt was only half buttoned; and she looked smug and sulky at the same time.

"Did you hear what happened, Ginny?" she said. "There was a man hiding up in the hills, and he took a shot at Freddie. And if he was where Simon thought he was, he must have seen me sunbathing without anything on."

"Tell Freddie that's what made him miss," Ginny suggested. "It might be worth some new silver foxes to you."

A dumb look came into Esther's beautifully sculptured face. She gazed foggily out at the landscape as the Saint cinched her saddle and thrust the reins into her limp hands.

She said: "Simon."

"Yes?"

"Didn't you say something last night about—about being sure it was someone in the house?"

"I did."

"Then . . . then just now—you were with Ginny, so she couldn't have done anything. And Lissa isn't here. But you know I couldn't—you know I couldn't have hidden a gun anywhere, don't you?"

"I don't know you well enough," said the Saint.

But it was another confusion that twisted around in his mind all the way home. It was true that he himself was an alibi for Ginny—unless she had planted one of those colossally elaborate remote-control gun-firing devices beloved of mystery writers. And Esther couldn't have concealed a gun, or anything else, in her costume—unless she had previously planted it somewhere up the stream. But both those theories would have required them to know in advance where they were going, and the Saint had chosen the place himself. . . . It was true he had mentioned it before they started, but mentioning it and finding it were different matters. He would have sworn that not more than a handful of people besides himself had ever discovered it, and he remembered sections of the trail that had seemed to be completely overgrown since they had last been trodden. Of course, with all his watchfulness, they might have been followed. A good hunter might have stayed out of sight and circled over the hills—he could have done it himself. . . .

Yet in all those speculations there was something that didn't connect, something that didn't make sense. If the theoretical sniper in the hills had been good enough to get there at all, for instance, why hadn't he been good enough to try a second shot before they got away? He could surely have had at least one more try, from a different angle, with no more risk than the first. . . . It was like the abortive attack on Lissa—it made sense, but not absolute sense. And to the Saint's delicately tuned reception that was a more nagging obstacle than no sense at all. . . .

They got back to the stables, and Freddie said: "I need a drink. Let's beat up the Tennis Club before we go home."

For once, the Saint was not altogether out of sympathy with the exigencies of Freddie's thirst.

They drove out to the club, and sat on the balcony terrace looking down over the beautifully terraced gardens, the palm-shaded oval pool and the artificial brook where imported trout lurked under spreading willows and politely awaited the attention of pampered anglers. The rest of them sipped Daiquiris, while Freddie restored himself with three double brandies in quick succession. And then, sauntering over from the tennis courts with a racquet in her hand, Lissa O'Neill herself came up to them. She looked as cool and dainty as she always seemed to look, in one of those abbreviated sun suits that she always seemed to wear, which some clairvoyant designer must have invented exclusively for her slim waist and for long tapered legs like hers, in pastel shades that would set off her clear golden skin. But it seemed as if all of them drew back behind a common barrier that made them look at her in the same way, not in admiration, but guardedly, waiting for what she would say.

She said: "Fancy meeting you here."

"Fancy meeting you," said the Saint. "Did you get bored with your book?"

"I finished it, so I thought I'd get some excercise. But the pro has been all booked up for *hours*."

It was as if all of them had the same question on their lips, but only the Saint could handle his voice easily enough to say, quite lazily: "Hours?"

"Well, it must have been two hours or more. Anyway, I asked for a lesson as soon as I got here, and he was all booked up. He said he'd fit me in if anybody cancelled, but I've been waiting around for ages and nobody's given me a chance . . ."

A part of the Saint's mind felt quite detached and independent of him, like an adding machine clicking over in a different room. The machine tapped out: She should have known that the pro would be booked up. And of course he'd say that he'd be glad to fit her in if he had a cancellation. And the odds are about eight to one that he wouldn't have a cancellation. So she could make him and several other people believe that she'd been waiting all the time. She could always find a chance to slip out of the entrance when there was no one in the office for a moment—she might even arrange to clear the way without much difficulty. She only had to get out. Coming back, she could say she just went to get something from her car. No one would think about it. And if there had been a cancellation, and the pro had been looking for her—well, she'd been in the johnny, or the showers, or at the bottom of the pool. He just hadn't found her. She'd been there all the time. A very passable casual alibi, with only a trivial percentage of risk.

But she isn't dressed to have done what must have been done.

She could have changed.

She couldn't have done it anyway.

Why not? She looks athletic. There are good muscles under that soft golden skin. She might have been sniping revenooers in the mountains of Kentucky since she was five years old, for all you know. What makes you so sure what she could do and couldn't do?

Well, what were Angelo and his pal, and Louis the Italian chef, doing at the same time? You can't rule them out.

Any good reader would rule them out. The mysterious murderer just doesn't turn out to be the cook or the butler any more. That was worked to death twenty years ago.

So of course no cook or butler in real life would ever dream of murdering anyone any more, because they'd know it was just too corny.

"What's the matter with you all?" Lissa asked. "Wasn't the ride any good?"

"It was fine," said the Saint. "Except when your last night's boy friend started shooting at Freddie."

Then they all began to talk at once.

It was Freddie, of course, who finally got the floor. He did it principally by saying the same things louder and oftener than anyone else. When the competition had been crushed he told the story again, challenging different people to substantiate his statments one by one. He was thus able to leave a definite impression that he had been walking up the canyon when somebody shot at him.

Simon signalled a waiter for another round of drinks and put himself into a self-preservative trance until the peak of the verbal flood had passed. He wondered whether he should ask Freddie for another thousand dollars. He felt that he was definitely earning his salary as he went along.

". . . Then that proves it must be one of the servants," Lissa said. "So if we can find out which of them went out this afternoon——"

"Why does it prove that?" Simon inquired.

"Well, it couldn't have been Ginny, because she was talking to you. It couldn't have been me——"

"Couldn't it?"

She looked at him blankly. But her brain worked. He could almost see it. She might have been reading everything that had been traced through his mind a few minutes ago, line by line.

"It couldn't have been *me*," Esther insisted plaintively. "I didn't have a stitch on. Where could I have hidden a gun?"

Ginny gazed at her speculatively.

"It'll be interesting to see how the servants can account for their time," Simon said hastily. "But I'm not going to get optimistic too quickly. I don't think anything about this business is very dumb and straightforward. It's quite the opposite. Somebody is being so frantically cunning that he must be practically tying himself—or herself—in a knot. So if it is one of the servants, I bet he has an alibi too."

"I still think you ought to tell the police," Ginny said.

The drinks arrived. Simon lighted a cigarette and waited until the waiter had gone away again.

"What for?" he asked. "There was a guy in Lissa's room last night. Nobody saw him. He didn't leave any muddy footprints or any of that stuff. He used one of our own kitchen knives. If there ever were any fingerprints on it, they've been ruined. So—nothing . . . This afternoon somebody shot at Freddie. Nobody saw him. He didn't leave his gun, and nobody could ever find the bullet. So nothing again. What are the police going to do? They aren't magicians . . . However, that's up to you, Freddie."

"They could ask people questions," Esther said hopefully.

"So can we. We've been asking each other questions all the time. If anybody's lying, they aren't going to stop lying just because a guy with a badge is listening. What are they going to do—torture everybody and see what they get?"

"They'd put a man on guard, or something," said Ginny.

"So what? Our friend has waited quite a while already. I'm sure he could wait some more. He could wait longer than any police department is going to detail a private cop to nursemaid Freddie. So the scare blows over, and everybody settles down, and sometime later, maybe somewhere else, Freddie gets it. Well, personally I'd rather take our chance now while we're all warmed up."

"That's right," Freddie gave his verdict. "If we scare whoever it is off with the police, they'll only come back another time when we aren't watching for them. I'd rather let them get on with it while we're ready for them."

He looked rather proud of himself for having produced this penetrating reasoning all on his own.

And then his mind appeared to wander, and his eyes changed their focus.

"*Hey,*" he said in an awed voice. "Look at that, will you?" They looked, as he pointed. "The babe down by the pool. In the sarong effect. Boy, is that a chassis! Look at her!"

She was, Simon admitted, something to look at. The three girls with them seemed to admit the same thing by their rather strained and intent silence. Simon could feel an almost tangible heaviness thicken into the air.

Then Ginny sighed, as if relief had reached her rather late.

"A blonde," she said. "Well, Lissa, it's nice to have known you."

Freddie didn't even seem to hear it. He picked up his glass, still staring raptly at the vision. He put the glass to his lips.

It barely touched, and he stiffened. He took it away and stared at it frozenly. Then he pushed it across the table towards the Saint.

"Smell that," he said.

Simon put it to his nostrils. The hackneyed odor of bitter almonds was as strong and unmistakable as any mystery-story fan could have desired.

"It does smell like prussic acid," he said, with commendable mildness. He put the glass down and drew on his cigarette again, regarding the exhibit moodily. He was quite sure now that he was going to collect his day's wages without much more delay. And probably the next day's pay in advance, as well. At that, he thought that the job was poorly paid for what it was. He could see nothing in it at all to make him happy. But being a philosopher, he had to cast around for one little ray of sunshine. Being persistent, he found it. "So anyway," he said, "at least we don't have to bother about the servants any more."

CHAPTER SEVEN

IT WAS a pretty slender consolation, he reflected, even after they had returned to the house and he had perfunctorily questioned the servants, only to have them jointly and severally corroborate each other's statements that none of them had left the place that afternoon.

After which, they had all firmly but respectfully announced that they were not used to being under suspicion, that they did not feel comfortable in a household where people were frequently getting stabbed at, shot at, and poisoned at; that in any case they would prefer a less exacting job with more regular hours; that they had already packed their bags; and that they would like to catch the evening bus back to Los Angeles, if Mr Pellman would kindly pay them up to date.

Freddie had obliged them with a good deal of nonchalance, being apparently not unaccustomed to the transience of domestic help.

After which the Saint went to his room, stripped off his riding clothes, took a shower, wrapped himself in bathrobe, and lay down on the bed with a cigarette to contemplate the extreme sterility of the whole problem.

"This ought to learn you," he told himself, "to just say NO when you don't want to do anything, instead of making smart cracks about a thousand dollars a day."

The servants weren't ruled out, of course. There could be more than one person involved, taking turns to do things so that each would have an alibi in turn.

But one of the girls had to be involved. Only one of them could have poisoned Freddie's drink at the Tennis Club. And any one of them could have done it. The table had been small enough, and everybody's attention had been very potently concentrated on the sarong siren. A bottle small enough to be completely hidden in the hand, tipped over his glass in a casual gesture—and the trick was done.

But why do it then, when the range of possible suspects was so sharply limited?

Why do any of the other things that had happened?

He was still mired in the exasperating paradoxes of partial sense, which was so many times worse than utter nonsense. Utter nonsense was like a code: there was a key to be found somewhere which would make it clear and coherent in an instant, and there was only one exact key that would do it. You knew that you had it or you hadn't. The trouble with partial sense was that while you were straightening out the twisted parts you never knew whether you were distorting the straight ones . . .

And somewhere beyond that point he heard the handle of his door turning, very softly.

His hand slid into the pocket of his robe where his gun was, but that was the only move he made. He lay perfectly still and relaxed, breathing at the shallow even rate of a sleeper, his eyes closed to all but a slit through which he could watch the door as it opened.

Esther came in.

She stood in the doorway hesitantly for a few seconds, looking at him, and the light behind her showed every line of her breath-taking body through the white crepe negligee she was wearing. Then she closed the door softly behind her and came a little closer. He could see both her hands, and they were empty.

He opened his eyes.

"Hullo," she said.

"Hullo." He stretched himself a little.

"I hope I didn't wake you up."

"I was just dozing."

"I ran out of cigarettes," she said, "and I wondered if you had one."

"I think so."

It was terrific dialogue.

He reached over to the bedside table, and offered her the package that lay there. She came up beside him to take it. Without rising, he struck a match. She sat down beside him to get the light. The negligee was cut down to her waist in front, and it opened more when she leaned forward to the flame.

"Thanks." She blew out a deep inhalation of smoke. She could have made an exit with that, but she didn't. She studied him with her dark dreamy eyes and said: "I suppose you were thinking."

"A bit."

"Have you any ideas yet?"

"Lots of them. Too many."

"Why too many?"

"They contradict each other. Which means I'm not getting anywhere."

"So you still don't know who's doing all these things?"

"No."

"But you know it isn't any of us."

"No, I don't."

"Why do you keep saying that? Ginny was with you all the time this afternoon, and I couldn't have had a gun on me, and Lissa couldn't have followed us and been at the Tennis Club too."

"Therefore there must be a catch in it somewhere, and that's what I'm trying to find."

"I'm afraid I'm not very clever," Esther confessed.

He didn't argue with her.

She said at last: "Do you think I did it?"

"I've been trying very conscientiously to figure out how you could have."

"But I haven't done anything."

"Everybody else has said that too."

She gazed at him steadily, and her lovely warm mouth richened with pouting.

"I don't think you really like me, Simon."

"I adore you," he said politely.

"No, you don't. I've tried to get on with you. Haven't I?"

"You certainly have."

"I'm not awfully clever, but I try to be nice. Really. I'm not a cat like Ginny, or all brainy and snooty like Lissa. I haven't any background, and I know it. I've had a hell of a life. If I told you about it, you'd be amazed."

"Would I? I love being amazed."

"There you go again. You see?"

"I'm sorry. I shouldn't kid you."

"Oh, it's all right. I haven't got much to be serious about. I've got a pretty face and a beautiful body. I know I've got a beautiful body. So I just have to use that."

"And you use it very nicely, too."

"You're still making fun of me. But it's about all I've got, so I have to use it. Why shouldn't I?"

"God knows," said the Saint. "I didn't say you shouldn't."

She studied him again for a while.

"You've got a beautiful body, too. All lean and muscular. But you've got brains as well. I'm sorry. I just like you an awful lot."

"Thank you," he said quietly.

She smoked her cigarette for a few moments.

He lighted a cigarette himself. He felt uncomfortable and at a loss. As she sat there, and with everything else in the world put aside, she was something that no man with a proper supply of hormones could have been cold to. But everything else in the world couldn't be put aside quite like that . . .

"You know," she said, "this is the hell of a life."

"It must be," he agreed.

"I've been watching it. I can think a little bit. You saw what happened this afternoon. I mean——"

"The blonde at the Tennis Club?"

"Yes . . . Well, it just happened that she was a blonde. She could just as well have been a brunette."

"And then—Esther starts packing."

"That's what it amounts to."

"But it's been fun while it lasted; and maybe you take something with you."

"Oh, yes. But that isn't everything. Not the way I mean. I mean . . ."

"What do you mean?"

She fiddled with a seam in her negligee for a long time.

"I mean . . . I know you aren't an angel, but you're not just like Freddie. I think you'd always be sincere with people. You're sort of different, somehow. I know I haven't got anything much, except being beautiful, but—that's something, isn't it? And I do really like you so much. I'd—I'd do anything . . . if I could only stay with you and have you like me a little."

She was very beautiful, too beautiful, and her eyes were big and aching and afraid.

Simon stared at the opposite wall. He would have given his day's thousand dollars to be anywhere the hell out of there.

He didn't have to.

Freddie Pellman's hysterical yell sheared suddenly through the silent house with an electrifying urgency that brought the Saint out of bed and up on to his feet as if he had been snatched up on wires. His instinctive movement seemed to coincide exactly with the dull slam of a muffled shot that gave more horror to the moment. He leapt towards the communicating door, and remembered as he reached it that while he had meant to get it unlocked that morning the episode of the obliterated fingerprints had put it out of his mind. Simultaneously, as he turned to the outer door, he realised that the sound of a door slamming could have been exactly the same, and he cursed his own unguardedness as he catapulted out on to the screened verandah.

One glance up and down was enough to show that there was no other person in sight, and he made that survey without even a check in his winged dash to Freddie's room.

His automatic was out in his hand when he flung the door open, to look across the room at Freddie Pellman, in black trousers and unbuttoned soft dress shirt, stretched out on the davenport, staring with a hideous grimace of terror at the rattlesnake that was coiled on his legs, its flat triangular head drawn back and poised to strike.

Behind him, the Saint heard Esther stifle a faint scream; and then the detonation of his gun blotted out every other sound.

As if it had been photographed in slow motion, Simon saw the snake's shattered head splatter away from its body, while the rest of it kicked and whipped away in series of reflex convulsions that spilled it still writhing spasmodically on to the floor.

Freddie pulled himself shakily up to his feet.

"Good God," he said, and repeated it. "Good God—and it was real! Another second, and it'd have had me!"

"What happened?" Esther was asking shrilly.

"I don't know. I was starting to get dressed—you see?—I'd got my pants and shirt on, and I sat down and had a drink, and I must have fallen asleep. And then that thing landed on my lap!"

Simon dropped the gun back into his pocket.

"Landed?" he said.

"Yes—just as if somebody had thrown it. Somebody must have thrown it. I felt it hit. That was what woke me up. I saw what it was, and of course I let out a yell, and then the door slammed, and I looked round too late to see who it was. But I didn't care who it was, then. All I could see was that God-damn snake leering at me. I almost thought I was seeing things again. But I knew I couldn't be. I wouldn't have felt it like that. I was just taking a nap, and somebody came in and threw it on top of me!"

"How long ago was this?"

"Just now! You don't think I lay there for an hour necking with a snake, do you? As soon as it fell on me I woke up, and as soon as I woke up I saw it, and of course I let out a yell at once. You heard me yell, didn't you, Esther? And right after that the door banged. Did you hear that?"

"Yes, I heard it," said the Saint.

But he was thinking of something else. And for that once at least, even though she had admitted that she was not so bright, he knew that Esther was all the way there with him. He could feel her mind there with him, even without turning to find her eyes fastened on his face, even before she spoke.

"But that *proves* it, Simon! You must see that, don't you? I couldn't possibly have done it, could I?"

"Why, where were you?" Freddie demanded.

She drew herself up defiantly and faced him.

"I was in Simon's room."

Freddie stood hunched and stiff and staring at them. And yet the Saint realised that it wasn't any positive crystallising of expression that made him look ugly. It was actually the reverse. His puffy face was simply blank and relaxed. And on that sludgy foundation, the crinkles of unremitting feverish bonhomie, the lines and bunchings of laborious domineering enthusiasm, drained of their vital nervous activation, were left like a mass of soft sloppy scars in which the whole synopsis of his life was hieroglyphed.

"What is it now?" Lissa's voice asked abruptly.

It was a voice that set out to be sharp and matter-of-fact, and failed by an infinitesimal quantity that only such ceaselessly critical ears as the Saint's would catch.

She stood in the doorway, with Ginny a little behind her.

Freddie looked up at her sidelong from under his lowered brows.

"Go away," he said coldly. "Get out."

And then, almost without a pause or a transition, that short-lived quality in his voice was only an uncertain memory.

"Run along," he said. "Run along and finish dressing. Simon and I want to have a little talk. Nothing's the matter. We just had a little scare, but it's all taken care of. I'll tell you presently. Now be nice children and go away and don't make a fuss. You too, Esther."

Reluctantly, hesitantly, his harem melted away.

Simon strolled leisurely across to a side table and lighted himself a cigarette as Freddie closed the door. He genuinely wasn't perturbed, and he couldn't look as if he was.

"Well," Freddie said finally, "How does it look now?"

His voice was surprisingly negative, and the Saint had to make a lightning adjustment to respond to it.

He said: "It makes you look like quite a bad risk. So do you mind if I collect for today and tomorrow? Two G, Freddie. It'd be sort of comforting."

Freddie went to the dressing-table, peeled a couple of bills out of a litter of green paper and small change, and came back with them. Simon glanced at them with satisfaction. They had the right number of zeros after the 1.

"I don't blame you," said Freddie. "If that snake had bitten me——"

"You wouldn't have died," said the Saint calmly. "Unless you've got a very bad heart, or something like that. That's the silly part of it. There are doctors within phone call, there's sure to be plenty of serum in town, and there's a guy like me on the premises who's bound to know the first aid. You'd have been rather sick, but you'd have lived through it. So why should the murderer go through an awkward routine with a snake when he had you cold and could've shot you or slit your throat and made sure of it? . . . This whole plot has been full of silly things, and they're only just starting to add up and make sense."

"They are?"

"Yes, I think so."

"I wish I could see it."

Simon sat on the arm of a chair and thought for a minute, blowing smoke-rings.

"Maybe I can make you see it," he said.

"Go ahead."

"Our suspects were limited to six people the first night, when we proved it was someone in the house. Now, through various events, everyone of them has an alibi. That would make you think of a partnership. But none of the servants could have poisoned your drink this afternoon, and it wasn't done by the waiter or the bartender—they've both been at the club for years, and you could bet your shirt on them. Therefore somebody at the table must have been at least part of the partnership, or the whole works if there never was a partnership at all. But everyone at the table has still been alibied, somewhere in the story."

Freddie's brow was creased with the strain of following the argument. "Suppose two of the girls were in partnership?"

"I thought of that. It's possible, but absolutely not probable. I doubt very much whether any two women could collaborate on a proposition like this, but I'm damned sure that no two of these girls could."

"Then where does that get you?"

"We have to look at the alibis again. And one of them has to be a phony."

The corrugations deepened on Freddie's forehead. Simon watched him silently. It was like watching wheels go round. And then a strange expression came into Freddie's face. He looked at the Saint with wide eyes.

"My God!" he said. "You mean—Lissa . . ."

Simon didn't move.

"Yes," Freddie muttered. "Lissa. Ginny's got a perfect alibi. She couldn't have shot at me. You were with her yourself. Esther might have done it if she'd hidden a gun there before. But she was in your room when somebody threw that snake at me. She couldn't have faked that. And the servants have all gone. . . . The only alibi Lissa has got is that she was the first one to be attacked. But we've only got her word for it. She could have staged that so easily." His face was flushed with the excitement that was starting to obstruct his voice. "And all that criminology of hers . . . of course . . . she's the one who's always reading these mysteries—she'd think of melodramatic stuff like that snake—she'd have the sort of mind . . ."

"I owe you an apology, Freddie," said the Saint, with the utmost candor. "I didn't think you had all that brain."

CHAPTER EIGHT

HE WAS ALONE in the house. Freddie Pellman had taken the girls off to the Coral Room for dinner, and Simon's stall was that he had to wait for a long-distance phone call. He would join them as soon as the call had come through.

"You'll have the place to yourself," Freddie had said when he suggested the arrangement, still glowing from his recent accolade. "You can search all you want. You're bound to find *something*. And then we'll have her."

Simon finished glancing through a copy of *Life*, and strolled out on the front terrace. Everything on the hillside was very still. He lighted a cigarette, and gazed out over the thin spread of sparkling lights that was Palm Springs at night. Down below, on the road that led east from the foot of the drive, a rapidly dwindling speck of red might have been the tail light of Freddie's car.

The Saint went back into the living-room after a little while and poured himself a long lasting drink of Peter Dawson. He carried it with him as he worked methodically through Esther's and Ginny's rooms.

He wasn't expecting to find anything in either of them, and he didn't. But it was a gesture that he felt should be made.

So after that he came to Lissa's room.

He worked unhurriedly through the closet and the chest of drawers, finding nothing but the articles of clothing and personal trinkets that he had found in the other rooms. After that he sat down at the dresser. The center drawer contained only the laboratory of creams, lotions, powders, paints, and perfumes without which even a modern goddess believes that she has shed her divinity. The top right-hand drawer contained an assortment of handkerchiefs, scarves, ribbons, clips, and pins. It was in the next drawer down that he found what he had been waiting to find.

It was quite a simple discovery, lying under a soft pink froth of miscellaneous underwear. It consisted of a .32 automatic pistol, a small blue pharmacist's bottle labeled "*Prussic Acid*—POISON," and an old issue of *Life*. He didn't really need to open the magazine to know what there would be inside, but he did it. He found the mutilated page, and knew from the other pictures in the layout that the picture which had headed the letter that Freddie had shown him at their first meeting would fit exactly into the space that had been scissored out of the copy in front of him.

He laid the evidence out on the dresser top and considered it while he kindled another cigarette.

Probably any other man would have felt that the search ended there; but the Saint was not any other man. And the strange clairvoyant conviction grew in his mind that that was where the search really began.

He went on with it more quickly, with even more assurance, although he had less idea than before what he was looking for. He only had that intuitive certainty that there should be something—something that would tie the last loose ends of the tangle together and make complete sense of it. And he did find it, after quite a short while.

It was only a shabby envelope tucked into the back of a folding photo frame that contained a nicely glamorised portrait of Freddie. Inside the envelope were a savings bank pass book that showed a total of nearly five thousand dollars, and a folded slip of paper. It was when he unfolded the slip of paper that he knew that the search was actually over and all the questions answered, for he had in his hands a certificate of marriage issued in Yuma ten months before . . .

"Are you having fun?" Lissa asked.

She had been as quiet as a cat, for he hadn't heard her come in, and she was right behind him. And yet he wasn't surprised. His mind was filling with a great calm and quietness as all the conflict of contradictions settled down and he knew that the last act had been reached.

He turned quite slowly, and even the small shining gun in her hand, aimed squarely at his chest, didn't surprise or disturb him.

"How did you know?" he drawled.

"I'm not so dumb. I should have seen it before I went out if I'd been really smart."

"You should." He felt very detached and unrealistically balanced. "How did you get back, by the way?"

"I just took the car."

"I see."

He turned and stood up to face her, being careful not to make any abrupt movement, and keeping his hands raised a little; but she still backed away a quick step.

"Don't come any closer," she said sharply.

He was just over an arm's length from her then. He measured it accurately with his eye. And he was still utterly cool and removed from it all. The new stress that was building up in him was different from anything before. He knew now, beyond speculation, that murder was only a few seconds away, and it was one murder that he particularly wanted to prevent. But every one of his senses and reflexes would have to be sharper and surer than they had ever been before to see it coming and to forestall it . . . Every nerve in his body felt like a violin string that had been tuned to within an eyelash weight of breaking . . .

And when it came, the warning was a sound so slight that at any other time he might never have heard it—so faint and indeterminate that he was never absolutely sure what it actually was, if it was the rustle of a sleeve or a mere slither of skin against metal or nothing but an unconsciously tightened breath.

It was enough that he heard it, and that it exploded him into action too fast for the eye to follow—too fast even for his own deliberate mental processes to trace. But in one fantastic flow of movement it seemed that his left hand plunged at the gun that Lissa was holding, twisted it aside as it went off, and wrenched it out of her hand and threw her wide and stumbling while another shot from elsewhere chimed into the tight pile-up of sound effects; while at the same time, quite independently, his right hand leapt to his armpit holster in a lightning draw that brought his own gun out to bark a deeper note that practically merged with the other two . . . And that was just about all there was to it.

The Saint clipped his own gun back in its holster, and dropped Lissa's automatic into his side pocket. It had all been so fast that he hadn't even had time to get a hair of his head disarranged.

"I'm afraid you don't have a very nice husband," he said.

He stepped to the communicating door and dragged the drooping figure of Freddie Pellman the rest of the way into the room and pushed it into a chair.

CHAPTER NINE

"HE'LL LIVE, if you want him," said the Saint casually. "I only broke his arm."

He picked up the revolver that Freddie had dropped, spilled the shells out, and laid it with the other exhibits on the dresser while Freddie clutched at his reddening sleeve and whimpered. It seemed as if the whole thing took so little time that Lissa was still recovering her balance when he turned and looked at her again.

"The only trouble was," he said, "that you married him too soon. Or didn't you know about the will then?"

She stared at him, white-faced, without speaking.

"Was he drunk when you did it?" Simon asked.

After a while she said: "Yes."

"One of those parties?"

"Yes. We were both pretty high. But I didn't know he was that high."

"Of course not. And you didn't realise that he wouldn't mind framing you into a coffin to keep his gay playboy integrity."

She looked at the collection of exhibits on her dresser, at Freddie, and at the Saint. She didn't seem to be able to get everything co-ordinated quickly. Simon himself showed her the marriage certificate again.

"This is what I wasn't supposed to find," he said. "In fact, I don't think Freddie even imagined you'd have it around. But it made quite a difference. How much were you going to shake him down for, Lissa?"

"I only asked him for two hundred thousand," she said. "I'd never have said anything. I just didn't want to be like some of the others—thrown out on my ear to be a tramp for the rest of my life."

"But you wanted too much," said the Saint. "Or he just didn't trust you, and he thought you'd always be coming back for more. Anyhow, he figured this would be a better way to pay off."

His cigarette hadn't even gone out. He picked it up and brightened it in a long peaceful draw that expressed all the final settling down of his mind.

"The mistake that all of us made," he said, "was not figuring Freddie for a moderately clever guy. Because he was a bore, we figured he was moderately stupid. Which is a rather dangerous mistake. A bore isn't necessarily stupid. He doesn't necessarily overrate his own intelligence. He just underrates everyone else. That makes him tedious, but it doesn't make him dumb. Freddie isn't dumb. He just sounds dumb because he's talking down to how dumb he thinks the rest of us are. As a matter of fact, he's quite a lively lad. He put a lot of gray matter into this little scheme. As soon as he heard that I'd arrived in town, he had the inspiration that he'd been waiting for. And he didn't waste a day in getting it started. He wrote himself the famous threatening letter at once—it was quite a coincidence, of course, that there was that last Christmas party to hang it on, but if there hadn't been that he'd certainly have thought of something else almost as good. He only had to establish that he was being menaced, and get me into the house to protect him. Then he had to put you in the middle of the first situation, in a set-up that would look swell in the beginning but would get shakier and shakier as things went on. That wasn't difficult either."

The only sound when he paused was Freddie Pellman's heavy sobbing breathing.

"After that, he improvised. He only had to stage a series of incidents that would give everyone else in turn an absolutely ironclad alibi that would satisfy me. It wasn't hard to do—it was just a matter of being ready with a few props to take advantage of the opportunities that were bound to arise. Perhaps he was a bit lucky in having so many chances in such a short space of time, but I don't know. He couldn't go wrong, anyway. Everything had to work in for him, once the primary idea was planted. Even an accident like Angelo picking up the knife was just a break for him—there weren't any fingerprints on it, of course, and it just helped the mystery a little . . . And this evening he was able to finish up in style with the snake routine. It wasn't exactly his fault that the routine fitted in just as well with another pattern that was gradually penetrating into my poor benighted brain. That's just one of the natural troubles with trying to create artificial mysteries— when you're too busy towing around a lot of red herrings, you don't realise that you may be getting a fishy smell on your own fingers. . . . That was what Freddie did. He was being very clever about letting it work out that your alibi was the only flimsy one; but he forgot that when I had to start questioning alibis it might occur to me that there was one other person whose alibis were flimsier still. And that was him."

Simon drew on his cigarette again.

"Funnily enough, I was just leading up to telling him that when he made his first major mistake. You see, I had an idea what was going on, but I was going nuts trying to figure out *why*. There didn't seem to be any point to the whole performance, except as a terrific and ponderous practical joke. And I couldn't see Freddie with that sort of humor. So I was just going to come out flatly and face him with it and see what happened. It's a shock technique that works pretty well sometimes. And then he took all the wind out of my sails by insisting on helping me to see how it all pointed to you. That's what I mean about him underrating other people's intelligence. He was just a little too anxious to make quite sure that I hadn't missed any of the points that I was supposed to get. But it had just the opposite effect, because I happened to know that your alibi must have been genuine. So then I knew that the whole plot didn't point *to* you—it was pointed *at* you. And when Freddie went a little further and helped me to think of the idea of staying behind tonight and searching your room, I began to guess that the climax would be something like this. I suppose he got hold of you privately and told you he'd started to get suspicious of what I was up to—maybe I was planning to plant some evidence and frame one of you?"

"Yes."

"So he suggested that the two of you sneak off and see if you could catch me at it?"

She nodded.

"Then," said the Saint, "you peeked in through the window and saw me with the exhibits on the dressing-table, and he said 'What did I tell you?' . . . And then he said something like: 'Let's really get the goods on him now. You take this gun and walk in on him and keep him talking. If he thinks you're alone he'll probably say enough to hang himself. I'll be listening, and I'll be a witness to everything he says.' Something like that?"

"Something like that," she said huskily.

"And then the stage was all set. He only had to wait a minute or two, and shoot you. I was supposed to have suspected you already. I'd found a lot of incriminating evidence in your room. And then you'd walked in on me with a gun . . . While of course his story would have been that he was suspicious when you sneaked off, that he followed you home, and found you holding me up, and you were just about to give me the works when he popped his pistol and saved my life. Everyone would have said that 'of course' you must have been Smoke Johnny's moll at some time, and nobody would ever have been likely to find the record of that marriage in Yuma unless they were looking for it—and why should they look for it? So you were out of the way, and he was in the clear, and I'd personally be his best, solid, hundred-percent witness that it was justifiable homicide. It would have made one of the neatest jobs that I ever heard of—if it had worked. Only it didn't work. Because just as I knew you had a good alibi all the time, I knew that all this junk in your drawer had been planted there, and so I knew that I still had something else to look for—the real motive for all these things that were going on. Maybe I was lucky to find it so quickly. But even so, from the moment when you walked in, something exciting was waiting to happen. . . . Well, it all worked out all right—or don't you think so, Freddie?"

"You've got to get me a doctor," Freddie said hoarsely.

"Do I have all the right answers?" Simon asked relentlessly.

Freddie Pellman moaned and clutched his arm tighter and raised a wild haggard face.

"You've got to get me a doctor," he pleaded in a rising shout. "Get me a doctor!"

"Tell us first," insisted the Saint soothingly. "Do we know all the answers?"

Pellman tossed his head, and suddenly everything seemed to disintegrate inside him.

"Yes!" he almost screamed. "Yes, damn you! I was going to fix that little bitch. I'll do it again if I ever have the chance. And you, too! . . . Now get me a doctor. Get me a doctor, d'you hear? D'you want me to bleed to death?"

The Saint drew a long deep breath, and put out the stub of his cigarette. He took a pack from his pocket and lighted another. And with that symbolic action he had put one more episode behind him, and the life of adventure went on.

"I don't really know," he said carelessly. "I don't think there'd be any great injustice done if we let you die. Or we might keep you alive and continue with the shakedown. It's really up to Lissa."

He glanced at the girl again curiously.

She was staring at Freddie in a way that Simon hoped no woman would ever look at him, and she seemed to have to make an effort to bring herself back to the immediate present. And even then she seemed to be a little behind.

She said: "I just don't get one thing. How did you know all that stuff had been planted in my drawer? And why were you so sure that my flimsy alibi was good?"

He smiled.

"That was the easiest thing of all. Aren't you the detective-story fan? You might have gotten good ideas from some of your mysteries, but you could hardly have picked up such bad ones. At least you'd know better than to keep a lot of unnecessary incriminating evidence tucked away where anyone with a little spare time could find it. And you'd never have had the nerve to pull an alibi like that first attack on yourself if it was a phony, because you'd have known that anyone else who'd ever read a mystery too would have spotted it for a phony all the time. About the only thing wrong with Freddie is that he had bright ideas, but he didn't read the right books."

"For Christ's sake," Freddie implored shrilly, "aren't you going to get me a doctor?"

"What would they do in a Saint story?" Lissa asked.

Simon Templar sighed.

"I imagine they'd let him call his own doctor, and tell the old story about how he was cleaning a gun and he didn't know it was loaded. And I suppose we'd go back to the Coral Room and look for Ginny and Esther, because they must be getting hungry, and I know I still am. And I expect Freddie would still pay off in the end, if we all helped him to build up a good story. . . ."

Lissa tucked her arm under his.

"But what are the rest of us going to do tonight?"

"The Hays Office angle on that bothers the hell out of me," said the Saint.

THE SIZZLING SABOTEUR

FROM *The Saint on Guard*

So NOW AT LAST we are compelled to drag in some of that definitely dated World-War-II product that I referred to in the Foreword.

This story was my automatic first choice because, in all awareness of my own elaborately publicized laziness, it looked on the first survey like the easiest story of all to introduce.

Because, after all, there was probably less fiction in it than in anything I ever wrote.

All the names, of course, are changed. And it didn't happen anywhere near Galveston. Or even anywhere in Texas. But a lot of the facts are in the newspaper files of another town, in another Southern state. And the facts that aren't there are in the files of the FBI.

So all the introduction it calls for, I thought, is to say, "Okay, most of it happened. I was there."

Now I find that this doesn't make a great introduction. And yet I don't know what to add to it that wouldn't be even worse hokum than the few trimmings that are already on it.

So it just has to go like that.

Most of it happened. I was there.

THE SIZZLING SABOTEUR

SIMON TEMPLAR had met a lot of unusual obstructions on the highway in the course of a long and varied career of eccentric traveling. They had ranged from migrant sheep to diamond necklaces, from circus parades to damsels in distress; and he had acquired a tolerant feeling towards most of them—particularly the damsels in distress. But a partly incinerated tree, he felt, was carrying originality a little far. He thought that the Texas Highway Department should at least have been able to eliminate such exotic hazards as that.

Especially since there were no local trees in sight to account for it, so that somebody must have taken considerable trouble to import it. The surrounding country was flat, marshy, and reedy; and the sourish salty smell of the sea was a slight stench in the nostrils. The road was a graveled affair with a high crown, possibly for drainage, and not any too wide although comparatively smooth. It wound and snaked along through alternating patches of sand and reeds like an attenuated sea serpent which had crawled out of Galveston Bay to sun itself on that desolate stretch of beach, so that Simon had seen the log a longish while before he was obliged to brake his car on account of it.

The car was a nice shiny black sedan of the 1942 or BF (Before Freezing) vintage; but it was no more incongruous on this ribbon of road than its driver. However, Simon Templar was noted for doing incongruous things. Enroute to Galveston via Texas City on Highway 146, he hadn't even reached Texas City. Somehow, back where the highway forked left from the Southern Pacific right-of-way, Simon had taken an even lefter turn which now had him heading southwards along a most erratic observation tour of the Gulf coastline. A long way from the metropolitan crowding of New York, where he had recently wound up a job—or even of St Louis, where he had been even more recently. Now his only company was the purring motor and an occasional raucous gull that flapped or soared above the marshland on predatory business of its own. Which didn't necessarily mean that that business was any less predatory than that of Simon Templar, who under his more publicised nickname of The Saint had once left sundry police departments and local underworlds equally flatfooted in the face of new and unchallenged records of predatoriality—if this chronicler may inflict such a word on the long-suffering Messieurs Funk, Wagnalls, and Webster. The most immediately noticeable difference between the Saint and the seagull was the seagull's protective parosmia, or perversion of the sense of smell. . . . Yet the sun was still three hours high, and it was still twenty miles to Galveston unless the cartographer who had concocted the Saint's road map was trying in his small way to cheer the discouraged pilgrim.

And there was the smouldering blackened log laid almost squarely across the middle of the road, as if some diehard vigilante had made it his business to see that no casehardened voyager rushed through the scenery without a pause in which its deeper fascinations might have a chance to make their due impression on the soul.

Simon considered his own problem with clear blue eyes as the sedan came to a stop.

The road was too narrow for him to drive around the log; and in view of the tire rationing situation it was out of the question to try and drive over it. Which meant that somebody had to get out and move it. Which meant that the Saint had to move it himself.

Simon Templar said a few casual things about greenhorns who mislaid such sizeable chunks of their camp fires; but at the same time his eyes were glancing left and right with the endless alertness hardening in their sapphire calm, and his tanned face setting into the bronze fighting mask to which little things like that could instantly reduce it.

He knew from all the pitiless years behind him how easily this could be an effective ambush. When he got out to move the smouldering log, it would be a simple job for a couple of hirelings of the ungodly to attack him. A certain Mr Matson, for instance, might have been capable of setting such a trap—if Mr Matson had known that Simon Templar was the Saint, and was on his way to interview Mr Matson in Galveston, and if Mr Matson had had the prophetic ability to foretell that Simon Templar was going to take this coastal road. But since Simon himself hadn't known it until about half an hour ago, it appeared that this hypothesis would have credited Mr Matson with a slightly fantastic grade of clairvoyance.

The Saint stared at the log with all these things in his mind; and while he was doing it he discovered for the first time in his life the real validity of a much handled popular phrase.

Because he sat there and literally felt his blood run cold.

Because the log moved.

Not in the way that any ordinary log would have moved, in a sort of solid rolling way. This log was flexible, and the branches stirred independently like limbs.

Simon Templar had an instant of incredulous horror and sheer disbelief. But even while he groped back into the past for any commonplace explanation of such a defection of his senses, he knew that he was wasting his time. Because he had positively seen what he had seen, and that was the end of it.

Or the beginning.

Very quietly, when there was no reason to be quiet, he snapped open the door of the car and slid his seventy-four inches of whipcord muscle out on to the road. Four of his quick light strides took him to the side of the huge ember in the highway. And then he had no more doubt.

He said, involuntarily: "My God . . ."

For the ember was not a tree. It was human.

It had been a man.

Instead of a six-foot log of driftwood, the smouldering obstacle had been a man.

And the crowning horror was yet to come. For at the sound of the Saint's voice, the blackened log moved again feebly and emitted a faint groan.

Simon turned back to his car, and was back again in another moment with his light topcoat and a whisky flask. He wrapped the coat around the piece of human charcoal to smother any remaining fire, and gently raised the singed black head to hold his flask to the cracked lips.

A spasm of pain contorted the man, and his face worked through a horrible crispness.

"Blue . . . Goose . . ." The voice came in a parched whisper. "Maris . . . contact . . . Olga—Ivan—Ivanovitch . . ."

Simon glanced around the deserted landscape, and had never felt so helpless. It was obviously impossible for him to move that sickening relict of a human being, or to render any useful first aid.

Even if any aid, first or last, would have made any difference.

"Can you hold it until I get some help—an ambulance?" he said. "I'll hurry. Can you hear me?"

The burned man rallied slightly.

"No use," he breathed. "I'm goner . . . Poured—gasoline—on me . . . Set fire . . ."

"Who did?" Simon insisted. "What happened?"

"Three men . . . Met last night—in bar . . . Blatt . . . Weinbach . . . And Maris . . . Going to party—at Olga's . . ."

"Where?"

"Don't know . . ."

"What's your name? Who are you?"

"Henry—Stephens," croaked the dying man. "Ostrich-skin—leather case—in gladstone lining . . . Get case—and send . . . send . . ."

His voice trailed off into an almost inaudible rasp that was whisked away along with his spirit on the wings of the wind that swept across the flats. Henry Stephens was dead, mercifully for him, leaving Simon Templar with a handful of unexplained names and words and a decided mess.

"And God damn it," said the Saint unreasonably, to no better audience than the circling gulls, "why do people like you have to read that kind of mystery story? Couldn't one of you wait to die, just once, until after you'd finished saying what you were trying to get out?"

He knew what was the matter with him, but he said it just the same. It helped him to get back into the shell which too many episodes like that had helped to build around him.

And then he lighted a cigarette and wondered sanely what he should do.

Any further identification of Henry Stephens was impossible. His hair was all burned off, his hands were barbecued from trying to beat out the flames of his own pyre, and the few remnants of his clothes were charred to him in a hideous smelting. Simon debated whether to take the body with him or leave it where it was. He glanced at his watch and surveyed the lonely country about him. There was still no living person in sight, although in the distance he could see a couple of summer shacks and the indications of a town beyond.

Simon moved the body gently to one side of the road, reentered his car, and drove carefully around it. Then his foot grew heavy on the accelerator until the side road eventually merged with the main highway and took him on to Virginia Point.

It was inevitable that the Saint's irregular past should have given him some fundamental hesitations about going out of his way to make contact with the Law, and on top of that he had projects for his equally unpredictable future which argued almost as strongly against inviting complications and delays; but he heaved a deep sigh of resignation and found his way to the local police station.

The sergeant in charge, who was sticking his tongue out over a crossword puzzle in a prehistoric and dog-eared magazine, listened bug-eyed to the report of his find, and promptly telephoned the police across the Causeway in Galveston proper.

"I'll have to ask you to stay here until the Homicide Squad and the ambulance comes over to pick up the corpse," he said as he hung up.

"Why?" Simon asked wearily. "Don't you think they'll bring enough men to lift him? I've got business in Galveston."

The sergeant looked apologetic.

"It's—it's a matter of law, Mr—er——"

"Templar," supplied the Saint. "Simon Templar."

This apparently meant no more to the local authority than John Smith or Leslie Charteris. He excavated a sheet of paper and began to construct a report along the lines which he had probably memorised in his youth, which had been a long time ago.

"You're from where, Mr Temple?" he asked, lifting his head.

"Tem-*plar*," Simon corrected him, with his hopes beginning to rise again. "I just came from St Louis, Missouri."

The sergeant wrote this down, spelling everything carefully.

"You got any identification papers on you?"

"What for?" Simon inquired. "It's the corpse you're going to have to identify, not me. I know who I am."

"I reckon so; but we don't," the other rejoined stolidly. "Now if you'll just oblige me by answering my questions——"

Simon sighed again, and reached for his wallet.

"I'm afraid you're going to be difficult, so help yourself, Lieutenant."

"Sergeant," maintained the other, calmly squinting at the Saint's draft cards and driving licenses and noting that the general descriptions fitted the man in front of him.

He was about to hand the wallet back without more than glancing into the compartment comfortably filled with green frogskins of the realm quaintly known as folding money when his eye was caught by the design stamped on the outside of the leather where a monogram might ordinarily have been. It was nothing but a line drawing of a skeletal figure with a cipher for a head and an elliptical halo floating above it. The pose of the figure was jaunty, with a subtle impudence that amounted almost to arrogance.

The sergeant examined it puzzledly.

"What's this?"

"I'm a doodler," Simon explained gravely. "That is my pet design for telephone booths, linen tablecloths, and ladies' underwear."

"I see," said the sergeant quite blankly, returning the wallet. "Now if you'll just sit down over there, Mr Templar, the Galveston police will be here directly. It's only a couple of miles across the Causeway, and you can lead the way to the spot."

"Aren't you going to call out the posse to chase the murderers?" Simon suggested. "If they brought a horse for me, I could save some of my gas ration."

"You got something there," said the sergeant woodenly. "I'll call the sheriff's office while we're waitin'."

Simon Templar groaned inwardly, and saw it all closing around him again, the fantastic destiny which seemed to have ordained that nothing lawless should ever happen anywhere and let him pass by like any other peaceful citizen.

He fished out another cigarette while the second call was being made, and finally said: "I'm beginning to hope that by the time you get out there the seagulls will have beaten you to it and there won't be any body."

"There'll be one if you saw one," opined the sergeant confidently. "Nobody'll likely come along that beach road again today. Too early in the season for picnics, and a bad day for fishin'."

"I trust your deductive genius is on the beam, Captain, but at least two other parties have been on that road today already—the victim and the murderers."

"Sergeant," grunted the other. "And I don't know how you come to be on that road yet."

Simon shrugged, and spread his hands slightly to indicate that under the laws of mathematical probability the point was unanswerable. Silence fell as the conversation languished.

Presently there was a noise of cars arriving, and installments of the Law filtered into the house. The sergeant put down his crossword puzzle and stood up to do the honors.

"Hi, Bill. . . . Howdy, Lieutenant Kinglake. . . . 'Lo, Yard. . . . Hi-yah, Dr Quantry. . . . This is the man who reported that burned corpse. His name is Templar and he's a doodler."

Simon kept his face perfectly solemn as he weighed the men who were taking charge of the case.

Lieutenant Kinglake was a husky teak-skinned individual with gimlet gray eyes and a mouth like a thin slash above a battleship prow of jaw. He looked as if he worked hard and fast and would want to hit things that tried to slow him up. Yard, his assistant, was a lumbering impression from a familiar mould, in plain clothes that could have done nicely with a little dusting and pressing. Dr Quantry, the coroner, looked like Dr Quantry, the coroner. Bill, who wore a leather windbreaker with a deputy sheriff's badge pinned on it, was middle-aged and heavy, with a brick-red face and a moustache like an untrimmed hedge. He had faintly popped light-blue eyes with a vague lack of focus, as if he was unused to seeing anything nearer than the horizon: he moved slowly and spoke even slower when he spoke at all.

It didn't take Kinglake more than a minute to assimilate all the information that the sergeant had gathered, and to examine Simon's identification papers. He stopped over the line drawing which reminded him of the figures of boxers which he used to draw in the margins of successive pages of his Fiske's history and riffle to simulate a sparring match.

"Doodler?" he said in a sharp voice. "I——" He broke off as his eyes widened and then narrowed. "I've seen this picture before. Simon Templar, eh? Are you the Saint?"

"I bow to your fund of miscellaneous information," Simon responded courteously.

"Meaning?"

"That I am known in certain strata of society, and to a goodly number of the carriage trade, by that cognomen."

"Ah." Detective Yard spoke with an air of discovery. "A funny man."

"The Saint, eh?" rumbled the sheriff's deputy, with a certain deliberate awe. "Gee, he's the Saint."

"He said he was a doodler," persisted the sergeant.

Dr Quantry consulted a gold watch in exactly the way that Dr Quantry would have consulted a gold watch, and said: "Gentlemen, how about getting on?"

Lieutenant Kinglake held the Saint's eyes for another moment with his hard stare, and gave back the wallet.

"Right," he snapped. "Cut out the eight-cylinder words, Mr Templar, and lead us to the body. You can leave your car here and ride with me. Yard, tell the ambulance driver to follow us. Come on."

Simon turned back to the sergeant as the party trooped out.

"By the way," he said, "the word for 'a hole in the ground' is w-e-l-l, not what you have. Goodbye, Inspector."

He climbed resignedly into the seat beside Kinglake, reflecting that there was nothing much you could do when Fate was running a private feud against you, and that he must be a congenital idiot to have ever expected that his business in Galveston would be allowed to proceed as smoothly as it should have for anyone else. He got a very meager satisfaction out of rehearsing some of the things he would have to say to a certain Mr Hamilton in Washington about that.

CHAPTER TWO

THE MORTAL REMAINS, as our school of journalism taught us not to call them, of Mr Henry Stephens lay precisely where Simon had left them, proving that the sergeant at Virginia Point had been right in one contention and no one had come along that road in the meantime.

Lieutenant Kinglake and the coroner squatted beside the body and made a superficial examination. Detective Yard took his cue to demonstrate that he was something more than window-dressing. He began searching the area close to the body, and then thoroughly quartered the surrounding acre in ever-widening circles like a dutiful mastiff. Slow and apparently awkward, perhaps a little on the dull side, he was meticulous and painstaking. Bill the deputy sheriff found a convenient horizon and gazed at it in profound meditation.

Simon Templar stood patiently by while it went on. He didn't want to interfere any more than he had already; and for all his irrepressible devilment he never made the mistake of underestimating the Law, or of baiting its minions without provocation or good purpose.

Dr Quantry eventually straightened up and wiped his hand on his handkerchief.

"Death by carbonisation," he announced. "Gasoline, apparently. It's a miracle that he was able to speak at all, if this is how Mr Templar found him. . . . Autopsy as a matter of course. Give you a full report later."

The hard-eyed Lieutenant nodded and got to his feet, holding out the Saint's topcoat.

"This is yours, Templar?"

"Thanks."

Dr Quantry beckoned to the ambulance crew.

"Remove," he ordered briskly. "Morgue."

Kinglake made his own inspection of the crown of the road where Simon showed him he had first seen the body.

"He didn't do all that burning here—the surface is hardly scorched," he concluded, and turned to wait for the approach of his assistant.

Detective Yard carried some souvenirs carefully in his handkerchief. They consisted of a partly burned crumple of newspaper, and an ordinary match folder bearing the name of the 606 Club in Chicago. Kinglake looked at the exhibits without touching them.

"Galveston paper," he said; and then: "When were you last in Chicago, Templar?"

"A few days ago."

"Ever been to the 606 Club?"

"As a matter of fact, I have," said the Saint coolly. "I'm making a survey of the United States on the subject of stage and floor-show nudity in the principal cities in relation to the per capita circulation of the *Atlantic Monthly*. It's a fascinating study."

Lieutenant Kinglake was unruffled.

"What's the story, Yard?"

"There's a spot about twenty yards in off the Gulf side of the road where the reeds are all trampled down and burned. Can't tell how many men made the tracks, and they're all scuffed up by the deceased having crawled back over them. Looks as if a couple of men might have taken the deceased in there, and one of them could have poured gas or oil over him while the other lit the paper to set fire to him so as not to have to get so close like he would've had to with a match. Then they scrammed; but there aren't any distinguishable tire marks. Victim must have staggered around, trying to beat out the flames with his hands, and found his way back to the road where he collapsed."

It was a pretty shrewd reconstruction, as Simon recognised with respect; and it only left out one small thing.

"What about the bottle or container which held the gasoline?" he inquired.

"Maybe we'll find that in your car," Yard retorted with heavy hostility. "You were at this club in Chicago where the matches came from——"

"The dear old match folder clue," said the Saint sadly. "Detective Manual, chapter two, paragraph three."

The deputy sheriff removed his eyes wistfully from the horizon, cleared his throat, and said weightily: "It ain't so funny, pardner. You're tied up closer'n anybody with this business."

"We'll check the newspaper and the match book for fingerprints," Kinglake said shortly. "But don't let's go off at half cock. Look."

He reached into his own pocket and brought out three match folders.

One carried the advertisement of a Galveston pool hall, one spoke glowingly of the virtues of Tums, and the other carried the imprint of the Florentine Gardens in Hollywood.

"See?" he commented. "Where did I get this Florentine Gardens thing? I've never been to Hollywood. Advertising matches are shipped all around the country nowadays. This is as good a clue as saying that the other book proves I must have a bad stomach. Let's go back and get Templar's statement."

"Just so I get to Galveston before I'm too old to care," said the Saint agreeably.

But inwardly he took a new measure of the Lieutenant. Kinglake might be a rough man in a hurry, but he didn't jump to conclusions. He would be tough to change once he had reached a conclusion, but he would have done plenty of work on that conclusion before he reached it.

So the Saint kept a tight rein on his more wicked impulses, and submitted patiently and politely to the tedious routine of making his statement while it was taken down in labored longhand by Detective Yard and Bill the deputy simultaneously. Then there were a few ordinary questions and answers on it to be added, and after a long dull time it was over.

"Okay, Bill," Kinglake said at last, getting up as if he was no less glad than the Saint to be through with the ordeal. "We'll keep in touch. Templar, I'll ride back to Galveston in your car, if you don't mind."

"Fine," said the Saint equably. "You can show me the way."

But he knew very well that there would be more to it than that; and his premonition was vindicated a few seconds after they got under way.

"Now," Kinglake said, slouching down in the seat beside him and biting off the end of a villainous-looking stogie, "we can have a private little chat on the way in."

"Good," said the Saint. "Tell me about your museums and local monuments."

"And I don't mean that," Kinglake said.

Simon put a cigarette in his mouth and pressed the lighter on the dashboard and surrendered to the continuation of Fate.

"But I'm damned if I know," he said, "why the hell you should be so concerned. Brother Stephens wasn't cremated within the city limits."

"There's bound to be a hook-up with something inside the city, and we work with the Sheriff and he works with us. I'm trying to save myself some time."

"On the job of checking up on me?"

"Maybe."

"Then why not let Yard worry about it? I'm sure he'd love to pin something on me."

"Yeah," Kinglake assented between puffs of smoke. "He could get on your nerves at times, but don't let him fool you. He's a first-rate detective. Good enough for the work we do here."

"I haven't the slightest doubt of it," Simon assured him. "But I've told you everything I know, and every word of it happens to be true. However, I don't expect that to stop you trying to prove I did it. So get started. This is your inspiration."

Kinglake still didn't start fighting.

"I know that your story checks as far as it goes," he said. "I smelt the liquor on that dead guy's mouth, and I saw your coat. I'm not believing that you'd waste good whisky and ruin a good coat just to build up a story—yet. But I do want to know what your business is in Galveston."

The Saint had expected this.

"I told you," he replied blandly. "I'm making this survey of American night life. Would you like to give me the lowdown on the standards of undress in your parish?"

"Want to play hard to handle, eh?"

"Not particularly. I just want to keep a few remnants of my private life."

Kinglake bit down on his cigar and stared impartially at the Saint's tranquil profile.

After a little while he said: "From what I remember reading, your private life is always turning into a public problem. So that's why I'm talking to you. As far as I know, you aren't wanted anywhere right now, and there aren't any charges out against you. I've also heard of a lot of officers here and there leading with their chins by thinking too fast as soon as they saw you. I'm not figuring on making myself another of 'em. Your story sounds straight so far, or it would if anybody else told it. It's too bad your reputation would make anybody look twice when you tell it. But okay. Until there's evidence against you, you're in the clear. So I'm just telling you. While you're in Galveston, you stay in line. I don't want your kind of trouble in my town."

"And I hope you won't have it," said the Saint soberly. "And I can tell you for my part that there won't be any trouble that someone else doesn't ask for."

There was a prolonged and unproductive reticence, during which Simon devoted himself wholeheartedly to digesting the scenic features of the approach over the channel of water known as West Bay which separates the island of Galveston from the mainland.

"The Oleander City," he murmured dreamily, to relieve the awkward silence. "The old stamping grounds of Jean Lafitte. A shrine that every conscientious freebooter ought to visit . . . Would you like me to give you a brief and somewhat garbled résumé of the history of Galveston, Lieutenant?"

"No," Kinglake said candidly. "The current history of the town is enough to keep me busy. Turn at the next light."

Simon drove him to Headquarters, and lighted another cigarette while the Lieutenant gathered his rather ungainly legs together and disembarked.

"The inquest will probably be tomorrow," he said practically. "Where are you staying?"

"The Alamo House."

Kinglake gave him directions.

"Don't leave town till I'm through with you," he said. "And don't forget what I told you. That's all."

He turned dourly away; and Simon Templar drove on to register faithfully and with no deception at the Alamo House.

The colored bellhop who showed him to his room was no more than naturally amazed at being tipped with a five-dollar bill for the toil of carrying one light suitcase. But the Saint had not finished with him then.

"George," he said, "I presume you are an expert crap shooter?"

"Yassah," answered the startled negro, grinning. "My name is Po't Arthur Jones, sah."

"Congratulations. I'm sure that Port Arthur is proud of you. But the point is, you should be more or less familiar with the Galveston police force—know most of them by sight, I mean."

"Well, sah, I—er—yassah."

"Then I must tell you a secret. Lieutenant Kinglake and some of his pals are investigating me for membership in a private club that they have. I expect some of them to be nosing around to find out if I'm really respectable enough to associate with them. Don't misunderstand me. If they ask you any questions, you must always tell them the truth. Never lie to detectives, Po't Arthur, because it makes them so bad tempered. But just point them out to me quietly and tell me who they are, so I can say hullo to them when we meet. And every time you do that, I'll be good for another fin."

The negro scratched his head, and then grinned again.

"Don't reckon they's no harm in that, Mistah Templah. That Mistah Kinglake sho' is a hard man. They ain't a single killin' he don't solve here in Galveston. He . . . Say!" The big brown eyes rolled. "How come you know 'bout Mistah Kinglake?"

"We had a mutual interest in what is known as a *corpus delicti*," said the Saint solemnly, "but I sold him my share. He's now checking the bill of sale. Do you follow me?"

"Nawsah," said Port Arthur Jones.

"Then don't let it worry you. Read the morning paper for details. By the way, what is the leading newspaper here?"

"The *Times-Tribune*, sah. They put out a mawnin' an' evenin' paper both."

"They must be as busy as bees," said the Saint. "Now don't forget our agreement. Five bucks per cop, delivered on the hoof."

"Yassah. An' thank yuh, sah."

The Saint grinned in his turn, and went to the bathroom to wash and change his shirt.

It was much later than he had meant to begin his real errand in Galveston; but he had nothing else to do there, and he didn't know enough about the entertainment potentialities of the town to be tempted by other attractions. It was most inconsiderate of Lieutenant Kinglake, he thought, to have refused to take his question seriously and enlighten him. . . . But besides that, he knew that his unfortunate discovery of the expiring Mr Henry Stephens meant that he couldn't look forward to following his own trail much further in the obscurity which he would have chosen. It looked like nothing but cogent common sense to do what he could with the brief anonymity he could look forward to.

Thus it happened that after a couple of grilled sandwiches in the hotel coffee shop he set out to stroll back down into the business district with the air of a tourist who had nowhere to go and all night to get there.

And thus his stroll brought him to the Ascot Hotel just a few blocks from the waterfront. The Ascot was strictly a business man's bunkhouse, the kind of place where only the much-maligned couriers of commerce roost briefly on their missions of peculiar promotion.

Simon entered the small lobby and approached the desk. The plaque above the desk said, without cracking a smile: "Clerk on duty: MR WIMBLETHORPE." Simon Templar, not to be outdone in facial restraint, said without smiling either: "Mr Wimblethorpe, I'm looking for a Mr Matson of St Louis."

"Yes, sir," said the clerk. "Mr Matson was staying here, but——"

"My name," said the Saint, "is Sebastian Tombs. I'm a mining engineer from west Texas, and I have just located the richest deposit of bubble gum in the state. I wanted to tell Mr Matson about it."

"I was trying to tell you," said the clerk, "that Mr Matson has checked out."

"Oh," said the Saint, a bit blankly. "Well, could you give me his forwarding address?"

The clerk shuffled through his card file.

"Mr Matson didn't leave an address. A friend of his came in at five o'clock and paid his bill and took his luggage away for him."

Simon stared at him with an odd sort of frown that didn't even see the man in front of him. For the Saint happened to know that Mr Matson was waiting for a passport from Washington, in order to take ship to foreign parts, and that the passport had not yet come through. Wherefore it seemed strange for Mr Matson to have left no forwarding address—unless he had suddenly changed his mind about the attractions of foreign travel.

"Who was this friend?" Simon inquired.

"I don't know, Mr Tombs. If you could stop by or call up in the morning you might be able to find out from Mr Baker, the day clerk."

"Could you tell me where Mr Baker lives? I might catch him at home tonight."

Mr Wimblethorpe was a little hesitant, but he wrote his fellow employee's address on a slip of paper. While he was doing it, the Saint leaned on the desk and half turned to give the lobby a lazy but comprehensive reconnaissance. As he had more or less expected, he discovered a large man in baggy clothes taking inadequate cover behind a potted palm.

"Thank you, Mr Wimblethorpe," he said as he took the slip. "And now there's just one other thing. In another minute, a Mr Yard of the police department will be yelling at you to tell him what I was talking to you about. Don't hesitate to confide in him. And if he seems worried about losing me, tell him he'll find me at Mr Baker's."

He turned and sauntered leisurely away, leaving the bewildered man gaping after him.

He picked up a taxi at the next corner and gave the day clerk's address, and settled back with a cigarette without even bothering to look back and see how the pursuit was doing. There were too many more important things annoying him. A curious presentiment was trying to take shape behind his mind, and he wasn't going to like any part of it.

Mr Baker happened to be at home, and recalled the incident without difficulty.

"He said that Mr Matson had decided to move in with him, but he'd had a few too many, so his friend came to fetch his things for him."

"Didn't you think that was a bit funny?"

"Well, yes; but people are always doing funny things. We had a snuff manufacturer once who insisted on filling his room with parrots because he said the old buccaneers always had parrots, and Lafitte used to headquarter here. Then there was the music teacher from Idaho who——"

"About Mr Matson," Simon interrupted—"what was his friend's name?"

"I'm not sure. I think it was something like Black. But I didn't pay much attention. I knew it was all right, because I'd seen him with Mr Matson before."

"Can you describe him?"

"Yes. Tall and thin, with sort of gray-blond hair cut very short——"

"And a military bearing and a saber scar on the left cheek?"

"I didn't notice that," Baker said seriously. "Mr Matson made a lot of friends while he was at the hotel. He was always out for a good time, wanting to find girls and drinking a lot. . . . I hope there isn't any trouble, is there?"

"I hope not. But this guy Black didn't say where Matson was going to move in with him?"

"No. He said Mr Matson would probably stop in and leave his next address when he sobered up." Baker looked at him anxiously. "Do you have some business connection with Mr Matson, Mr—ah——"

"Titwillow," said the Saint. "Sullivan Titwillow. Yes, Mr Matson and I are partners in an illicit diamond buying syndicate in Rhodesia. I hope I haven't kept you up. . . . Oh, and by the way. Don't jump into bed as soon as I go, because you'll have at least one other caller tonight. His name is Yard, and he is the Law in Galveston. Please be nice to him, because I think his feet hurt."

He left the baffled day clerk on the front stoop, and returned to the cab which he had kept waiting.

He was whistling a little tune to himself as he got in, but his gaiety was only in the performance. The presentiment in his mind was growing more solid in spite of anything he could do. And he knew that he was only trying to stave it off. He knew that whatever happened, Fate had taken the play away from him.

"My name, if anybody should ask you," he said to his driver, "is Sugarman Treacle. I am a Canadian in the lumber business. I have sold myself on the job of investigating public vehicles with a view to equipping them with soft pine blocks and coil springs as a substitute for rubber during the present tire shortage. Please feel quite free to discuss my project with any rival researchers who want to talk it over with you."

"Okay, Colonel," said the cabby affably. "Where to now?"

And then the Saint's presentiment was much too firmly materialised to be brushed off. It was something too outrageously coincidental to have ever been intelligently calculated, and at the same time so absurdly obvious that its only concealment had been that it had been too close to see.

The Saint said: "Do you know a joint called the Blue Goose?"

"Yeah," said the other briefly. "You wanna go there?"

"I think so."

"I can get you in. But after that you're on your own."

Simon raised one eyebrow a millimeter, but he made no comment. He said: "Do you think you could shake off anybody who might be following us before we get there? My wife has been kind of inquisitive lately, and I'm not asking for trouble."

"I getcha, pal," said the driver sympathetically, and swung his wheel.

The Blue Goose had a sign outside and several cars parked in front; but the door was locked, and the chauffeur had to hammer on it to produce a scrap of face at a barred judas window. There was a line of muttered introduction, and then the door opened. It was all very reminiscent of Prohibition, and in fact it was much the same thing, for the state of Texas was still working on the package store system and hadn't legalised any open bars.

"There y' are, doc," said the cabby. "An' take it easy."

Simon paid his fare and added a generous tip, and went in.

It was apparent as soon as he was inside that at least the adjective in the name was justified. The decorator who had dreamed up the trimmings must have been hipped on Gershwin. Everything was done in a bluish motif—walls and tablecloths and glass and chairs. There was the inevitable from hunger orchestra, with too much brass and a blue tempo, and the inevitable tray-sized dance floor where the inevitable mixture of sailors, soldiers, salesmen, and stews were putting their work in with the inevitable assortment of wild kids who had drunk too much and wise women who hadn't drunk enough. Even the lighting scheme was dim and blue.

The only thing that wasn't clear from the entrance was whether the customer got goosed, or was merely a goose to be there.

Simon crossed to the bar and ordered a Scotch and water, saving himself the trouble of ordering Peter Dawson, which would have been no different any way in spite of the label on the bottle. He got it with plenty of water in a shimmed glass, and saved his breath on that subject also.

He said to the bartender: "Throgmorton——"

"Call me Joe," said the bartender automatically.

He was a big blond man with big shoulders and a slight paunch, with a square face that smiled quickly and never looked as if the smile went very far inside.

"Joe," said the Saint, "do you know a gal here by the name of Olga Ivanovitch?"

The man paused only infinitesimally in his mopping.

At the Saint's side, a voice with strange intonations in it said: "My name is Olga Ivanovitch."

Simon turned and looked at her.

She sat alone, as certain other women did there, with a pale drink in front of her. He hadn't paid any attention to her when he chose his stool, but he did now. Because she had a real beauty that was the last thing he had expected there—in spite of the traditional requirements of a well-cast mystery.

Beauty of a stately kind that had no connection with the common charms of the other temptations there. A face as pale and aristocratic as that of a grand duchess, but with the more earthy touches of broad forehead and wide cheekbones that betrayed the Slav. Blonde hair as lustrous as frozen honey, braided severely around her head in a coiffure that would have been murder to any less classic bone structure. Green eyes that matched her deep-cut green gown. By her birth certificate she might have been any age; but by the calendars of a different chronology she had been old long ago—or ageless.

"Why were you looking for me?" she asked in that voice of unfamiliar harmonies.

The bartender had moved down the counter and was busy with other ministrations.

"I wanted to know," said the Saint steadily, "what you can tell me about a character called Henry Stephen Matson—possibly known to you as Henry Stephens."

CHAPTER THREE

HE HAD to admire the way she handled the mask of her face, even with the underlying configuration to help her.

"But why should you ask me?" she protested, with seductive bewilderment.

The Saint put one elbow on the bar and pillowed his chin on the hand attached to it.

"Darling," he said, with every kind of friendliness and good humor and amiable sophistication, "you are an exceedingly beautiful creature. You've probably been told that at least once before, if not ten times an evening. You are now hearing it again—but this time from a connoisseur. Nevertheless, ready as I am to swoon before you, the few fragments of sense that I have left will not let me go along with the gag of treating you as an ingénue."

She laughed; and it was something that he registered in her favor, if only because she was probably the only woman in the place who could have unraveled his phraseology enough to know whether to laugh or not.

She said: "Then I won't do?"

"You'll do perfectly," he assured her, "if you'll just take my word for it that I'm strictly in favor of women who are old enough to have had a little experience—and young enough to be interested in a little more. But they also have to be old enough to look at an old tired monument like me and know when I don't want to sit up all night arguing about storks."

It was a delight to watch the play of her shoulders and neck line.

"You're priceless. . . . Would you buy me a drink?"

"I'd love to. I expect to buy the whole joint, a small hunk at a time. If I have a drink too, it should be worth two tables and a dozen chairs."

He signaled the square-faced bartender.

"And a cigarette?" she said.

He shook one out of his pack.

"You've got quite a sense of humor, Mr——"

"Simon Templar," he said quietly, while the bartender was turning away to select a bottle.

Her perfectly penciled eyebrows rose in perfectly controlled surprise.

"Simon Templar?" she repeated accurately. "Then you must be—— Here let me show you."

She reached away to remove a newspaper from under the nose of a recuperating Rotarian on the other side of her. After a moment's search, she refolded it at an inside page and spread it in front of the Saint.

Simon saw at a glance that it was the early morning edition of the *Times-Tribune,* and read the item with professional appraisal.

It was not by any means the kind of publicity that he was accustomed to, having been condensed into four paragraphs of a middle column that was overshadowed on one side by the latest pronunciamento of the latest union megaphone, and on the other by a woman in Des Moines who had given birth to triplets in a freight elevator. But it did state quite barrenly that an unidentified burned body had been found on the shore road east of Virginia Point by "Simon Temple, a traveling salesman from Chicago." The police, as usual, had several clues, and were expected to solve the mystery shortly.

That was all; and the Saint wondered why there was no mention of the name that the dying man had given him, or his gasped reference to the Blue Goose, and why Lieutenant Kinglake had been so loth to give out with any leads on the night life of Galveston. Perhaps Kinglake hadn't taken the Saint's question seriously at all. . . .

Simon turned his blue steel eyes back to Olga Ivanovitch again, and gave her a light for her cigarette. Once more he was aware of her statuesque perfection—and perfect untrustworthiness.

He lifted his newly delivered dilution of anonymous alcohol.

"Yes," he acknowledged modestly, "I am the traveling salesman. But you aren't the farmer's daughter."

"No," she answered without smiling. "My name is Ivanovitch."

"Which means, in Russian, exactly what 'Johnson' would mean here."

"But it's my name."

"And so is 'Templar' mine. But it says 'Temple' in the paper, and yet you placed me at once."

"For that matter," she said, "Why did you ask me about—Henry?"

"Because, my sweet, if you'd like the item for your memoirs, your name was on dear Henry's lips just before he passed away."

She shuddered, and closed her eyes for a moment.

"It must have been a gruesome experience for you."

"How did you guess?" he inquired ironically, but she either didn't feel the irony or chose to ignore it.

"If he was still alive when you found him . . . Did he say anything else?"

The Saint smiled with a soft edge of mockery.

"Yes, he said other things. But why should you be so interested?"

"But naturally, because I knew him. He was to have come to my house for cocktails this afternoon."

"Was he really?" said the Saint gently. "You know, I can think of one man in this town who'd be quite excited to hear that."

Her dark gaze was full of innocence.

"You mean Lieutenant Kinglake?" she said calmly. "But he has heard it. He's already talked to me tonight."

Simon took a gulp of his drink.

"And that's how you got my name right?"

"Of course. He asked me about you. But I couldn't tell him anything except what I've read in the papers."

Simon didn't take his eyes off her, although it called for a little effort to hold them there. His first reaction was to feel outstandingly foolish, and he hid it behind a coldly unflinching mask. He hadn't held anything back in his statement—he had no reason to—and so there was no reason why Kinglake shouldn't have been there before him. It was his own fault that he had made a slow start; but that was because he hadn't been receptive to a coincidence that was too pat to be plausible.

He couldn't tell whether her green eyes were laughing at him. He knew that he was laughing at himself, but in a way that had dark and unfunny undertones.

"Tovarich," he said frankly, "suppose we let our back hair down. Or are you too steeped in intrigue to play that way?"

"I could try, if I knew what you meant."

"I'm not one of Kinglake's stooges—in fact, the reverse. I just happened to find Henry. He mumbled a few things to me before he died, and naturally I repeated what I could remember. But on account of my evil reputation, which you know about, I end up by qualifying as a potential suspect. So I'd have to be interested, even if I wasn't just curious. Now it's your move."

Olga Ivanovitch eyed him for a long moment, studying his clean-cut devil-may-care face feature by feature.

She said at last: "Are you very tired of being told that you're a frighteningly handsome man?"

"Very," he said. "And so how well did you know Henry?"

She sipped her drink, and made patterns with the wet print of her glass on the bar.

"Not well at all. I work here as a hostess. I met him here like I meet many people. Like I met you tonight. It was only for a few days. We had a lot of drinks and danced sometimes."

"But he was coming to your house."

"Other people come to my house," she said, with a dispassionate directness that disclaimed innuendo and defied interrogation.

The Saint blew a careful smoke-ring to bridge another uncomfortable gap; but this time he bowed to a rare dignity that he had seldom met, and would never have looked for in the Blue Goose.

"Did Henry tell you anything about himself?"

"Nothing much that I can remember. Perhaps I didn't pay enough attention. But men tell you so many things. I think he said he'd been working in a defense plant somewhere—I think it was near St Louis."

"Did he say anything about where he was going next, or what his plans were?"

"He said he was going to work in another plant in Mexico. He said he was waiting for a ship to Tampico or Vera Cruz."

"What sort of people was he with?"

"All sorts of people. He drank a lot, and he was very generous. He was— what do you call it?—a Good Time Charlie."

"He had plenty of moula?"

"Please?"

"Dough. Cabbage. The blue chips."

"Yes, he seemed to have plenty of money. And he bought plenty of drinks, so of course he made many friends."

"Can you remember any particular guy with a name like Black?"

She wrinkled her brow.

"I don't think so."

"Tall and thin, with sort of gray-blond hair cut very short."

"How can I be sure?" she said helplessly. "I see so many people."

The Saint drew a long breath through his cigarette that was not audibly a sigh, but which did him as much good.

He was very humbly baffled. He knew that Olga Ivanovitch had told him almost as little as he had told her; he knew at the same time that she was holding back some of the things she knew, exactly as he was. He knew that she had probably told him precisely as much as she had told Kinglake. But there was nothing that he could do about it. And he guessed that there had been nothing that Kinglake had been able to do about it, either. She had a good straight story in its place, and you couldn't shake it. It was quite simple and plausible too, except for the omissions. The only thing a police officer could have done about it was to obscure the issue with some synthetic charges about morals and the illegality of the Blue Goose, which Kinglake probably wouldn't stoop to even if the political system would have let him.

And yet the Saint knew to his own satisfaction that Olga Ivanovitch was watching and measuring him just as he was watching and measuring her. And if he was tired of being told how fascinating he was, she was indubitably just as tired of hearing about her exotic harmonies of ivory skin and flaxen hair, and the undeniable allure that they connived at. He took stock of the plain pagan perfection of her lip modeling, and could have done without the illegitimate ideas it gave him.

"In that case," he said, "let's have some more colored water and go on seeing each other."

The small hours of the morning were starting to grow up when he finally admitted that he was licked. By that time he must have bought several gallons of the beige fluid which was sold by the Blue Goose as Scotch, and it had made no more impression on Olga Ivanovitch than it had on himself. He decided that if the late Mr Matson had cut a wide swath there, he must have worked diligently over lubricating his mower before he went in. But Olga Ivanovitch had given out nothing more. She had been gay and she had been glowing, and with her poise and intelligence she had really been a lot of fun; but every time the Saint had tried to cast a line into the conversation she had met him with the same willing straightforward gaze and been so genuinely troubled because she could add nothing to what she had already told.

"So," said the Saint, "I'm going to get some sleep."

They were back at the bar, after some time of sitting at a table through a floor show of special talent but questionable decorum. Simon called for his check, and decided that by that time he should own everything in the place except possibly the ceiling. But he paid it without argument, and added a liberal percentage.

"I'm going to check out too," Olga said. "Would you give me a lift?"

The square-faced bartender gave them his quick skin-deep smile.

"Come again, folks," he said, and made it sound almost like a pressing invitation.

"Goodnight, Joe," said the Saint, and made it sound almost like a promise.

He took the girl out to a taxi that was providentially waiting outside. It was so providential that he was prepared to believe that some less altruistic agency had brought it there; but that detail didn't distress him. If the ungodly wanted to find out what they would have a chance to find out that night, it wouldn't be hard for them to find it out anyway. When he seriously wanted to exercise them, he would do a job on it.

After they had gone a short way, Olga Ivanovitch said very prosaically: "You owe me ten dollars for the evening."

In identically the same prosaic manner, he peeled a ten-dollar bill out of his pocket and handed it to her.

She put it away in her purse.

After a while she said: "I don't know what you're trying to find in Galveston, Saint, but don't find anything you don't want."

"Why should you care?" he inquired mildly.

He had his answer in something yielding and yearning that was suddenly all over him, holding his mouth with lips that fulfilled all the urgent indications that he had been doing his earnest best to ignore.

It was more or less like that until the cab stopped again on Seawall Boulevard.

"Won't you come in for a nightcap?" she said.

Her face was a white blur in the dark, framed in shadow and slashed with crimson.

"Thanks," he said, "but I have to think of my beauty. So do you."

"You won't have to spend any more."

"I'll see you again," he said.

"Are you sure?"

"Quite sure."

"You'll remember the address?"

"Yes."

He took the taxi back to the Alamo House, and found Detective Yard snoring in a leather armchair in the lobby. It grieved him sincerely to have to interrupt such a blissful orchestration; but these were circumstances in which he felt that noblesse obliged.

"Good evening, Brother Yard," he murmured. "Or, if you want to be literal, good morning. And don't tell me your first name is Scotland, because that would be more than I could bear at this moment. . . . I trust you have enjoyed your siesta."

The field representative of the Kinglake Escort Service had a chance to gather his wits together during the speech. He glared at the Saint with the overcooked malignance which was only to have been expected of a man who had been rudely awakened with such a greeting.

"What's your name, anyhow?" he growled indignantly. "Giving your name as Sebastian Tombs at the Ascot! Telling Baker your name was Sulli-van Titwillow! Telling that taxi driver you was Sugarman Treacle!"

"Oh, you tracked him down, did you?" said the Saint interestedly. "So by this time you know that I've been to the Blue Goose. Wait till you check back there and find that I've been masquerading all evening as Shirley Temple."

"What," demanded the detective cholerically, "is the idea of all these names?"

Simon shook a disappointed head at him.

"Tut, Mr Yard. In fact, a trio of tuts. How can a man with a name like yours ask such kindergarten questions? Don't all suspicious characters use aliases? Isn't it an inviolable rule on page thirty-six of the Detective Manual that a fugitive may change his name but will always stick to his proper initials? I was merely following the regulations to make things easy for you. I could just as well have told any of these people that my name was Mont-gomery Balmworth Wobblehouse, and loused the hell out of things. The trouble is, you don't appreciate me."

Detective Yard explained in a few vivid phrases just how much he appre-ciated Simon Templar.

"Thank you," said the Saint gratefully. "And now if you'd like to rest for a while, you can go back to sleep. Or go home to your wife, if she's attractive enough. I promise you that I'm going to bed now and stay there for several hours. And if it'll help you at all, I'll phone you before I go out again."

He stepped into the elevator and departed towards his floor with the depressing conviction that he had added one more notch to his record of failing to Win Friends and Influence Policemen. More practically, he knew that his visit to the Blue Goose was now certain to be misinterpreted.

He consulted the mirror in the elevator about wiping lipstick off his mouth, and hoped that Detective Yard had had as much fun out of noting it as he himself had had out of acquiring it.

CHAPTER FOUR

IN SPITE of the lateness of his bedtime, the Saint was up reasonably early the next morning. He was expecting to be officially annoyed before noon, and he preferred to get some breakfast under his belt first.

Port Arthur Jones met him as he stepped out of the elevator.

"Mawnin', Mistah Templah, sah. Ah been waitin' for you. One of them gennelmen you was askin' about is sittin' in the co'nah of the lobby."

"I know," said the Saint. "His name is Yard. He's worried about me."

The bellboy's grin shrank in from between his ears so abruptly that Simon was sorry for him.

He said: "Never mind, Po't Arthur. Here's five dollars anyway. Keep up the counter-espionage."

The negro beamed again.

"Yassah, thank you, sah. And there was somethin' else——"

"What?"

"Another gennelman was nosin' around this mawnin', askin' questions about you. He didn't give no name, and Ah never saw him befo'."

"Was he tall and thin, with gray-blond hair cut very short?"

"Nawsah. He was kinda short and fat, and he had a red face and red hair and pale gray eyes. Ah dunno nothin' 'bout him, but he wasn't no Galveston policeman."

"Po't Arthur," said the Saint, "you have exceeded my fondest hopes. Here is another V for Victory. Carry on."

He went into the coffee shop and ordered tomato juice and ham and eggs. His mind revolved ineffectually while he fortified himself with them.

The late Mr Matson had considerately bequeathed him three names, besides Olga Ivanovitch. Blatt, Weinbach, Maris. Blatt, who sounded like Black, was probably the tall thin gray-blond one who had been seen at the Ascot. The guy with the red face and red hair was one of the other two. So there was still one without any kind of identification. But even that made very little difference. There was no other detail in their pictures—no links, no attachments, no place to begin looking for them. Unless it was the Blue Goose. But unless they were very stupid or very well covered, they wouldn't be going back there.

He certainly had something on his hands, and all he could do was to wait for something to lead at him.

It did, while he was smoking a cigarette and stretching out his coffee. It looked just like Detective Yard, in a different suit that needed pressing just as badly as the last one.

"If you've finished," Yard said heavily, standing over him, "Lieutenant Kinglake would like to see you at Headquarters."

"That's fine," said the Saint. "I was only waiting for you to issue the invitation, so I could get a ride in a police car or make you pay for the taxi."

They traveled together in an uncongenial aloofness which the Saint's efforts at light badinage did nothing to alleviate.

The atmosphere at Headquarters was very similar; but the Saint continued to hand it to Kinglake for a restraint which he hadn't anticipated from a man with that air of nervous impatience. The Lieutenant looked just as tough and irascible, but he didn't rant and roar.

He let the official authority behind him make the noise for him, and said with impeccable control: "I hear you were getting around quite a bit last night."

"I tried to," said the Saint amiably. "After all, you remember that survey I told you about. If the Blue Goose meant things to you, you should have tipped me off. You could have saved me a lot of dollars and a slight hangover."

"I didn't think it was any of your business," Kinglake said. "And I still want to know why it was."

"Just curiosity," said the Saint. "In spite of anything you may have read, it isn't every day that I pick up a lump of talking charcoal on the highway. So when it says things to me, I can't just forget them."

"And you didn't forget Ivanovitch, either."

"Of course not. She was mentioned too. I'm sure I told you."

"According to Yard, you came home last night with lipstick on you."

"Some people are born gossips. But I think he's just jealous."

Lieutenant Kinglake picked up a pencil from his desk and fondled it as if the idea of breaking it in half intrigued him. Perhaps as an act of symbolism. But he still didn't raise his voice.

"I'm told," he said, "that you asked a lot of questions about this Henry Stephens—only you knew that his name was Matson. And you were asking about him all over town under that name. Now you can explain that to me, or you can take your chance as a material witness."

Simon rounded a cigarette with his forefingers and thumbs.

"You want to ask me questions. Do you mind if I ask a couple? For my own satisfaction. Being as I'm so curious."

Kinglake's chilled gimlet eyes took another exploratory twist into him. "What are they?"

"What did Quantry get out of his autopsy?"

"No traces of poison or violence—nothing that came through the fire, anyway. The guy burned to death."

"What about the newspaper and the matches?"

"Just a piece of a local paper, which anybody could have bought or picked up. No fingerprints."

"And where did you get the idea that I was a salesman?"

"I didn't give out anything about you. If some reporter got that idea, he got it. I'm not paid to be your press agent." Kinglake was at the full extension of his precarious control. "Now you answer my question before we go any further."

The Saint lighted his cigarette and used it to mark off a paragraph.

"The deceased's name," he said, "was Henry Stephen Matson. Until recently, he was a foreman at the Quenco plant near St Louis. You may remember that Hobart Quennel got into a lot of trouble a while ago, on account of some fancy finagling with synthetic rubber—and mostly because of me. But that hasn't anything to do with it. The Quenco plants are now being run by the Government, and the one outside St Louis is now making a lot of soups that go bang and annoy the enemy. Matson pulled out a while ago, and came here. He used his real name at the Ascot, because he'd applied for a passport to Mexico and he wanted to get it. But in his social life he called himself Henry Stephens, because he didn't want to die."

"How do you know all this?" Kinglake rapped at him. "And why didn't you——"

"I didn't tell you yesterday, because I didn't know," said the Saint tiredly. "The thing I found on the road said it was Henry Stephens, and it was all too obvious to bother me. So I was too smart to be sensible. It wasn't until I started hunting for Matson that it dawned on me that coincidences are still possible."

"Well, why were you hunting for Matson?"

The Saint pondered about that one.

"Because," he said, "a Kiwanis convention just picked him as Mr Atlantic Monthly of 1944. So in the interests of this survey of mine I wanted to get his reaction to the Galveston standards of strip-teasing. Now, the grade of G-string at the Blue Goose . . ."

There had to be a breaking-point to Detective Yard's self-control, and it was bound to be lower than Kinglake's. Besides, Mr Yard's feet had endured more.

He leaned down weightily on the Saint's shoulder.

"Listen, funny man," he said unoriginally, "how would you like to get poked right in the kisser?"

"Pipe down," Kinglake snarled; and it was an order.

But he went on glaring at the Saint, and for the first time his nervous impatience seemed to be more nervous than impatient. Simon was irresistibly reminded of his own efforts to cover confusion with a poker pan, only the night before.

"Let me tell you something, Templar," Kinglake said dogmatically. "We've made our own investigations; and no matter what you think, our opinion is that Stephens, or Matson, committed suicide by pouring gasoline on himself and setting himself alight."

It took a great deal to shatter the Saint's composure, but that was great enough. Simon stared at the Lieutenant in a state of sheer incredulity that even took his mind off the crude conventional ponderance of Detective Yard.

"Let me get this straight," he said slowly. "Are you going to try and work off Henry as a suicide?"

Lieutenant Kinglake's hard face, if anything, grew harder.

"On all the evidence, that's what it looks like. And I'm not going to make a monkey out of myself to get you some headlines. I told you, I don't want any trouble in this town."

"So what're you gonna do about it?" demanded Detective Yard, with an aptness which he must have learned from the movies.

Simon didn't even notice him.

"Evidence my back door," he said derisively. "So this guy who was so reckless with his gas ration was careful enough to swallow the flask he carried it in so it could eventually be recovered for the scrap drive."

"We just didn't happen to find the container yesterday. But if we search again, we may find it."

"Probably the coke bottle that Scotland Yard takes out with him to keep his brain watered."

"One more crack like that outa you," Yard said truculently, "an' I'll——"

"You might just tell me this, Kinglake," said the Saint bitingly. "Is this your idea of a brilliant trick to trap the killers, or are you just a hick cop after all? The only thing you've left out is the standard suicide note. Or have you got that up your sleeve too?"

The Lieutenant's thin lips tightened, and his battleship jaw stuck out another half inch. He had all the chip-on-the-shoulder characteristics of a man in the wrong who wouldn't admit it while there was a punch left in him; yet he met the Saint's half jeering and half furious gaze so steadily as to almost stare Simon out of countenance.

"Get this, Templar," Kinglake said coldly. "We think Stephens committed suicide——"

"In the most painful way he could think of——"

"He must have been nuts. But I've met nuts before."

"And even while he was dying he tried to make up a story——"

"He was out of his mind. He must have been, after a burning like that. You haven't been burned yet, so you use your head. And if you want to keep your nose clean, you will forget the whole thing—or you may find yourself with your can in the can. Do I make myself clear?"

The Saint met his eyes lengthily.

"If you were rolled flat, you could rent yourself out as a window," he said. "Instead of which, you have the colossal crust to sit there and spew that pap at me even after I've told you that I know more about Matson than you did."

"Yes," was all Kinglake replied.

"You aren't even going to make an issue out of the Blue Goose and my going there."

"No," Kinglake said curtly.

For once in his life, Simon Templar was frankly flabbergasted. He searched the shreds of his brain for a better word, and couldn't find one. Theories whirled through his head; but they were too fast and fantastic to be co-ordinated while he had to think on his feet.

Which was where he was thinking, since Kinglake's impenetrable stone-wall had brought him up there, shrugging off Detective Yard's clumsy physical obstruction as if it had been a feather which had accidentally drifted down on to him out of a cloud.

"I've met an astonishing variety of cops in my time," he remarked absorbently; "but you, chum, are an entirely new species. You don't even attempt to give me the guileless runaround or the genteel brushoff. . . . Have you said your last word on the subject?"

"Yes," snapped the Lieutenant. "Now will you kindly get the hell out of here and go on with the survey you were talking about?"

"I will," retorted the Saint. "And don't blame me if you find G-men in your G-string."

He stalked out of there with another unique feeling which was the precise antithesis of the sensation he had had when a certain log moved on the shore road. His blood had run cold then. Now it was boiling.

He had had to cope with local politics and obstruction before, in different guises and for different reasons. But this game was something else. And in that swift invigorating anger, the Saint knew just what he was going to do about it.

Kinglake had taunted him about publicity. Well, the Saint didn't need to hire any press agents. . . . He had seen himself waiting and hoping for a lead; but he could always ask for one. He had used newspapers before, in sundry ways, when he wanted to lead with his chin and invite the ungodly to step up and introduce themselves while they looked at it.

Almost literally without looking to left or right, he followed Center Street towards the waterfront on the north or channel side of the city. He walked into the building that housed the *Times-Tribune,* and worked his way doggedly through the trained interference until he stood in front of the city editor's desk.

"My name is Simon Templar," he said for about the fourteenth time. "If you spelt me right, I'd be the traveling salesman who found that botched biscuit on the shore road yesterday. I want to cover that case for you; and all I want out of you is a by-line."

The editor scrutinised him quite clinically.

"Our police reporter must have messed up his spelling," he said. "It's funny—the name started to ring a bell when I read it. . . . So you're the Saint. But what are you selling?"

"I'm selling you your lead story for the afternoon edition," said the Saint. "I may be nuts, but I'm still news. Now shall we play gin rummy, or will you lend me a typewriter and stop the press?"

CHAPTER FIVE

IF ONLY to be different in one more way from most typical men of action, Simon Templar was perfectly happy with words and paper. He could play just as fluently on the legitimate or L C Smith form of type-writer as he could on the well-known Thompson variety, and he handled both of them in much the same way. The keys rattled under his fingers like gunfire, and his choice of words had the impact of bullets. He worked at white heat, while his wrath still had all its initial impetus.

He told his own full story of the finding of "Henry Stephens," and every word that the dying man had said, together with a general summary of the other facts as he knew them, in a fusillade of hardboiled sinewy prose that would have qualified him for a job on the toughest tabloid in the country. Then he squared off to a fresh sheet of paper and went into his second movement. He wrote:

It now grieves me to have to break it to all you nice people that these sensitive nostrils, which long ago became extraordinarily appreciative of certain characteristic smells, have caught wind of the grand inspiration that this guy committed suicide, which Lieutenant Kinglake was feeling out this morning.

Now I am in here with quite a different story, and it has got to be known that Bulldog Templar does not brush off that easy.

I am remembering a legend, true or not, that once when S S Van Dine happened to be close to the scene of another murder, it was suggested by some newspaper that he might co-operate with the gendarmerie and help run the villain to earth in the best Philo Vance manner; whereupon Mr Van Dine placed himself in the center of four wheels and trod on the loud pedal so rapidly that his shadow had to be sent after him by express.

We Templars are made of sterner stuff. Just give us a chance to stick our neck out, and a giraffe is not even in our league.

So we are going to sign our name to this invitation to all of you voting citizens to take a good long look at the suicidal Mr Stephens.

He was, we observe, the stern and melancholy type which can get along without life anyway. He proved that by the way he spent his last days here, drinking all night in speakeasies and dancing with the girls. He didn't go much for fun of any kind, which is said to soften people up. He was strictly an ascetic; and when he knocked himself off he was still going to be tough. He wouldn't jump out of a window, or take an overdose of sleeping tablets, or put a gun in his ear and listen to see if it was loaded. He deliberately picked the most painful way that a man can die.

He figured he had some suffering coming to him. After all, he wasn't broke, for instance, which has been known to make some people so unhappy that they have let air into their tonsils with a sharp knife. He seems to have had plenty of spending money. So he was going to have his hard times on his deathbed instead of before.

He even went 20 miles out of town to do it, walking all the way, since the street cars don't go there, so that he'd have lots of time to look forward to it and enjoy the prospect.

He was a consistent guy, too. He didn't mean to be selfish about his suffering. He wanted somebody else to have some of it too. So after he'd taken his gasoline shower, and before he struck the match, he carefully chewed up and ate the bottle he'd brought it in, so that Lieutenant Kinglake could have something to worry about. Not knowing, of course, that Lieutenant Kinglake wouldn't worry about a little thing like that at all.

It always gives us Templars a great respect for the benignness of Providence to observe how frequently a hard-pressed police department, facing a nervous breakdown before the task of breaking a really difficult case, has been saved in the nick of time by discovering that there never was a murder after all. It makes us feel pretty good to think that cops are practically people, and God takes care of them as well as Pearl White.

The Saint was beginning to enjoy himself by then. He lighted a cigarette and gazed at the ceiling for a while, balancing his ideas for the finale. Then he went on when he was ready.

But let's pretend that we don't have the clear and penetrating vision of Lieutenant Kinglake. Let's just pretend that we are too dumb to believe that a man in the dying agonies of third degree burns cooked up that wonderful story about three men who did it to him, just because he was too modest to want to take the credit. Let's pretend there might really have been three other men.

Men with names. Blatt, Weinbach, Maris. A nice trio of Herrenvolk.

Then we might go along with the gag and say, suppose Henry Stephen Matson was a traitor. Suppose he'd gotten into some sabotage organisation, and he'd been given a job to do in this explosives plant in Missouri. Suppose he'd even drawn payment in advance—just to account for what he was using for dough in Galveston.

Then suppose he welshed on the job—either from an attack of cold feet or a relapse of patriotism. He knew that the heat was on. He couldn't stay in this country, because they might have turned him in to the FBI. If they didn't do anything worse. He took it on the lam for here, hoping to get a passport, and hoping he'd shaken off his pals. But they were too good for him. They tracked him down, struck up an acquaintance with him, and gave him what he had coming. In a very nasty way, just to discourage imitators.

That's my fairy-tale. And I like it.

Blatt, Weinbach, Maris. I have a description of two of those men, and I've got my own good ideas about the third. And I am hereby announcing that I shall now have to get them for you myself, since we must not disturb Lieutenant Kinglake in his august meditations.

The city editor read it all through without a change of expression. Then he tapped the last page with his forefinger and said: "It's an ingenious theory, but what's your basis for it?"

"Nothing but logic, which is all you can say for any theory. The facts are there. If you can do better with them, you can join Kinglake's club."

"This last statement of yours, about the three men—is that a fact?"

"Some of it. But the main point of it is that that's what you pay me with. If I can make them believe that I know more than I do, I may scare them into making some serious mistakes. That's why I'm making you a present of all the rest of that luscious literature."

The editor pulled at his under lip. He was a pear-shaped man with a long forbidding face that never smiled even when his eyes twinkled.

"It's good copy, anyway, so I'll print it," he said. "But don't blame me if you're the next human torch. Or if Kinglake has you brought in again and beats hell out of you."

"On the contrary, you're my insurance against that," said the Saint. "Going my own way, I might have had a lot more trouble with Kinglake at any moment. Now, he won't dare to do anything funny, because it would look as if he was scared of me."

"Kinglake's a good officer. He wouldn't do a thing like this unless there was a lot of pressure on him."

Simon recalled the Lieutenant's tight-lipped curtness, his harried and almost defensive belligerence.

"Maybe there was," he said. "But whose was it?"

The editor put his fingertips together.

"Galveston," he said, "has what is now called the commission form of government. Commissioner Number One—what other cities would call the mayor—is coming up for re-election soon. He appoints the Chief of Police. The Chief controls such men as Lieutenant Kinglake. Nobody wants any blemish on the record of the police department at this time. I'm quite confident that neither the Commissioner nor the Chief of Police is mixed up in anything crooked. It's just best for everybody concerned to let sleeping dogs—in this case, dead dogs—lie."

"And that is perfectly jake with you."

"The *Times-Tribune,* Mr Templar, unlike yourself, is not addicted to sticking its neck out. We are not a political organ; and if we did start a crusade, it would not be on the basis of this one sensational but insignificant killing. But we do try to print the whole truth, as you'll see by the fact that I'm ready to use your article."

"Then you still haven't told me where the pressure would come from."

The city editor's long equine face grew even more absorbed in the contemplation of his matched fingers.

"As a stranger in town, Mr Templar, it may surprise you to know that some of our most influential citizens sometimes go to the Blue Goose for their—er—relaxation. The Blue Goose is one of the leads in this story as you have it. So while none of these people, from the Commissioner down, might want to be a party to hushing up a crime, you can see that they might not be keen on too comprehensive an investigation of the Blue Goose. So that the management of the Blue Goose, which naturally doesn't want the spot involved in a murder mystery, might find a lot of sympathetic ears if they were pointing out the advantages of forgetting the whole thing. I shall not allow you to print that in your next article, but it might help you personally."

"It might," said the Saint. "And thank you."

He spent several hours after that on a conscientious job of verifying his background material that would have amazed some people who thought of him as a sort of intuitive comet, blazing with pyrotechnic violence and brilliance to ends and solutions that were only indicated to him by a guardian angel with a lot of spare time and an incurable weakness for piloting irresponsible characters. His research involved visits to various public places, and ingenuous conversations with a large number of total strangers, each of them a cameo of personality projection that would have left Dale Carnegie egg-bound with awe. But the net yield was negatively and concisely nothing.

The Commissioner appeared to be a bona fide native of Galveston who had made his money in sulphur and still controlled an important business. There seemed to be no particularly musty bones in his family skeleton. He came of Texas stock from away back, and he was set solid with business and family ties.

The Sheriff of the county came out with the same sort of background and clean bill of health. Nobody seemed to know much about the type of deputies in his office, but there had never been any scandal about his administration. He was frankly a member of the same political machine as the Commissioner.

Nor were there any crevices in the armor of the Chief of Police. Kinglake was not too popular, very likely because of his personality; but his record was good. Quantry was negligible.

Which meant that the *Times-Tribune* editor's analysis stood unshaken, and there was no evidence to brand the official eagerness to turn a blind eye on a murder as anything but a local issue of political expediency.

Except for the one thin thread that curled into a question mark and asked who it was at the Blue Goose who had turned the heat on even a complaisant political machine.

Olga Ivanovitch?

The Saint knew she was beautiful, he thought she was clever, and he suspected that she was dangerous. But how clever and how dangerous? He could learn nothing about her that sounded at all important. If she had any political connections, they weren't common gossip. But he knew that she had a definite place in the picture.

He made another call at the Ascot Hotel; but Mr Baker hadn't remembered any more overnight, and could add nothing to his information about Blatt or Black.

"But I'm sure, Mr Titwillow, he wasn't a local man. I've been here so long that I think I know all the important people in Galveston by sight."

Blatt, Weinbach, Maris.

The names made no impression on anyone to whom he mentioned them. But he did find some representatives of their clans in the telephone directory, and studiously checked on each of them. Each of them had the kind of unimpeachable clearance that it would have been simply a waste of time to investigate any further.

It was a long and strenuous day, and dusk was creeping over the city as Simon headed back towards the Alamo House. He bought an evening paper and a bottle of Peter Dawson on the way.

The *Times-Tribune* carried his article on the front page, unabridged and unexpurgated, but with a box that gave a brief explanation of the Saint's background for the benefit of the ignorant, and stated that Mr Templar's theories were his own and did not necessarily represent the editorial opinion of the *Times-Tribune*.

There was special justification for that in a short column which ran alongside his, which reported succinctly that at an inquest held that after-noon the coroner's jury had brought in a verdict of suicide.

Simon Templar crushed the newspaper in his hand with a grip that almost reverted it to its original pulp, and said several things which even our freedom of the press will not allow us to print.

So Kinglake hadn't backed down. He had gone right out from their interview and helped to railroad that fantastic verdict through. Maybe he had a wife and children and just wanted to go on feeding them; but he had done it.

In his room at the Alamo House, Simon sent for ice and opened his bottle, and tried to simmer down again over a highball.

He only had one other clue to think about, and that was in another snatch of words that the dying man had managed to get out. He could hear them just as clearly now as when they had been dragged hoarsely through the charred tortured lips.

"Ostrich-skin—leather case—in gladstone lining . . . Get case—and send . . . send . . ."

Send where?

And why?

And anyhow, Black or Blatt had the gladstone now.

One of three practical killers, probably strangers to Galveston themselves, possibly from Chicago (he remembered the 606 Club match booklet) who had trailed Matson on their mission of vengeance, carried out the assign-ment, and vanished.

He had another drink, and didn't get any further on that one.

It was later still when the telephone rang.

He had an electric moment as he went to answer it. He knew that the call had to have some bearing on the case, since he had no personal friends in Galveston; but the exquisite suspense was in wondering—who? A soft-pedaling politician? A raging Kinglake? Or the first nibble at his bait?

It was a voice that he knew, even if he had not known it long—a deep musical voice with appealing foreign inflections.

"You aren't only handsome, but you have talent," she said. "Why didn't you tell me you were a writer too?"

"My union doesn't allow it."

"Am I going to see you again? I'd like to very much."

He reached for a cigarette.

"I'm flattered. But I've only just paid one installment on the Blue Goose."

"I don't have to be there till ten. What are you doing for dinner?"

"Eating with you," he said with abrupt decision. "I'll meet you in the lobby here at eight o'clock."

He hung up, and still wondered which category that belonged in. But anything would be better than waiting in idleness.

He washed and freshened himself and changed his shirt, and went downstairs a little before eight. There was a note in his box when he turned in his key.

"It was delivered by hand just a few minutes ago," said the clerk.

Simon slit open the envelope. The letter inside was written in pencil on a cheap lined paper of an uncommon but typical pattern. There was no address; but Simon knew what that would be even without the clues in the context.

DEAR MR TEMPLAR,

I just read your piece in the paper, and I can tell you you sure have got it over these dumb bastards. I am getting a chap to take this out for me. I can tell you a lot more about this case and I will tell you if you can fix it to talk to me alone. You are right all the way and I can prove it, but I will not talk to anyone except you. After that you can do what you like with what I tell you but I will not give these dumb cops anything.

Yours truly,
NICK VASCHETTI.

Simon looked up from the note because someone was practically leaning on him and breathing in his face.

"Got a love-letter?" asked Detective Yard. "Or is it fan mail?"

Simon put the letter in his pocket.

"Yes," he said. "But not for you. In fact, I hate to tell you, but my admirer calls you a dumb bastard."

The detective's face swelled as if he were being strangled.

"Listen, you," he got out. "One of these days——"

"You're going to forget your orders and be unkind to me," said the Saint. "So I'll be kind to you while I can. In a few minutes I'll be going out to dinner. I'll try to pick a restaurant where they'll let you in. And if I start to leave before you've finished, just yell at me and I'll wait for you."

Simon thought afterwards that it was criminal negligence on his part that he was so seduced by the frustration of Detective Yard that he didn't even notice the thin gray-blond man and the fat red-haired man who occupied chairs in the farther reaches of the lobby. But there was an excuse for him; because while he had heard their names and heard their sketchy descriptions, he had never before laid eyes on Johan Blatt and Fritzie Weinbach.

CHAPTER SIX

HE WENT BACK up to his room and phoned the city desk of the *Times-Tribune*.

"Could you work it for me to have a private chat with a prisoner in the City Jail?"

"It might be done," said the editor cautiously, "if nobody knew it was you. Why—have you had a bite?"

"I hope so," said the Saint. "The guy's name is Nick Vaschetti." He spelt it out. "He says he won't talk to anybody but me; but maybe the jail doesn't have to know me. See what you can do, and I'll call you back in about an hour."

He sat on the bed in thought for a minute or two, and then he picked up the telephone again and asked for Washington. He hardly had to wait at all, for although the hotel operator didn't know it the number he asked for was its own automatic priority through all long distance exchanges.

"Hamilton," said the phone. "I hear you're a newspaper man now."

"In self-defense," said the Saint. "If you don't like it, I can pack up. I never asked for this job, anyway."

"I only hope you're getting a good salary to credit against your expense account."

The Saint grinned.

"On the contrary, you'll probably be stuck for my union dues. . . . Listen, Ham: I'd rather lay it in your lap, but I think I'd better bother you. These three men——"

"Blatt, Weinbach, and Maris?"

"Your carrier pigeons travel fast."

"They have to. Is there anything else on them?"

Simon gave him the two rough descriptions.

"There's a good chance," he said, "that they may have come on from Chicago. But that's almost a guess. Anyway, try it."

"You never want much, do you?"

"I don't like you to feel left out."

"You're not leaving out the beautiful swooning siren, of course."

"In this case, she's a blonde."

"You must like variety," Hamilton sighed. "How much longer are you expecting to take?"

"Depending on what you can dig up about the Three Neros, and what breaks tonight," said the Saint, "maybe not long. Don't go to bed too early, anyhow."

Which left him laughing inwardly at the breath-taking dimensions of his own bravado. And yet it has already been recorded in many of these chronicles that some of the Saint's tensest climaxes had often been brewing when those almost prophetic undercurrents of swashbuckling extravagance danced in his arteries. . . .

Olga Ivanovitch was waiting in the lobby when he came downstairs again.

"I'm sorry," he said. "There was a letter I had to answer."

"*Nitchevo*," she said in her low warm memorable voice. "I was late myself, and we have plenty of time."

He admitted to himself after he saw her that he had had some belated misgivings about the rendezvous. The lighting in the lobby of the Alamo House was a different proposition from the blue dimness of the Blue Goose: she might have looked tired and coarsened, or she might have been over-dressed and overpainted into a cheap travesty of charm. But she was none of those things. Her skin was so clear and fresh that she actually looked younger than he remembered her. She wore a long dress; but the décolletage was chastely pinned together, and she wore an inappropriate light camel-hair polo coat over it that gave her a kind of carelessly apologetic swagger. She looked like a woman that any grown man would be a little excited to take anywhere.

"I've got a car," he said. "We can take it if you can direct me."

"Let me drive you, and I'll promise you a good dinner."

He let her drive, and sat beside her in alert relaxation. This could have been the simplest kind of trap; but if it was, it was what he had asked for, and he was ready for it. He had checked the gun in his shoulder holster once more before he last left his room, and the slim two-edged knife in the sheath strapped to his right calf was almost as deadly a weapon in his hands —and even less easy to detect. It nested down under his sock with hardly a bulge, but it was accessible from any sitting or reclining position by the most innocent motion of hitching up his trouser cuff to scratch the side of his knee.

Simon Templar was even inclined to feel cheated when the drive ended without incident.

She steered him into a darkened bistro near the Gulf shore with bare wooden booths and marble-topped tables and sawdust on the floor.

"You have eaten *bouillabaisse* in Marseille," she said, "and perhaps in New Orleans. Now you will try this, and you will not be too disappointed."

The place was bleakly bright inside, and it was busy with people who looked ordinary but sober and harmless. Simon decided that it would be as safe as anything in his life ever could be to loosen up for the length of dinner.

"What made you call me?" he asked bluntly.

He had always felt her simple candor as the most cryptic of complexities.

"Why shouldn't I?" she returned. "I wanted to see you. And you turn out to be such an unusual kind of traveling salesman."

"There are so few things you can sell these days, a guy has to have a side line."

"You write very cleverly. I enjoyed your story. But when you were asking me questions, you weren't being honest with me."

"I told you everything I could."

"And I still told you everything I knew. Why do you think I was—what do you call it?—holding out on you?"

"I told you everything I knew, tovarich. Even if you did place me for a salesman."

"You didn't ask me about Blatt, Weinbach, and Maris."

"Only about Blatt."

He had to say that, but she could still make him feel wrong. Her air of straightforwardness was so unwavering that it turned the interrogator into the suspect. He had tried every device and approach in a rather fabulous repertoire the night before, and hadn't even scratched the surface of her. He knew exactly why even Lieutenant Kinglake might have left her alone, without any political pressure. Take her into court, and she could have made any public prosecutor feel that he was the prisoner who was being tried. It was the most flawlessly consistent stonewall act that Simon Templar had ever seen.

"You could have asked me about the others," she said. "If I could have told you anything, I would have. I'd like to help you."

"What could you have told me?"

"Nothing."

At least she had told him the truth about the *bouillabaisse*. He gave himself up to that consolation with fearful restraint.

It was half an hour later when he made one more attempt to drag the conversation back from the delightful flights of nothingness into which she was able to lead it so adroitly.

"Aside from my beautiful profile and my great literary gifts," he said, "I'd still like to know what made you want to see me again."

"I wanted you to pay for my dinner," she said seriously. "And I do like you—very much."

He remembered the way she had kissed him at her door, and forced himself to consider that if he had gone for that he would probably have been going for something as calculated as her simplicity.

"It couldn't have been, by any chance, because you wanted to find out if I knew any more?"

"But why should I? I am not a detective. Do I keep asking you questions?"

She was wide open and disarming. "No, I am just guilty of liking you. If you wanted to tell me things, I would listen. You see, my dear, I have that Russian feeling which you would think stupid or—corny: that a woman should be the slave of a man she admires. I am fascinated by you. So, I must be interested in what you are doing. That is all."

The Saint's teeth gripped together while he smiled.

"Then, sweetheart, you'll be interested to know that I'm going to make an important phone call, if you'll excuse me a minute."

He went to a coin phone at the rear of the restaurant and called the *Times-Tribune* again.

"It's all set," said the flat voice of the city editor. "Any time you want to pick me up."

"I'm just finishing dinner," said the Saint grimly. "If nothing happens on the way, I'll pick you up within thirty minutes."

He went back to the table, and found Olga placidly powdering her perfect nose.

"I hate to break this up," he said, "but I have a short call to make; and I have to deliver you back to the Blue Goose in time to catch the next influx of salesmen."

"Whatever you like," she replied calmly. "I don't have to be exactly on time though, so you do whatever you want to do."

It was impossible to stir her even with virtual insult.

But he drove the Ford himself this time, knowing that it could have seemed a much better moment for ambush than before dinner. Yet even then nothing happened, in such a way that the mere failure of anything to happen was a subtle rebuke in exactly the same key as all her refusals to rise to his varied provocations.

His sleepless sense of direction enabled him to drive without a mistake to the offices of the *Times-Tribune;* and he arrived there with no more alarm than a slight stiffness in muscles which had been poised too long on an uncertain fuse. But then, the egregious efficiency of Detective Yard had still conspired to blind him to the shift of concealing newspapers which had punctuated his exit from the Alamo House.

"I have to complain to my editor about the size of my headlines," he said. "It's a union rule. Do you mind waiting a little while?"

"Of course not," she said with that sublime and demoralising pliability. "Waiting is an old Russian pastime."

Simon went up to the editorial floor, and this time he swept through the interceptor command without interference, powered by the certainty of his route and destination.

The city editor saw him, and took his feet off the desk and crammed a discolored and shapeless panama on to the small end of his pear-shaped head.

"I'll have to go with you myself," he explained. "Not that I think you'd sell out to the UP, but it's the only way I could fix it. Let me do the talking, and you can take over when we get your man."

"What's he in for?"

"Passing a rubber check at his hotel. I hope you have some idea what strings I had to pull to arrange this for you."

Simon handed him the note that had been delivered to the Alamo House. The editor read it while they waited for the elevator.

"Smuggled out, eh? . . . Well, it might come to something."

"Is there a back alley way out of the building?"

"When I was a copy boy here, we used to know one. I haven't noticed the building being altered since." The city editor turned his shrewd sphinxlike face towards Simon with only the glitter of his eyes for a clue to his expression. "Are we still expecting something to happen?"

"I hope, yes and no," said the Saint tersely. "I left Olga in my car outside for a front and a cover. I'm hoping she's either fooled herself or she'll fool somebody else."

He knew that he had seldom been so vulnerable, but he never guessed how that flaw in his guard was to mature. He just felt sure that a prisoner in the City Jail couldn't be the trigger of any of the potential traps that he was waiting to recognise. Provided he took the obvious precautions, like leaving Olga Ivanovitch in his car outside the newspaper building while he slipped out through a back alley . . .

The *Times-Tribune* man's dry bulbous presence was a key that by-passed tired clerks and opened clanging iron doors, and exacted obedience from soured disinterested jailers, and led them eventually into a small barren and discouraging office room with barred windows where they waited through a short echoing silence until the door opened again to admit Mr Vaschetti with a turnkey behind him.

The door closed again, leaving the turnkey outside; and Mr Vaschetti's darting black eyes switched over the city editor's somnolent self-effacement and made one of their touch landings on the Saint.

"You're Templar," he stated. "But I said this had to be private."

"This is Mr Bettlespats of the *Times-Tribune*," said the Saint inventively. "He published the article you read, and he organised this meeting. But we can pretend he isn't here. Just tell me what you've got on your mind."

Vaschetti's eyes whirled around the room like small dark bugs exploring the intricacies of a candelabra.

"I can tell you," he said, "you were dead right about Matson. I've been a courier for the Bund for a long time. I took a letter to Matson in St Louis, and I brought a letter to your Mr Blatt and other people in Galveston too."

CHAPTER SEVEN

HE WAS a rather small man, spare and wiry, with the heavy eyebrows and hollow cheeks which so often seem to go together. His hair needed combing and his chin needed scraping. His clothes were neither good nor bad, but they were rumpled and soiled as if they had been slept in, which they doubtless had.

The Saint gave him a cigarette and said: "I don't think there are any dictographs planted here, so just keep talking. What made you write to me?"

"Because I don't like cops. I see where you've made suckers out of the cops plenty of times, and I'd like to see you do it again. Especially to those sons of bitches who threw me in here."

"You did pass a bum check, didn't you?" Simon mentioned.

"Yeah, but only because I had to, because Blatt didn't come through with my dough and I was broke. I wouldn't have squawked just for that, though. I've taken raps before. I've stood for a lot of things in my time, but I don't want any part of this." Vaschetti puffed at his cigarette shakily, and moved about the room with short jerky strides. "Not murder. No, sir. I don't want to sit in the hot seat, or dance on the end of a rope, or whatever they do to you in this state."

Simon kindled a cigarette for himself, and propped himself on the window sill.

"Why should anyone do things like that to you? Or were you one of the three fire-bugs?"

"No, sir. But that Kinglake might find out any time that I'd seen Blatt and been asking for him at the Blue Goose, and what chance would I have then? I don't want Blatt gunning for me either, and I guess he might be if he thought I might put the finger on him. I'd rather squeal first, and then if they know it's too late to shut my mouth maybe they won't bother with me."

"I see your point," said the Saint thoughtfully. "Suppose you sit down and tell me about your life as a courier."

Vaschetti attempted a laugh that didn't come off, licked his lips nervously, and sat down on a creaky chair.

"I met Fritz Kuhn when I was doing time in Dannemora. We got on pretty well, and he said if I wanted to make some money when I got out

I should see him. Well, I did. I got this job carrying packages from place to place."

"How did that work?"

"Well, for instance, I'd have a package to deliver to Mr Smith at the Station Hotel in Baltimore. I'd go there and ask for him. Maybe he'd be out of town. I'd hang around until he showed up—sometimes I'd have to wait for a week and more. Then I'd give Smith the package; and he'd pay me my dough and my expenses, and maybe give me another package to take to Mr Robinson at Macfarland's Grill in Miami. Any time there wasn't anything more for me, I'd go back to Jersey and start again."

"These Smiths and Robinsons weren't anything to do with the joints you met them in?"

"Mostly not. I'd just ask a bartender if he knew Mr Smith, and he'd point out Mr Smith. Or sometimes I'd be hanging around and Mr Robinson would come in and say he was Robinson and had anyone been asking for him."

"How much did you get for this?"

"Seventy-five a week and all my expenses."

"You got paid by the Smiths and Robinsons as you went along."

"Yeah."

"You knew that this was obviously connected with something illegal."

Vaschetti licked his lips again and nodded.

"Sure, sure. It had to be things they didn't want to send through the mail, or they didn't want to chance having opened by the wrong person."

"You knew it was more than that. You knew it was for the Bund, and so it was probably no good for this country."

"What the hell? I'm an Italian, and I got brothers in Italy. And I never did like the goddam British. This was before the war got here. So what?"

"So you still went on after Pearl Harbor."

Vaschetti swallowed, and his eyes took another of those fluttering whirls around the room.

"Yeah, I went on. I was in it then, and it didn't seem to make much difference. Not at first. Besides, I still thought Roosevelt and the Jews were getting us in. I was scared, too. I was scared what the Axis people here might do to me if I tried to quit. But I got a lot more curious."

"So——?"

"So I started opening these packages. I was taking one to Schenectady at the time. I steamed it open, and inside there was four smaller envelopes addressed to people in Schenectady. But they had wax seals on them with swastikas and things, and I was afraid it might show if I tried to open them. So I put them back in the big envelope and delivered it like I was told to. Sometimes I had big parcels to carry, but I didn't dare monkey with them.

I still had to eat, and I didn't want no trouble either. . . . But then I got more scared of the FBI and what'd happen to me if I got caught. Now there's this murder, and I'm through. I been a crook all my life, but I don't want no federal raps and I don't want to go to the chair."

Simon's sapphire blue eyes studied him dispassionately through a slowly rising veil of smoke. There was nothing much to question or decipher about the psychology of Signor Vaschetti—or not about those facets which held any interest for the Saint. It was really nothing but a microcosmic outline of Signor Mussolini. He was just a small-time goon who had climbed on to a promising bandwagon, and now that the ride ahead looked bumpy he was anxious to climb off.

There could hardly be any doubt that he was telling the truth—he was too plainly preoccupied with the integrity of his own skin to have had much energy to spare on embroidery or invention.

"It's a fine story," said the Saint lackadaisically. "But where does it get us with Matson?"

"Like you wrote in the paper, he must have been paid to do some sabotage. He didn't do it, but he kept the money and took a powder. But you can't run out on that outfit. That's why I'm talking to you. They traced him here and gave him the business."

"That *is* about how I doped it out," Simon said with thistledown satire. "But what are you adding besides the applause?"

"I'm telling you, I took one of those letters to Matson in St Louis. That proves he was being paid by the Germans, and that proves you're right and Kinglake is a horse's——"

"But you made this delivery in St Louis. Why are you here in Galveston now?"

Vaschetti sucked on the stub of his cigarette, and dropped it on the floor and trod on it.

"That's on account of Blatt. I came here from El Paso two weeks ago with a package to give to Blatt at the Blue Goose. I didn't know Matson was coming here. I didn't know anything about Matson, except he told me he was working for Quenco. Blatt only paid me up to date and kept me hanging around waiting for some letters he said he'd be sending out. I ran up a pretty big bill at the hotel, and Blatt never came around and I couldn't reach him. That's why I flew the kite."

"Did you meet any of my other friends?"

"I met Weinbach. He's a fat kraut with a red face and red hair and the palest eyes you ever saw."

Simon placed the word-picture alongside the description that Port Arthur Jones had given him of the stranger who had been inquiring about him at the Alamo House, and it matched very well. So that was Weinbach.

And that left Maris, whom nobody seemed to have seen at all.

The Saint went on staring at the twitching representative of the Roman Empire.

"You could have told Kinglake this," he said.

"Yeah. And I'd be here as an accessory to murder, if that sour-pussed bastard didn't try to make out I was all three murderers in one. No, sir. It's yours now. Gimme a break, and I'll write it down and sign it. I'm not going to give any of these dumb cops a free promotion. I'd rather you showed 'em up instead. Then I'll feel better about the spot I'm in."

Simon spun out his smoke in a few moments' motionless contemplation.

"If it was some time ago that you met Matson in St Louis," he said, "how come you connected all this up?"

"I remembered." The other's eyes shifted craftily. "And I got notes. I didn't dare play with those inside envelopes, but I been writing down the names of people. And the places I went to in different cities. A fellow never knows when some things will come in handy. You can have that list too, if you take care of me, and I don't care what you do with it. None of those bastards tried to do anything for me when I got in this jam, so the hell with them."

The Saint barely showed polite interest; yet he felt so close to one of the real things that he had come to Galveston for that he was conscious of rationing his own breathing.

"It's only fair to tell you, Comrade," he said very carefully, "that if you give me any information that seems worth it, I shall have to turn it straight over to the FBI."

Vaschetti's face was pale in the clearings between his eyebrows and the stubble on his chin, yet in a foolish way he looked almost relieved.

"What you do after you've got it is your affair," he said. "Just gimme a couple hundred dollars and a chance to blow this town, and it's all yours."

Simon glanced at the city editor of the *Times-Tribune*, who was reclining in a junk-pile armchair in the corner with his shabby hat tilted over his eyes, who might have been passed over as asleep except that the eyes were visible and open under the stained straw brim. The eyes touched the Saint briefly and brightly, but nothing else in the composition looked alive. The Saint knew that he was still on his own, according to the agreement.

He said: "What hotel were you working on?"

"The Campeche."

"How much for?"

"Fifty bucks. And my bill."

"I'll take care of all that. You can probably be sprung in a couple of hours. Then I'll meet you at the Campeche and give you two hundred bucks for that statement and your list of names. Then I'll give you two hours to start traveling before I break the story. After that, you're on your own."

"You made a deal, mister. And as soon as I get that dough, I'll take my chance on getting out of here or I'll take what's coming to me. I don't want anything except to be all washed up with this."

His cathartic relief or else his blind faith in his ability to elude the seines of the FBI was either way so pathetic that Simon didn't have the heart to freeze him down any more. He hitched himself out of the window frame and opened the office door to call back the jailer.

The city editor rocked his antique panama back on his head and tried to keep step beside him as they left.

"I suppose," he said, "you want me to take care of everything and get the Campeche to withdraw the complaint."

"I suppose you can do it. You didn't say anything, so there it is."

"I can put a man on it. I'll have him out in a couple of hours, as you said. But don't ask what happens to me for conspiring to suppress evidence, because I don't know."

"We write up the story," said the Saint, "and we hand Kinglake a proof while the presses are rolling. He gets the complete dope, and we get the beat. What could be fairer?"

The city editor continued to look dyspeptic and unhappy with all of his face except his bright eyes.

He said: "Where are you going now?"

"Call me at the Alamo House as soon as your stooge has Vaschetti under control," Simon told him. "I've got to take Olga to her treadmill, if she hasn't run out by this time."

But Olga Ivanovitch was still sitting in the Saint's car, to all appearances exactly as he had left her, with her hands folded in her lap and the radio turned on, listening happily to some aspiring and perspiring local comedy program.

She was able to make him feel wrong again, even like that, because she was so naïvely and incontestably untroubled by any of the things that might have been expected to rasp the edges of deliberate self-control.

"I'm sorry I was so long," he said, with a brusqueness that burred into his voice out of his own bewilderment. "But they've started teaching editors two-syllable words lately, and that means it takes them twice as long to talk back to you."

"I've been enjoying myself," she said; and in her own Slavic and slavish way she was still laughing at him and with him, enjoying the tranquillity of her own uncomplaining acceptance of everything. "Tell me how you talk to editors."

He told her something absurd; and she sat close against him and laughed

gaily aloud as he drove towards the Blue Goose. He was very disconcertingly
conscious of the supple firmness of her body as she leaned innocently towards him, and the loveliness of her face against its plaque of yellow
braided hair; and he had to make himself remember that she was not so
young, and she had been around.

He stopped at the Blue Goose, and opened her door for her without
leaving the wheel.

"Aren't you coming in?" she asked.

He was lighting a cigarette with the dashboard gadget, not looking at
her.

"I'll try to get back before closing time," he said, "and have a nightcap
with you. But I've got a small job to do first. I'm a working man—or did
you forget?"

She moved, after an instant's silence and stillness; and then he felt his
hand brushed away from his mouth with the cigarette still freshly lighted
in it, and her mouth was there instead, and this was like the night before
only more so. Her arms were locked around his neck, and her face was the
ivory blur in front of him, and he remembered that she had been a surprising warm fragrance to him when she did that before, and this was
like that again. He had a split second of thinking that this was it, and
he had slipped after all, and he couldn't reach his gun or his knife with
her kissing him; and his ears were awake for the deafening thunderbolts
that always rang down the curtain on careers like his. But there was nothing
except her kiss, and her low voice saying, docilely like she said everything:
"Be careful, tovarich. Be careful."

"I will be," he said, and put the gears scrupulously together, and had
driven quite a fair way before it co-ordinated itself to him that she was
still the only named name of the ungodly whom he had met and spoken to,
and that there was no reason for her to warn him to be careful unless she
knew from the other side that he could be in danger.

He drove cautiously back to the Alamo House, collected his key from
the desk, glanced around to make sure that Detective Yard had found a
comfortable chair, and went up to his room in search of a refreshing pause
beside a cool alcoholic drink.

Specifically, the one person he had most in mind was the venerable Mr
Peter Dawson, a tireless distiller of bagpipe broth who, as we recollect,
should have been represented among the Saint's furniture by the best part
of a bottle of one of his classic consommés. Simon Templar was definitely
not expecting, as an added attraction, the body of Mr Port Arthur Jones,
trussed up and gagged with strips of adhesive tape, and anchored to his
bed with hawsers of sash cord, and looking exactly like a new kind of
Ethiopian mummy with large rolling eyes; which is precisely what he was.

CHAPTER EIGHT

SIMON UNTIED HIM and stripped off the tape. The bellhop at least was alive, and apparently not even slightly injured, to judge by the ready flow of words that came out of him when his mouth was unwrapped.

"Two men it was, Mistah Templah. One of 'em was that fat man with red hair that Ah done tole you about. Ah'd been off havin' mah supper, and when I come back, there he is in the lobby. He's with another tall thin man, like it might be the other gennelman you was askin' me about. So Ah was goin' to call your room so you could come down and have a look at them, but the clerk tole me you just went out. Then these men started to get in the elevator, and Ah knew there was somethin' wrong, Ah knew they wasn't stayin' here, and with you bein' out Ah just figured they was up to no good. So Ah ran up the stairs, and sho' 'nuff there they were just openin' your doah. So Ah asked them what they was doin', and they tried to tell me they was friends of yours. 'You ain't no friends of Mistah Templah's,' Ah says, 'because Mistah Templah done tole me to keep mah eyes open for you.' Then the fat man pulled out a gun and they hustled me in here and tied me up, and then they started searchin' the room. Ah don't think they found what they was huntin' for, because they was awful mad when they went off. But they sho' made a mess of your things."

That statement was somewhat superfluous. Aside from the disorder of the furnishings, which looked as if a cyclone had paused among them, the Saint's suitcase had been emptied on to the floor and everything in it had been tossed around and even taken apart when there was any conceivable point to it.

"Don't let it get you down, Po't Arthur," Simon said cheerfully. "I know they didn't get what they wanted, because I didn't leave anything here that they could possibly want. Unless one of them coveted an electric razor, which it seems he didn't. Just give me a hand with straightening out the wreckage."

He began to repack his suitcase while Port Arthur Jones became efficient about replacing the carpet and rearranging the furniture.

He was puzzled about the entire performance, for he certainly had no precious goods or papers with him; and if he had had any he certainly wouldn't have left them in his room when he went out. The ransacking must have stemmed from his connection with the Matson murder, but it seemed a long way for the ungodly to have gone with the mere hope of picking up some incidental information about him. The only reasonable explanation would be that they suspected that Matson might have given him something, or told him where to find something, before he died. But

Matson had only muttered about an ostrich-skin case in a gladstone lining; and they had the gladstone. If they had taken the trouble to collect the gladstone, hadn't they looked in the lining? Or had they just picked it up along with other things, in the broad hope of coming across what they were searching for?

He said: "This happened just after I went out?"

"Yassah. The desk clerk said you hadn't been gone more'n a few minutes. He said you went out with a lady."

"What about that Detective Yard?"

"Ah didn't see him, sah. Ah guess most likely he went out when you did."

It had been a nice job of contrivance anyhow. If the ungodly knew or assumed that the police were watching Simon Templar, they could also assume that the police would go out when Simon Templar went out. So the coast would be relatively clear when they knew he was going out.

He had been on his guard against uninvited shadows, when it seemed like a good idea to watch out for uninvited shadows. He hadn't bothered much about those who stayed behind, because he hadn't been thinking about anything worth staying behind for. But they had been.

The three faceless men. Blatt, Weinbach, and Maris. Two of whom he had only heard described. And Maris, whom nobody had heard of and nobody had ever seen.

But Olga Ivanovitch must have known at least one of them. Or even more positively, at least one of them must have known her. They must have sat and looked at each other in the lobby while she was waiting for him. One way or another, the Saint was being taken out of the way for a safe period; and some of them had known it and watched it when he went out. Quite probably, Olga.

Simon's lips hardened momentarily as he finished refolding the last shirt and laid it on top of the stack in his bag. He turned back from the job to watch Port Arthur Jones fastidiously fitting a chair back into the scars which its standard position had printed on the nap of the carpet. The room looked as tidy again as if nothing had ever happened there.

"Thanks, chum," said the Saint. "Have we forgotten anything?"

The colored man scratched his close-cropped head.

"Well, sah, Ah dunno. The Alamo House is a mighty respectable hotel——"

"Will you be in trouble on account of the time you've been shut up in here?"

"Nawsah, Ah can't say that. Ah goes off for mah supper, and then Ah comes back and just stays around as long as there's a chance of earnin' an honest tip. Ah don't clock out at no definite time. But with people breakin' into rooms and pullin' a gun on you and tyin' you up, it seems like the management or the police or somebody oughta know what's goin' on."

He was honestly confused and worried about the whole thing.

Simon took a ten-dollar bill out of his pocket and flattened it between his hands so that the numbers were plainly visible.

"Look," he said, as one man to another, "I don't want any trouble with the hotel. And I don't want any help from the cops. I'd rather take care of these guys myself if I ever catch up with them. Why can't we just pretend that you went home early, and none of this ever happened, except that you did spot two more of those people I asked you about and pointed them out to me; and I'll pay you off on that basis."

The scruples of Mr Port Arthur Jones were probably no less sincere and confirmed than those of Mr Henry Morgenthau; but he eyed the dangling sawbuck and was irresistibly swayed by its potentialities in his budget. You could see box cars rolling majestically over the murky tracks of his mind.

"Yassah," he said, beaming. "Ah don't wanna start no trouble. Ah'll just forget it if that's what you say, sah."

Simon watched him stow away the green consolation and close the door contentedly after him.

Then he poured himself the highball which he had come home for in the first place. He was glad that at least his guests hadn't been searching for something that might have been soluble in alcohol.

He was just getting acquainted with the drink when his telephone rang.

"I've taken care of your friend," said the *Times-Tribune*. "He should be back at the Campeche in just a little while. One of the boys is taking care of him."

"Good," said the Saint. "I'll be over there in just a little while too."

"I was able to fix it with the hotel and get to the judge," persisted the voice, rather mournfully. "At this time of night, that's not so easy."

"Congratulations," said the Saint. "You must be *persona* very *grata*."

There was a brief hiatus where the city editor silenced as if he was digging out a new lead.

"I liked the way you talked to that man Vaschetti," he excavated at length, "and I think I ought to talk to you the same way. I'll hold everything while you bring in your story; but I have to live here too. So whatever you bring in, I'll have to turn over to the police and the FBI."

"I'll give you a personal commendation for your fine public spirit," said the Saint.

He could see the pear-shaped figure with its feet on the desk and the battered hat tilted over the eyes that were the only sparkle in the dried poker face, as if it were sitting directly in front of him.

"You've said things that sounded as if you had a hell of a lot of inside dope on this case," said the city editor finally. "What are you doing in

Galveston anyway, and why don't you give me the whole story and earn yourself some real dough?"

"I'll think about it," said the Saint, "after I've talked to Vaschetti again." He dropped the phone, and tried to resume relations with his highball. He had absorbed one good solid sip when the bell rang again.

This time it was Washington.

"Hamilton," said the line. "I hope this is an awkward moment."

Simon grinned for his own benefit, and said: "No."

"This is all I've got so far on those names. During Prohibition, there were two trigger men in Milwaukee named Johan Blatt and Fritzie Weinbach. They usually worked together. Racketeers. One or two charges—assault, carrying concealed weapons, and so on. Associated with un-American activities in Chicago just before the War. I can read you their full records, but they just sound like a couple of mercenary hoodlums."

"Don't bother," said the Saint. "What about Maris?"

"Nothing yet. A name doesn't mean anything. Hasn't anyone even seen the color of his eyes?"

"Nobody ever sees Maris," said the Saint. "They don't notice anything about him at all. But I'll find him before you do. I'm still working. Have some more black coffee and wait up for me."

He pronged the transceiver again, and reached for his glass once more with indomitable determination.

Maris—the man nobody saw. The man who might be much more than the mere trick answer to a riddle that had been posed by the premature cremation of Henry Stephen Matson. The man who might materialise into one of those almost legendary spear-carriers who were primarily responsible for Simon Templar's excursions as a talent scout even to such outposts as Galveston. The man who might be more concerned than anyone about the contents of the ostrich-skin leather case which had consumed Matson's dying breath.

Or about the lists or memory of Nick Vaschetti, a glorified errand-boy with a bad case of fright or fluctuating conscience.

He crumpled out the stub of his cigarette and went downstairs.

Port Arthur Jones, shining like refurbished ebony, intercepted him as he left the elevator.

"Mistah Templah, sah, that Detective Yard just gone home. Another detective took over for him. His name's Mistah Callahan. He's sittin' half behind the second palm across the lobby. A stout gennelman with a bald head in a gray suit——"

Simon slipped another Lincoln label into the bellboy's pink palm.

"If you keep on like this, Po't Arthur," he said, "you're going to end up a capitalist whether you want to or not."

It was a well indicated move which should have been taken before, to replace the too familiar Mr Yard with somebody else whom the Saint might not recognise. Simon's only surprise was that it hadn't happened sooner. But presumably the whimsical antics of the Selective Service System had not excluded the Galveston Police Department from the scope of their ruthless raids upon personnel.

That wasn't the Saint's business. But for the most immediate future, at least until he had consummated the Vaschetti diversion, Simon Templar preferred to get along without the politically complicated protection of the Galveston gendarmerie.

Wherefore he shelved Mr Callahan by the rather kindergarten expedient of climbing very deliberately into his parked car, switching on the lights, fiddling with the starter, and then just as leisurely stepping out of the other door, boarding a passing cab, and going away in it while Mr Callahan was still glued to the bridge of his municipal sampan and waiting for the Saint's wagon to weigh anchor so that he could pursue it.

Which was an entirely elementary technique, but didn't even begin to tackle the major problem of the Law in Galveston.

What Simon wanted more than anything at that moment was Mr Vaschetti's autographed statement, and the list of names and addresses which he had promised. Those things, as weapons, would be worth even more to him than the gun that still bulked under his left arm, or the knife which he could feel with every swing of his right leg.

The Campeche Hotel was down on Water Street, and it appeared to be a very popular bivouac, for there was such a large crowd of citizens clustered around the entrance that they obstructed the traffic, and the Saint left his taxi a few doors away and walked into the throng. As he edged his way through them he was conscious of the crunching of broken glass under his feet; but he didn't think much about it until he noticed some of the crowd glancing upwards, and he glanced upwards with them and saw the jagged gaping hole in the shattered marquee overhead. Then with the advantage of his height he looked over a few heads and shoulders and saw the thing that was the nucleus of the assembly. A rather shapeless lump of something in the center of a clear circle of blood-spattered sidewalk, with one foot sticking out from under a blanket that covered its grosser deformations.

Even then, he knew; but he had to ask.

"What gives?" he said to the nearest bystander.

"Guy just got discouraged," was the laconic answer. "Walked outa his window on the eighth floor. I didn't see him jump, but I saw him light. He came through that marquee like a bomb."

Simon didn't even feel curious about getting the blanket moved for a glimpse of anything identifiable that might have been left as a face. He observed the uniformed patrolman standing rather smug guard over the remains, and said quite coldly: "How long ago did this happen?"

"Only about five minutes ago. They're still waitin' for the ambulance. I was just goin' by on the other side of the street, and I happened to look around——"

The Saint didn't weary his ears with the rest of the anecdote. He was too busy consuming the fact that one more character in that particular episode had elected to go voyaging into the Great Beyond in the middle of another of those unfinished revelations which only the most corny of scenario cookers would have tolerated for a moment. Either he had to take a very dim view of the writing talent in the books of Destiny, or else it would begin to seem that the abrupt transmigration of Nick Vaschetti was just another cog in a divine conspiracy to make life tantalising for Simon Templar.

CHAPTER NINE

THE LINKS went clicking through Simon's brain as if they were meshing over the teeth of a perfectly fitted sprocket.

The ungodly had ransacked his room at the Alamo House while they knew he would be out of the way, and had drawn a blank. But they would have had plenty of time to pick him up again, and it would have been childishly simple for them to do it, because they knew he was with Olga Ivanovitch, and the place where she was going to steer him for dinner had been decided in advance. The Saint had been alert for the kind of ambuscade that would have been orchestrated with explosions and flying lead, but not for ordinary trailing, because why should the ungodly trail him when one of them was already with him to note all his movements? He had left Olga Ivanovitch in his car outside the *Times-Tribune* building, as he said, for a front and a cover: it hadn't occurred to him that she might be a front and a cover for others of the ungodly. She sat there covering the front while they took the precaution of covering the other exits. When he came out by the back alley, they followed. When he went to the City Jail, they remembered Vaschetti and knew that that must have been the man he had gone to see. Therefore one of them had waited for a chance to silence Vaschetti; and when Vaschetti was released and led back to the Campeche, the opportunity had been thrown into their laps. It had been as mechanically simple as that.

And Olga Ivanovitch had done a swell job all the way through. All those items went interlocking through his mind as he stood at the desk inside and faced an assistant manager who was trying somewhat flabbily to look as though he had everything under perfect control.

Simon flipped his lapel in a conventional gesture, but without showing anything, and said aggressively: "Police Department. What room was Vaschetti in?"

"Eight-twelve," said the assistant manager, in the accents of a harassed mortician. "The house detective is up there now. I assure you, we——"

"Who was with him when he jumped?"

"No one that I know of. He was brought in by one of the men from the *Times-Tribune*, who redeemed his check. Then the reporter left, and——"

"He didn't have any visitors after that?"

"No, nobody asked for him. I'm sure of that, because I was standing by the desk all the time. I'd just taken the money for his check, and told Mr Vaschetti that we'd like to have his room in the morning; and I was chatting with a friend of mine——"

"Where are the elevators?"

"Over in that corner. I'll be glad to take you up, Mr——"

"Thanks. I can still push my own buttons," said the Saint brusquely, and headed away in the direction indicated, leaving the assistant manager with only one more truncated sentence in his script.

He had very little time to spare, if any. It could be only a matter of seconds before the accredited constabulary would arrive on the scene, and he wanted to verify what he could before they were in his hair.

He went up and found 812, where the house detective could be seen through the open door, surveying the scene with his hands in his pockets and a dead piece of chewing cigar in the corner of his mouth.

Simon shouldered in with exactly the same authoritative technique and motion of a hand towards the flap of his buttonhole.

"What's the bad news?" he demanded breezily.

The house detective kept his hands in his pockets and made a speech with his shoulders and the protruding cud of his cigar that said as eloquently as anything: "You got eyes, ain'tcha?"

Simon fished out a pack of cigarettes and let his own eyes do the work.

It didn't take more than one wandering glance to rub in the certainty that he was still running behind schedule. Although not exactly a shambles, the room showed all the signs of a sound working over. The bed was torn apart, and the mattress had been slit open in several places, as had the upholstery of the single armchair. The closet door stood wide, and the few garments inside had been ripped to pieces and tossed on the floor. Every drawer of the dresser had been pulled out, and its contents dumped and pawed over on the carpet. The spectacle was reminiscent of the Saint's own room at the Alamo House—with trimmings. He wouldn't have wasted a second on any searching of his own. The search had already been made, by experts.

So someone already had Vaschetti's diary; or else no one was likely to come across it there.

The Saint scraped a match with his thumbnail and let the picture shroud itself in a blue haze.

"What about the men who were up here with Vaschetti?" he asked.

"I never saw anyone with him," responded the house dick promptly. He had a broad beam and an advancing stomach, so that he had some of the air of a frog standing upright.

"I didn't get your name," he said. "Mine's Rowden."

"You didn't hear any commotion up here, Rowden?"

"I didn't hear a thing. Not until the crash Vaschetti made going through the marquee. I didn't even know he was back out of jail until just now. Where's Kinglake? He usually comes out on death cases."

"He'll be along," Simon promised, with conviction.

There was one fascinating detail to consider, Simon observed as he narrowed down the broad outlines of the scene. In the middle of the strewn junk on the floor there was an almost new gladstone bag, empty and open, lying on its side. He moved to examine it more closely.

"Anybody else been up here?" he inquired.

"Nope. You're the first. Funny I don't know you. I thought I'd met all the plainclothes men in Galveston."

"Maybe you have," said the Saint encouragingly.

Indubitably that was the gladstone which he had heard about. It even had the initials "HSM" gold-stamped beside the handle. But if there had ever been an ostrich-skin leather case in the lining, it wasn't there any more. The lining had been slashed to ribbons, and you could have found a long-lost pin in it.

It was a picturesque mystery-museum piece, but that was all. The current questions were, how had it come to rest there, and why? Johan Blatt had removed it from the Ascot; and by no stretch of imagination could his description have been confused with that of the latest failure in the field of empirical levitation. Vaschetti and Blatt were even more different than chalk and cheese: they didn't even begin with the same letter.

Simon Templar pondered that intensely for a time, while the house detective teetered batrachianly on his heels and gnawed on his bowsprit of cigar. The house detective, Simon thought, would surely have been a big help in detecting a house. Aside from that, he was evidently content to let nature and the Police Department take their course. He would have made Dick Tracy break out in a rectangular rash.

They remained in that sterile atmosphere until the sound of voices and footsteps in the corridor, swelling rapidly louder, presaged the advent of Lieutenant Kinglake and his cohorts.

"Ah," said Detective Yard wisely, as he sighted the Saint.

Kinglake didn't even take time out to show surprise. He turned savagely on the frog-shaped house detective.

"How in hell did this bird get in here?"

"I came in under my own power," Simon intervened. "I was thinking of moving, and I wanted to see what the rooms were like. Don't blame Rowden. He was trying to tell me about the wooden mattresses. If you look again, you'll see where he was even ripping them open to show me the teak linings."

The Lieutenant was not amused. He had never looked like a man who was amused very often, and this was manifestly not one of his nights to relax in a bubble bath of wit and badinage.

He glared at the Saint balefully and said: "All right, Templar. You asked for it. I told you what was going to happen to you if you didn't keep your nose clean in this town. Well, this is it. I'm holding you as a material witness in the death of Nick Vaschetti."

The arch of the Saint's brows was angelic.

"As a witness of what, Comrade? The guy bumped himself off, didn't he? He stepped out of a window and left off his parachute. He'd heard about the Galveston Police, and he knew that the most precious legacy he could bequeath them was an absolutely watertight suicide. What makes you leave your ever-loving wife warming her own nightie so you can come here and improve your blood pressure?"

Kinglake's mouth became a thin slit in his face, and his neck reddened up to his ears; but he kept his temper miraculously. The blood stayed out of his slate-gray stare.

"Why don't you save the wisecracks for your column?" he said nastily. "You've been mixed up in too many fishy things since you've been here——"

"What makes you assume that I was mixed up in this?"

"You talked to Vaschetti in the City Jail this evening. You arranged for him to be sprung, and you arranged to meet him here. I call that being mixed up in it."

"You must be psychic," Simon remarked. "I know I got rid of your Mr Callahan. Or who told you?"

"I did," said the voice of the *Times-Tribune*.

He stood in the doorway with a vestige of apology on his mild stolid face. Simon turned and saw him, and went on looking at him with acid bitterness.

"Thanks, pal. Did you bring out a special edition and tell the rest of the world too?"

"I did not," said the city editor primly. "I acted according to the agreement I made with you, as soon as I heard what had happened to Vaschetti."

"How did you hear?"

"The reporter who was supposed to be taking care of him and waiting for you arrived back at the office. I asked him what he thought he was doing, and he said he'd been given a message that I wanted him back at once. Since I hadn't sent any such message, I guessed something was going on. I wasn't any too happy about my own position, so I thought I'd better come over and look into it myself. I met Lieutenant Kinglake downstairs, and I told him what I knew."

"And so we come up here," Kinglake said comfortably, "and catch the Saint just like this."

The repetition of names ultimately made its impression on the comatose house detective.

"Gosh," he exhaled, with a burst of awed excitement, "he's the Saint!" He looked disappointed when nobody seemed impressed by his great discovery, and retired again behind his cigar. He said sullenly: "He told me he was the police."

"He told the assistant manager the same thing," Kinglake said with some satisfaction. "A charge of impersonating an officer will hold him till we get something better."

Simon studied the Lieutenant's leathery face seriously for a moment.

"You know," he said, "something tells me you really mean to be difficult about this."

"You're damn right I do," Kinglake said without spite.

At that point there was a sudden sharp exclamation from Detective Yard, who had been quartering the room with the same plodding method that he had used out on the flats where the late Henry Stephen Matson had become his own funeral pyre.

"Hey, Lieutenant, look what we got here."

He brought over the shredded gladstone, pointing to the initials stamped on it.

"H,S,M," he spelt out proudly. "Henry Stephen Matson. This could of belonged to that guy we found yesterday!"

Lieutenant Kinglake examined the bag minutely; but the Saint wasn't watching him.

Simon Templar had become profoundly interested in something else. He had still been fidgeting over that bag in the back of his mind even while he had to make more immediate conversation, and it seemed to be sorting itself out. He was scanning the hodgepodge of stuff on the floor rather vacantly while Yard burgeoned into the bowers of Theory.

"Lieutenant, maybe this Vaschetti was the guy who called himself Blatt an' got away with Matson's luggage. So after they throw him out the window, they tear that bag apart while they're rippin' up everything else."

"Brother," said the Saint in hushed veneration, "I visualise you as the next Chief of Police. You can see that whole slabs of that lining have been torn right out; but in all this mess I bet you can't find one square inch of lining. I've been looking to see if the ungodly had been smart enough to think of that, but I don't think they were. Therefore that bag wasn't chopped up in here. Therefore it was planted just for the benefit of some genius like you."

"What else for?" Kinglake demanded curtly.

"To throw in a nice note of confusion. And most likely, in the hope that the confusion might take some of the heat off Blatt."

"If there ever was a Blatt before you thought of him."

"There was a Blatt," the city editor intervened scrupulously. "I think I told you, Vaschetti spoke about him and described him."

The Lieutenant handed the gladstone back to his assistant, and kept his stony eyes on the Saint.

"That doesn't make any difference," he stated coldly. "All I care about is that whatever went on here was done inside the city limits of Galveston. There's no question about my jurisdiction this time. And I'm tired of having you in my hair, Templar. You wanted Vaschetti out of the calaboose. You arranged to meet him here. And I find you in his room in the middle of a mess that makes it look as if he could have been pushed out of that window instead of jumped. You've been much too prominent in every bit of this—from finding Matson's body to going around with Olga Ivanovitch. So I'm just going to put you where I'll know what you're doing all the time."

"Has there been a political upheaval in the last half-hour," Simon inquired with sword-edged mockery, "or do you happen to be kidding yourself that if you bring me into court on any charge I won't manage to tie this job in with the Matson barbecue and raise holy hell with all the plans for a nice peaceful election?"

Kinglake's jaw hardened out like a cliff, but the harried expression that Simon had noticed before crept in around his eyes.

"We'll worry about that when the time comes. Right now, you're going to do all your hell-raising in a nice quiet cell."

Simon sighed faintly, with real regret. It would have been so much more fun playing it the old way, but he couldn't take any more chances with that now. This game mattered so much more than the old games that he had played for fun.

"I hate to disappoint you," he said, "but I can't let you interfere with me tonight."

He said it with such translucent simplicity that it produced the kind of stunned silence that might exist at the very core of an exploding bomb.

Detective Yard, the least sensitive character, was the first to recover.

"Now, ain't that just too bad!" he jeered, advancing on the Saint, and hauling out a pair of handcuffs as he came, but moving warily because of his own affronted confidence.

Simon didn't even spare him a glance. He was facing Kinglake and nobody else, and all the banter and levity had dropped away from his bearing. It was like a prizefighter in the ring shrugging off his gay and soft silk robe.

"I want five minutes with you alone," he said. "And I mean alone. It'll save you a lot of trouble and grief."

Lieutenant Kinglake was no fool. The hard note of command that had slid into the Saint's voice was pitched in a subtle key that blended with his own harmonics.

He eyed Simon for a long moment, and then he said: "Okay. The rest of you wait outside. Please."

In spite of which, he pulled out his Police Positive and sat down and held it loosely on his knee as the other members of the congregation filed out with their individual expressions of astonishment, disappointment, and disgust.

There was perplexity even on Kinglake's rugged bony face after the door had closed, but he overcame it with his bludgeon bluff of harsh peremptory speech.

"Well," he said unrelentingly. "Now we're alone, let's have it. But if you were thinking you could pull a fast one if you had me to yourself—just forget it, and save the City a hospital bill."

"I want you to pick up that phone and make a call to Washington," said the Saint, without rancor. "The number is Imperative five, five hundred. Extension five. If you don't know what that means, your local FBI gent will tell you. You'll talk to a voice called Hamilton. After that you're on your own."

Even Kinglake looked as briefly startled as his seamed face could.

"And if I let you talk me into making this call, what good will it do you?"

"I think," said the Saint, "that Hamilton will laugh his head off; but I'm afraid he'll tell you to save that nice quiet cell for somebody else."

The Lieutenant gazed at him fixedly for four or five seconds.

Then he reached for the telephone.

Simon Templar germinated another cigarette, and folded into the remnants of an armchair. He hardly paid any attention to the conversation that went on, much less to the revolver that rested for a few more minutes on the detective's lap. That phase of the affair was finished, so far as he was concerned; and he had something else to think about.

He had to make a definite movement to bring himself back to that shabby and dissected room when the receiver clonked back on its bracket, and Kinglake said, with the nearest approach to humanity that Simon had yet heard in his gravel voice: "That's fine. And now what in hell am I going to tell those muggs outside?"

CHAPTER TEN

THE SAINT could string words into barbed wire, but he also knew when and how to be merciful. He smiled at the Lieutenant without the slightest trace of malice or gloating. He was purely practical.

"Tell 'em I spilled my guts. Tell 'em I gave you the whole story, which you can't repeat because it's temporarily a war secret and the FBI is taking over anyhow; but of course you knew all about it all the time. Tell 'em I'm just an ambitious amateur trying to butt into something that's too big for him: you scared the daylights out of me, which is all you really wanted to do. Tell 'em I folded up like a flower when I tried to sell you my line and you really got tough. So I quit; and you were big-hearted and let me hightail out of here. Make me into any kind of a jerk that suits you, because I don't want the other kind of publicity and you can get credit for the pinch anyway."

"Why didn't you tell me this in the first place?" Kinglake wanted to know, rather petulantly.

"Because I didn't know anything about you, or your political problems. Which were somewhat involved, as it turns out." The Saint was very calmly candid. "After that, I knew even less about your team. I mean guys like Yard and Callahan. This is a small town, as big towns go, and it wouldn't take long for one man's secret to become everybody's rumor. You know how it is. I might not have gotten very far that way."

Kinglake dragged another of his foul stogies out of his vest pocket, glared at it pessimistically, and finally bit off the end as if he had nerved himself to take a bite of a rotten apple. His concluding expression conveyed the notion that he had.

"And I always knew you for a crook," he said disconsolately.

The Saint's smile was almost nostalgically dreamy.

"I always was, in a technical sort of way," he said softly. "And I may be again. But there's a war on; and some odd people can find a use for some even odder people. . . . For that matter, there was a time when I thought you might be a crooked cop, which can be worse."

"I guess you know how that is, too," Kinglake said, sourly but sufficiently. "You sounded as if you did."

"I think that's all been said," Simon replied temperately. "We're just playing a new set of rules. For that matter, if I'd been playing some of my old rules, I think I could have found a way to pull a fast one on you, with or without the audience, and taken that heater away from you, and made time out of here no matter what you were threatening. I've done it before. I just thought this was the best way tonight."

The Lieutenant glanced guiltily at his half forgotten gun, and stuffed it back into his hip holster.

"Well?" He repeated the word without any of the aggressive implications that he had thrown into it the last time. "Can you feed me any of this story that I'm supposed to have known all along, or should I just go on clamming up because I don't know?"

Simon deliberately reduced his cigarette by the length of two measured inhalations. In between them, he measured the crestfallen Lieutenant once more for luck. After that he had no more hesitation.

If he hadn't been able to judge men down to the last things that made them tick, he wouldn't have been what he was or where he was at that instant. He could be wrong often and anywhere, incidentally, but not in the fundamentals of situation and character.

He said quite casually then, as it seemed to him after his decision was made: "It's just one of those stories . . ."

He swung a leg over the arm of his chair, pillowed his chin on his knee, and went on through a drift of smoke when he was ready.

"I've got to admit that the theory I set up in the *Times-Tribune* didn't just spill out of my deductive genius. It was almost ancient history to me. That's what brought me to Galveston and into your hair. The only coincidence I wasn't expecting, and which I didn't even get on to for some time afterwards, was that the body I nearly ran over out there in the marshes would turn out to be Henry Stephen Matson—the guy I came here to find."

"What did you want him for?"

"Because he was a saboteur. He worked in two or three war plants where acts of sabotage occurred, although he was never suspected. No gigantic jobs, but good serious sabotage just the same. The FBI found that out when they checked back on him. But the way they got on to him was frankly one of those weird accidents that are always waiting to trip up the most careful

villains. He had a bad habit of going out and leaving the lights on in his
room. About the umpteenth time his landlady had gone up and turned them
out, she thought of leaving a note for him about it. But she didn't have a
pencil with her, and she didn't see one lying around. So she rummaged
about a bit, and found an Eversharp in one of his drawers. She started to
write, and then the lead broke. She tried to produce another one, and nothing happened. So she started fiddling with it and unscrewing things, and
suddenly the pencil came apart and a lot of stuff fell out of it that certainly
couldn't have been the inner workings of an Eversharp. She was a bright
woman. She managed to put it together again, without blowing herself
up, and put it back where she found it and went out and told the FBI—of
course, she knew that Matson was working for a defense plant. But it's a
strictly incredible story, and exactly the sort of thing that's always happening."

"One of these days it'll probably happen to you," Kinglake said; but his
stern features relaxed in the nearest approximation to a smile that they
were capable of.

The Saint grinned.

"It has," he said. . . . "Anyway, Matson had an FBI man working next
to him from then on, so he never had a chance to pull anything."

"Why wasn't he arrested?"

"Because if he'd done other jobs in other places, there was a good chance
that he had contacts with a general sabotage organisation, and that's what
we've been trying to get on to for a long time. That's why I went to St Louis.
But before I arrived there, he'd scrammed. I don't think he knew he was
being watched. But Quenco was much tougher than anything he'd
tackled before. You don't have any minor sabotage in an explosives factory.
You just have a loud noise and a large hole in the ground. I think Matson
got cold feet and called it a day. But he wasn't a very clever fugitive. I'm
not surprised that the mob caught up with him so quickly. He left a trail
that a wooden Indian could have followed. I traced him to Baton Rouge
in double time, and when I was there I heard from Washington that he'd
applied for a passport and given his address as the Ascot Hotel in Galveston.
He was afraid that his goose was cooked. It was, too—to a crisp."

"You were figuring on getting into his confidence and finding out what
he knew."

"Maybe something like that. If I could have done it. If not, I'd have
tried whatever I had to—even to the extent of roasting him myself. Only
I'd have done it more slowly. I thought he might have some informative
notes written down. A guy like that would be liable to do that sort of
thing, just for insurance. Like Vaschetti. . . . I want that ostrich-skin case
that was in his gladstone lining; and I want Vaschetti's diary of his trips

and meetings. With those two items, we may be able to clean up practically the whole sabotage system from coast to coast."

"What do you mean by 'we'?" Kinglake asked curiously. "I've heard of this Imperative number; but is it a branch of the FBI?"

Simon shook his head.

"It's something much bigger. But don't ask me, and don't ask anyone else. And don't remember that I ever mentioned it."

Kinglake looked at the chewed end of his stogie.

"I just want you to know," he said, "that I had Matson figured as an ordinary gang killing, and that's why I would have let it ride. If I'd known it was anything like this, nobody could have made me lay off."

The Saint nodded.

"I guessed that. That's why I've talked to you. Now we've spent enough time for you to be able to put over your story; and I've got to be moving."

"You know where you're going?"

"Yes." Simon stood up and crushed out his cigarette. "You may hear from me again tonight."

The Lieutenant held out his hand and said: "Good luck."

"Thanks," said the Saint, and went out.

Rowden and Yard and the *Times-Tribune,* standing in a little huddle down the corridor, turned and fanned out to stare at him as he strolled towards them. Then the Lieutenant's voice came from the doorway behind him.

"Mr Templar is leaving. Now you can all come back here."

"You know," Simon said earnestly, to Detective Yard, "I do wish your first name was Scotland."

He sauntered on, leaving his favorite plainclothes man gawping after him like a punch-drunk St Bernard whose succored victim has refused to take a drink out of its keg.

Kinglake's trephining eyes reamed the blank questioning faces of his returned entr'acteurs. He clamped his teeth defiantly into his stogie, and drew a deep breath. In that breath, every wisp of the convenient alibi that Simon Templar had suggested was swept away, and he was standing solidly on a decision of his own.

"If you want to know what we were talking about," he clipped out, "Templar was giving me a stall, and I pretended to fall for it. Now I'm going to see where he takes me. Yard, you can take charge here. I'm going to follow the Saint myself, and I'm going to bust this whole case if it takes me till Christmas."

"But, Lieutenant," protested the dumbfounded Yard, "what about the Chief? What about . . ."

"The Chief," Kinglake said shortly, "and the Commissioner, and the Sheriff, and everybody behind them, can——"

He did not say that they could jump in the lake, or go climb a tree, or perform any of the more conventional immolations. It is indeed highly doubtful whether they could have done what the Lieutenant said they could do. But Kinglake was not very concerned just then with literal accuracy. He had an objective of his own which mattered a lot more to him, and he left his extraordinary statement fluttering forgotten in the air behind him as he stalked out.

Simon Templar was also dominated by one single idea. The murder of Matson had been unfortunate, but he could exonerate himself from it. The murder of Vaschetti had been still more unfortunate, but the excuses he could make for himself for that were flimsy gauze before his own ruthless self-criticism. But his reaction to that had already reversed itself into a positive driving force that would go on until the skies fell apart—or he did. For the ungodly to have murdered two men almost under his nose and within split seconds of giving him the precious information that he had to get was an insolence and an effrontery that he was going to make them wish they had never achieved. The Saint was angry now in a reckless cold savage way, not as he had been when he first went from Police Headquarters to the offices of the *Times-Tribune,* but in a way that could only be soothed out in blood.

And now he thought he knew where he was going to find the blood that night.

A taxi took him to the Blue Goose; but this time he didn't need the driver to vouch for him. The doorkeeper remembered him, and let him in at once. He walked through the blue melodious dimness towards the bar, loose-limbed and altogether at his ease; yet there were filaments stirring through all the length of him that kept no touch at all with that lazily debonair demeanor. He caught sight of Olga Ivanovitch sitting at a table with another girl and two obvious wholesale bottle-cap salesmen, but he only gave her a casual wave and went on to find a stool at the bar. He knew she would join him, and he waited good-humoredly while the brawny blond bartender worked over complicated mixtures for a complicated quartet at the other end of the counter.

Then she was beside him; and he knew it by the perfume she used and the cool satin of her hand before he looked at her.

"I'm glad you got here," she said. "Did you get your job done?"

She was exactly the same, lovely and docile, as if she was only glad of him and wanting to be glad for him; as if death had never struck near her or walked with the men she knew.

Simon made a movement of his head that seemed to answer the question unless one stopped to wonder whether it meant yes or no. He went on before that could happen: "I nearly didn't come here. What I'd really hoped to do was curl up at home with a good book from the circulating library."

"What was the book?"

"Just a piece of some guy's autobiography. However, when I went to pick it up, it was gone. A man named Nick Vaschetti had it earlier in the evening. He hadn't finished with it—but he has now. I suppose you wouldn't know where it is?"

Her eyes were still pools of emerald in the mask of her face.

"Why do you say that?" She seemed to have difficulty in articulating. "Lots of people read. It occurred to me——"

"I mean that this—this Vaschetti—hadn't finished with the book—but he has now?"

"He's given up reading," explained the Saint carelessly. "He was so upset about having the book taken away from him that he stepped out of an eighth-floor window—with the help of a couple of your pals."

He watched the warm ivory of her face fade and freeze into alabaster. "He's—dead?"

"Well," said the Saint, "it was a long drop to the sidewalk, and on account of the rubber shortage he didn't bounce so well."

The bartender was standing over them expectantly. Simon said: "Dawson for me; and I guess you know what the lady's drinking." He became absorbed in the way the man worked with his big deft hands.

And then suddenly he knew all about everything, and it was like waking up under an ice-cold shower.

He took his breath back gradually, and said without a change in his voice except that the smile was no longer there: "You don't know Brother Blatt and his playmates very well, do you, Olga? Especially Maris. But if I'd only been a little brighter I'd have just stayed here and found Maris."

She was staring at him rigidly, with wide tragical eyes. It was a good act, he thought cynically.

The bartender stirred their drinks and set them up, fastidiously wiping spots of moisture from the bar around them. Simon appealed to him.

"I should have asked you in the first place, shouldn't I, Joe? You could have shown me Maris."

The man's big square face began to crinkle in its ready accommodating smile.

And the Saint knew he was right—even though the conclusion had come to him in one lightning-flash of revelation, and the steps towards it still had to be retraced.

Maris, the man nobody knew. Maris, the man nobody had ever heard of. The truly invisible man. The man whom the assistant manager of the

Ascot might have been referring to, and have forgotten, even, when he said that he had been chatting with a friend when Nick Vaschetti came home to die. The man nobody ever saw, or ever would see; because they never looked.

Simon lifted his glass and took a sip from it.

"You could have told me, couldn't you?" he said, with his eyes like splinters of blue steel magnetised to the man's face. "Because everybody calls you Joe, but they don't give a damn about your last name. And I don't suppose you'd tell them it's Maris, anyway."

It was strange that everything could be so clear up to that instant, and then be blotted out in an explosion of blackness that sprang from somewhere behind his right ear and dissolved the universe into a timeless midnight.

CHAPTER ELEVEN

THERE WERE bells tolling in the distance.

Enormous sluggish bells that paused in interminable suspense between each titanic *bong!* of their clappers.

Simon Templar was floating through stygian space towards them, so that the clanging became louder and sharper and the tempo became more rapid as he sped towards it.

He was hauling on the bell cords himself. It seemed vaguely ridiculous to be ringing peals for your own funeral, but that was what he was doing.

His arms ached from the toil. They felt as though they were being pulled out of their sockets. And the knell was blending into pain and sinking under it. A pain that swelled and receded like a leaden tide . . . like a pulse beat . . .

His mind came back gradually out of the dark, awakening to the realisation that the carillon was being played inside his own cranium, and the pain was synchronised with the beating of his own heart.

He became aware that he was in a windowless chamber with some sort of plastered rock walls. A naked light bulb shone in the middle of the low ceiling. It was a cellar. There were collections and scatterings of the kind of junk that accumulates in cellars. There was an ugly iron furnace; and lines and criss-crosses of pipe hung high under the ceiling, wandering from point to point on undivinable errands, like metal worms in exposed transit from one hole to another.

He was close to one of the walls, sagging downward and outward, his whole weight hanging from his outstretched arms. He had been tied by the wrists to two of the overhead pipes, about six feet from the floor and the same distance apart. That accounted for the ache in his arms. Otherwise, he was unconfined.

He found the floor with his feet and straightened his knees. That eased the racking strain on his joints and ligaments, and reduced the pain of the ropes biting into his wrists, and might eventually give the throbbing of his strangled circulation a chance to die down. But it was the only constructive movement he could make.

Then he saw Olga Ivanovitch.

She was against the wall at right angles to his, tied to the pipes in exactly the same manner; but she was quite conscious and standing upright. She didn't look trim and sleek as he had last seen her. One of the braids of her coiled hair had broken loose and fallen over her shoulder like a drooping wing, and the demure dark dress she had been wearing was disheveled and torn away from one creamy shoulder and the lift of a breast. She was watching the Saint's recovery with eyes like scorched holes in the desperate pallor of her beauty.

It was the shock of recognition as much as anything which helped to clear the rest of the fuzzy cobwebs from his brain. His headache was more bearable now, but he had an idea that he wouldn't want anyone to lay a heavy hand on the place behind his right ear where it seemed to come from.

"To digress a moment from what we were saying," he managed to remark aloud in a thick voice that grew clearer and stronger with each passing breath, "what the hell did Joe hit me with—a boomerang? I only took a sip of that drink, and it wasn't any worse than the stuff they served me before."

"Blatt hit you from behind," she said. "He came up behind you while you were talking. I tried to warn you with my eyes. He was very quick, and nobody would have seen it. Then he caught you, and they said you were drunk and passed out. They took you into a back room, and that was the end of it."

Simon glanced at his surroundings again. They were depressingly reminiscent of many similar surroundings that he had been in before. He seemed to have had a great deal of his life being knocked on the head and tied up in cellars.

"And so, by one easy transfer," he observed, "we arrive in the bomb-proof doghouse."

"This is the cellar of my house. There is a back way out of the Blue Goose. They took you out and brought you here."

"Well, well, well. We certainly do lead a hectic life. Never a dull moment."

Her gaze was wondering.

"You jest in the face of certain death. Are you a fatalist, or are you only a fool?"

"I've certainly acted like a fool," Simon admitted ruefully. "But as for this death business—that shouldn't lose you any sleep. You didn't have any nightmares over Matson, did you?"

"I have seen too much to have nightmares," she said wearily. "But I give you my word that I have never had a hand in any murder. I didn't know they were going to kill Matson. I knew nothing about him, except that he was one of their men, and I was told to amuse him. But after he had been killed—what could I do? I couldn't bring him back to life, or even prove that they did it. And Vaschetti. I thought Vaschetti was safe in jail when I . . ."

"When you what?"

"When I went to his room this afternoon to see if I could find—anything."

The Saint wondered if the blow on his head had done something to him. He looked at her through a film of unreality.

He said: "Such as a diary of names and places?"

"Anything. Anything I could find. I thought he might have kept something, and I wanted it."

"What for—blackmail?"

"To turn over to the FBI, when I had enough."

He had learned before that he couldn't needle her, but it was a discovery that she could astound him.

"You mean you were planning to sell your own gang down the river?"

"Of course."

Maybe it was better to occupy his twinging head with material things. On due consideration, he admired the basic ingenuity of the way he was tied up. It was so simple and practical and economical of rope, and yet it completely eliminated all the standard tricks of escape. There was no chance of reaching a knot with the fingertips or the teeth, or cleverly breaking a watch-glass and sawing the cords on a sharp fragment, or employing any of the other devices which have become so popular in these situations. It was one of the most effective systems the Saint had encountered in an exceptionally privileged experience, and he made a mental note to use it on his next prisoner.

Meanwhile he said, without much subtlety: "But would that have been cricket, tovarich? Do you want me to believe that anyone so beautiful could sink so low?"

For an instant he thought that he actually struck a flash from her green eyes.

"Why do you think I'm here now—tovarich?"

"I had wondered about that," he said. "But I decided you might have a fetish about being crucified."

"I'm here because they don't trust me any more. I helped to bring you here. I wanted them to believe I was still helping them. I couldn't do anything else. . . . And I was only waiting for a chance to help you. . . . They tied you up. I helped them. And then, suddenly, they took hold of me and tied me up too. I fought them, but it was no use."

"You have such a sweet honest face—why wouldn't they trust you?"

"That was because of what you said in the Blue Goose," she told him without resentment. "You asked me if I had Vaschetti's book. Before that, they thought it was you who had been there first. But when Maris heard you accuse me he was suspicious. They knew that I liked you, and I had seen you. And for Maris, a little suspicion is enough."

Simon decided that there was not so much profit in standing upright as he had hoped. If he rested his arms, the cords gnawed at his wrists again; if he favored his wrists, the strain of fatigue on his shoulders tautened slowly into exquisite torture. He had had no sensation in his hands and no control of his fingers for some time.

"And you really expect me to swallow that without water?" he asked scornfully.

"It doesn't matter much what you believe now," she replied tiredly. "It's too late. We shall both be dead in a little while. We cannot escape; and Siegfried is pitiless."

"Pardon me if I get a bit confused among all these people, but who is Siegfried?"

"Siegfried Maris. You call him Joe. I think he is the head of the Nazi sabotage organisation in the United States."

The Saint thought so too. He had had that all worked out before Blatt hit him on the head. It explained why Matson had ever gone to the Blue Goose at all. It explained why Vaschetti had touched there in his travels. It explained why the Blue Goose played such a part in the whole incident— why it was the local focus of infection, and why it could send its tendrils of corruption into honest local political dishonesty, squeezing and pressing cunningly here and there, using the human failings of the American scene to undermine America. A parasitic vine that used the unassuming and unconscious flaws in its host to destroy the tree. . . . It was not incredible that the prime root of the growth should turn out to be Siegfried Maris, whom everyone knew as Joe. Simon had always had it in his mind that the man he was hunting for would turn out to be someone that everybody called Joe. And this was the man. The man who could have anything around and not be part of it; who could always say, whatever happened, that he just happened to be legitimately there. The man nobody saw, in the place nobody thought of . . .

"Comrade Maris," said the Saint, "has been offstage far too much. It's not fair to the readers. What is he doing now?"

"I expect he's upstairs, with the others. Searching my house."

"He must like the place. How long have we been here?"

"Not very long. Not long at all."

"What's he searching for?"

"The book," she said. "Vaschetti's little book."

"Why here?"

"Because I did find it. Because it has half the code names and meeting places in this country listed in it. But Maris will find it. I couldn't hide it very well."

Simon was able to shrug his left shoulder tentatively. No weight dragged on it. They would have found and taken the gun in his spring holster, of course. It wouldn't have been much use to him if they hadn't. However . . .

"So it was you who tore Vaschetti's room at the Ascot apart," he said. "But your mob thought it was me. That's why my room was gone over this evening while we were out together, and a colored friend of mine nearly had colored kittens. You aren't overlooking any bets, are you? And since Vaschetti's indiscreet memoirs are still missing—not to mention Brother Matson's notes and papers——"

"They have those," she said listlessly. "They were in the gladstone bag."

He was shaken as if he had been jolted in the ribs; but he went on.

"So anyway, we now have a well-staged scene in the old torture chamber, where you trick me into revealing where I have hidden all these priceless documents. You're doing a great show, Olga. If I could get my hands together I would applaud. You must be a full-fledged member of this lodge of Aryan cut throats."

"Think what you please," she said indifferently. "It makes no difference."

She could always make him feel wrong. Like now, when she was not angry, but wounded in everything but dignity. Because that devastating ingenuousness of hers was real; because the bridges she walked on were firm and tried, and she had built them herself, and she was as sure of them and her way as he was sure of his own. There could be no facile puncturing of a foundation like that, with a skilled flick of the wrist.

She said, without any emotion: "You think of me as a mercenary adventuress. I don't deny it. I have worked for Maris—and other men—only for money. But that was before the Nazis invaded Russia. You will not believe that a greedy adventuress could have a heart, or a conscience. But it made all the difference to me. . . . I pretended that it didn't. I went on working for them—taking their money, doing what they told me, trying to keep their trust. But I was only waiting and working for the time when I could send all of them to the hell where they belong. . . . Yet, I had my own sins to redeem. I had done wrong things, too. That's why I thought that if I could bring something with me, something big enough to prove that all my heart had changed—then perhaps your FBI would understand and forgive me, and let me begin again here. . . . I could swear all this to you; but what is swearing without faith?"

The Saint's head was much clearer now. He saw her again through the ruthless screen of his disbelief. And still she wasn't trying to sell him from behind the counter of any phony job of tying-up. Her wrists were lashed as cruelly tight as his own. He could see the livid ridges in her skin where the ropes cut. Her face was damp like his was from strain and pain.

"Damn it, tovarich," he said musingly, "you could act anyone in Hollywood off the screen. You've almost convinced me that you're on the level. You couldn't possibly be, but you sound just like it."

Her eyes were unwavering against his, and they looked very old. But that was from the patience of a great sadness.

"I only wish you could have believed me before the end. It would have been nicer. But it will not be long now. Siegfried Maris is one of the most important men that Hitler has in this country. He won't take any chances with us."

"At least," said the Saint, "we should feel flattered about getting the personal attention of the big shot himself."

He had crossed his left leg over his right now, but it was not with the idea of striking an elegant and insouciant pose. He was pressing the outsides of his legs together, feeling for something. He had been searched and disarmed, he knew; but there was his own special armory which the ungodly didn't always . . .

"If we could have caught Maris," Olga was saying, out of that passionless and regretful resignation, "it would have meant as much as winning a battle at the front. I would have liked to do that very much. Then we could have been quite happy about this."

It was too good to be true; but it was true. He could feel the solid flat hardness of the haft and blade between the movements of his legs. And with that, he had a fantastic inspiration that might grow into a fantastic escape. But he had seen fantasy come real too often to discard it for nothing but its name.

The glint in his eyes was like sunlight on cut sapphires.

"Maybe we can still be happy, Olga," he said; and there was a lilt of exultant vitality in his voice. "We'll try to repeat a significant scrap of United Nations history. You, like some other Russians, were petting the wrong dog. Until you saw the error of your ways. And it bit you. Now I shall try to come through with the lend-lease matériel."

CHAPTER TWELVE

OLGA IVANOVITCH stared at him as though she was certain now that he was out of his mind.

"No, darling, I'm not," he said, before she could put her own words to it. "I was just remembering a movie serial that I saw as a boy, which starred the greatest of all escape artists—Harry Houdini."

"How interesting," she said blankly.

It was lucky, he thought, that he liked his shoes loose and comfortable. Otherwise, getting them off might have been quite a problem. As it was, he was able to tread on one heel with the opposite instep and force one shoe off with only a moderate amount of violence. The other shoe presented a little more difficulty, without a hard welt to scrape against, but he went on working at it.

"Now don't go all Russian on me and relapse into brooding despair," he pleaded. "You ought to be interested in the late Mr Houdini. He was a real maestro at getting out of situations like this. I was thinking of one installment in which he was tied to some sort of Oriental torture wheel, in very much the same way as we're tied up now. He managed to worry his shoes and socks off, and neatly unfastened the knots on his wrists with his toes."

He had the other shoe off at last. The socks were easier. He only had to tread on a bit of slack at each toe in turn and pull his feet out.

"So what?" Olga said skeptically. "Can you even reach your wrists with your toes?"

"Now you're coming to life," Simon approved. "I used to be a fairly agile guy before I started drinking myself to death, and I think I can manage that." He twisted his body and balanced himself on one foot, and swung his other leg lithely up to kick his hand. "There. I always knew all those years I spent in the Follies chorus would come in handy some day," he said contentedly.

"But the knots," she said in the same tone as before; yet it was already being contradicted by the curiosity kindling in her eyes.

"I'm afraid I'm not quite that good," he confessed. "However, I have an alternative solution for them which Harry might not have considered entirely ethical."

He was already working up his right trouser leg with his naked left foot. Under the amazed eyes of the girl, the upper end of the sheath and the haft of his knife came into view. He grasped the shaft with his toes and drew the blade gently out of the scabbard and laid it on the floor.

"When I was swinging through the trees in my last incarnation," he said, "this would have been duck soup for me. But I'm a bit out of practice these days."

He was concentrating singly on the knife, maneuvering it between his two feet, getting the firmest possible grip on the handle between his big toe and the one next to it, adjusting and testing it before he made a decisive move. There was no sound in the room but the faint scuff of his efforts. His wrists hurt like hell; but he had forgotten about them. The sweat was standing out on his forehead by the time he was satisfied.

· "Now we get to the really fancy part of the trick," he said. "Like the man on the flying trapeze without a net, I won't be able to go back and start over if I muff it."

He poised himself in the same way as he had done for his preliminary experiment, but much more carefully, gauged his distances, and drew a deep breath and held it.

Then he swung his leg, aiming the razor edge of the blade at the link of rope between his left wrist and the pipe.

Once, twice, three times he repeated the same pendulum movement, trying to strike the same spot on the rope each time, feeling the keen blade bite the fibers at every stroke.

Then the knife twisted between his toes; but he managed to keep a precarious hold on it. He brought it gingerly down to the floor and adjusted it again, with the aid of his left foot, in an intolerable hush of intense patience and concentration.

He swung his leg again.

Once more.

Twice more.

The knife spun out of his hold and clattered to the floor.

It was beyond his reach, and beyond hers.

He heard the girl's pent-up breath break out of her lungs in a long throaty sob, and saw tears swimming in her eyes.

He knew then, at last, without thinking about it any more, that she had told him the truth. He had been unsure. He had taken a chance on it, because he was forced to, but wondering all the time if this would end up as the supreme sadism of tantalisation—if after he had revealed his secret weapon, and freed himself, if he could free himself, she would only call out, and Maris would walk in with a gun, and all the hope and struggle would have been for nothing. Now he knew. She couldn't have gasped and wept like that, otherwise; wouldn't have needed to, no matter how well she was playing a part.

It was worth something to be sure of that.

The Saint smiled grimly as he inspected the section of rope that he had been working on. He had done a good job, in spite of everything. It wasn't anything like the rope it had been before.

"I forgot to mention," he murmured, "that when I was in the circus I also used to break chains and tow tanks around with one hand."

Then with an abrupt and feral outburst of titanic effort he threw all his weight and strength together against the partly severed cords, dropping his weight on them with a plunging jerk, and simultaneously thrusting himself away from the wall with his feet and contracting his arms together with all the power of his torso. The veins swelled in his neck, and the muscles rippled over his body in quivering waves. For an instant it felt as if his wrists were being bitten off. . . .

And then, with a suddenness that was physically sickening, the frayed and slashed portion of rope parted with a snap that flung him whirling outward and around.

He heard the girl sob again; but this time it was with a note of almost hysterical laughter.

He regained his balance without a waste motion, and fell to attacking the knots that bound his right hand.

"I must be slipping," he said. "I used to do things like that just to warm up."

The knots weren't so easy. His hands were numb, and he had to drive deliberate commands through for every movement of his fingers. He worked as fast as he could through that nightmarish impediment.

At last he was free. His wrists were chafed and bleeding a little. But that was nothing. The sense of freedom, of triumph, was like an intoxicating wind blowing through the reviving spaces of his soul.

He scooped up his knife, a little awkwardly because of the cramp in his hands, and cut Olga loose. She almost fell against him, and he had to hold her up for a moment. Until her clinging grew up from the weakness of reaction into something else.

Then he steadied her on her feet and left her standing while he went back to put on his shoes and socks. The return of circulation was filling his hands with pins and needles; but gradually, with the relentless exertion, his fingers began to feel less like swollen frozen sausages.

"There is a way out of here without going through the house," she was saying breathlessly. "We can slip out without them ever knowing that we've gone."

"Slip out?" He glanced up at her. "Darling, that would be a hell of an anticlimax. I'm going upstairs now and get Matson's notes and Vaschetti's diary away from dear old Joe!"

"But how can you?" she cried. "He'll shoot you like a dog. They took your gun. I saw them. We can call the police——"

Simon straightened up, and looked down in silent reckless laughter at her desperate imploring face.

"I've got my knife," he said; "but I haven't got any guarantee that the police would get here in time. And meanwhile Maris and Co might find out that we'd got away, and decide to take the brakes off themselves. We don't want to risk that now. And besides, we've got to deliver you as a certified heroine. Remember?" Her soft scarlet lips were only a few inches away, turned up to him below the liquid pools of her eyes; and once again he was aware of their distracting provocation. He said: "Thanks just the same for being so concerned about me. It ought to be worth at least . . ."

Then she was in his arms, her breath warm against his cheek, and all of her asking for him; and then he was bruising her moist mouth with his own, and it would never be like that again, but there was no time for that now and perhaps there never had been. It was like so many things in his life: they were always too late, and there was never any time.

He disengaged himself very gently.

"Now," he said, "we will have the last word with Joe."

The door on the other side of the cellar was not locked. Simon went up the crude wooden stairs, very quietly, and was conscious of Olga Ivanovitch following him. But he didn't look back. He came out through another un-latched door into the hall of the house. There was no guard there either. Obviously, Maris and his crew had great faith in the durability of manila hemp and the efficacy of their trussing system.

Which was reasonable enough; just as the Saint's faith in his knife was reasonable. He knew what it could do, and what he could do with it. He knew how it could transform itself into a streak of living quicksilver, swift as the flash of light from its polished blade, true as a rifle, deadly as any bullet that was ever launched by erupting chemicals.

He held it delicately in his resensitised fingers, frail and strong as a bird, only waiting for him to release it into life.

He was outside another door then, listening, when the voice came firmly through it to his ears. Just a voice: the voice of Siegfried Maris, generally known as Joe. But coming with a clear suddenness that was like traveling back in time and never having heard a talking picture, and suddenly hearing a screen speak.

It said: "Keep your hands well up, Lieutenant. Please don't try anything stupid. It wouldn't do you any good."

And then Kinglake's savage growl: "You son of a bitch—how did you get out of the Blue Goose?"

The Saint's mouth opened and closed again in a noiseless gasp, and a ripple of irresistible laughter rose up through him like a stream of bubbles to break soundlessly at his lips. Even at a moment like that he had to enjoy the perfection of that finishing touch.

"We have our own way out," Maris replied calmly. "It's very useful, as you see. But if you didn't know about it, how did you follow us here?"

"I didn't. When I didn't find Templar at the Blue Goose, I thought he might have come here with Ivanovitch."

"An excellent deduction, Lieutenant. And quite correct. He did come here with Ivanovitch. But that wasn't his choice. . . . It's very fortunate that you're a detective and not a burglar, isn't it? If you'd been a burglar you wouldn't have made such a clumsy entrance, and it mightn't have been half so easy to catch you."

Simon settled his fingers on the door knob as if it had been a wafer-shelled egg. He began to turn it with micrometric gentleness.

"You bastards," Kinglake said. "What have you done with them?"

"You'll see for yourself, when you join them in just a few minutes."

"So you're Maris, are you? I should have known it."

"A pardonable oversight, Lieutenant. But you may still call me Joe, if it will make you feel more comfortable."

Simon waited through an infinitesimal pause, with the door handle fully turned.

Kinglake said: "I guess you can have oversights too. You aren't getting away with anything, Joe. I've got men outside——"

The low hard chuckle of Maris came through the door.

"An old bluff, Lieutenant, but always worth trying. I know that you came alone. Fritzie was watching you outside, and we made sure of that before we let you break in. Now if you'll be very careful about holding your arms up while Blatt takes your gun——"

That was the pleasantly dramatic moment when it seemed right to the Saint to throw the door wide open.

It was a nice composition that framed itself through the opening, a perfect instant of arrested motion, artistic and satisfactory. There was Lieutenant Kinglake standing with his hands up and his jaw tensed and a stubborn snarl around his eyes, with Johan Blatt advancing towards him. Fritzie Weinbach stood a little off to the right, with a big snub-nosed automatic leveled at the detective's sternum. Simon could identify them both without ever having seen them before—the tall blond man and the fat red man with the cold bleached eyes.

He saw Siegfried Maris too, for the first time as the man he was instead of the forgotten bartender called Joe. It was amazing what a difference there was. He sat behind a desk, without the disguise of the white coat and the quick obsequious serving movements, wearing an ordinary dark business suit, and obviously the dominant personality of the group. For ultimate proof, he even had a flat light tan case and a shabby pocket memorandum book among some papers on the blotter in front of him. Simon knew even from where he stood that they must be the notes of Henry Stephen Matson and the diary of Nick Vaschetti. It was all there.

And Maris was there, with his square powerful face that hadn't a natural smile in any line of it; and he was turning towards the interruption with his eyes widening and one of his strong swift hands already starting to move; and the Saint knew without any further study, without a second's hesitation, that this was the one man he had to get and be sure of, no matter what else happened afterwards.

The knife sped from his hand like a glitter of leaping silver, flying like a splinter of living light straight for the newly retired bartender's throat.

Then Lieutenant Kinglake had taken advantage of the diversion to make a grab for his gun, and the room was full of thunder and the dry stinging tang of cordite.

CHAPTER THIRTEEN

SIMON TEMPLAR didn't carve notches in the handle of his knife, because they would eventually have affected the balance, and he was used to it and he hoped it would last for a long time. He did worry about rust and the way it could dull a blade. He wiped the blade very carefully on Maris's shirt before he put the knife back in its sheath.

"Let's face it," he said; "he did pour some of the lousiest drinks I ever paid for."

Kinglake was reloading his Police Positive with the unconscious detachment of prehistorically rooted habit.

He said, almost awkwardly for him: "I just wanted to be in at the death."

"You were," Simon assured him, somewhat unnecessarily.

"Are there any more of 'em?"

"Quite a lot—I hope. But not around here. And we don't have to bother about them. Just turn that stuff on the desk over to the FBI. The rest will be their routine."

"I'd sure like to know what happened to you."

The Saint told him.

Kinglake scratched his head.

"I've seen plenty in my time, believe it or not," he said. "But you've topped all of it." He ended up with an admission. "I'll have to think of a new story now, though; because I messed up the one you gave me."

"It doesn't matter," said the Saint. "Whatever you said, you can tell 'em you only said it for a stall, because you couldn't give out with what you really knew. The true story is your story now. Only leaving me out. There's plenty of evidence on that desk. Go on and grab yourself some glory."

"But these are the three guys you named in the *Times-Tribune*."

"So what? So I happened to know too much, and I was too smart for anybody's good. You knew just as much if not more, but you were playing a cagey game. You say that by shooting my mouth off like that I told Maris and Co that they were hot, and nearly ruined all your well-laid plans. That's why you were so hopping mad about me. In fact, you had to perform superhuman feats to salvage the situation after I balled it up. Say anything you like. I won't contradict you. It suits me better that way. And there's nobody else left who can call you a liar."

The Lieutenant's steely eyes flickered over the room. The truth of that last theorem was rather gruesomely irrefutable.

Then his glance went to Olga Ivanovitch.

She stood very quietly beside the Saint, her pale face composed and expressionless, her green eyes passing unemotionally over the raw stains and ungainly attitudes of violent death. You could tell nothing about what she thought or expected, if she expected anything. She waited, in an incurious calm that suddenly struck Simon as almost regal; she hadn't asked anything or said anything.

"What about her?" Kinglake asked.

Simon's pockets had been emptied completely. He bent over one of the bodies and relieved it of a packet of cigarettes that it wouldn't be needing any more.

"I'm afraid I was holding out on you about her," he answered deliberately. "She's one of our people. Why the hell do you think she was tied up in the cellar with me? But I couldn't tell you before."

He was so easy and matter-of-fact with it that the Lieutenant only tried to look unstartled.

"But what story am I supposed to give out?"

"Like me—the less you say about her the better," Simon told him. "She was just one of the hostesses at the Blue Goose, and Maris was making use of her through his rôle of bartender. He set her up in this house, so he had a key. But she wasn't here tonight. When the setup began to look too sticky, she scrammed. You don't think she's worth fussing about."

Simon hadn't looked at the girl until then. He did now.

"By the way," he said casually, "you'd better get a move on with this scramming act. Kinglake is going to have to call Headquarters in a few minutes. You can scram in my car—it won't take me more than ten minutes to check out of the Alamo House. Go and put some things in a bag."

"Yes," she said, impassively and obediently; and went out of the room. Simon smoked his inherited cigarette with unalloyed enjoyment.

Kinglake gathered the papers on the desk together and frowned over them wisely.

The Saint made another search of the unlamented ungodly, and found his own automatic in Weinbach's pocket. He nested it affectionately back in his clip holster.

The Lieutenant gazed yearningly at the telephone, tightened a spartan stopper on a reawakening ebullience of questions, and got out another of his miasmic cigars.

Olga Ivanovitch came in again.

She had changed into a simple gray suit with plain white trimmings. Her honey-colored hair was all in place again, and her face was cool and freshly sweetened. She looked younger than Simon had ever remembered her. She carried a pair of suitcases. Kinglake really looked at her.

Simon hitched himself off the corner of the desk where he had perched.

"Well," he said, "let's be on our way."

He shook hands with Kinglake for the last time, and picked up Olga's bags and went out with her. They went down the crushed coral walk through a rambling profusion of poinsettias and bougainvillea that were only dark clusters under the moon. The Gulf waters rolled against the beach beyond the seawall with a hushed friendly roar. Simon Templar thought about Jean Lafitte again, and decided that in the line of piracy he could still look the old boy in the eye on his home ground.

They left the gate; and the girl's step faltered beside him. He slowed with her, turning; and she stopped and faced him.

"*Spassibo*," she said, with an odd husky break in her voice. "Thank you, thank you, tovarich. . . . I don't think it's any use, but thank you."

"What do you mean, you don't think it's any use?"

Light seeping from a window of the house behind them like a timid thief in a dimout touched her pale halo of hair and glistened on her wide steady eyes.

"Where can I go now?"

The Saint laughed.

"My God, you Russians! Look, darling. You played along with Maris for quite a while. Several of the ungodly must know it. But they'll never know that Maris ever changed his mind about you. They'll only know that you got out of Galveston one jump ahead of the barrage. So you're all set to move in again somewhere else. That's what you wanted, isn't it? Well, I wasn't kidding either. That's what you're going to do. Only next time you'll do it legitimately—for the FBI or something like that. I'm taking you to Washington with me so you can meet a guy named Hamilton. I have to see him anyway. . . . Besides," he added constructively, "it's a dull trip, and we might make fun on the way."

THE MASKED ANGEL

From *Call for the Saint*

ANOTHER STORY I kept saying for years I would have to write some day was a story about prize fighting. Not that I am a particularly rabid fan of boxing, although I was a passable amateur in my youth, before I valued my brains too much to ignore the disadvantage of possibly having them beaten out. But just because I thought the Saint sooner or later had to get into everything.

I was reminded of this when the Saint radio show started on the air in 1945, and the prospective need for an endless (if you took an optimistic view of the future) number of original stories, at the relentless rate of one a week, stretched rather frighteningly ahead. In the first feverish struggle to line up a reserve of scripts, I was squeezing my memory for every unused idea I ever had, and this was one of the first to come back to me.

Of course I was not writing all the shows myself—to have done that, as well as producing them, as well as running a publishing business on the side, as I was then, as well as doing other writing of my own, would have been the schedule of a human dynamo, which I have never resembled. But I was supplying most of the ideas, and working closely with the writers who put the scripts together.

The collaborator I picked for this one was a solid radio writer named Irvin Ashkenazy; and it is about time he got some of the credit for it. I picked him because in his earlier and hungrier days in New York he himself fought several professional fights. He was never a threat to Jack Dempsey, and never aspired to be: it simply seemed like a relatively easy way to pick up a few honest dollars, which he badly needed. But it gave him the necessary background to do a good job on this subject, and any fortuitous air of authenticity this story may have it certainly owes to him.

Later I developed the radio script into the novelet you are about to read, and it was published in the *American* Magazine, and afterwards in a book.

But the thing that I treasure most that came out of that association with Mr Ashkenazy could not find a place in the radio script, or the subsequent novelet, and has had to remain my private joy until now.

It is that when Mr Ashkenazy was fighting these curtain-raisers, he felt perhaps understandably bashful about letting the fact be known to his family, his employers, or his more dignified acquaintances. Therefore he fought under an alias which, while it preserved traces of his own name, undoubtedly served to conceal his identity from anyone who might have happened on it in the sport sections of the newspapers. And one of the things for which I shall always love the guy is that he devised for himself a name that must be unique in the annals of the ring—the wonderful, the gorgeous, the superb *nom de guerre* of Izzy Ashcan.

THE MASKED ANGEL

A T THIS MOMENT Simon Templar was not quite enjoying the thrill of a lifetime.

Relaxed as much as the immediate carpentry would permit in his ringside seat between Hoppy Uniatz and Patricia Holm, he blended the smoke of his own cigarette with the cigar-and-sweat aroma of the Manhattan Arena, and contemplated the dying moments of the semi-final bout with his sapphire eyes musing under lazily drooping lids. Never addicted to obtaining his thrills vicariously, the man who was better known to the world as the Saint would have found small cause for excitement even if he had been addicted to such sedentary pursuits. Being there anyhow, he slouched in easy grace, the clean-cut lines of his face etched in a bronze mask of sardonic detachment as he watched the two gladiators move about the ring with all the slashing speed of ballet dancers in leg irons performing under water, and dedicated himself uncomplainingly to whatever entertainment the soirée of sock might provide.

In the great world outside, there were uncountable characters who would have considered his presence there with no equanimity. Some of them, who in one way or another had participated in much shadier promotions than prize fights, would have considered it a personal injustice that anyone like Simon Templar should still be at large when so many of their best friends were not. Others, whose standard of righteousness was vouched for by at least a badge, would have moaned just as loudly that there was nothing basically unhappy about a policeman's lot except what the Saint might plant in it.

If Inspector Fernack, for instance, had seen him there, that bulldogged minion of the law would have pondered darkly. He would have sensed from long experience in previous encounters with this amazing modern buccaneer that the Saint could have no orthodox interest in such a dreary offering of Promoter Mike Grady's salon of swat. Of course the main bout between Torpedo Smith and the celebrated Masked Angel would probably be more interesting, but Simon Templar wasn't there just for the entertainment. That was something John Henry Fernack would never have believed.

And on this occasion, for instance, he would have been right.

Jeers swept in derisive breakers over the two Ferdinands in the ring without in the least disturbing the equilibrium of their mitt minuet. The massed feet of the cash customers began to stamp in metronomic disapproval, and Simon's chair jumped as the boxcar brogans on his left added their pile-driving weight to the crashing cantata. Their owner's klaxon voice lifted in a laryngismal obbligato, a brassy, belly-searching ululation with overtones reminiscent of the retching bellow of a poisoned water buffalo. This, the Saint recognized, was merely Hoppy Uniatz's rendition of a disgusted groan.

"Boss," Hoppy heaved, "dis is moider!" The narrow strip of wrinkles that passed for Hoppy's forehead was deep with scorn. "I oughta go up dere and t'row 'em bot' outta de ring."

Hoppy's impulses were beautiful in their straightforward simplicity and homicidal honesty. The small globule of protoplasm that lurked within his rock-bound skull, serving the nominal function of a brain, piloted his anthropoidal body exclusively along paths of action, primitive and direct, unencumbered by any subtleties of thought or teleological considerations. The torture of cerebration he left entirely to the man to whose lucky star he had hitched his wagon. For, to Hoppy, the Saint was not of this ordinary world; he was a Merlin who brought strange wonders to pass with godlike nonchalance, whose staggering schemes were engineered with supernatural ease to inevitable success through miracles of intellect which Hoppy followed in blind but contented obedience.

The Saint smiled at him tenderly.

"Relax, chum. This isn't the fight we came to see anyway."

The dream with the spun-gold hair on Simon's right smiled.

"Never," admonished Patricia Holm, "look gift horses in the mouth."

"To corn a phrase," the Saint observed dryly.

"Huh?" Hoppy stared at the Saint's lady in openmouthed perplexity. "Horses?" His face, which bore a strong family resemblance to those seen on totem poles designed to frighten evil spirits, was a study in loose-lipped wonder. "What horses?"

"After all," Pat said, "we're here as guests and——"

The clanking of the bell terminated both the fight and the need for further explanation. The sound pulled the trigger on a thunderclap of boos as the unfatigued gladiators were waved to their respective corners to await the decision. It came swiftly. A well-booed draw.

"What a clambake," Hoppy muttered.

"No hits, no runs, no fight," Simon murmured sardonically.

"They had a lot of respect for each other, hadn't they?" Pat observed innocently.

"Respect!" Hoppy exploded. "Dem bums was doggin' it. I could beat bot' deir brains out togedder wit' bot' hands tied behind me." He simmered with righteous outrage. "I only hope de Masked Angel don't knock out Torpedo Smith *too* quick. Dey oughta let him stay for at least a coupla rounds so maybe we'll see *some* fightin'."

"If there's any fighting to be seen," Simon said, absently, "at least we're in a good position to see it."

The chiseled leanness of cheekbone and jaw were picked out vividly as he lighted a cigarette. Pat, glancing at the flame momentarily reflected in those mocking blue eyes, felt a familiar surge of yearning and pride. For he was a very reincarnation of those privateers who once knew the Spanish Main, a modern buccaneer consecrated to the gods of gay and perilous adventure, a cavalier as variable as a chameleon, who would always be at once the surest and the most elusive thing in her life.

"Yeah," Hoppy agreed grudgingly. "Dey ain't nut'n wrong wit' de seats. Ya must have some drag wit' de promoter, boss."

"I've never even met him."

Simon wasn't listening really. His eyes were angled to his left, gazing through a meditative plume of smoke to where Steve Nelson was rising about a dozen seats away and climbing into the ring to be introduced as the champion who would defend his title against the winner of tonight's bout. However, it wasn't Nelson whom Simon was watching. It was the girl in the seat beside Nelson—a girl with curly raven hair, big green eyes, and a nose whose snub pertness was an infinitely lovelier reproduction of her Irish sire's well-publicized proboscis.

"I suppose he just thought this would be a nice way to introduce himself," Patricia mocked. "Three little ringside tickets, that's all. Sent by special messenger, no less. Compliments of Mike Grady and the Manhattan Arena!"

The girl with the dark hair had turned and, for a brief instant, met Simon's gaze. He spoke without taking his eyes off her.

"Pat darling, you're taking too much for granted. It wasn't Mike who sent them."

"No?"

"No. It was his daughter, Connie. Third from the aisle in the front row." She followed his gaze.

There was no hint of coquetry in the eyes of the black-haired girl. There was something in them quite different—a swift glow of gratitude tempered by an anxiety that shadowed her clear elfin beauty. Then she turned away.

Pat smiled with feline sweetness.

"I see. How nice of her to think you might need some excitement!"

Hoppy's porcine eyes blinked.

"Boss, ain't she de Champ's girl friend?"

"So I've heard." Simon smiled and blew a large smoke ring that rose lethargically over the seat in front of him and settled about the bald pate of its occupant like a pale blue halo.

A scattered burst of cheering greeted Torpedo Smith's entrance into the ring.

"Shouldn't you be more careful about picking your leading ladies?" Pat inquired with saccharine concern.

"I have to face the hazards of my profession," Simon explained, with a glint of scapegrace mockery in his blue eyes. "But there may be some excitement at that—although I don't mean what *you're* thinking, darling."

The memory of Connie's visit, her confused plea for him to see the fight, lingered in his mind like the memory of strange music, a siren measure awakening an old familiar chill, prescient and instinctive, warning of danger that was no less perilous because it was as yet unknown.

The crowd broke into a thunderous roar.

"It's de Angel!" Hoppy proclaimed. "He's climbin' in de ring!"

The current sensation of the leather-pushing profession was indeed mounting the punch podium. He squeezed his hogshead torso between the ropes; and as he straightened up the Saint saw that the mask was really nothing more than a black beanbag that fitted over his small potato head with apertures for eye, nose, and mouth, and fastened by a drawstring between chin and shoulder at the place where a normal person's neck would ordinarily be, but which in the Angel was no more than an imaginary line of demarcation. He shambled to his corner like a hairless gorilla and clasped his bandaged hands over his head in a salute to the enraptured mob.

Patricia shuddered.

"Simon, is it—is it human?"

The Saint grinned.

"He'll never win any contests for the body beautiful, but of course we haven't seen his face yet. He may be quite handsome."

"Dere ain't *nobody* seen his face," Hoppy confided. "Dese wrestlers what pull dis gag wit' de mask on de face, dey don't care who knows who dey really are, but Doc Spangler, he don't let nobody see who his boy is. Maybe it's for luck. De Masked Angel ain't lost a fight yet!"

"Doc Spangler?"

Hoppy's head bobbed affirmatively. He pointed to a well-dressed portly gentleman who looked more like a bank president out for an evening's entertainment than a fighter's manager, who was standing in smiling conversation with one of the Angel's seconds.

"Dat's de Doc. He's de guy who discovers de Angel from someplace. Dat Doc is sure a smart cookie, boss."

The Saint smiled agreeably.

"You can say that again."

The salient features of the estimable Doc Spangler's history passed through Simon Templar's mind in swift procession—a record which, among many others, was filed with inexorable clarity in the infinite index of a memory whose indelibility had time and again proven one of the more useful tools of his profession.

"In fifteen fights," Hoppy expounded, "he brings de Angel from nowhere to a fight wit' de Champ t'ree weeks from now!"

Pat lifted an eyebrow.

"Even if Torpedo Smith beats him?"

"Aaah!" Hoppy chortled derisively. "Dat bum ain't got a chanst! De Angel'll moider him! You wait and see."

The Champ, having shaken hands with the two contenders, climbed out of the ring and resumed his seat beside Connie Grady, and the fighters rose from their corners as the referee waved them to the center of the ring for instructions.

Pat, wide-eyed, shook her head unbelievingly.

"Simon, that man with the mask—he—he's fantastic! Those arms—his gloves are touching his knees!"

"A fascinating example of evolution in reverse," Simon remarked.

The Masked Angel was indeed a remarkable specimen. With his arms dangling alongside his enormous hairless body he was the very antithesis of the classic conception of an athlete, his sagging breasts and vast pink belly undulating in rolls, billows, and pleats of fat; and though his hips narrowed slightly to the negligible proportions of a bull gorilla's, his flabby thighs ballooned out like a pair of mammoth loose-skinned sausages, tapering to a pair of stubby tree-trunk legs.

"A freak," Pat decided. "He wears that ridiculous mask because he's a pinhead."

"But even he can do somebody some good. You've got to admit that he makes Hoppy look like a creature of svelte and sprightly beauty."

"In dis racket, boss," Hoppy mulled with a heavy concentration of wisdom, "you don't have to be good-lookin'." Suddenly he sat up straight and strained forward. "Well, for cryin' out loud!"

"What's the matter?" The Saint followed his gaze to the ring.

Hoppy waved a finger the size of a knackwurst in the general direction of the two contestants and their handlers standing in the middle of the ring listening to the referee.

"Lookit, boss! Standin' behind Torpedo Smith—his handler! It's me old chum, Whitey Mullins!"

The fighters and their seconds were turning back to their respective corners. Whitey Mullins, a slender rubbery-faced little man with balding flaxen hair, wearing a turtle-necked sweater and sneakers, convoyed Smith to his corner and climbed out of the ring, taking the stool with him. The Saint recognized him as one of the professional seconds connected with the Manhattan Arena.

"One of the Torpedo's propellers, I take it?"

Hoppy nodded.

"He works a lot wit' me when I am in the box-fight racket, boss." Fond memories of yesteryear's mayhem lit his gorgon countenance with reminiscent rapture. "Cyclone Uniatz, dey called me."

"That, no doubt, explains why you never get up before the stroke of ten," Simon observed.

"Huh?"

Pat giggled as the bell clanked for the first round.

The Angel shuffled forward slowly, his arms held high, peering cautiously between his gloves at the oncoming Torpedo Smith. Smith, who had crashed into the top ranks of pugilism via a string of varied victories far longer than the unbroken string of knockouts boasted by the Masked Angel, moved warily about his opponent, jabbing tentative lefts at the unmoving barrier of arms that the Angel held before him. The Angel turned slowly as Smith moved around him, the fantastic black cupola of his masked head sunk protectively between beefy pink shoulders, the little eye slits peering watchfully. He kept turning, keeping Smith before him without attempting a blow. The Torpedo moved about more deliberately, with a certain puzzlement, as though he couldn't understand the Angel's unwillingness to retaliate, but was himself afraid to take any chances.

There was a stillness in the crowd, a sense of waiting as for the explosion of a bomb whose fuse was burning before their very eyes.

Pat spoke at last.

"But, Simon, they're just looking at each other."

The Saint selected another cigarette and tapped it on his thumb.

"You can't blame them. It'll probably take a round for them just to get over the sight of each other."

Hoppy lifted a voice that rang with the dulcet music of a foghorn with laryngitis.

"Come on, you Angel! Massecrate de bum!"

But the Angel, with supreme indifference to encouragement, merely kept turning, shuffling around to meet the probing jabs of Torpedo Smith, peering through his sinister mask, tautly watchful.

The crowd broke into a roar as the Torpedo suddenly drove a left hook to the Angel's stomach, doubling him up, and, casting caution to the winds, followed with a swift onslaught of lefts and rights. The Angel, arms, gloves, and elbows shielding his exposed surfaces, merely backed into a corner and crouched there until the bell punctuated the round.

Pat shook her head bewilderedly.

"Simon, I don't understand. This Masked Angel doesn't look as if he can fight at all. All he did was make like a turtle while that other man tried to find some place to hit him."

"Oh, you just wait," Hoppy growled reassuringly. "Dis fight ain't over yet. De smart money is bettin' t'ree to one de Angel kayoes Smith insida six rounds. He wins *all* his fights by kayoes."

The Saint was watching the two gladiators being given the customary libations of water and between-round advice by their handlers. He smiled thoughtfully.

"The Masked Angel has a very clever manager."

The bell for the second round brought Torpedo Smith out with a rush. Gaining confidence with every blow, he drove the quivering hulk of the Angel back on his heels, bringing the crowd to its feet in a steady roar of excitement.

"Hoppy," the Saint spoke into Hoppy's ear, "has the Angel ever been cut under that black stocking he wears over his head?"

"Huh? Naw, boss! His fights never last long enough for him to get hoit." Hoppy's eyes squinted anxiously. "Chees! Why don't he do sump'n? Torpedo Smith is givin' him de woiks!"

Pat was bouncing in her seat, the soft curve of her lips parted with excitement as she watched.

"I thought the Angel was so wonderful!" she gibed. "Come on, Torpedo!"

"Dey're bot' on de ropes!" Hoppy exclaimed hoarsely.

The Saint's hawk-sharp eyes suddenly narrowed. No, it was Torpedo Smith who was on the ropes now. With the Angel in control! . . . Something had happened. Something he hadn't seen. He gripped Hoppy's arm.

"Something's wrong with Smith."

Something was very definitely wrong with Torpedo Smith. He stood shaking his head desperately as if to clear it, holding onto the top strand with one hand and with the other trying to push away the black-masked monster who was now opening up with the steady relentless power of a pile driver.

"De Angel musta hit him!" Hoppy yelled. "I told ya, didn't I? I told ya!" His foghorn bellow rose over the mob's fierce blood cry. "Smith's down!"

Torpedo Smith, obviously helpless, had slumped beneath the repeated impact of the Angel's deliberate blows and now lay where he had fallen, face down, motionless, as the referee tolled him out.

The sea of humanity began ebbing like a tide toward the exits, the vast drone of their voices and shuffling feet covered by the reverberating recessional of a pipe organ striking up "Anchors Aweigh" from somewhere in the bowels of the coliseum.

"Well, ya see, boss?" Hoppy jubilated as they drifted into the aisle. "It's just like I told ya. De Angel's dynamite!"

Pat shook her golden head compassionately.

"That poor fellow—the way that horrible creature hit him when he was helpless! Why didn't the referee stop it?"

She turned, suddenly aware that Simon was no longer behind her. She looked about bewilderedly. "Simon!"

"Dere he is!" Hoppy waved a hamlike hand toward the end of the row they had just left. "Boss!"

The Saint was standing there, the occupants of the first rows of the ringside eddying past him, watching the efforts of Whitey Mullins and his assistants to revive the slumbering Smith.

Hoppy breasted the current with the irresistible surge of a battleship, and returned to Simon's side with Pat in his wake.

" 'S matter, boss?"

"What is it, Simon?"

The Saint glanced at her and back at the ring. He took a final pull at his cigarette, and dropped it to crush it carefully with one foot.

"They've just called the Boxing Commission doctor into Smith's corner," he said.

Pat stared at the ring.

"Is he still unconscious?"

"Aw, dat's nuttin'." Hoppy dismissed Smith's narcosis with a scornful lift of his anthropogenous jaw. "I slug a guy oncet who is out for twelve hours, an' when dey——"

"Wait a minute," the Saint interrupted, and moved toward Smith's corner as Whitey Mullins leaped from the ring to the floor.

"Whitey!" Hoppy bellowed joyfully. "Whassamatter, chum? Can't ya wake up dat sleeping beauty?"

Whitey glanced at him with no recognition, his wide flexible mouth contorted curiously.

Hoppy blinked.

"Whitey! Whassamatter?"

Pat glanced at the ring with quick concern.

"Is Smith hurt badly?"

The towheaded little man with the lean limber face stared at her a moment with twisting lips. When he spoke, his high-pitched Brooklyn accent was muted with tragedy.

"He's dead," he said, and turned away.

The spectral cymbals of grim adventure clashed an eerie tocsin within the Saint, louder now than when first he heard their faint far notes in Connie Grady's flustered appeal for him to search the sinister riddle of the Angel's victories, and save her fiancé from unknown peril. They had rung in the nebulous confusion of her plea, in the tortured suspicions unvoiced within her haunted eyes. . . . Now he heard their swelling beat again, a phantom reprise that prickled his skin with ghostly chills.

He spoke softly into Pat's ear.

"Darling, I just remembered. Hoppy and I have some vitally urgent business to attend to immediately. Do you mind going home alone—at once?"

Patricia Holm looked up sharply, the startled pique on her lovely face giving way swiftly to disquieted resignation. She knew him too well.

"What is it, Simon? What are you up to?"

"I'll explain later. I'm already late. Be a good girl." He kissed her lightly. "I'll make it up to you," he said, and left her gazing after him as he sauntered down the long concrete ramp leading to the fighters' dressing rooms with Hoppy shambling in his wake like a happy bear.

CHAPTER TWO

THE DOOR of the number-one dressing room beneath the floor of the Manhattan Arena rattled and shook as the sportswriters milled about the corridor outside and protested their exclusion. Who, one of them shouted, did the big ham think he was, Greta Garbo?

Behind the locked door, Dr Kurt Spangler rubbed his shining bald head and listened benignly to the disgruntled din.

"Maybe I should oughta give 'em an interview, huh, Doc?" The pink mountain of flesh lying on the rubbing table lifted a head the general size and shape of a runt eggplant. "I don't want they should think I'm a louse."

The un-Masked Angel blinked, his little brown eyes apologetic beneath the shadow of brows ridged with the compounded scar tissue of countless ancient cuts and contusions.

"Never mind what they think," Doc Spangler beamed comfortingly. "Let them disparage you—revile you—hate you." His sonorous voice sank confidingly. "It's exactly what we want."

The Angel sighed unhappily. His head dropped back on the rubbing table as the two handlers pulled off the gloves, tossed them in a corner, and proceeded to rip off the hand wrappings of gauze and tape.

"The more the newspapers hate you," Doc Spangler expounded, "the more cash they'll pay to see you get beaten." He rubbed his hands, considering the Angel with all the pride a farmer might display surveying his prize hog. "Kid McCoy, for instance," the doctor illustrated. "He made a fortune on the hatred of the mob. They paid to see him fight in the hope he would be slaughtered. Only he never was—not till after he became champion, anyway. And neither will you be, my lad. Not as long as you continue to follow my instructions."

The Angel grunted as Karl, one of his handlers, kneaded the mountainous mesa of his belly. His naked body, a pink mass of monstrous convexities, gleamed beneath the bright incandescents with a sheen of oily sweat that highlighted the ruby splotches where Torpedo Smith's gloves had exploded. His flat button nose, the distorted rosettes of flesh that were his ears, furnished further evidence that Dr Spangler's discovery, far from being a supernova in the pugilistic firmament, was actually a battle-battered veteran, the survivor of an unnumbered multitude of beatings.

"I did like you said wit' Smith, didn't I, Doc?" the Angel mumbled.

"You did indeed! You followed my instructions to the letter tonight. Always remember to keep covered till your man seems a bit careless." Spangler patted one beefy shoulder. "You were great tonight, my boy."

The Angel lifted his undersized noggin, a grateful grimace on his pear-shaped face.

"Thanks, Doc." He sank back. "I always try to do like you say." He sighed like a deflating dirigible. "But why do the crowd gotta t'ink I'm a crum? I radder they should like me. I like *them*."

Doc Spangler sighed patiently, but was spared the need for further exposition by an increased burst of banging on the door. He turned resignedly to the fox-faced thug who was unlacing the Angel's ring shoes.

"Maxie, perhaps you'd better go out and have a word with our journalistic friends."

Maxie nodded briefly. He went to the door, yanked it open, and stepped outside into a stream of vivid excoriation.

Doc Spangler listened a moment with admiration as the reporters' protests faded gradually down the hall.

Karl, the other henchman, had ceased his ministrations and was listening with a certain degree of envy. "Doc," he suggested, "maybe better I should go and help chase 'em away, yah?" His accent was a curious blend of Yorkville kraut and Bowery bum.

Doc Spangler smiled, glancing at the half-open door. Only Maxie's distant profanities were still audible, and that, too, finally ceased.

"I think Maxie has everything under control," Spangler said pleasantly. "Better finish taking off the Angel's shoes so he can take his shower and get dressed. We've got to have some supper."

The Angel heaved up to a sitting position.

"I'm hungry," he announced heavily. "I wanna double porterhouse and shoestring potaters."

Spangler's colorless eyes flitted tenderly over the Angel's three-storied bay window.

"You'll have a triple filet mignon with truffles à la Waldorf Astoria three times a day if we win the title."

The Angel grinned dully.

"Leave it to me, Doc. I'll take Nelson."

"Of course you will—if you'll always remember to do exactly as I tell you. It was only by obeying my instructions that you got through that first round tonight—and don't forget it. *I* won that fight for you, my lad."

"Congratulations," said the Saint.

"Yeah," Hoppy rasped, kicking the door shut behind them. "Nice woik, Doc."

For a paralyzed second, Dr Spangler, Karl, and the massive Angel composed a tableau of staring surprise. Then Spangler's florid wattles grew even more crimson.

"Who the devil——"

"Forgive us," the Saint interrupted. He took the cigarette from his mouth and flicked the ash reflectively, indicating Mr Uniatz, who stood beside him with the black snout of a big automatic protruding from one hairy fist. "My friend and I couldn't resist the temptation, Doctor—especially when your man left the door to pursue those reporters down the hall." He forbore to add that Maxie was, at the moment, reposing peacefully in a corridor broom closet where Hoppy had stuffed him after an exceedingly brief encounter. "Put away the gun, Hoppy," he reproved. "This is strictly social."

Hoppy obeyed slowly. He was staring at the naked mass of the Angel as if what mental equipment he possessed failed utterly to accept the evidence of his eyes.

"Ged oudda here," Karl grated tonelessly.

His voice, like his bushy-browed eyes, was flat, dull, and deadly. The Saint appraised him with a glance—a short, squat, powerfully constructed character whose prognathous jaw matched the cubist lines of his shoulders.

"For de luvva mike!" Incredulous amazement raised Hoppy's bullfrog bass a full octave. Rapturous recognition slowly illumined his corrugated countenance like dawning sunlight on a rock pile. "Bilinski!" he shouted. "Barrelhouse Bilinski!"

The Angel, who had been favoring Hoppy with the same openmouthed concentration, slid slowly off the edge of the table to his feet. A reciprocal light dawned on the fuzzy horizon of his memory and spread over his humpty-dumpty face in a widening grin.

"For crize sake! Hoppy Uniatz!"

They practically fell into each other's arms.

"Well, well, well," the Saint drawled. "Old Home Week. Perhaps you two would like to be alone?"

"Are *you* de Masked Angel?" Hoppy burbled with hoarse delight. *"You?"*

"Yea, sure, Hoppy, dat's me!"

"Boss, dis is Barrelhouse Bilinski. Barrelhouse, meet de Saint!"

"Ged oudda here!"

Karl's voice rose half a decibel, his right hand sliding toward a pocket.

"I wouldn't if I were you, comrade." The Saint smiled deprecatingly, a glint in his eyes like summer lightning in a blue sky. His hand was thrust negligently in a pocket of his beautifully tailored sports jacket. "I'd hate having to put a hole through this coat, but your navel is such a tempting target."

Karl's hand dropped to his side.

"Doc, this is me old chum from way back when!" The Angel turned to Spangler eagerly. "Hoppy Uniatz!"

"Delighted. . . . Now, Karl," Doc Spangler said reproachfully, "don't be a boor."

"Me and Barrelhouse useta beat each udder's brains out every week!" Hoppy effervesced hoarsely. "We barnstorm all over de country oncet. One week I win, next week he wins. What a team!"

"I can imagine," the Saint murmured.

Spangler smiled at Simon with revived benevolence.

"I might have known who you were, Mr Templar, but you rather caught me by surprise, you know. I hardly expected a visit from the Saint at this particular moment."

"The pleasure," Simon bowed, "is all mine."

"Not at all, my dear fellow. I—er—I've rather expected this visit—at some time or another, knowing of your parasitic propensities."

The Saint lifted an eyebrow.

"Parasitic?"

Dr Spangler chuckled.

"Forgive me. I was merely referring to your habit of living on other people's enterprises."

"Meaning, no doubt, that you think I've come for a cut of your take in the Masked Angel—is that it?"

Spangler shrugged deprecatingly.

"What else?"

"Doc, whassa matter, huh?" the Angel queried with a puzzled grin which exposed several broken teeth. "What's he want?"

"Take it easy, Barrelhouse," Hoppy rumbled. "Dis is strictly social."

The Saint laughed.

"You're wrong, Doctor."

"Am I?" Spangler said. "I've always known that at some unexpected point in the strange geometry of providence our paths must surely cross someday. We have much in common, Templar. We would work well together."

Mockery danced in Simon's azure eyes.

"You must be psychic, Doctor, to have recognized me so quickly. I can't recall our ever having met before."

"True." Spangler nodded graciously. "However, your face has appeared in the public prints on several occasions I can recall."

"And so has yours," said the Saint reminiscently—"generally tacked on post-office walls beneath the word 'Wanted.'"

Spangler chuckled.

"You amuse me."

The light in Simon's eyes settled into two steely points.

"Then laugh *this* off. Torpedo Smith is dead."

The startled sag of the fat man's jaw was too sincere a reflex for simulation. His stare shifted uncertainly to Karl standing beside him.

"Vot der hell!" Karl's beetling black brows matched his sneering snarl. "You tryink to scare somebody, hah?"

The Angel scratched his jaw bewilderedly, the whole unlovely mass of his gross nakedness quivering like jelly as he turned to his manager.

"Dead?" he muttered stupidly. "He's dead?"

Hoppy nodded admiringly.

"He won't never be no deader. Whereja ever get dat punch, chum? Why, when we was togedder, you stunk."

"My dear sir," Spangler said, eyeing the Saint with watchful deliberation, "if this is an attempt at humor——"

"You needn't laugh now," Simon assured him pleasantly. "Save it for later—when the police get here. They should be in at any moment."

The Angel licked his lips tremulously.

"Jeez, Doc . . . I croaked him. I croaked de Torpedo . . ."

"He's lying!" Karl sneered. "Smith cannot be dead!"

"Listen." The Saint glanced at the door. "I think I hear them now."

They followed his gaze, listening.

And while they stood intently frozen, the Saint sauntered quite casually to the corner where Karl and Maxie had tossed the Angel's gloves, and scooped them up in one sweeping motion.

Dr Spangler turned quickly.

"What are you doing? Put down those gloves!" Alarmed suspicion darkened his colorless eyes. "Karl! Angel!"

His voice broke shrilly.

Bilinski went into motion uncertainly, as if still wondering what he was called on to do; but with a playful push as gentle as the thrust of a locomotive piston, Hoppy shoved him back to a sitting position on the edge of the rubbing table.

"Aw, don't mind him, Barrelhouse," he grinned. "He's just noivous."

He stuck out a foot to trip Karl who, gun in hand, was diving for cover behind the table.

The Saint moved with the effortless speed of lubricated lightning, kicking the gun from the sprawling thug's hand with all the vicious grace of a *savate* champ.

"Whassamatter?" the Angel blinked bewilderedly. "Doc——"

Karl struggled to all fours. It was a strategic error; for he presented, for one irresistible moment, his rear end to Mr Uniatz's ecstatic toe in an explosive junction that flung him end over end into the shower stall across the room.

"Help!" Spangler shouted. "Max! Max! Hel——"

His cry broke in a gasping grunt as the Saint's fist buried itself a good six inches in his paunch, collapsing him to the floor like a deflated blimp.

"Nice woik, boss," Hoppy congratulated.

"Hey's what's the big idea?" the Angel demanded, his confusion crystallizing into a fuzzy awareness that the isotope of friendship had somehow exploded.

He struggled off the edge of the rubbing table.

"Aw, relax, ya fat slob!" Hoppy recommended affectionately.

He clarified his suggestion with a shove that had all the delicate tact of an impatient rhinoceros slamming full tilt into a bull elephant; and the Angel, unbalanced, staggered backwards, knocking over the rubbing table and going down with it in a thunderous crash.

"All right, Hoppy," Simon called from the door as he removed the key. "Don't let's wear out our welcome."

He handed the gloves to Hoppy as they stepped out into the corridor and locked the door behind them. As they turned to leave, other gruff voices echoed faintly through the corridor leading from the end of the ramp; and the Saint's white teeth flashed in a satiric grin as he recognized the terse tonalities of the Law.

"The other way, Hoppy," he said, and turned in the opposite direction.

They sped swiftly through the underground maze toward the basement exits that opened into the street at the other end.

CHAPTER THREE

HOPPY UNIATZ eased the big convertible adroitly through the midnight traffic and past the bright lights of the Times Square district; and presently gave vent to a cosmic complaint.

"Boss," he announced with the wistful appeal of an arid hippopotamus being driven past a water hole, "I gotta t'oist. Exercise always gives me a t'oist, boss."

"Keep going," the Saint commanded inexorably. His long brown fingers were carefully probing the gloves on his lap. "You can refresh yourself after we get home."

Hoppy sighed and trod on the accelerator again.

"Anyt'ing in dem gloves, boss?"

"I can't feel anything."

Simon lifted a glove and sniffed it thoughtfully. He rubbed his finger over the damp leather and tasted it.

"Barrelhouse musta loined how to speed up his punch," Hoppy ruminated. "De fat slob always can hit like a mule, but he never is able to land it much when I know him. He's too slow." Hoppy shook his head in perplexity. "Imagine *him* bein' de Masked Angel! Doc Spangler musta teached him plenty."

"I wonder," said the Saint.

But, whatever the secret of the Angel's success, Simon was certain now that it didn't lie in his gloves. There was nothing wrong with them that he could determine. No weights in the padding, no chemicals impregnated in the leather. He'd seen enough of Bilinski's hand wraps to determine that there had been no illegal substance compounded therein. And yet the practically overnight transformation of a battered dull-witted hulk into an invincible gladiator with lethal lightning in his fists was too obvious a discord in the harmony of logic.

The action of that fatal second round leading up to Torpedo Smith's collapse passed through the Saint's memory again, slowed down to a measured succession of mental images.

"Hoppy," the Saint reflected, "did you see that first blow which started the Torpedo on his way out?"

"Sure, boss." Hoppy nodded positively. "Barrelhouse catches him in de ropes."

"Did he hit him with a right or a left?"

"He hits him wit' both hands—lotsa times. *You* seen it."

The Saint said: "I know. But I mean that very first punch—the one that dazed Smith and laid him open for the other blows. Did you see that particular punch?"

"Sure I see it, boss. We bot' see it."

Hoppy yanked the car around a final corner and slid it to a halt in front of a canopy that stretched from the Gothic doorway of a skyscraper apartment building to the curb.

"If you remember it so well," Simon pursued patiently, "what was it—a right or a left?"

"Why, it wuz a right, a—no, it wuz a left. A hook. Or maybe——" Hoppy hesitated, his vestigial brow furrowing painfully. "Maybe it wuz an uppercut dere against de ropes. He is t'rowin' so many punches, I wouldn't know."

"That's what I thought."

The memory of Connie Grady's enigmatic anxiety and her confused half-explained fears for Steve Nelson's life rose in swelling reprise, cued in with the discord of tonight's events like the opening movement of a concerto that gave promise of more—much more—to come.

Simon got out, the gloves dangling from his hand by their laces, entered the lobby of the building with Hoppy at his heels, and headed for the elevators.

"Maybe we oughta send out for sump'n to drink, huh, boss?" Hoppy suggested.

The Saint glanced at him. "Send *who?*"

Hoppy glanced around, becoming aware that the lobby was deserted, the desk man and lift operators off duty.

"It's after midnight, chum," the Saint pointed out as they entered the automatic elevator. He pressed the button marked *Penthouse*. The doors closed softly and the elevator purred skyward. "Besides," the Saint added as an afterthought, "I believe there's half a bottle of bourbon left."

Mr Uniatz looked at him gloomily. "Yeah, boss. I know. Half a bottle— and me wit' a t'oist!"

"Mix it with a little water and make it go farther," Simon suggested helpfully.

"Water?" Hoppy stared incredulously. "De stuff what you wash wit'?"

The Saint smiled absently, thinking of other things.

"You're definitely no child of Aquarius, Hoppy!"

Hoppy blinked with mild stupefaction, pondered a moment and gave up.

"No, I guess not," he sighed. "I wuz de child of Mr an' Mrs Uniatz."

The elevator stopped and they stepped out.

"I meant the sign you were born under." Simon unlocked the door and entered the apartment. "From the way you drink, you must have been born under Pisces."

Hoppy's eyes widened in wonder at this hitherto unimagined vista of biological phenomena.

"Who, me? How did dat happen?"

The Saint shrugged, tossing the gloves on the living-room divan as he turned on lights.

"I don't know," said the Saint. "It must have been shady there."

He flung himself down on the divan and stretched his long legs luxuriously, while Hoppy struggled briefly with his Delphic observation and then discarded the entire subject as the bottle on the sideboard caught his eye.

"Keerist!" he muttered. "Me tongue's hangin' out."

He made a beeline for the half bottle of Kentucky dew, throttling it with an enormous hairy paw as he lifted it to his mouth, back-tilted like the maw of a baying wolf. His Adam's apple plunged in convulsive rhythm as the contents lowered an inch a second, a full four seconds elapsing before he straightened his neck again, halted in mid-swallow by the pop of a cork.

The Saint had a fresh bottle of Old Forester on his lap and was reaching for a glass from the top of a cabinet by the divan.

Hoppy's mouth pursed in hurt reproach.

"So *dat's* why it's locked," he deduced aggrievedly.

"And a good thing, too," the Saint said.

He recorked the bottle, gathered the Angel's gloves on his lap, and savored the drink with sybaritic enjoyment. Then he proceeded to re-examine the gloves; not that he expected them to yield any more secrets, but he had to be quite sure.

"Ja figure de mitts is loaded, boss?" Hoppy picked up one of the gloves. "Is dat why you want 'em?"

Simon considered him.

"Did you work that out all by yourself?"

He tossed the remaining glove aside and picked up his glass again. Hoppy took the glove he had thrown down and felt that one too.

"Ain't nut'n de matter wit' dese gloves, boss."

The telephone rang.

It was Pat, her voice a stiletto in a silken sheath.

"Simon dear, it isn't that I mind being abandoned like a sinking ship——"

"Darling," said the Saint, "I've never been called a rat more delicately. However——"

"However," she interrupted determinedly, "you could at least have phoned me as soon as you got home. I've been sitting here expecting a call every minute. What happened? Where did you go? I waited at the Arena until the cleaning people nearly swept me out."

"Good lord! I told you to go on home."

"I know, but after you disappeared down that ramp I figured you to come up again. You never did."

"Darling——"

"Don't darling me. After the police went down and never came up again either, I went out to find your car, and that was gone too."

"You poor baffled child," he commiserated tenderly. "Hoppy and I took it. There was another exit. Several, in fact——"

"I happen to have figured that out quite some time ago," she said sweetly. "What happened? What was that shouting and crashing going on down there?"

"Oh, that," the Saint murmured. "Doc Spangler lost his key, so I suppose the police had to break down the door."

"Lost his key! What key?"

"The key I have in my pocket."

"B-but——" She broke off. "Simon, if you're going to be coy——"

"Not at all. Come over for breakfast, and I'll try to give you a general idea what happened."

"And just what has your little colleen, Connie Grady, got to do with all this?"

"I haven't decided yet. We'll talk about it at breakfast."

"I'll be there," she said ominously. "And it had better be good."

"It will be. The freshest eggs, the crispest bacon, the best butter——"

"I don't mean that. Good night, Lothario."

Simon thoughtfully pulled off a shoe.

Hoppy Uniatz had disposed of the remains of his pint, and had taken advantage of the interruption to begin a strategic circling maneuver towards the Saint's bottle. This was a more or less instinctive gravitation; his receding brow was grooved by a stream of excogitation that flowed with all the gusto of a glacier towards its terminal moraine.

"Boss," Hoppy ruminated, "I got an idea."

The Saint kicked off the other shoe.

"Be kind to it, Hoppy," he yawned, "it's in a strange place."

But Hoppy, lost in contemplation of a glorious tomorrow evolving from the stuff of his dreams, went on unheeding.

"Dis fat slob, Bilinski, who is de Masked Angel. He beats de Champ. Dat makes *him* de Champ, don't it?"

The Saint eyed him curiously. "He hasn't beaten him yet."

"But if Barrelhouse Bilinski gets de crown," Hoppy continued with growing inspiration, "dey is one guy who can take it away from him. Dey is one guy who can knock him on his can any day in de week. Dat's me, boss! If dat fat slob gets de champeenship, I'm de guy what can take it away from him. Den I'll be de champ and you'll be my manager!"

The telephone rang again.

"Excuse me," said the Saint. "My bottle seems to be moving towards your hand."

He rescued it in the nick of time, and picked up the phone.

He recognized at once the soft husky lilt of the voice.

"I—I do hope you'll forgive my calling you at this hour," Constance Grady apologized hurriedly. "I called several times after I—I thought you might have gotten home, but there was no answer."

"I just got in," Simon explained. "I didn't have a chance to call you right after the fight as I'd promised, and I thought it was rather late to phone you now. But," he added quickly, "I'm glad you called. Thanks for the tickets."

"Thank you for using them." She hesitated, her voice dropping almost to a whisper. "You—you saw what happened . . ."

"Yes. Very interesting."

A slight pause.

"Daddy——" she began, and stopped. "My father came home a few minutes ago. He's very upset. I—I made an excuse that I had to go to an all-night drugstore on the corner to get some aspirin. I'm talking to you from there."

"I see." The Saint's voice was speculative. "Naturally he would be upset by tonight's accident."

"Accident? . . . Yes, I know." She hesitated again. "There was something else—something about you and that—that man you call Hoppy——"

"Oh?"

"You went into the Masked Angel's dressing room after the fight. Daddy said there was a brawl."

"I wouldn't say that," Simon said gravely. "One of Dr Spangler's assistants happened to trip on one of Hoppy's big feet and knock himself out. The Angel fell over a table, causing Dr Spangler to get the wind knocked out of him."

"But . . . You—didn't go down to see this—Masked Angel because you saw something—something wrong?"

"Wrong? No, Connie, if you mean fouling or anything like that, I didn't see a thing. By the way, it seems the Masked Angel is one of Hoppy's old chums."

"Oh."

"What makes you think there was anything wrong?"

"I—I don't know. I'm—I'm just afraid." Her answer was just as vague now as it had been the first time. "I thought you might have been able to—to see something, or—or figure something out. I——"

"Why not drop in for breakfast and we'll talk it over?"

"All right." She seemed reluctant to finish, and yet unable to find an excuse to go on. "And thanks again."

The Saint poured himself another drink, and surrendered the bottle.

"Who was dat, boss?" Hoppy asked.

"A lady," Simon replied, "who is holding out on me."

"You can't trust 'em, boss," Hoppy affirmed, shaking his head. "None of 'em. I know a doll once." He sighed, shaking his head like a wistful grizzly. "She has coives like a—a——"

"A scenic railway?" Simon suggested.

Hoppy beamed.

"Dat wuz Fanny, boss! All over! I can see her now." He sighed with the stentorian nostalgia of a libidinous walrus. "She was de goil of my dreams!"

The Saint yawned and turned to the bedroom.

"Then let's go see her there," he said.

The doorbell rang a sudden prolonged pizzicato.

Simon halted in his tracks. Ghostly caterpillars crawled along his back-bone. Instinct, sensitive and prescient, had whispered its warning of further explosions in the chain reaction he had started that night; the clamor of the bell came as if on a long-awaited cue. A faint smile flitted over his reckless mouth.

"Who da hell is dat dis time of night?" Hoppy wondered.

"Open the door and find out," Simon told him.

Mr Uniatz slipped a meaty hand into his gun pocket and strode out into the foyer to the doorway.

The Saint heard the door open fractionally; he grinned slowly as he recognized the impatient imperative voice that answered Hoppy's gruff inquiry. The door opened all the way . . . The determined clomp of hard-heeled brogans entered the foyer, heading for the living-room door.

"Boss," Hoppy trumpeted in warning, "it's——"

"Don't tell me," the Saint broke in cheerfully. "Give me one guess—Inspector Fernack!"

CHAPTER FOUR

DEVOTED STUDENTS of our hagiography who have been following these chronicles for the past several years may be a little tired of reading the exposition of Inspector John Henry Fernack's emotional state which usually punctuates the narrative at moments like this. Your favorite author, to be perfectly candid, is a little tired of writing it. Perhaps this is one occasion when he might be excused. To compress into a few sentences the long epic of failures, disappointments, and frustrations which made up the history of Inspector Fernack's endless pursuit of the Saint is a task before which the staunchest scribe might quail. And it is almost ludicrous to attempt to describe in mere words the quality of incandescent ire that seethed up in him like a roiled volcano as the Saint's welcoming smile flashed in the chiseled bronze of that piratical face.

"Of course," Simon murmured. "I knew it."

The detective glowered at him.

"How did you know?"

"My dear John Henry!" the Saint grinned. "That concerto you played on my doorbell was unmistakably a Fernack arrangement." He waved him to a chair. "Sit down, won't you? Let me pour you a drink—if Hoppy can spare it."

"Sure," said Mr Uniatz hospitably. "Just don't take all of it."

Inspector Fernack did not sit down. In fact, he looked more as if he might easily rise into the air, from the sheer pressure of the steam that seemed to be distending his chest.

For the same routine was going to be played out again, and he knew it, without being able to do anything to check or vary its course. It was all implicit in the Saint's gay and friendly smile; and the bitterness of the premonition put a crack in his voice even while he plowed doggedly onwards to his futile destiny.

"Never mind that!" he squawked. "What were you and this big baboon raising Cain about in the Masked Angel's dressing room tonight?"

"You mean *last* night, don't you? It happens to be tomorrow morning at the moment."

"I'm asking you," Fernack repeated deliberately, "what were you doing——"

"It's funny," the Saint interjected, "all the places where a flying rumor will land."

"It's no rumor!" Inspector Fernack said trenchantly. "I was at the fight myself." He removed the stogie from his mouth and took a step forward, his gimlet eyes challenging. "Why did you steal those gloves?"

The Saint's brows lifted in polite surprise.

"Gloves?"

"Yes, gloves! The gloves that killed Torpedo Smith! Doc Spangler told me what happened. Why'd you take 'em?"

"My hands were cold," Simon said blandly.

An imaginative audience might have fancied that it could hear the perspiration sizzling on Inspector Fernack's face as its rosy glow deepened to purple. He thrust the stogie back into his mouth with a violence that almost choked him, and bit into it savagely.

"You be careful, Templar!" he bellowed. "If I felt like it, I could pull you in for assault, trespass, malicious mischief, *and* petty larceny!"

Simon shook his head sadly.

"You disappoint me, Inspector. A hunter of your caliber talking about sparrows when there are tigers in them thar hills."

"You don't say!" Fernack's cigar angled upward like a naval rifle. "Meaning what?"

The Saint shrugged.

"Well, almost anything is more interesting than——" Amusement flickering in the lazy-lidded, hawk-sharp blueness of his eyes as he enumerated on his fingers: "Assault, trespass, malicious mischief, *and* petty larceny."

The cigar made another trip from Inspector Fernack's face to his fist, and suffered further damage in transit.

"All right, Saint," Fernack ground out, "what are you up to? And don't give me that look of injured innocence. You didn't crash that dressing room just for the exercise."

"We wanted de Angel's autograft," Hoppy contributed helpfully.

The Inspector whirled on him.

"I didn't ask *you!*" he blared, with such ferocity that even Hoppy recoiled.

"John Henry," the Saint mused wistfully, "our association through the years has been a beautiful thing—in a futile sort of way—but there are moments when you really embarrass me."

"I'll bet!"

"Why should you take Spangler's word that *I* stole those gloves? You know what *he* is. Besides, what makes you think there's anything wrong with them? What was the doctor's opinion as to the cause of death?"

Inspector Fernack placed the cigar in his mouth, his eyes fixed on the Saint.

"Concussion," he said. "We'll get the medical examiner's report in the morning."

The Saint nodded.

"Concussion. Undoubtedly caused by the psychic dynamite that Doc Spangler has put in the Angel's punch."

"Or by a hunk of lead in one of those gloves!" the Inspector growled. His eyes wandered searchingly about the room.

The Saint said: "You spoke to the Masked Angel, of course?"

"I spoke to him, of course. Why?"

"What is *his* theory, if any?"

"*His* theory!" Inspector Fernack snorted scornfully. "Why, that moron Bilinski doesn't know he's alive! But he's staying in jail till we find those gloves, understand?" His eyes narrowed. "How long have you known Bilinski? How did you recognize him as the Masked Angel? Is he a friend of yours?"

The Saint smiled wryly.

"Please, Inspector," he protested. "My social standing is not indestructible." He turned to Hoppy. "Well," he sighed, "if it's a matter of getting your little playmate out of the cooler, you'd better bring the Inspector his souvenirs."

"Okay, boss."

"I thought so!" Inspector Fernack bared his teeth in uneasy triumph. Hoppy shuffled to the divan, bent over, and reached under it.

"Here dey are," he announced, hauling them out. He thrust the damp leather mitts at Fernack with all the graciousness of a dyspeptic mastodon. "Take 'em!"

The Saint selected a cigarette from the silver box on the table.

"I borrowed them for the same reason you want them," he said. "I was afraid there'd be a substitution before you thought of it."

He held a lighter to his cigarette, smiling at the Inspector over its little golden spear point of flame.

Fernack scowled, staring at the Saint for a longish moment.

"So that's your story!" he began with an imminent crescendo. "Now let me tell you——"

And there, in a hopeless anticlimax, he stopped. Galling memories of past pitfalls into which his headlong suspicions had tripped him in previous encounters with the Saint seemed for once to take all the conviction out of his attack. What, after all, was he going to tell the Saint? That he was under arrest for stealing a pair of boxing gloves?

The Saint was engagingly frank.

"I examined them quite carefully, John Henry," he said, "and they're really quite in order, believe me. None of the stitches has been tampered with, or the lining torn, or any chemical such as oil of mustard soaked into the leather. I also had a look at Bilinski's hand wraps. No plaster of paris, pads of tinfoil, or calking compound. No hunks of lead——"

"All right, wise guy!" Fernack exploded. "If these are the gloves, the police lab will tell me all I want to know!"

The Saint spread his hands with mock resignation, laughter sparkling in his cobalt eyes like sunlight on an Alpine lake.

"Of course, John Henry, if you don't believe me. However, if you should ever feel the need of any further enlightenment, always remember that our motto is service. Sure you won't change your mind about that drink?"

"All right!" Fernack grated, repeating himself. "Be a wise guy. Play the lone wolf. But remember this, Templar. Sooner or later you're going to make a false move, a mistake you can't get out of. And when that happens, brother, I'll be right there waiting to tag you for it!"

"You an' who else?" Hoppy inquired brilliantly.

Inspector Fernack ignored him. He thrust a finger at the Saint.

"One of these days you're going to reach out just a little too far—and you're going to draw back a bloody stump!"

The Saint's face crinkled in a shrugging smile as he put his cigarette to his mouth with a careless gesture. And as if by accident its glowing tip touched the finger Inspector Fernack held under his nose.

The detective jerked his hand back with a yelp.

"Oh, sorry, John!" Simon exclaimed contritely. "That should teach me a lesson, shouldn't it?"

Fernack glared at him speechlessly. Then, thrusting the gloves under his arm, he turned and stalked out of the living room. Simon followed him politely to the apartment's threshold.

"Good night," said the Saint, as Fernack yanked open the door. "If you should ever need me, you know where to find me."

"If I ever want you," Inspector Fernack growled, "I'll find you, don't worry."

He strode out; and with a cheerful grin at the two harness bulls waiting outside by the elevators, Simon quietly closed the door.

"Well," he sighed. "Now maybe we can get some sleep at last!"

Hoppy yawned in soporific sympathy, but had enough presence of mind to reach for the Old Forester, which still contained an appreciable amount of fluid.

"I better have a nightcap," he explained. "I don't wanna stay awake t'inkin' about Torpedo."

"A nightcap that size," Simon observed, watching the level of the bottle descending, "could double as a sleeping bag."

He retrieved what was left and poured it into a glass, for a private relaxer of his own.

He tried to tot up what scores there were on hand, to determine exactly where he stood at the moment. He had to confess to himself that so far he'd been working with mists, trying to assemble a concrete pattern, a design out of stuff that emanated almost entirely from his intuitive processes. The promise of hovering danger had dissolved in two unsatisfactory climaxes: the dressing-room brawl, and Fernack's visit. Unsatisfactory because they resolved nothing, answered no questions, gave no reason for the ghostly centipedes he still felt parading up his spine. . . . The mystery of Connie Grady's disproportionate agitation, the Masked Angel's incredible victory, still stood as prime question marks.

But perhaps, he told himself, they weren't real question marks. Perhaps he'd been overdramatizing his perceptions. Connie was young and in love. Her fear for Steve's safety could well have inspired her strangely distraught plea. And the Masked Angel might have initially stunned Smith with such a short swift jab that his eye had missed it entirely.

He told himself this and knew he was kidding himself. He knew he had missed nothing in the fight. Therefore there must have been something else—something that he still had to search for.

He stood up and stretched himself.

And once again the telephone rang.

"This is getting monotonous," said the Saint.

He lifted the instrument from its cradle.

"Templar's Telephone Chums, Incorporated," he said.

Silence.

It was a kind of receptive cylindrical silence, open at both ends.

"We're having a breakfast meeting at 9 A.M.," Simon confided into the receiver. "Would you like to come too?"

He heard a faint click—a sudden blank deadness.

The Saint hung up thoughtfully; and an airless draught prickled along his nerves like a spectral breeze. It was a well-remembered sensation, a wave length registered on the sensitive antenna of a sixth sense which selected and amplified it throughout his being into an unmistakable alarum. It had warned him before more times than he could remember of impending danger and sudden death—just as it whispered to him now.

Someone had hung up as soon as he'd recognized the Saint's voice. Someone who wanted to make sure whether he was there.

"Hoppy," he said, "something tells me we're going to have more visitors tonight."

Mr Uniatz's cogitative machinery ground to an excruciating halt.

"What for, boss?"

"It's the price we pay for being so irresistibly attractive."

He was taking a rapid mental inventory of the room, until his eyes settled on a table lamp with a fairly long cord. He pulled the plug out of the baseboard outlet and broke the lamp cord off close to the lamp, while Hoppy stared at him.

"What gives, boss? What's dat for?"

The Saint nodded at the empty whisky bottle still clutched in Hoppy's hand.

"Take that dead soldier, go to the bathroom, fill it with water, and bring it over there."

Hoppy opened his mouth to speak, closed it, and lumbered off obediently, confident that on whatever path the Saint pointed for him to follow, devious though it might be, a goal would unfold somehow at the end.

From the chest of drawers in his bedroom the Saint took a slim leather case which, on being unzipped, revealed a highly specialized collection of peculiar articles. Skipping the more obviously illegal tools, he selected a small spool of copper wire, a roll of adhesive tape, and a razor-blade

knife. Armed with these, he returned to the entrance hall, where Mr
Uniatz extended the whisky bottle to him as though it contained an unclean
substance.

"Here's de water, boss. Whatcha gonna do wit' it?"

"Just hold it for me a minute," said the Saint. He began to cut several
inches of insulation from the broken end of the lamp cord. "We are preparing a phylactery against zombies," he explained.

Hoppy's jaw sagged.

"We're preparin' a what against who?"

"An apotropaion, so to speak," the Saint elucidated.

Hoppy moved nervously aside as the Saint went to the front door and
taped one of the two strands of the lamp cord against the metal doorknob.
He watched in silent wonder as the Saint unrolled a length of copper wire,
wound the spool end a couple of times around the radiator pipe, and
slipped the other end under the door until it projected a foot into the hall
outside.

"All right, Hoppy, give me the bottle."

Simon stepped outside and carefully poured the water on the tile floor
in front of his door so that the protruding wire lay in a shallow puddle. He
went a couple of paces down the corridor, turned and studied the approach
to the living-room door, then came back.

"Boss," Hoppy sighed, voicing his perennial complaint, "I don't get it."

"You will," said the Saint.

He fastened the other bared end of the drop cord to the radiator with
another strip of adhesive and carefully closed the door. Finally he pushed
the plug into a nearby baseboard outlet and turned to Hoppy. "Well," he
said, "there it is."

Hoppy stared at the closed door; and his lucubratory processes, oozing
like a glutinous stream between narrow banks, at last achieved a spreading
delta of cognition. A slow enchanted grin dissolved his facial fog like sunlight on a jungle swamp.

"Chees, boss," he said in awesome incredulity, "I do get it!"

"Congratulations."

"In case de zombies you're expectin' should touch de doorknob," Hoppy
deduced triumphantly. His eyes were worshipful. "Ya even got de water
puddle grounded, huh?"

The Saint laid his hand on Hoppy's shoulder in an accolade.

"Nothing escapes your eagle eye, does it?"

"Oh, I got experience in dis line, boss," Mr Uniatz acknowledged deprecatingly. "Once I do a job on a mug's car wit' a stick of dynamite wired
to de starter. De whole mob says it's one of de biggest laughs I ever give
dem."

The Saint surveyed his work with an artist's satisfaction.

"That water grounded to the radiator should lend some authority even to 110 volts—especially if he's in his stockinged feet." He turned, picking up the wire, knife, and tape, and headed back toward his bedroom. "Let's grab some shut-eye while we can. It'll be daybreak in a few hours."

CHAPTER FIVE

IT WAS two hours later when he opened his eyes, instantly and completely awake, with every nerve alive and singing. He lay motionless save for the silent closing of his fingers on the gun at his side, every sense toned to razor keenness, straining to receive consciously whatever it was that had alerted him. From the next bed Hoppy's snoring rose and fell in majestic rhythm, its pipe-organ vibrato accompanied by a piccolo phrase with every exhalation. . . .

Then he heard it—a faint scratching of metal—and recognized it instantly. A skeleton key was probing the front door lock.

He was out of bed and on his feet in one smooth soundless motion, and laying a hand on Hoppy's mouth. The snoring ceased abruptly; Simon swiftly spoke in his ear, and Hoppy's groggy eruption died aborning. He relaxed, and the Saint removed his hand.

"Listen."

The faint scratching of metal was barely audible.

Hoppy nodded, one hand scratching for the gun under his pillow, his anticipatory grin almost as luminous as the moonlight that poured into the window.

"De zombies!" he hissed in a resounding whisper that brought Simon's hand back upon his mouth again.

"Quiet!" the Saint breathed savagely.

There was a brief silence, and it seemed for a moment as if the man working on the door had indeed heard him. Then it came again—a scrape of metal—and suddenly the metallic click of tumblers falling into alignment, and the snick of an opening bolt.

"He's coming in," Simon whispered in Hoppy's ear. "Don't make a sound or I'll brain you with this gun butt."

He took his hand off Hoppy's mouth and moved with the effortless ease of a cat through the living room. He could hear the creak of the bed as Hoppy got out and padded after him. They paused by the archway to the entrance hall, staring into the almost darkness, intent on the pale rectangle of the front door.

As they waited there, the Saint couldn't help feeling that somehow, despite his conviction that this visit arose from his recent conflict with Spangler, it didn't quite add up. For he thought he knew Spangler's character pretty thoroughly; and so primitive a motive as simple revenge simply didn't agree with his knowledge of the man. Revenge for revenge's sake was a luxury too expensive—and dangerous—to be compatible with Doc Spangler's conservative nature. The worthy doctor might have better reason later on, but so far the Saint couldn't imagine him going to so much trouble merely to assuage a sore belly.

There was another moment of silence. . . . Then, without hearing it, but almost as if he sensed a momentary and fractional change in the air pressure, the Saint knew that the front door was starting to open.

Hoppy edged past Simon, as though straining on a leash.

Simultaneously, several things happened in such swift succession that they had the effect of happening almost all at once: a sizzling shower of golden sparks flamed from the doorknob, a wild howl split the silence, there was a mad scramble of slipping feet, the thud of a falling body, the blast of a gunshot, and the rattle of plaster cascading to the floor.

The Saint and Hoppy leaped forward almost on top of the gunman's yell, with Hoppy ahead of Simon by virtue of his head start.

Simon's warning cry came too late.

Hoppy's joyous battle bellow leaped to a yell of consternation as he grabbed the doorknob amid another constellation of sparks bursting about his hand. He hurtled backwards, skidding on a rug, and sat down with a mighty crash in front of the doorway.

The Saint ripped the cord from the electric outlet with one hand, reached over with the other, and tried to pull open the door against Hoppy's obstructing weight.

"Okay, boss, okay!" Hoppy grunted protestingly as Simon rolled him over with a yank at the door.

He scrambled to his feet as the Saint disappeared into the hallway. But even as he snatched open the front door, Simon knew that the quarry had escaped. The "In Use" signal light of the automatic elevator gleamed at him in yellow derision.

Hoppy charged past him and skidded to a halt.

"Where'd he go, huh? Where'd he go?" he demanded feverishly.

Then he caught the glow of the elevator signal light and whirled for the stairs.

The Saint grabbed his arm and stopped him.

"Come back, Pluto," he said disgustedly. "That elevator will be at the bottom before you've gone down three flights."

He dragged Hoppy back into the apartment as a murmur of alarmed voices, with a few doors opening and closing, drifted faintly up the stair well. Muttering to himself, Hoppy joined the Saint in the darkness before the living-room window and stared down at the moon-silvered street before the building entrance far below. Suddenly, as the realization that the would-be raider would probably be leaving by that exit dawned upon him, a vast feral grin spread over his face. He raised his gun.

The Saint noted the car parked before the building, a little distance behind his—a dark sedan that hadn't been there when he'd arrived there that night. He caught a glimpse of hands in the moonlight—hands that carried an odd sparkle—resting on the visible portion of the steering wheel.

Hoppy crouched beside him, his big black automatic clutched in a hairy fist resting on the window sill, and stared lynx-eyed at the canopied building entrance eighteen floors below. Presently he rasped in an awful tide of anxiety: "Boss, maybe he goes out de back——"

He broke off as a man darted out from under the canopy, a figure reduced to miniature, scurrying towards the parked sedan.

Mr Uniatz raised his gun and was aiming carefully when Simon's hand clamped on his wrist in a grip of iron.

"No!" he ordered. "We'll only have Fernack back—and next time he won't be so easy to get rid of."

"Chees, boss!" Hoppy complained mournfully, staring at the sedan roaring down the street. "I had a bead on him."

"In the dark? Shooting downward at that distance?" Simon snapped. He turned away, crossing the living room. "Don't be a goddam fool. Besides"— he stepped out of the darkness of the living room into the hallway—"there's been enough noise for one night."

Hoppy shuffled after him, muttering indignantly: "Nobody can gimme de business an' get away wit' it."

The Saint looked at him resignedly.

"Don't blame *him!* Grabbing that doorknob after I'd wired it was your own damn fault."

"I wouldn'a done it if it wasn't for him," Hoppy insisted sullenly. "Besides, how do I know he can run like dat? All de zombies I ever see in pitchers more slower dan Bilinski. Dis musta bin a new kind, boss. Maybe somebody gives him a hypo."

"Maybe somebody does," Simon agreed. "And the doc's name could be Spangler."

He switched the lights on at the entrance and looked around. The loose rug that had been involved in Hoppy's downfall was a tousled heap in the middle of the floor; and as he lifted one corner to straighten it he saw the gun underneath it.

He picked it up gingerly—a heavy "banker's" model revolver with a two-inch barrel.

"Chees," Hoppy said. "De lug forgets his equalizer. Now all we gotta do is find out who it belongs to, an' we know who he is."

"That piece of logic," said the Saint, "has more holes in it than Swiss cheese. However——"

He broke off as he became aware that the elevator doors were opening in front of him. For one instant he was tense, with his forefinger curling instinctively on the trigger of the weapon in his hand. Then he saw the passenger clearly.

He was a rabbity little man draped in a flowered bathrobe, with pince-nez supporting a long black ribbon.

"I," he enunciated pompously, "am your neighbor downstairs, Mr Swafford. Has there been any trouble?"

He stepped back suddenly, with his eyes popping, as Hoppy moved into full view from behind the Saint.

"Trouble?" Simon inquired politely. "What sort of trouble?"

Mr Swafford seemed hypnotized by the baleful apparition glaring at him over the Saint's shoulder.

"I," he swallowed. "I—— Please forgive me," he said hastily, "but there was some rumor—about a shot, I think it was. Some people in the building seem to think it came from up here."

Simon turned to Hoppy.

"Did you hear a shot?"

Mr Uniatz fixed Mr Swafford with a basilisk glare. He growled: "Boss, dis guy must be nuts!"

Mr Swafford gulped and amended hastily: "Of course I don't say it came from your apartment. It was just what some of the tenants thought. They seem to have jumped to the conclusion that someone was being shot, but I assure you——"

"I'm sure," the Saint broke in pleasantly, "that there must be a more productive form of exercise than jumping to conclusions, don't you think, comrade?"

Mr Swafford retreated another step, his eyes bulging wider as they confirmed their impression of the gun in the Saint's hand and the fallen shower of plaster from the ceiling.

"Oh, yes, of course," he said weakly. "I never——"

"I'm sorry you were disturbed," said the Saint benevolently. "My friend here is just in from Montana, where men are men and have notches in their guns to prove it. When they're having fun, they just blaze away at the ceiling. I've just taken his six-shooter away and tried to explain to him——"

"Scram before I step on ya like a roach!" Hoppy bellowed, squeezing past the Saint.

Mr Swafford stumbled backwards, his pince-nez dropping from his long nose and dangling by their ribbon; he turned and scurried precipitately back into the elevator.

"Good night, Mr Swafford," Simon called breezily, as the closing elevator doors blotted out the little man's pallid stare.

He turned back into the apartment, shutting the door behind him.

"Boss," Hoppy said, following him, "dis is gettin' monogamous. Just one t'ing after anudder."

"That sounds almost bovine to me," said the Saint. "But it'll probably get worse before it gets better."

He was sure that he had recognized the squat silhouette of Spangler's henchman, Max, fleeing from the building toward the waiting sedan. But he was still wondering, as he fell asleep, just why Doc Spangler had sent him.

CHAPTER SIX

HOPPY was in the penthouse kitchen frying bacon with concentrated absorption late the next morning when the doorbell rang. The Saint, seated in the adjoining breakfast alcove, put down the morning paper and stood up.

"I'll get it, boss," Hoppy offered, laying down the fork in one hand and the comic section clutched in the other.

"Never mind." Simon strode across the kitchen. "I don't want to take your mind off Dick Tracy."

The opening door revealed a vision in daffodil yellow with hair to match and a quizzical smile.

"Pat!" Simon drew her in and held her at arm's length, boldly admiring. "You're a sight to be held!"

He suited the action to the word.

She laughed breathlessly, pulling away.

"Darling, you have one of the most elemental lines since Casanova."

His eyes caressed her figure. "The most elemental lines," he said, "are never spoken. They're looked at."

"Do I look as good as Connie?" she inquired with arched eyebrows.

"Much better." He took her hand and led her toward the kitchen. "Hoppy!" he called, "bring on the vitamins."

"Comin' up, boss!" Hoppy sang out, and came around to deposit a glass of pale amber liquid in front of her as she sat down. "Vitamins," he grinned, and retreated back to his stove.

"Thank you." Pat smiled and lifted the glass.

"Wait." Simon reached over and took the glass from her. He sniffed it. "I thought so!"

"What's the matter?" Pat asked. "Isn't it all right?"

He pushed the glass back.

"Smell it."

She sniffed the glass and sat up, laughing. "Brandy!"

Hoppy's head appeared over the top of the alcove partition.

"Whassamatter, boss?"

"Thanks for the compliment," said Patricia, "but I'm not quite up to your kind of fruit juice."

Mr Uniatz's brow furrowed in hurt bewilderment.

"It's from grapes, ain't it? Grapes is fruit, ain't it?" He reached behind him and raised up the bottle for all to behold. "It says so, right here on de bottle."

The Saint waved him away in despair.

"Never mind," he said. "Bring on the solid food."

"Okay, boss." Hoppy removed the offending liquor and drained it at a gulp. He went back into the kitchen and looked over the partition onto the top of Pat's blond head. "Dijja read about de fight in de paper dis mornin'?" he asked.

"They arrested the Masked Angel, didn't they?"

"But not for long," Hoppy said complacently. "We fix dat, don't we, boss?"

Pat's clear eyes studied the Saint.

"What does he mean—you fixed it up?"

"We informed the law that the Masked Angel is an old chum of Hoppy's," Simon explained glibly. "Naturally, with that kind of a character reference, they're bound to let Bilinski go."

"I don't trust you," Patricia said coldly. "Not for a minute. What goes on?"

"Goes on?" The Saint's eyebrows lifted.

"I know you too well. You wouldn't have left me last night the way you did unless something had——"

She broke off as the doorbell sounded briefly.

"I'll let her in, boss," Hoppy said cheerfully, and paddled out of the kitchen.

" 'Her'?" Patricia quoted acidly. "Miss Grady, I presume?"

"A purely professional visit," he said calmly. "After all, she *is* engaged to Steve Nelson."

Pat's cool red mouth curved cynically.

"A passing fiancé, no doubt."

Simon's eyes closed in pain.

"My dear girl," he protested.

He got to his feet as Hoppy trumpeted from the hallway.

"It's Connie Grady, boss!"

She hesitated in the kitchen door, slim and dewy-fresh, her short black curls making her look very young and almost boyish, with Hoppy looming up behind her like a grinning Cerberus.

"Come in, darling," said the Saint. He took her hand and led her to the breakfast alcove. "Miss Grady, this is my colleague, Miss Holm."

"Hullo, Connie," said Patricia sympathetically. "Welcome to the harem."

Connie Grady glanced uncertainly from Pat to Simon. "I—I didn't know you were having company," she said. "I didn't want to——"

"It's perfectly all right," Simon assured her. "Pat really is my colleague in—er—many of my enterprises. Anything you say to me you can say to her with equal freedom." He waved to Hoppy. "That's another of my colleagues—Hoppy Uniatz."

"Likewise, I'm sure," Hoppy beamed. "I seen ya lotsa times when your pop was runnin' de old Queensberry Gym, remember? Ya useta bring him his lunch."

Her elfin features crinkled in a smile.

"Yes . . . I remember."

"Sit down," said the Saint. "We're just starting."

He saw her settled in the booth and pulled up another chair for himself, while Mr Uniatz doled out plates of bacon and eggs and cups of coffee with hash-house dexterity.

Connie picked up her fork and tried to start, but the effort of restraint was too much. She looked full at the Saint, with the emotion unashamed on her face.

"You saw what happened," she said, her voice small and tense. "The Angel killed a man last night. . . . Now, do you wonder that I don't want Steve to fight that—that gorilla?"

"I can see your point."

"When I was talking to you last night," she began, "I—I——" She fumbled as if groping for the right words.

Simon passed Patricia the sugar with harlequin courtesy. She didn't seem to see it.

She said sweetly: "Last night?"

"On the phone, after you called," Simon elucidated smoothly. "She wanted to know what went on, too. Her father was rather upset by our little visit to the Masked Angel's dressing room after the fight."

Patricia's red mouth pursed in a skeptical "Oh!"

Connie found the words at last: "I was hoping and praying they'd keep

that—that man in jail—that the fight would be called off . . ." Her voice
broke. "But they're releasing him."

"Are they?" Simon asked with interest. "I didn't see anything about it in
my paper."

"Daddy was over at police headquarters first thing this morning with
Spangler—he's the Masked Angel's manager."

The Saint nodded.

"I see. So they got the Angel out of the jug in spite of Hoppy's recom-
mendation."

"Steve is going through with this fight—if you don't do something about
it." Connie Grady's voice strained against her self-control. "He'll be killed!"

Hoppy gulped on a mouthful that would have choked a horse.

"Killed? De Champ? Why, he'll moider de bum!"

Connie turned on him sharply.

"You think so? After what the Masked Angel did to Torpedo Smith
last night? That—that so-called bum has beaten every man he's fought."

"Under Doc Spangler's ministry, at least," the Saint amended.

"Aah, dey was fakes!" Hoppy derided. "Dey musta bin!"

"When Torpedo Smith was killed last night," she said tensely, "do you
think *he* was faking?"

"You know, of course," Simon said to Connie, "who the Masked Angel
really is, don't you?"

She nodded wearily.

"Yes, of course. Daddy owns part of him."

She looked up quickly, as if suddenly realizing what she had said. "I
mean," she stumbled confusedly, "he doesn't have any interest in him directly—that is, not really. It's just that Spangler owes Daddy money, and—
and——"

"Of course," Simon soothed gently, "I understand. It's just that Doc
Spangler is paying off your father from his earnings on the Masked Angel."

She seemed grateful for the lead.

"Yes. Yes, that's it."

"After all," the Saint observed casually, "it's not considered ethical for a
matchmaker to hold a financial interest in any of his contestants—or at
least a major share—so naturally Mr Grady would avoid that sort of thing.
Especially where a championship bout was concerned."

Connie Grady looked up suddenly.

"I don't want Steve to be one of those contestants!" she burst out, her
emerald eyes misting. She turned away. "I sound—ridiculous, don't I? I—I
wouldn't dream of asking this of anyone else in the world. You—you're the
only person I could possibly imagine being capable of—somehow arranging
it so that the fight would never happen."

"Exactly what are you suggesting?" Pat asked curiously. "Do you think the Saint could persuade Nelson not to fight?"

Connie flashed her a startled glance.

"Oh, no!" she said. "If he knew I'd come here to ask Mr Templar—he'd never forgive me." She turned to Simon pleadingly. "There must be some—other way. I can't say how. I only know that you've done things—in the past that—that were like miracles. . . . Daddy has told me about—some of your adventures."

"Well, well," said Patricia admiringly. "Simon Templar, the Paul Bunyan of modern crime. Have you another miracle up your sleeve?"

Then she caught the stricken look on Connie's face and her laughter softened. She put an arm about the girl's shoulders and looked up at the Saint questioningly.

"Simon, what do you think?"

"I think," said the Saint, "that we ought to go on with breakfast before it all gets cold, or Hoppy eats it."

He deliberately devoted himself to his own plate, and insisted on that matter-of-fact diversion until even Connie Grady had to follow with the others. He knew that the letdown was what she needed if she could be eased into it, and for his own part a healthy appetite was mixed with the need for an interlude of constructive thinking in approximately equal pro-portions. If it was obvious that Connie's concern for Steve Nelson was absolutely real, it was no less plain to the Saint that she still hadn't come out with everything that was on her mind.

He waited until the commonplace mechanics of eating had achieved an inevitable slackening of the tension, and then he said almost casually: "Of course one thing we might do is shoot Barrelhouse Bilinski——"

"No, no," Connie gasped; but her tone was now more impatient than fearful. "I didn't mean anything like that. I don't want—anybody hurt." She shook her head. "There must be something—something else you could do. You're clever . . ."

Simon considered the tip of his cigarette a moment, the smoke trickling from his mouth.

"Does your father know you're here?" he asked.

"Of course not!" The idea seemed to startle her. "I couldn't tell him I'm trying to have the fight stopped—any more than I could tell Steve!"

"Steve is pretty good at his profession," Simon remarked. "Does he know how you feel about his chances against the Angel?"

"How could I tell him? I've tried to make him quit now—with the cham-pionship. It hasn't done any good. He's so sure, so confident! If he only had sense enough to be afraid, to realize!"

"Realize what?" Simon queried mildly.

"That it's not—not worth risking his life——"

"He's retiring after this next fight, according to the papers," Patricia said.

"Yes, I know. He promised me. . . . But it may be too late by then." Hoppy was shaking his head uncomprehendingly.

"You talk like he's a cream puff," he said. "He's de Champ, ain't he?"

"Connie," said the Saint gently, holding her eyes, "is there any other reason why you think Steve won't win? Something you haven't told me yet?"

She drew back.

"No." She turned away. "I've told you everything. I—— Spangler used to be a doctor once," she said quickly. "I mean a real doctor, I—— Suppose he uses hypnotism? I know how crazy that sounds, but something will happen to Steve! I know it will!"

None of this was particularly fresh grist for Simon's cogitative mill. He sighed.

"If Steve gives his usual performance," he reasoned, "I don't see that Bilinski stands a prayer. As for Doc Spangler's hypnotic powers—I wouldn't worry too much about them, if I were you, Connie."

Her mouth trembled.

"I'm sorry. I might have known that you'd talk just like Steve does. . . . You and that—trainer of his."

Simon's brows lifted.

"Trainer?"

"Whitey Mullins."

Hoppy, reaching for the coffeepot, turned eagerly.

"Ya mean Whitey's trainin' de Champ? Say!" He beamed with the fanged grimace of a delighted dinosaur. "Whitey's a great guy."

The green eyes flashed at him.

"Is he? What does Mullins care what happens to Steve? All *he* cares about is getting even with Spangler. He's just using Steve for a cat's-paw!"

Hoppy blinked, his mouth open.

"I didn't know de Champ's a southpaw, but everybody knows Whitey has it in for de Doc ever since Spangler finagles Bilinski's contract away from him. Dat's an old story." He shook his head dazedly. "And all de time I t'ink Nelson is a right-hander! He fights like one."

Pat suppressed a smile.

"There doesn't seem to be much wrong with having a handler who's so interested in seeing the Angel beaten."

"But the Angel won't be beaten," Connie said hopelessly. "Steve'll be killed! He hasn't a chance!"

Simon studied her broodingly.

"You're very sure of that," he said, and reached into his pocket to bring something out. He went on without a change of tone: "Did you ever see this before?"

On the table between them he laid the revolver which last night's visitor had left behind.

By no perceptible sign, the Saint sensed a sudden change in her, an inner freezing, her eyes coming into focus on the gun, her whole being gripped by that thanatoid stillness that stands on the threshold of panic.

"Where," she said, in a small tight voice, "did you get—that?"

"It was left here last night as a sort of—calling card."

Patricia was staring at him.

"Last night?"

"Some hopped-up heister crashes de jernt," Hoppy snorted. "He gets away before we can even see who it is. But we give him such a scare he forgets de rod."

"You didn't tell me!" Pat accused. "You finished that brawl at the Arena over here, didn't you?" She searched Simon's face narrowly, and sensed the truth with the swift certainty of an intuition ground to psychic fineness by the countless abrasions of past experience. "Someone followed you here and tried to kill you!"

The Saint bowed.

"Darling, you know our kind of friends too well."

Connie Grady stood up. She gathered up her purse and gloves with unsteady hands. Her face was pale, the magnolia skin drawn and haggard. She tried to ignore the revolver on the table, but her eyes kept flitting back to it, under the spell of some kind of frightening fascination.

"I'm sorry I bothered you like this," she said with nervous breathlessness. "It was silly, really. I——" She broke off, walking quickly to the door. "Goodby."

"No, wait!"

"Please."

She almost ran out of the apartment, and the front door slammed behind her.

Patricia and Hoppy returned their blank stares to the Saint—Patricia's tinged with irony.

"Too bad," she said. "And you were just starting to make such an impression."

"Chees," Hoppy said between mouthfuls, resuming his assault on the food, "de Torpedo gettin' killed last night kinda made her blow her top, huh, boss?"

"It was that gun," Pat stated, "that upset her. Why?"

Simon picked up the revolver and turned it idly in his hands.

"My crystal ball doesn't work like yours," he said, and he smiled at her. "Rather an attractive little thing, isn't she?"

"Oh, rather," Pat agreed, her smile sweetly corrosive; "if you like them on the slightly hysterical side."

Simon laughed, his fingernail tracing the small intertwined letters engraved on the metal just above the stock of the gun.

"Poor Melusina," he sighed whimsically. "I'm afraid her dear old daddy is making her cry."

"Melusina? What are you talking about? I thought her name was Connie."

"So it is. The term was merely analogous. Melusina was a fairy. A French fairy." Simon grinned provocatively. "If you ever delved into such matters in your youth, dear, you'll remember the story."

"I never was as good at fairy tales as you," Pat said demurely.

"Melusina," Simon continued imperturbably, "was no end attractive and quite easy to take—even if she was on the slightly hysterical side. However, she happened to suffer an injury from her father, for which, if memory serves, she had him imprisoned inside a mountain. She, in turn, was punished by being turned into a snake from the waist down every Saturday night."

"She ought to have been able to wriggle out of that one," Patricia said dryly. "But what has it got to do with Miss Grady, if anything?"

"Boss, don't she t'ink Smith got killed by accident?" Hoppy demanded.

"Inasmuch as you raise the question," Simon said, "I'll give you an answer. No."

"Obviously," said Patricia. "But what do *you* think?"

"She's quite right. It wasn't an accident."

Mr Uniatz absorbed half a cup of coffee at a gulp, scowling interestedly. "Ya mean de Torpedo ain't knocked off fair and square?"

The Saint nodded thoughtfully.

"Indubitably not—if instinct serves, and I think it does. At any rate, we're going to look into the matter."

"What are you going to do, Simon?"

The Saint smiled at her, and then at the gun lying on the palm of his hand.

"We're going to call on the man who owns this," he said. "Wish we could take you along, but unfortunately . . ."

"But you said you didn't even see who it was who left that gun here!" she exclaimed. "How do you know who——"

"I know who owns these initials," said the Saint patiently, lifting the gun for her inspection. He showed her the monogram in fancy script on the metal. "They're rather difficult to untangle, but I think you can make them out."

Hoppy leaned over.

"Initials?" he queried, peering at the gun. "Where?"

"M . . . G," Pat read. "M-G? But who is M G?"

"Offhand, I'd say it was Connie's father, Michael Grady, wouldn't you?" Simon kissed her, and stood up. "Let's get started, Hoppy. We may be able to dig her old man out of the mountain."

CHAPTER SEVEN

THE SAINT entered by one of the side entrances of the Manhattan Arena and found himself, as he expected, in the office wing of the building. The corridors and reception rooms were alive with voices and sporting gentry of varied interests and importance; for this was a crossroads of the indoor sporting world, and through these catacombs paraded its foremost and hind-most representatives.

Simon moved silently and inconspicuously along the shadowed wall of the main hall and stepped into the main reception room.

It was a bare and unkempt antechamber, its hard chairs and bare benches occupied by a garrulous covey of promoters, managers, sportswriters, ticket speculators, and professional athletes of varied talents and notoriety, all obviously waiting to see the great Mike Grady. A fog of tobacco smoke hung over the room like stale incense burnt to strange and violent gods; the voices of the votaries droned a ragged litany punctuated by coarse yaks of laughter. There was something about them that marked them as a distinct species of metropolitan life; each was subtly akin to the other, no matter how different their outer hides might be. It lay, perhaps, in the mutual boldness of their eyes, the uninhibited expression of primitive emotion, the corner-of-the-mouth asides and the sudden loudly profane rodomontades in lower-bracket dialects. Their eyes appraised him pitilessly as he threaded his way through them, like circus animals taking the measure of a new trainer; but in the same moment their inquisitorial glances flipped away again, as if even under his easy elegance they recognized instinctively a fellow member of their own predatory species.

The girl at the switchboard near Grady's office door, who doubled as receptionist, surveyed the Saint in the same way as he approached her. But even her dead-pan appraisal softened responsively to the intimate flattery of his smile, the irrepressible proposition of his blue eyes, and the devil-may-care lines of chin and mouth. . . . He was opening the door of Grady's private office before she suddenly remembered her duties as sentry of the sanctum.

"Hey, come back here!" she cried. "You can't go in there!"

Like other women who had tried to tell the Saint what he couldn't do, she thought of her objections a little late. The Saint was already in.

Michael Grady was sitting tilted back in his swivel chair, his feet resting on the edge of his huge desk, his broad snub-nosed face turned upward at the ceiling as he cuddled a telephone in the crook of his jaw and shoulder. His gaze swung downward as he heard the door close, and his eyes, which matched the Saint's for blueness, bulged with embryonic eruption.

The Saint waved a debonair greeting and sank into a worn leather club chair facing him.

The promoter grunted a couple of times into the telephone, his eyes fixed on Simon Templar's, and hung up, his feet returning to the floor with a crash.

"And who the hell might you be?" he blasted.

A rich brogue was still ingrained in his gravelly tenor, although as the Saint well knew it had been thirty years since he had left his native Ireland. The ups and downs of Mike Grady's turbulent career to his present eminence as promoter of the Manhattan Arena was a familiar story to the city's sporting gentry; it was a career which on the whole, Simon knew, had won Grady more friends than enemies—and those enemies the kind an honest but headstrong man easily makes on his way to the top.

"The name," Simon announced, "is Simon Templar."

Grady stared at him, digesting the name, seeking a familiar niche for it, his brows drawn in a guarded frown. He opened his mouth as if to speak, then closed it again as recognition dawned in his eyes and wiped away the frown. He leaned forward on his desk.

"The Saint?" he asked unbelievingly, and sprang to his feet without waiting for a reply. "Of course! I should've known!" He came from behind the desk, extending an eager hand. "Glad to meet you, Saint!"

Simon rose to his feet and allowed his arm to be used like a pump handle.

"And it's a shame you've not visited me before," Grady enthused. "Why, only yesterday one of the boys brings up your name as a possibility for master of ceremonies for the Summer Ice Follies we're puttin' on soon. The Saint and Sonja Henie! Can't you just see that billin'! It'd be sensational! You'd pack 'em in! We'd have it in all the papers—on billboards—on the radio——"

"And in skywriting," said the Saint. "Well, I suppose the world will always beat a path to the door of the man who builds a better claptrap, but I didn't come as a performer in that line. I—er—already have a—sort of profession, you know."

"A profession? You?" Grady smiled jestingly. "And what would that be?"
"I'm what you might call a haunter," said the Saint.
Grady's brows knitted.
"A haunter?"
"Of guilty consciences."
"That," said Mr Grady after a pause, "I don't get."
Simon helped himself to a cigarette from the dispenser on the desk.
"Well," he said engagingly, "take your conscience, for example."
Grady grinned at him.
"And why would you be hauntin' *my* conscience? It's crystal clear."
Simon struck a match.
"Is it?"
"Indeed it is."
"Even about your secret partnership with Doc Spangler?"
Grady's grin faded. He turned abruptly, went back behind his desk, and
sat down. His fingertips tapped a nervous tattoo on the top of his desk for a
moment.
"Even if that were true," he said finally, "would it be a crime?"
The Saint also sat down again, lowering himself through a leisured breath
of smoke.
"I always heard you were an honest man, Mike," he said quietly. "Span-
gler's a crook, and you know it."
Grady flushed.
"I don't know anything of the sort!" he snapped. "So he served time once.
What of it? A man can make a mistake."
"I know," Simon nodded. "And you put him back on his feet; gave him a
job at the Queensberry Gym."
"The best damn' masseur I ever had!"
"Very likely. He was an MD before they took away his license for ped-
dling dope." Simon consulted his cigarette ash. "Mike, you even advanced
him money to go into business as a fight manager, didn't you?"
Grady stirred impatiently.
"Well, what of it?" he demanded. "When I got this job here at the Arena
I gave up the gym. Doc didn't want to work there without me, so I loaned
him a couple of grand."
"For which he gave you a share in Barrelhouse Bilinski as collateral."
"Well——" Grady chuckled, but his humor was laciniated with unease.
"It didn't seem like much collateral at the time. He wasn't the Masked
Angel then, you know."
"I know."
"Well, then," Grady said, spreading his square freckled hands expres-
sively, "you know how good Spangler is. A great fighter he's made out of a
broken-down stumble bum."

The Saint shook his head sadly.

"Mike," he protested, "anyone, a child—even Connie, your own daughter —might be skeptical of that. In fact, if she knew about your partnership with Spangler, she might even be afraid that you're mixed up in something not quite——"

Grady stiffened, his face reddening.

"And what the hell has my daughter to do with this?"

The Saint's disclaimer was as bland as cold cream.

"Why, nothing at all, Mike. I merely mentioned her as a possibility."

"Well, you just leave her out of this!" Grady glared at him and then looked away restlessly. "Maybe it isn't according to Hoyle for me to have a financial interest in Bilinski," he grumbled, "but it doesn't matter a damn to me if he wins or loses, just so I get my two grand back."

"By the way," said the Saint, "how does Spangler get away with Bilinski wearing that old sock over his head?"

"He has special permission from the Boxin' Commission," Grady replied curtly. "It's a legitimate publicity stunt."

"If there is such a thing," Simon admitted. "But it certainly improves his appearance."

"He'll have to take it off for the Championship fight," Grady informed him sourly, "when he gives Steve Nelson the beatin' he deserves!"

The Saint's probing eyes drooped with offensive restraint.

"You seem to lack a certain enthusiasm for your future son-in-law," he observed.

"Not *my* son-in-law!" roared the promoter. "No common knuckle-head box fighter is going to marry the daughter of Mike Grady, I can tell you. I don't know what tales you been hearing, but she's not marrying that punk, you can depend on it!"

"What are you going to do—forbid the banns?"

"I'll not see her tied to a lowser with no more future than a cake of ice," Grady said belligerently. "I've seen what happens to the most of 'em after their fightin' days are done, with their brains addled and the eyes knocked out of 'em, no money saved and their wives drudges!"

The Saint built an "O" with a smoke ring.

"So that's why you quarreled."

"I wouldn't call it a quarrel." The promoter's eyes glittered. "I told him just what I've told you, and I told him to let Connie alone."

"But if Steve is retiring after his fight with the Angel, as he says——"

"Sure! That's what he says," Grady snorted. "How many times have I heard *that* one before! So he's retiring. On what?"

Simon shrugged.

"On the purse, I suppose. Unless, of course, he gets killed before he can collect it. The way Smith was."

Mike Grady put his elbows on the desk and cupped his forehead in his hands, staring down at his desk.

"That was a terrible thing to happen," he said somberly. "But it was an accident." He looked up defiantly. "It wouldn't happen once in a million fights."

The Saint gazed at him thoughtfully. A pattern seemed to be unfolding. So Grady wanted no part of Connie's fiancé. He was in semi-partnership with Doc Spangler. But did he disapprove of Nelson enough to arrange his death? Was he of the same stripe as Spangler? . . . Somehow the Saint couldn't quite accept that. Grady was not wanting in the essential elements of humanity. A hotheaded obstinate old blowhard, perhaps—but not a wicked man. Shrewd, conniving, scheming maybe—but not a crook. Somewhere the thorn of conscience pricked. Somewhere beneath the flinty carapace was a naïvely sentimental heart. An expert in such things, the Saint felt certain of his diagnosis. And yet . . .

"Perhaps," said the Saint. "But I collect those one-in-a-million chances." He slipped the snub-barreled revolver out of his pocket and laid it almost casually on Grady's desk. "No doubt it was also one chance in a million that I found this in my apartment last night."

Grady stared at the gun in openmouthed amazement.

"Where the hell did you get that?" he demanded stupidly.

"It's yours, of course?"

"Sure it's mine. My initials are on it! Where'd you get it?"

"I told you. In my apartment last night. After my little interview with Spangler last night, some character broke into our ivory tower with the apparent idea of air-conditioning us with your heater. Unfortunately we had just booby-trapped the door in preparation for a visit from the tax collector. This other character didn't have a sense of humor, so he went away in a sort of huff."

Grady thrust himself from his chair and walked to the window. He stared out blindly, his hands folded across his chest, his face a thundercloud.

"I don't understand," he muttered. "Unless he sold it, or——" He turned to Simon abruptly. "That gun was stolen from me," he said flatly, "by Steve Nelson!"

The Saint tapped the ash from his cigarette dispassionately.

"Stolen?" he murmured.

"Yes, stolen!" Grady returned to his chair. "Last week. Right in this office. He took the gun and I've never seen it since—that is, until this moment."

"How do you know he took it?" the Saint asked.

"How do I know he took it!" Grady bawled. "The bastard nearly broke my arm!"

"Oh," Simon deduced innocently. "This, I take it, was during the quarrel you didn't have."

Grady glowered at the gun on the desk.

"If it wasn't a matter of business and money out of my pocket, I'd have had him thrown in jail for so long——"

"That Connie wouldn't even know him when he did come out?"

"Skip it."

"You pulled that gun on him, didn't you? And he took it away from you. Was that it?"

Grady's high-blood pressure became painfully evident.

"I said skip it!" he shouted. "I was defending myself—not that I couldn't handle the lowser with me bare hands if I had to!"

Simon rose to his feet and retrieved the gun.

"You won't mind if I borrow this until I trace the character who tried to use it on me last night?"

"Help yourself," Grady grunted darkly. "Did you have any idea who it was?"

"Do you think Steve Nelson could answer that question?"

Grady scowled and shook his head.

"It doesn't sound like him—sneakin' into a man's house . . . No, it couldn't have been! The lowser must have sold it or—lost it. Whoever got it from Nelson is the man you'll be wantin'.'."

The Saint stood up.

"That's who I'm going to find," he said. "I'll see you again, Mike."

Before the promoter realized that the interview was over, he had opened the door and sauntered out.

There was a sudden dampening of volume in the conversation about him as he emerged from Grady's office. Whereas he had attracted little attention on entering the reception room, his effrontery in crashing Grady's office ahead of everyone else now made him a marked man, the target of a concentrated battery of indignant eyes. But the Saint seemed wholly unaware of the hushed hostility as he paused by the girl at the switchboard and watched her plug in a connection.

"Yes, Mr Grady," she said. And after a moment: "Dr who? . . . Yes, sir, I'll get him for you right away."

She reached for the telephone directory on a shelf beside her.

"Crescent 3-1465," the Saint prompted helpfully.

She looked up like a startled gopher; and Simon Templar gave her the same friendly smile with which he had short-circuited her before.

"It was Dr Kurt Spangler you wanted, wasn't it?" he said, and strolled on out before she could find her voice.

Hoppy Uniatz had the engine of the convertible racing as Simon opened the door, and he scarcely gave the Saint time to sit down before he banged in the clutch and sent the car roaring up the street and lurching around the first corner against the lights.

"What are you trying to do?" Simon asked. "Pick up a ticket?"

"Don't worry, boss," Hoppy said. "De getaway is a cinch. I drove lotsa dese jobs before. Dijja blast him good?"

Simon considered him.

"What on earth are you talking about?"

"Dat bum, Grady! Ya just give him de business, don'tcha?"

The Saint shook his head patiently.

"No, Hoppy, no. I never said that our visitor last night was Mike Grady. Let's head for Riverside Drive—I want to talk to Steve Nelson in person."

CHAPTER EIGHT

THE BLUE CONVERTIBLE swept up Riverside Drive through the sixties, past the seventies, with the sun-drenched wind whispering through Simon Templar's crisp dark hair; it was a clean brisk wind cooled by the majestic mile-wide ribbon of the Hudson which ran parallel on their left, its shining waters stippled by the wind in a million breaking facets that caught the bright sunlight in broad mosaics of burnished gold. All in all, the Saint thought, it was much too gay and lovely a day for exploring spiritual sewers, or delving into the fetid labyrinths of murder.

They were in the eighties before the Saint signaled Hoppy to slow down.

"It's that house at the end of the block," he said.

The big car swooped to the curb and drew to a halt before one of the three-storied brownstone buildings which stand along Riverside Drive like autumnal spinsters, their old-fashioned elegance reminiscent of a more sedate and happier era.

"De champ live here?" Hoppy asked with some wonder.

"It says so in the directory."

"Wit' his dough, I'd be livin' on Park Avenue."

"That's why you wouldn't have his dough for long." Simon got out of the car. "Wait for me, Hoppy. I won't be long."

A glance at the letter boxes revealed that Steve Nelson had an apartment on the second floor. Simon opened the door and went to the foot of the thickly carpeted stairway. The gloom inside was stygian by contrast with the brightness of the street, but he was able to make out the doorway of Steve Nelson's apartment at the head of the stairs. From the same direction came the sound of male voices raised in argument.

Simon gripped the ornately carved banister and bounded upward lightly and with absolute silence; before he reached the top, however, the voices suddenly rose to shouting violence. There was a girl's scream, and the door flew open with a crash. A bull-necked citizen staggered backward out of the door, followed by a taller quick-moving younger man who gripped him by the shoulder, spun him around with a jerk, and sent him crashing down the stairs with a savage kick.

If the Saint hadn't been in the way, it is probable he would have continued to the bottom without more than two bounces. But, as it happened, Simon caught the impact of his weight on one arm and shoulder, lifted him to his feet, and had a good look at his face.

"Why, Karl!" Simon greeted him affably, keeping a firm grip on the dazed thug's lapel. "How you do get around."

Recognition and fear flared simultaneously in the gunman's eyes. With a sudden turn he jerked away and leaped the rest of the way down the stairs and disappeared out the door, leaving his coat in the Saint's hands.

"The Saint!" Connie Grady gasped.

There was a pale thread of repressed panic in her startled voice. She was standing in the doorway of Steve Nelson's apartment, staring down at Simon past one of Steve Nelson's broad shoulders.

The Saint went on up the stairs, with Karl's coat over his arm.

"Your playmate must have been in a hurry," he murmured. "Doesn't he know there's a clothing shortage?"

Nelson, blond and slim-waisted, gazed at the Saint puzzledly. He turned to Connie.

"It's the Saint," she said. "Simon Templar. I told you I met him yesterday. . . . My fiancé, Steve Nelson," she introduced them.

As Nelson turned to take Simon's hand, the Saint caught a glimpse of Connie's eyes over his shoulder, strained and pleading. So she was afraid he'd spill the beans about her visit to his apartment that morning.

"I'm afraid you came at rather a difficult moment," she was saying with a nervous laugh.

"If that character ever comes back again," Steve Nelson said deliberately, "he'll lose more than just a coat." He grinned. "Glad to know you, Saint. I've sure heard a lot about you. Won't you come in?"

Steve Nelson's apartment inside was considerably more attractive than the conservative exterior of the building seemed to indicate. Simon looked about him approvingly.

"Do sit down, won't you?" Connie invited, and he could feel her nervousness like a secret between them.

The Saint sat down, stretching his long legs luxuriously as he fished for his cigarettes.

Nelson dropped into a chair across the table and pushed a little wooden donkey toward him. He pumped its tail and a cigarette flopped out of its mouth into the Saint's lap.

Simon retrieved it admiringly.

"Quite a gadget," he remarked easily. "Too bad you haven't got one that tosses out undesirable guests with equal facility."

"That's one thing I'd rather do by hand," Nelson said. "You know him, eh?"

The Saint's shoulders lifted slightly. "Karl? We've met." He glanced at Connie. She was still standing, watching him tensely. "One of Doc Spangler's favorite thugs." He struck a light and lit his cigarette, aware of Nelson's silent curiosity about his visit. "Unfortunately," he commented, "his mind has too much specific gravity—which is only natural, perhaps, when you consider that there's more solid ivory on top of it than even my friend Hoppy Uniatz can boast."

"Who?" Nelson asked wonderingly.

They all turned to the door as a sudden rush of giant footfalls came pounding up the stairs.

"That would be him now," Simon announced calmly.

"Boss!" Hoppy's laryngismal bellow shook the panels of the door almost as forcefully as the crash of his fist. "Boss, you all right? Boss!"

The Saint sprang to his feet, but Connie was already opening the door.

Hoppy surged in, looking around alertly. He spotted Simon with a gusty sigh of relief.

"Hoppy," Connie cried in alarm. "What's the matter?"

"Chees!" wheezed Mr Uniatz. "I see dat monkey Karl comin' out after you go in, an' when you don't come out after him——"

"You really thought that brainless ape had taken me? You didn't stop him to find out?"

Mr Uniatz floundered with embarrassment.

"Well, I chase him, boss, but he dives into somebody's basement on West End Avenoo, an' I'm kinda worried about what goes wit' youse, so I come back to find out."

The Saint handed him Karl's coat.

"He was just streamlining his wardrobe. You can have it—it's about your size and certainly your style."

He turned to Nelson. "This is Hoppy Uniatz. Hoppy—meet the Champ, Steve Nelson."

Hoppy thrust out a hamlike paw as he grabbed the coat with the other. "Likewise, I'm sure," he beamed.

"This your sparring partner?" Nelson asked, looking Hoppy up and down with respect.

"Not Hoppy," said the Saint regretfully. "He forgot all the Queensberry rules long ago. When Hoppy fights, he uses everything he has—including his head, elbows, knees, and feet. That is, when he can't use brass knuckles, a beer bottle, or a blackjack."

"Well, yeah," Hoppy admitted, "a sap makes t'ings easier, but ya can't handle it wit' dem big gloves on."

"I guess not," Nelson said politely.

"But I'll sure be glad to spar wit' youse, just de same," Hoppy said. "I myself can knock dis Masked Angel kickin' and so can you."

"That's what the Angel's manager seems to be afraid of," Nelson said. He turned to Simon. "He sent that bum I threw out to proposition me."

The Saint regarded him steadily.

"Tell me more."

"Spangler's offering him the Angel's share of the purse!" Connie broke in, a note of hysteria in her voice. "Steve'll get the whole purse if he—if——"

She was trembling.

"Take it easy, baby," Nelson soothed, putting an arm around her shoulders. He looked at Simon. "I get the Angel's cut of the purse if I throw the fight. That's the proposition." He showed his teeth humorlessly. "The Boxing Commission will get a kick out of it when I tell them."

Simon shook his head.

"I'm afraid Spangler will only deny it."

"But Connie's a witness!"

"Of course. But Karl was drunk. He didn't know what he was doing or saying. And he was kidding anyway. Karl's a great little kidder. At least, that's what Spangler will say, and Karl will agree with him absolutely. Spangler may even fire him—in public anyway—for being a bad boy." The Saint shrugged. "I wouldn't bother about reporting it to the Commission if I were you, Steve. Just go ahead and flatten the Angel. Tell the Commission afterwards."

"No!" Connie cried. "Steve ought to report it first. Spangler shouldn't be allowed to get away with it. He's a crooked manager and it's going to be a crooked fight!"

"I can take care of myself," Nelson said irritably. "The fight's going on, baby, come hell or high water. And I'm not going to get hurt. After all the good men I've fought, you have to worry about a stumble bum like the Angel!"

"Lookit, Champ," Hoppy said proudly. "I got a idea."

"What?"

"Whyncha tell de Doc you'll take his proposition—cash in advance? Get de dough an' den knock de fat slob for a homer. What's wrong wit' dat?"

"I'm afraid it would offer undesirable complications," Simon vetoed amiably. "There are enough complications to straighten out as it is." He pulled Mike Grady's gun from his pocket. "This, for instance," he said, and handed it, butt first, to Steve Nelson.

For the space of two seconds a startled stillness froze the room.

Then Nelson put out his hand slowly and took the weapon. He glanced at it, looked at the Saint a moment, then turned to meet Connie's wide stare. Her eyes were dark with apprehension.

The narrow margin of Mr Uniatz's brow knotted in puzzlement.

"Boss," he said hoarsely, "ya don't mean it was *him*?"

The champion's eyes flashed to the Saint.

"What's this about?" he clipped. "Where'd you get this?"

"From some character who paid us a call last night. We've been trying to find out who he was and return it to him, in case he feels undressed without it. Mike Grady admits the gun is his, but he claims you stole it from him."

"That's ridiculous!" Connie jumped up, her eyes flashing. "Daddy was—he wasn't himself!" Sudden tears spilled down the curve of her cheeks. She continued with difficulty: "He—he'd been drinking too much. Steve had to take the gun away from him."

She flung herself on the sofa and buried her face in her hands. Steve Nelson put his arm about her shoulders.

"That's okay, baby," he comforted, "that's okay."

Hoppy stirred uncomfortably; but the Saint accepted the emotional demonstration and Nelson's uncertain glare with Indian equanimity. He was completely impersonal, completely unconfused.

He lighted another cigarette, and exhaled with judicious patience.

"All I'm interested in," he said, "is how that gun happened to find its way into my apartment last night."

Nelson seemed uncertain whether to explain or fight.

"Sure, I—I took the gun away from Grady, but how it got into the hands of a burglar I don't know. I gave it back to Connie to give back to her father." He turned to her. "You did return it to him, didn't you, honey?"

She sat up, drying the teary dampness from her nose, and shook her head in silent negation.

Nelson stared at her.

"You didn't?"

She stuffed the handkerchief away.

"I didn't want him to have it!" she said vehemently. "He wasn't safe with it. After what he did to you——"

"But——"

"I gave it to Whitey to get rid of," she said. "I told him to drop it in the river!"

"I know Whitey," said Mr Uniatz. "He's a good trainer, Champ."

"He's my manager too, now," Nelson said.

Simon stroked the ash tray with the end of his cigarette, clearing the glowing end.

"Since when?" he inquired.

"We signed the papers yesterday." Nelson turned back to Connie. "Whitey never said anything about you giving him the gun."

"Why should he? I just told him to get rid of it and not say anything to anybody."

"Whitey's okay," Mr Uniatz insisted, to make his point absolutely clear. "He can do ya a lotta good."

"Sure," Nelson asserted moodily, "and he's honest—which is a damn sight more than you say for most of 'em—not that your dad isn't honest, honey," he amended quickly. "We never quarreled over that."

The Saint drew his trimmed cigarette end to a fresh glow.

"It sounds cosy as hell," he murmured. "But I'd still like very much to find out what brother Mullins did with that gun after he got it."

The girl said: "I don't know . . . I don't know."

Footfalls sounded on the stairway outside and the doorbell rang.

"That's probably him now," Nelson said. "He's going to the gym with me."

He opened the door and Whitey Mullins stepped in, as advertised.

"Hiya, Champ," he greeted, and stopped short as he caught sight of Hoppy heaving to his feet.

"Whitey!" Mr Uniatz welcomed, surging forward and flinging a crane-like arm about Whitey's shoulders in leviathan camaraderie.

Mullins staggered beneath the shock of its weight; his derby slipped over his forehead and he pushed it back crossly.

"Easy, you big ape!" he snarled.

"We just hear you are de Champ's new manager," Hoppy bellowed happily.

"This is the Saint," Steve Nelson introduced. "You've heard of him."

Whitey Mullins's pale eyes widened a trifle; his mouth formed a nominal smile.

"You bet I have."

He thrust out a narrow monkeylike hand. "I seen you at the fights last night, didn't I?"

The Saint nodded, shaking the hand.

"I was there."

"Sure you seen us," Hoppy said. "You're de foist one tells us de Torpedo is croaked, remember?"

"I never wanna have nuttin' like that happen to me again," Mullins said grimly. "It's awful. I still can't figure how it coulda happened. The Torpedo was in great condition. The poor guy musta had a weak ticker—or sump'n." He turned to Simon, a faint gleam coming alive in his pale eyes. "I hear you raised a stink with that louse Spangler after the fight."

The Saint launched a smoke ring in the direction of the gun lying on the table and smiled dreamily.

"The stench you mention," he said, "was already there. Hoppy and I merely went to investigate its source."

"Yeah," Hoppy corroborated. "De Angel stinks out loud! Why, dat bum can't fight."

"How can you say that," Connie objected tensely, "when he's just killed a man in the ring?"

"That was an accident." Mullins waved away her fears with an impatient gesture of one thin hairy hand. "That crook Spangler will be eatin' off'n his social security when we get through with him, huh, Champ? You'll murder that big beef he stole from me!"

His hatchet face was venomous, as though distorted by an inward vision of vengeance.

"Whitey," Connie said, "what did you do with that gun?"

Whitey's rapt stare came back to earth and jerked in her direction.

"Gun?" he said blankly, and followed her glance at the table. "Oh, *that*." He looked quickly at Steve, at Simon and Hoppy, and back to Connie again.

"Yes, that," she said. "I told you to get rid of it."

"I did," Whitey said. "How did it get here?"

Hoppy grunted: "Some heister crashes de Saint's flat last night. He leaves de rod."

"Yeah? Who was it?"

"That," said the Saint amiably, "is what I'd like to know. If you got rid of this gun, what did you do with it?"

Mullins snapped his fingers as if smitten by recollection.

"Oh, Christ! I almost forgot!" He reached into his coat, extracted a wallet, and selected a ten and a five. He offered the two bills to Connie. "Here. It's your dough."

"Mine?" She didn't touch the money. "Why?"

"It's the dough I got fer it at th' hock shop," he explained. "Ten bucks on the rod—five bucks for the pawn ducat I sell for chips in a poker session the other night."

She shook her head quickly.

"No. You keep it. For your trouble."

Whitey unhesitatingly replaced the money in his wallet.

"Okay, if you say so."

"Who did you sell the ticket to?" Simon inquired casually.

"Mushky Thompson," Whitey said. "But it goes through his kick like a dose of salts. Pretty soon it's movin' from one pot to another like cash."

"Yes, but who got it in the end?" Nelson asked.

"I quit at three in th' morning. Who it winds up with, I couldn't say."
Whitey glanced at his wrist watch. " 'Bout time we was headin' for the gym,
Stevie."

"Was Karl sitting in on the game?" Simon persisted.

Whitey blinked.

"I don't think so."

"That's an expensive gun, Whitey," Simon pursued mildly. "Is ten all you
could get on it?"

Mullins spread his hands expressively.

"No papers, no license. Ten bucks and no questions asked is pretty good
these days."

"I haven't been following the market lately," Simon confessed. "Where
did you hock it?"

The trainer lifted his derby and thoughtfully massaged the bald spot in
his straw-colored hair with two fingers of the same hand.

"It's a place on Sixth Avenue, as I recall," he said finally, dropping his
chapeau back on its accustomed perch. "Near Forty-fourth. The Polar Bear
Trading and Loan Company."

The Saint picked up the gun again.

"Thanks. I may need this a bit longer—if nobody minds." He slipped it
into his pocket and glanced at Nelson. He said inconsequentially: "I
wouldn't do any boxing until that hand heals, Steve."

Whitey's eyes flashed to the hand Steve Nelson had been carrying palm
upwards to conceal the raw gash along its back. He swore softly as he examined it.

"It's just a scratch," Nelson scoffed. "I was going to take care of it before
we left."

"The next time our friend Karl visits you," Simon advised him, "don't give
him a chance to touch you. That finger jewelry he wears is more dangerous
than brass knuckles."

"Karl!" Whitey turned with outraged incredulity. "He was here?"

"He had a little proposition," Nelson said. "Wanted me to throw the fight
for both ends of the gate."

"The louse!" Mullins exploded. "The dirty no-good louse. I mighta known
Spangler'd try sump'n like that. He knows that ham of his ain't got a
chance."

Simon crushed out his cigarette in the ash tray.

"I'd feel even more sure of that if I could drop in and watch you train,
Steve," he said. "In fact, I'd rather like to work out with you myself."

"Any time," Nelson said.

"Tomorrow morning," said the Saint. "Come on, Hoppy—let's keep on
the trail of the roving roscoe."

CHAPTER NINE

THE ONLY CONNECTION that the Polar Bear Trading and Loan
Company might possibly have had with the animal for which it was named,
Simon decided as he entered the premises, was the arctic quality of its
proprietor's stare. This personality, however, was a far cry from the conventional bearded skullcapped shylock that was once practically a cliché in the
public mind. He was, in fact, a pale smooth-shaven young man with curly
black hair, elegantly attired in a sports jacket and striped flannels, who
scanned the Saint as he entered with eyes of a peculiar ebony hardness. He
barely lifted a brow in recognition as he caught sight of Hoppy on Simon's
heels.

"Hi, Ruby," Hoppy said. "I have a idea I remember dis jernt from 'way
back. Long time no see, huh?"

To the Saint's unsentimental blue eyes, Ruby slipped into a familiar
niche like a nickel into a slot. Just as a jungle dweller knows at a glance the
vulture from the eagle, the ruminant from the carnivore, so the Saint knew
that in the stone jungles of the city this specimen was of a scavanger breed—
with a touch of reptile, perhaps. And the fact that Mr Uniatz knew the
place of old was almost enough to confirm the discredit of its stony-eyed
proprietor.

Ruby flinched instinctively as Mike Grady's revolver appeared in the
Saint's fist, held for an instant with its muzzle pointed at the pawnbroker's
midriff, before Simon laid it on the counter.

"This gun," said the Saint, "was pawned here a few days ago. Remember?"

The pawnbroker studied it a moment. His delicately curved brows lifted
slightly, the tailored shoulders accompanying them upwards in the mere
soupçon of a shrug.

"I see lots of guns," he said tonelessly. "Every day."

He looked at Simon with eyes that had the blank unfocused quality of
the blind.

"Whitey Mullins hocks it," Hoppy amplified. "Ya know Whitey."

"However, he didn't claim it himself," Simon went on. "Someone else
did—a few days ago. I want to know who."

"Who are you?" Ruby asked in his flat monotone. "What gives?"

Hoppy grabbed his shoulder in a bone-crushing clutch and, with his
other hand, pointed a callused digit directly under Simon's nose.

"Dis," he explained unmistakably, "is de Saint. When de boss asks ya a
question, ya don't talk back."

Ruby shook off Hoppy's paw and flicked imaginary contamination from where it had been. He looked back to the Saint.

"So?" he said.

"This gun," Simon continued pleasantly, "was redeemed. Who turned in the ticket? I promise there's no trouble in it for you."

The young man across the counter sighed and stared moodily at the gun.

"Okay, so you give me a promise. Can my wife cash it at the bank if I get knocked off for talkin' too much?"

"No," Simon conceded. "But your chances of living to a ripe and fruitless old age are far better, believe me, if you do give me the information I want."

The pawnbroker's eyes slid over him with obsidian opacity.

It began to be borne in upon Mr Uniatz that his old pal was being very slow to co-operate. His reaction to that realization was a darkening scowl of disapproval. Backgrounded by the peculiar advantages of Hoppy's normal face, this expression conveyed a warning about as subtle as the first smoke rising from an active volcano. . . . Ruby caught a glimpse of it; and whatever cogitation was going on behind the curtain of his face reached an immediate conclusion.

"Why ask me?" he complained wearily. "I don't ask his monicker. I ain't interested. He's a tall skinny jerk with a face like a horse. He bought a set of throwing knives from me once. That's all I know."

The Saint's perspective roamed through a corridor of memory that Ruby's description had faintly illuminated. A nebulous image formed somewhere in the vista, and tried to coalesce within recognizable outlines; but for the moment the shape still eluded him.

"Give you ten on the rod," Ruby offered disinterestedly.

Simon picked up the revolver and slipped it back into his pocket.

"I'm afraid it isn't mine," he said truthfully; and a sardonic glimmer flickered in the young pawnbroker's eyes for an instant.

"You don't say."

"As a matter of fact, it belongs to George Murphy, whose initials are M G, spelled backwards," Simon informed him solemnly, and sauntered from the shop with Hoppy in his wake.

It was perhaps the way the black sedan roared away from the curb at the end of the block that pressed an alarm button in the Saint's reflexes. It forced itself into the stream of traffic with a suddenness that compelled the drivers behind to give way with screaming brakes. For one vivid instant, as if by the split-second illumination of a flash of lightning, Simon saw the driver, alone in the front seat, hunched over the wheel, his hat pulled low over his eyes, his face hidden in the shadow of the brim, a glimpse of stubbled jowl barely visible. He had an impression of two others crouched in the deeper shadow of the back seat, their faces obscured by handkerchiefs, the vague angle of their upraised arms pointing towards him. . . . All this the Saint saw, absorbed, analyzed, and acted upon in the microscopic fragment of time before he kicked Hoppy's feet from under him so that they both dropped to the sidewalk together as the black sedan raced by, sending a fusillade of bullets cracking over them into the pawnshop window beyond.

Hoppy Uniatz, prone on his stomach, fumbled out his gun and fired a single shot just as the gunmen's car cut in ahead of a truck and beat a red light.

"Hold it!" Simon ordered. "You're more likely to hurt the wrong people."

They scrambled up and dusted off their clothes.

"You okay, boss?" Hoppy asked anxiously.

"Just a bit chilled from the draft of those bullets going by."

Hoppy glared up the street at the corner where their assailants had vanished.

"De doity bastards," he rumbled. "Who wuz it, boss?"

The Saint had no answer; but if he had had, it would have been interrupted by the yelp of the curly-haired young man peering pallidly from behind the edge of the pawnshop doorframe.

"Get the hell away from here!" he bawled, with a shrill vibrato in his voice. "Get yourselves knocked off some other place!"

Hoppy turned on him redly, like a buffalo preparing to charge; but Simon grabbed one beefy bicep and yanked him back on his heels.

"Stop it, you damn fool!" he snapped. "Don't take it out on *him!*"

He stepped to the doorway, drawing the knife strapped to his forearm.

From within the pawnshop Ruby's voice, strident with fear, screeched: "Come in here and so help me God, I'll blast ya!"

Simon spotted him crouching behind a counter, goggling over the sights of a sawed-off shotgun. He thrust out a knee as a barrier to Hoppy's impulsive acceptance of the challenge, and began working quickly.

He was aware of the scared faces starting to peer out of windows, of people moving out of doorways and peeping around corners. A crowd seemed to be converging from every direction, drawn by the shots and the wildfire smell of excitement.

In a few seconds he cut out one of the bullets imbedded in the doorframe. He dropped the scarred slug in his pocket, and moved away.

"Let's get out of here," said the Saint, taking Hoppy's arm. "I still think it would be a social error to be arrested on Sixth Avenue, even if they have tried to change the name to 'Avenue of the Americas.'"

CHAPTER TEN

"WHO DONE IT?" Mr Uniatz asked once more, his neanderthaloid countenance still furrowed with the remnants of rage. "He makes me get mud on dis new suit."

The Saint grinned as he swung the convertible around a corner.

"Never mind, Hoppy," he said. "It helps to tone down the pattern. . . . Anyway, all I saw was two gentlemen with handkerchiefs over their faces in a black sedan with no rear license plate."

Hoppy scowled.

"I seen dat too," he grumbled. "What I wanna know is, who wuz dey?"

"Did you notice the outside hand of the fellow driving the car? It flashed in the sun."

Mr Uniatz blinked.

"Huh?"

"He was wearing a lot of finger jewelry."

"Finger jewelry?"

"Rings—large flashy rings."

For a long moment Hoppy strove painfully to determine the relation of the driver's digital ornamentation to his identity.

"Ya can't never tell about pansies," he concluded despondently.

The car swung east to Fifth Avenue and then south, moving leisurely with the traffic.

The Saint was in no hurry. He wanted a breathing spell to summarize the situation.

So far, two attempts had been made to murder him since the affair in the dressing room the previous night. An emotional thug might have found the Saint's insolence sufficiently provocative to inspire an urgent desire for his death; and certainly a blow in the solar plexus would be regarded in some circles as an act of war, and worthy of an act of reprisal. But somehow the Saint could not conceive of Dr Spangler, even with that kind of provocation, taking the risk of a murder charge. For Spangler was neither emotional nor reckless. He was an operator who had learned from experience to be thrifty of risks, to allow as wide a margin of safety as possible to every enterprise. An attempt to bribe Nelson was in line with that; but the only motive Spangler was likely to consider strong enough to justify an attempt at murder would be the fear that the Saint's interference might affect the Angel's chance of taking the title.

Would Spangler, even with a guilty conscience, have taken alarm so precipitately? Would he be afraid, on such scanty evidence, that the Saint had discovered the secret of the Angel's victories? . . . For that matter, was there any secret more sinister than common chicanery and corruption? So far, he could only conjecture.

"And that," said the Saint, "leaves us just one more call to make."

"Who we gonna see now, boss?" asked Mr Uniatz, settling philosophically into the social whirl.

"That depends on who's home."

Simon swung the car toward Gramercy Park, and presently slowed down as he turned into a secluded side street lined with graystone houses as conservatively old-fashioned in their way as the Riverside Drive brownstones were in theirs, but with a polished elegance that bespoke substantially higher rents.

"What home, boss?" Hoppy insisted practically.

The Saint peered at the numbers of the houses slipping by.

"Doc Spangler's."

Hoppy's eyes became almost as wide as shoe buttons.

"Ya mean it's de Doc what tries to gun us?"

"It was more likely one of the bad boys he chums around with," said the Saint. "But he probably knew about it. Bad companions, Hoppy, are apt to get a man into trouble. Of course you wouldn't know about that."

"No, boss," said Mr Uniatz seriously.

The Saint was starting to pull in towards one of the graystone houses when he saw the other car. The rear license plate was on now, but there was no doubt about the genesis of the neat hole with its radiation of tiny cracks that perforated the rear window. Simon pointed it out to Hoppy as he kept the convertible rolling and parked it some twenty yards further down the block.

"Chees," Hoppy said in admiration, "I hit it right in de middle. Dey musta felt de breeze when it goes by."

"I hope it gave them as bad a chill as theirs gave us," said the Saint.

They walked back to the house and went up the broad stone steps and rang the bell. After awhile the door opened a few inches. Simon leaned on it and opened it the rest of the way. It pushed back a long lean beanpole of a man with a sad horse face and dangling arms whose wrists stuck out nakedly from the cuffs of his sweater. And as he saw him, a gleam of recognition shot through the Saint's memory.

The tall man's recognition was a shade slower, perhaps because his faculties were slightly dulled by the surprise of feeling the door move into his chest. He exhaled abruptly, and staggered back, his long arms flying loosely as though dangling on strings. As he recovered his balance he took in Hoppy's monstrous bulk, and then the slim supple figure of the Saint closing the door after him and leaning on it with the poised relaxation of a watchful cat, the gun in his hand held almost negligently. . . . Slowly, the long bony wrists lifted in surrender.

The young pawnbroker's description repeated itself in the Saint's memory. Also he recalled Mike Grady's office and a tall thin character among the loiterers in the reception. This was the same individual. The odyssey of the gun was beginning to show connections.

"Who are you, chum?" Simon asked, moving lightly towards him.

"I know him, boss," Hoppy put in. "De name is Slim Mancini. He useta be a hot car hustler."

"I work here," the beanpole said in a whining nasal tenor that had a distinct equine quality about it. He sounded, the Saint thought, just like a horse. A sick horse. "I'm the butler," Mancini added. He glanced back at a door down the hall and opened his mouth a fraction of a second before the Saint stepped behind him and clamped a hand over it.

"No announcements, please," the Saint said, his other arm curving about Mancini's neck like a band of flexible steel. "This is strictly informal. You understand, don't you?"

The man nodded and gasped a lungful of air as the Saint removed the pressure on his throat.

"Slim Mancini—buttlin'!" Hoppy sneered hoarsely. "Dat's a laugh." He grunted suddenly as Simon jabbed a warning elbow into his stomach.

The muffled voices in the room down the hall had gone silent.

"Walk ahead of us to that door," the Saint whispered to Spangler's cadaverous lackey, "and open it and go in. Don't say anything. We'll be right behind you. Go on."

Mancini's sad eyes suddenly widened as he stared over the Saint's shoulder, apparently at something behind him.

Simon rather resented that. It implied a lack of respect for his experience, reading background, and common intelligence that was slightly insulting. However, he was accommodating enough to start to turn and look in the indicated direction. It was only a token start, and he reversed it so quickly that Mancini's hand was still inches from his shoulder holster when the Saint's left exploded against his lantern jaw.

Simon caught the toppling body before it folded and lowered it noiselessly to the carpet.

Mr Uniatz kicked it carefully in the stomach for additional security.

"De noive of de guy," he said. "Tryin' a corny trick like dat. Whaddas he t'ink we are?"

"He'll know better next time," said the Saint. "But now I suppose we'll have to open our own doors——"

Blam!

The stunning crash of a heavy-caliber pistol smashed against their eardrums and sent them diving to either side of the hallway.

The Saint lay there, gun at the ready, waiting. The shot had come from the room ahead, where they'd heard the voices; but he noticed that the door was still shut. . . . Seconds passed. . . . A weak moan, muffled by the closed door, punctuated the silence.

Simon signaled Hoppy with a lift of his chin, and they stood up again and advanced noiselessly. He motioned Hoppy back into the shadows as they reached the door. Then he turned the knob, kicked the door open, and stayed to one side, out of reach of possible fire.

There was silence for a moment. All he could see in the sunlit portion of the room visible to him was a huge fireplace and a corner of a desk. . . . Then from within came a challenge in an accent that was unmistakable.

"Well?" Dr Spangler barked impatiently. "Come in!"

The Saint stood there a moment, looking into the triangle of the interior visible to him, estimating his chances of meeting a blast of gunfire if he showed himself. In the two seconds that he stood there, weighing the odds, he also realized that an unexpected diversion had taken place. What it was he didn't know. But it did lend some excuse for hoping his presence might yet be miraculously undiscovered. . . . It was a flimsy enough hope, but he decided to gamble on it. He signaled Hoppy to stay back and cover him as best he could, and stepped into the room.

Doc Spangler was seated at the desk, leaning forward, his arms on the desk, staring at him. Beyond him in a corner of the big room was Karl, down on one knee beside the prostrate body of a man whose head was concealed by the squat body of Spangler's ursine lieutenant. There was a gun in his hand, pointed at the Saint from his hip, as if he had been interrupted in his examination of the man he had apparently just shot.

For one second it was quite a skin-prickling tableau; and then Simon took a quick step to one side which placed Spangler's body between him and Karl's gun muzzle.

"Better tell your baboon to lay his gun on the floor, Doc," he suggested, and his smile was wired for sudden destruction. "You might get hurt."

Spangler half turned in his swivel chair toward Karl.

"You imbecile!" he spat, his usual fat complacency temporarily disconnected. "I told you to put up that gun! It's gotten me into enough trouble for one day. Put it on the floor as he says."

Karl laid the gun down slowly, grudgingly, glooming balefully past Spangler at the Saint.

"Thank you," said the Saint. "Now get up and stand away."

Karl rose to his feet slowly and shuffled aside as the Saint stepped around the desk and came to a startled halt.

He was looking down incredulously at the face of the man lying on the floor. One side of it was caked with blood and the hair was red with it, but that presented no obstacle to recognizing the owner. It was Whitey Mullins.

CHAPTER ELEVEN

MR UNIATZ'S heavy breathing reverberated in Simon's ear.

"Dey got Whitey!" His head jerked up suddenly at Karl and Spangler, his gun lifting. "Whitey was me pal!" he snarled. "Why, you——"

Simon stopped him.

"Don't shoot the Doc—yet. Whitey may need him." The Saint's eyes were cold blue chips. "Let's have the score, Spangler, and make it fast."

"He isn't dead," wheezed the fat man damply. "It's only a graze. He brought it on himself, coming here to my home to assault me. Karl had to stop him, but he didn't hurt him much. You can see that for yourself. The bullet just grazed his scalp and went into the wall there—see?"

He pointed a plump finger to a hole in the wall above Mr Mullins's prostrate form.

Whitey moaned and opened his eyes.

"Saint!" he mumbled feverishly.

Simon pocketed his automatic and bent over him.

"Take it easy, Whitey. It's okay." He went on without turning his head: "Doc, I'll bet you a case of Old Forester that Karl doesn't live to draw that gun he's trying to sneak out of his pocket."

"Eh?" Spangler grunted blankly.

Hoppy's attention flashed back to the danger on hand, swiveling his gun to the thug's belly. One of Karl's hairy paws had already dipped halfway into a coat pocket.

"Reach!" Mr Uniatz rasped.

"Hands empty, please," Simon smiled pleasantly over his shoulder.

The squat gunman slowly dragged his hand out of his pocket and raised both arms over his head.

Simon stepped over to him and extracted a Colt automatic from his pocket. Then he proceeded to run his hands with expert deftness down Karl's sides, under his arms, inside his thighs, and along his back. He patted his sleeves, paused, and plucked another gun from inside one of the gunman's cuffs. It looked like a toy, no larger than a magnified watch charm, but it held a .22-caliber shell in its chamber.

"Forgive me for underestimating you, comrade," he said. "You're a walking arsenal, aren't you?"

He pulled what seemed to be a fountain pen from Karl's breast pocket and examined it briefly. He chuckled, pushing Karl so that he stumbled backwards. Simultaneously, Simon exploded a capsule of tear gas from one end of the "fountain pen" squarely into the gangster's nose. Karl clutched his face with both hands and reeled halfway across the room, tripping over a chair and crashing to the floor.

"That stuff spreads!" Spangler gasped. "We'll all get it——"

"Take it easy," said the Saint. "The windows are open, and there isn't enough in one of those pills to do much harm unless it's shot straight at you."

"What do you want?" Spangler demanded, a glister of panic in his eyes. "Why did you come here?" He looked down at Whitey as the trainer gripped the edge of the desk for support and pulled himself to his feet with Hoppy's quick aid. Spangler pointed at him, his eyes narrowing. "I understand. You're working for *him* now!"

Simon lighted a cigarette.

"Don't confuse yourself, Doc. Hoppy and I represent our own business only—the Happy Dreams Shroud and Casket Company. I'm sorry we weren't able to accommodate your boy Karl last night. We'd have liked to give him a fitting, but he was in such a hurry . . ."

He glanced at Karl who, on all fours, was crawling blindly toward the door.

A leer of gargoyle delight transfigured Hoppy's features as he observed the proffered target. He took three steps across the room and, with somewhat better form than the previous night, launched a thunderous drop kick that caught the unfortunate thug squarely, lifting his entire body off the floor in a soaring ballotade, and dropped him sprawling in a corner.

Spangler stared fascinated at his limp cohort, and then again at Hoppy. His gaze swung uncertainly back to the Saint. He cleared his throat.

"I fail to comprehend," he began, with an attempt to regain his habitual pomposity, "why you should——"

"I'm quite sure you do comprehend," the Saint broke in suavely, "why I should resent your sending that goon over to my apartment last night to kill me."

Spangler opened and shut his mouth like a frog.

"I sent him to your apartment?" he said in shocked tones.

"You hoid him!" Hoppy growled.

"But my dear boy, I did no such thing!" Doc Spangler plucked a handkerchief from his breast pocket and mopped his shining pink brow. He frowned at Karl, who was beginning to stir again in the corner. "If he took it upon himself to—uh—visit you last night, it must have been a matter of personal inspiration. I had nothing to do with it, believe me."

"Strangely enough," said the Saint surprisingly, "I do."

"He's lyin'," Whitey grated fiercely. "He was gonna knock me off if you hadn't come when ya did."

"That's entirely untrue," Spangler said. "Mullins forced his way in here; he was abusive and threatening, and when he tried to attack me physically Karl had to fire a shot in my defense."

"However," the Saint continued, "a repeat performance was staged less than an hour ago near Sixth Avenue, with three characters and a black sedan taking the chief roles in another attempt to reunite Hoppy and me with our illustrious ancestors."

"I assure you, sir, that I——"

"Excuse me," the Saint interrupted. "I'm willing to believe that Karl might attempt a solo mission on account of the kicking around we gave him in the dressing room, but there were three men in the second try. I'm rather certain the driver was Karl. He might have done that to grind a private axe, but the other two must have had other inducements, Doc, old boy. Inducements supplied by you, perhaps."

Spangler shook his head bewilderedly.

"But—you're entirely off the track, dear boy. Karl has been here in the house for the past three hours."

"Then he must have a twin running around loose gunning for me. . . . As for the other two—I'd lay some odds that one of them was your new butler, Jeeves Mancini, the demon major-domo, who seemed to be sort of lying down on the job when I saw him. The third man," said the Saint dispassionately, "may very well have been you."

Spangler's expression of outraged innocence would have done credit to a cardinal accused of committing bigamy.

"But that's simply preposterous. I haven't left the house yet today. As a matter of fact, Karl and Slim and I were about to leave for the gym to meet the Angel when you arrived." He spread his hands. "Surely you're not serious when you say you actually expected to find three anonymous snipers—men who tried to shoot you from a car like movie gangsters—here in my house?"

"I don't say I had that idea all along," Simon admitted. "It just kind of grew on me when I found their car parked in front of this house. *Your* Stanley Steamer, I presume, Dr. Livingstone?"

"What!" Spangler's eyes were round with appalled amazement. "My dear boy, are you sure you're not feeling the heat? My car has been parked there all day."

"I did feel the heat," said the Saint gently, "of your car's engine. For a jalopy that hadn't been moved all day, it was awful feverish."

"Standing out there in the sun——"

"It might get the chill off. But I hardly think the sun was quite hot enough to burn those holes through the rear window and the windshield."

Spangler sank back into his chair, shaking his head helplessly.

"I don't know what you're trying to prove," he protested earnestly. "But if you mean those bullet holes, they've been there for nearly a month now. One of the boys became a little exuberant one night and——"

"Skip it," said the Saint amiably. "I didn't come here to torment you by putting the stretch on your imaginative powers. Any time a good story is needed, I'm sure you can come up with one. I just wanted to make one point for the record. The next time any uncomfortable passes are made at me or any of my friends—among whom I am going to include Steve Nelson—I am just automatically going to drop by and beat the bejesus out of you and any of your teammates who happen to be around. It may seem rather arbitrary of me, Doc; but an expert like you should be able to allow for my psychopathic fixations. . . . Let's go, Whitey."

Whitey let go the desk unsteadily.

"Okay. I can make it," he said, and waved away Hoppy's helpfully offered hand. He followed Simon, spitting contemptuously on the floor as he passed Karl's cowed figure huddled in the corner.

As they sped northward up Fifth Avenue, Mullins explained the predicament in which the Saint had found him.

"I guess I was nuts," he said, "goin' into that den of thieves alone, but I went off my chump just thinkin' of that lousy fink sendin' his stooge to proposition my boy."

"You shoulda gone heeled, pal," Hoppy said.

"I did." Whitey slapped his right hip. "But I just figured on bawling Spangler out, not killin' him; and then I get blasted from behind."

"How long were you there?" Simon asked.

"'Bout half an hour. Say!" Whitey's voice lifted as though remembering. "It couldn'a been Karl who was with those mugs what you said tried to gun you. He was in that room with Spangler most of the time I was cussin' the Doc." His pale eyes brightened with thought. "Y'know, there's a coupla heist guys with the Scarponi mob who Spangler hires sometimes for jobs. They look a lot like Karl."

The Saint shrugged.

"He still might have made it. I figure that Karl got some of his pals together in a hurry after he left Steve's place, and followed Hoppy and me when we left. I wouldn't give him an alibi unless he punched a time clock. You certainly weren't in shape to time everything to the minute." He glanced at Whitey. "We'd better drop you off at a doctor's so you can get that fixed up. How do you feel?"

"Oh, I'm okay, Saint," Whitey minimized. He felt his blood-clotted head gingerly. "The slug took a li'l hair off, that's all. Just drop me off at Kayo Jackson's gym. I'll wash up there."

"It's your noodle." Simon swung the wheel to his left and cut westward toward Sixth Avenue.

"Did you mean it," Whitey asked after a moment, "when you said you'd work with the Champ?"

The Saint fished a cigarette from his breast pocket and punched the dashboard lighter.

"You're the trainer, Whitey."

Whitey found a match in his pocket and struck it with his thumb, cupping the flame as he held it to the Saint's cigarette.

"Kayo'll go nuts when I tell him," he grinned. "Wit' you and the Champ workin' out there together, we'll pack 'em in."

"At two bits a head," Mr Uniatz mentioned, rather quickly for him. "So whaddas de boss get out of it?"

"I'll see that Kayo shells out with the Saint's cut of the gymnasium gate, don't worry."

"Hoppy is my agent," said the Saint.

He was thinking more about the slug he carried in his pocket—the slug he had dug out of the pawnshop doorframe. He had to ponder the fact that neither Karl's guns nor Slim Mancini's were of the same caliber—and in spite of what he had said, he couldn't really visualize Doc Spangler doing his own torpedo work. There was at least negative support for Whitey's evidence that Karl had been in the house during the time the Saint thought he'd seen him at the wheel of the gunmen's car. Yet Simon found it impossible to reconcile his indelibly photographic impression of the man who had driven that car with the possibility that it had been someone other than Karl. . . . If it hadn't been Karl, then it had certainly been his identical twin.

CHAPTER TWELVE

THE DAWNING SUN arched a causeway of golden light through the Saint's bedroom window, glinting on his crisp dark hair as he laced on the heavy rubber-soled shoes in which he did his road work with Steve every morning. Hoppy, bleary-eyed, leaned against the doorframe, watching him unhappily.

"Chees," he complained hoarsely, "will I be glad when de fight is over tomorrow night! I'm goddam sick of gettin' up wit' de boids every mornin' to do road work wit' Nelson." He yawned cavernously. "Dis at'letic life is moider."

"*What* athletic life?" the Saint inquired with mild irony. "The only road work *you* do is follow behind in the car with Whitey."

Hoppy sighed lugubriously.

"Dat ain't de pernt, boss. It's just I don't get de sleep a guy needs at my age."

"Well, I must say you wear the burden of your years with lavender and old dignity," Simon complimented him. He stood up and headed for the door. "Come on, Steve and Whitey will be waiting for us."

Hoppy groaned and followed like an exhausted elephant.

They found Nelson near the Fifty-ninth Street entrance of Central Park, alone.

"Whitey's got another of those headaches," he explained. "I think maybe that bullet Karl grazed him with last month must have shaken his brains up worse than he admitted."

The Saint nodded, breaking into an easy jogging trot beside Nelson as they struck out northward along the side of a winding park road.

"Could be," he agreed.

Mr Uniatz climbed into the car again, and waited disconsolately for several minutes in order to give them a good head start. Then he started the car up and followed slowly behind.

Some thirty minutes later the Saint and Steve Nelson were jogging eastward along the inner northern boundary of Central Park, following the edge of the park road. The Saint's long legs pumped in smooth, tireless rhythm as he breathed the dew-washed fragrance of blooming shrubs that covered the green slopes. At that early hour there was practically no traffic through Central Park, and he filled his lungs with air untainted by the fumes of carbon monoxide and tetraethyl lead. . . . During the past weeks the regimen of training in which he had joined Steve Nelson had tempered his lithe strength to the whiplash resilience of Toledo steel and surcharged his reflexes with jungle lightning; and as he ran his blood seemed to tingle with the sheer exultation of just living. He drank deeply of the perfume of the morning, smiling at a sky of the same clear blue as his eyes, his every nerve singing, feeling his youth renewed indestructibly.

He glanced back once at the brooding shadow of Hoppy's face behind the wheel of the car far behind, and chuckled softly. Nelson, trotting beside him, asked: "What's funny?"

The Saint nodded over his shoulder.

"Hoppy. He's miserable. Nobody to talk to. Nothing to drink."

Nelson looked back and grinned.

Ahead to his left over the park wall some distance away Simon could see the broad terminus of Lenox Avenue coming into view. Directly in front of them, through the trees, he caught the gleam of the lake that lies at the northern end of the park. The park road swoops sharply to the right at this point, paralleling the lake for a distance as it winds southward again.

The easy purr of an approaching car blended against and quickly drowned out the sound of the Saint's car hugging the edge of the road. The overtaking car accelerated as it came up to them and whooshed past, disappearing around the curve some distance ahead.

The Saint looked after it thoughtfully. Only two private cars had passed them since they'd started running—and both of them had been this same big limousine with the curtained windows.

"I hope you won't be too busy the day after the fight," Nelson said, glancing at him.

The Saint pondered his remark for a moment.

"That all depends. Why?"

"Connie and I have set the date for our wedding. Will you be my best man?"

The Saint's quick warm smile sparkled at him. "It'll be a pleasure, Steve."

Nelson slapped him on the back as they jogged along.

"Thanks."

"Will you be staying on at your place on Riverside Drive?"

"Yeah. Having it redecorated. As a matter of fact, they started work today. It was the only date I could make that would have it finished when we get back from our honeymoon, but the place is a mess right now."

"Why don't you move in with me until the day after tomorrow?" Simon suggested. "We've got a spare bed that you're welcome to."

"That's swell of you, Saint."

"No trouble at all. Besides, it'll be easier to keep an eye on you."

They padded on with tireless ease, tucking another mile behind them. The city was beginning to take on life. In the distance Simon could see the subway-entrance cupolas at the head of Lenox Avenue with early morning workers hurrying toward each of them. But the park as yet seemed quite deserted. The lake was like a sheet of silvered glass with a covey of green rowboats huddled along the near shore about their mother boathouse. . . . As they approached the curve in the road the path along the road narrowed and the Saint crossed over to the opposite side to run parallel with Steve.

He had just reached the curve when he heard, with startling suddenness, the roar of a car approaching behind him. He glanced over his shoulder. The black limousine that had already passed them twice was crossing over to his side of the road with swiftly increasing acceleration, rushing straight at him. In that split second he perceived with crystal clarity the tall bony high-shouldered figure hunched over the wheel, eyes crinkled with murderous intent, and knew instantly that the driver had stalked them in the hope of catching him apart from Nelson.

He flung himself down the gentle embankment that sloped to the sidewalk before he even heard Nelson's warning yell. The big limousine screamed around on two wheels as it tried to stick to the curve, but its mile-a-minute momentum was too great. It bounded sideways over the slope, entirely clearing the iron railing that bordered the sidewalk, struck the concrete pavement with a sickening crash, and took a fifteen-foot bounce into the lake, landing on its top, its wheels just visible above the water and still spinning.

The Saint leaped to his feet and ran to the water's edge with Nelson sprinting down the embankment after him. A screech of brakes knifed the morning stillness as Hoppy leaped out of his car to join them.

"He ran at you deliberately!" Nelson blurted as he came up.

"That's my trouble—I can't keep my fans away," said the Saint, and plunged into the water.

"Let him croak!" Hoppy bellowed breathlessly as he came running up. "De bum was trying to get ya!"

The Saint needed only one dive to tell him what he wanted to know. Nelson read the truth on his face as he came to the surface and rejoined him on the sidewalk.

"You know him?" he asked.

"Doc Spangler," the Saint said laconically, "is going to need a new butler."

He glanced up at the park's Lenox Avenue entrance. Several people, appearing magically, were running down to the scene of the "accident."

"Let's get out of here," he said, and bounded back over the iron fence and up the embankment.

Hoppy and Nelson followed him. They got into the car and sped away as an approaching police-car siren lifted its high clear alarum on the morning air.

"Spangler again," Nelson muttered grimly, staring straight ahead.

A stream of earnest profanity issued from Mr Uniatz's practiced lips.

"You shoulda stuck a knife in de rat when you was under wit' him," he concluded. "Dose dumb jackasses back dere are liable to pull him out before he drowns."

"They'll have to pull him off that steering column first," Simon said callously. "He's stuck on it like a bug on a pin."

"But why," Steve Nelson puzzled, "did he try to do it? What has he got against *you?*"

"Maybe he thinks I'm bringing you luck. If I'm out of the way, he's backing the Angel to take care of you."

Nelson said nothing for a moment. Then he shook his head.

"It doesn't make good sense," he said. "I don't get it."

The Saint shrugged.

"Forget it. Spangler and his outfit are a bunch of psychopaths, anyway."
He unhooked a key from his ring and handed it to Nelson. "Here—to the
apartment. I'll use Hoppy's key."

Nelson took it with troubled gratitude. "Thanks—thanks a lot, Saint. I
expect I'll take my stuff over sometime this afternoon. I've got some things
to do before I move."

"I've a few things to attend to myself," said the Saint. "Move in whenever
you're ready."

They let Steve Nelson out at the Fifty-ninth Street end of the park where
he'd parked his car. He put a hand on the Saint's arm, leaning over the door
of the convertible.

"Tell me," he asked worriedly, "what goes on between you and Spangler?
Why does he hate you so?"

A bantering smile touched the Saint's lean cynical face.

"We're allergic, I guess," he said. "Don't worry about it."

Steve sighed and shook his head perplexedly. He turned and walked to
his car.

"Where to now, boss?" Hoppy inquired as the Saint drove the car out
into the tide of Fifth Avenue.

"Mike Grady's," Simon Templar said flatly.

CHAPTER THIRTEEN

MR MICHAEL GRADY was incredulous. He leaned forward in his
swivel chair, his mouth open and his eyebrows lifted in soaring arches.

"Two attempts on your life!" he repeated. "By Spangler?"

The Saint, relaxed in one of Grady's worn leather chairs, studied him
through drifting cirrus clouds of cigarette smoke.

"Not by Spangler in person, perhaps. He's too smart—and too fat for that."
He sent a playful smoke ring soaring over Mike's carroty dome like a pale
blue halo. "He merely pays people to try to kill me. Of course," he added
thoughtfully, "when I say two attempts, I'm not counting the first try by
brother Karl. Let's say he did that on his own and give the good Doc the
benefit of any doubt I may have on that particular score. . . . The other
attempts were more up Doc Spangler's alley. One showed organized effort.
The other—well, it could have been an accident, you know, giving Mancini
an out if he got caught. Both those last tries had brains behind them."

A confused scowl furrowed Grady's brow.

"And why," he asked, "should you be so quick to make a case against Doc
Spangler? He told me all about your crashin' his house and roughin' up

his hired help and then accusin' him of those same things you've come to me about."

"Really?" Simon flicked ash into a nearby tray. "The Doc is burning his candor at both ends these days."

"There are men," Grady said sententiously, "who make more than a man's proper share of enemies for no proper reason." He pointed a stubby finger at the Saint. "And you, Mr Templar, are one of them."

The Saint bowed graciously.

"I've always been rather proud of my enemies, Mike. They're usually the sort that every man ought to make." His mouth curved in a crooked smile. "Did your friend Spangler tell you that Karl also shot Whitey Mullins? We found him bleeding on the carpet when we got there."

"I know all about that! If Whitey or anybody else goes to another man's house to threaten and raise a shindy, he should be prepared to take the consequences." Grady's lip curled scornfully. "And that's the manager Nelson picks for himself, is it? Ivory from the neck up! It's two of a kind they are, and no mistake." He leaned forward again. "Why, I ask you why, in God's name, should Spangler want to put you away? Why? Give me one reason I can believe."

The Saint smiled sympathetically.

"I know—mysterious, isn't it? Or have I already told you that he's afraid I might be able to show Steve how to beat the Angel?"

Grady snorted impatiently.

"Nuts to that! There's no man livin' who can beat the Angel! Neither you nor anyone else can make a winner out of a second-rater like Steve Nelson!"

The Saint's brows lifted politely.

"Second-rater? He only happens to be the champion. If you're betting your shirt on the Angel, I hope you have a good laundry. You might have to wait a long time for——"

He stopped short as he saw Grady tense, staring past him. The Saint looked back.

Connie Grady and Steve Nelson stood in the open doorway. They came in, hand in hand, Nelson shutting the door behind them as they entered, his youthful face set and determined.

The Saint rose lazily to his feet as Grady's eyes flashed with angry suspicion from Nelson to his daughter.

"What's the meaning of this?" bellowed the promoter, kicking his chair away and coming out from behind his desk.

Connie's lips parted to speak, but Nelson stepped forward before she could say a word.

"You'd better ask me that, Mr Grady," he said, and glanced at the Saint.

"Sorry, I didn't know you were here, or we'd have waited."

"All right!" Grady roared. "Then I'm askin' *you!* What the hell do you mean bustin' into my office? And how many times have I got to be tellin' you to keep away from my daughter, you penny-ante palooka!"

"Don't you dare talk to him like that!" Connie cried, her green eyes flashing angrily. "I'm going to marry him right after the fight, with or without your permission!"

Grady's mouth dropped open. He swallowed.

"The hell you say," he finally choked out.

"Perhaps," Simon murmured, "you family people would like to be alone." He edged toward the door, but Nelson grabbed his arm.

"No, stick around. You're my best man, aren't you?"

Grady wheeled on the Saint.

"Best man, is it?" he yelled. "So it's a plot!"

"Not so far as I'm concerned," the Saint said hastily.

"You listen to me, Mike." The fighter seized Grady by the lapel. "Seeing that you're going to be my father-in-law, you might as well——"

"In a pig's eye!" Grady sputtered. "Let go me coat, you punch-drunk jerk, or I'll—I'll——"

He turned wildly and grabbed a boxing trophy that stood on his desk. Nelson ducked nimbly and clutched his wrist, shaking the heavy metal statuette from his grasp.

"You might as well get used to the idea, Mike," said the Saint. "It seems to be settled that Steve loves Connie and Connie loves Steve, and they're going to be married, and since they're both of age I don't see what you can do about it."

"Oh, Daddy!" Connie pleaded, coming around to face him. "You're acting like a spoiled brat. You've got nothing against Steve——"

"Let go me arm!" Grady snapped at Nelson. "Or are you trying to break it, you foul-fightin' blackguard?"

Nelson released him and stepped back.

"I came here to tell you because I don't want you to say I ever did anything behind your back, Mike," he said palely.

Connie threw her arms around her father, looking up into his face.

"Darling, you know darn well you haven't any real reason for not liking Steve."

"I know it's all on account of your wanting Connie to have the best, Mike," Nelson said. "I know I'm not a millionaire, maybe, but——"

"We'll have enough," Connie put in. "Even"—she looked at Steve nervously, the shadow of her fear passing over her face—"even if he didn't fight tomorrow night."

"I'll be in plenty good shape to take care of a wife," Nelson grinned. "Especially *after* tomorrow night."

Grady gazed at him a moment with lackluster eyes. Then he pushed Connie away, grabbed his hat from a corner of his desk, jammed it on his head, and stalked to the door.

"Dad, wait!" she cried.

The door slammed behind him.

"Congratulations," the Saint smiled from the depths of the club chair into which he had retired, one leg slung over a leather upholstered arm. "He'll dance at your wedding yet."

"Oh, I do hope so," said the girl. The rosy flush of effort that had tinted her smooth pixie features was fading to an unhappy pallor. "Oh, Steve . . ."

"Cheer up," said the Saint. "He really likes him. He just guessed wrong about Steve at first and he's too bullheaded to admit it."

He climbed to his feet once more.

"Have lunch with us," Steve invited eagerly. "Will you? We have a table at the Brevoort. We're going over to your place first so I can leave my stuff, and then we——"

"Bless you, my children," the Saint interrupted, "but I have a prior engagement, unfortunately. Some other time, perhaps."

He lifted a hand in a debonair gesture of farewell, opened the door, and sauntered out rather abruptly before the argument could continue.

He did not mean to be rude, but he had a sudden pellucid intuition where Michael Grady had gone, and he did not want to be too far behind.

CHAPTER FOURTEEN

MIKE GRADY sat slumped in a corner of the sofa in Doc Spangler's study, moodily chewing an unlit cigar. Spangler, his elbows on the desk, pressed his fingertips together with injured reproach pointedly visible behind a film of charlatan good humor.

"My dear Mike," he argued, "every successful man in this game is the natural target of vile rumor and malicious gossip. I'm hurt that you, with all your experience with that sort of thing, should give even hesitant credence to this thing you've mentioned."

"I didn't say I believed it," Grady said heavily. "I just want to get your side of it, that's all."

"If Karl attacked Templar, it was entirely on his own volition, Mike, I assure you. After all, the Saint gave him sufficient reason, don't you think?"

"Okay," Grady said. "Maybe so. But what about the thing that happened this morning? I picked up this paper on my way down here. It's on the front page—look." He picked up the early afternoon edition from his lap and tossed it onto Spangler's desk. "According to that, it was an accident. But was it? Did Templar tell me the truth? Did Mancini try to run him down?"

Spangler shrugged, spreading his hands helplessly.

"Now how would I know? Certainly Slim had as much reason as Karl had to attempt a, shall we say, retributive act? That is, if it *wasn't* an accident, which it may well have been." He sighed. "After all, the manhandling that both of them have suffered from Templar and that gorilla of his would be enough to tax the forbearance of far less—er—angelic creatures than Karl and Slim, poor fellow. After all, Mike, I'm no nursemaid. Nor do I keep any of my employees on a leash."

"Yeah, yeah," Mike agreed restlessly, removing the cigar from his mouth. "But that isn't all. There's talk. About that last fight. Torpedo Smith's death is still being—well, talked about. There are rumors——"

"Rumors, rumors . . ." The fat man shook his head ruefully. "And you listen? Where do you suppose they originate? From Steve Nelson's camp, of course. Trying to discredit me, to smear the Angel. Nelson knows very well he hasn't a chance against my man, so he's preparing his alibi in advance. Can't you see that? You know and I know that the real reason the Angel wins is because of the psycho-hypnotic technique I use in my training methods. It gives that great hulk of a fellow power and speed many times greater than any man is normally capable of."

"Maybe so." Grady stuck his cigar back between his teeth and wagged a warning forefinger at Spangler. "But I tell you right here and now, Doc, if that man Smith was killed because of anything—shady——"

The good humor vanished completely from Spangler's meaty face.

"My dear Mike!" he protested aggrievedly. "Trust my intelligence if nothing else!" He spread his hands widely. "What possible reason could *I* have to wish him harm?"

"A very good reason indeed, Doctor," drawled the Saint.

Both men's eyes jerked to the open doorway.

Simon Templar stood there, the automatic in his hand held with deceptive negligence.

"The Saint!" Spangler got out.

An unhealthy flush suffused his florid face, and his hands dropped to his lap behind the desk.

"Yes, gentlemen," Simon Templar smiled. "However, you'll notice this little gadget I'm holding is not a harp. Hands on the desk, please, Doc."

Spangler obeyed slowly, the habitual good humor on his face distorted into a parody of itself.

Grady found his voice.

"What's this?" he rasped cholerically. "Are you following me around?"

"Rather fortunately for you, I am," said the Saint. "I overheard just enough of your conversation to settle a lot of early doubts about your honesty. Which only leaves your intelligence more in doubt than ever."

Spangler suddenly yelled: "Karl! Help!"

Simon shook his head regretfully.

"Don't strain your larynx, Doctor. It won't do you any good. We met Brother Mancini's successor at the door. My friend Mr Uniatz is watching over him in the hall to see that no one disturbs his slumber." The Saint glanced at the knuckles of his left hand affectionately. "If this happens much more often I'm afraid the Butler's Union will put you on the black list."

Grady climbed to his feet, an angry glint in his eye.

"Now look here——" he began.

There was a sudden scurry of footfalls in the hall, and the outer door slammed open just ahead of a wrathful howl from Hoppy.

The Saint sighed: "I guess Karl is on his way to report you now. I was hoping he'd sleep longer than that."

"What's the meaning of this?" Grady spluttered.

"Yes," Spangler said, all pretense at good humor blotted out by the venomous hatred that simmered behind the onyx sheen of his eyes, "what do you want?"

"Your signature," said the Saint easily. He walked up to Spangler's desk, fishing two checks from his pocket. He laid them before Spangler. "You'll notice that both of these are for the same amount. The amount, you can verify, is the total of the winner's shares of all the purses that your masked moron has won through practices that are extremely illegal."

Spangler looked up at him sharply, his hand slipping off the desk.

"You're stark raving crazy!" he blared.

"Do keep your hands on top of the desk, Doctor," Simon reminded him pleasantly. "That's better. . . . Both of these checks, you'll observe, are payable to the Simon Templar Foundation for the Relief of Distressed Pugilists."

"What?" Spangler squealed incredulously.

"What kind of racket is this?" Grady demanded.

A ghost of a smile touched the Saint's face. He stepped to one side and glanced at the door as Hoppy's heavy footsteps pounded back through the outer door, into the hallway, and clomped to a halt in the doorway of the room.

Mr Uniatz stood there a moment, catching his breath.

"He got away," he announced with dark disgust. "When I wasn't lookin'."

"Don't worry about it," Simon said. "We'll put an ad in the paper." He returned to Spangler, who had risen to his feet behind his desk as the massive frame of Mr Uniatz filled the doorway. "As you see, Doc, I've already signed one of those checks. Now you are going to sign the other."

Spangler turned sharply to Grady.

"You're a witness, Mike. It's blackmail, extortion!"

"Hardly that," Simon corrected him. "Those are simply the stakes in our bet, Doctor. I'm betting that Barrelhouse Bilinski is knocked out tomorrow night."

For a long narrow-lidded moment Doc Spangler gaped at the Saint. And then a slow glistening grin began to spread over his face.

"And that," he queried softly, "is what you want me to sign?"

The Saint nodded amiably.

"Exactly. If you don't, I'm afraid our friend Inspector Fernack will have to drop in and ask you some awkward questions. . . ."

A deep chuckle seemed to boil up deeply from within the fat man's rotund belly. The chuckle broke into a laugh that shook his chins.

"My dear Mr Templar!" he said deprecatingly, waving a pudgy hand. "Put away that gun." He wiped his eyes with his cuff as though overcome by some secret joke, and looked down at his desk, still chuckling. "Where's my pen?" He found it and pulled the check toward him, leaning over the desk. He looked up. "Mike Grady will hold these checks, of course?"

"That's okay with me."

"Now wait." Grady frowned, plagued by a vague troubled puzzlement. "I don't want no part——"

"Of course you do," the Saint insisted persuasively. "I assure you this is on the up-and-up, Mike."

"At least," Spangler agreed genially, "I know I can trust *you*." He bent over and signed the other check with a flourish and held them both out to Grady. "If you please, Mike."

Grady took them reluctantly.

"Nothing would please me more," Spangler gurgled, "than to have your check bounce, Mr Templar. I should enjoy sending you to jail for something like that. It would certainly look well in the newspapers." He licked his lips as if already tasting the Saint's ignominy. "Famous Adventurer Sentenced to a Year and a Day in County Hoosegow!"

"That wouldn't be nearly so embarrassing," the Saint said imperturbably, "as twenty years in Sing Sing for second-degree murder. I don't think you really wanted to kill Torpedo Smith. But nevertheless he died on account of you."

Spangler's jaw fell open. He started to speak.

"Now look here," Grady tried again. "I don't like this a bit, Saint. I don't want to be mixed up in any——"

"Just the same, you're going to hold those bets," said the Saint. "And you want me to drive you back to your office—now. Come along."

"I warn you," Spangler said bleakly, "that I shall hold both of you to the exact terms of that bet. If you try to welsh on it, the Betting Commissioner——"

"Your fadder's mustache!" Mr Uniatz quoted delicately.

He spread a large horny hand over Spangler's beefy face, and pushed with the force of an impatient mule. Doc Spangler crashed backwards against his chair and toppled thunderously to the floor, chair and all. He was still lying there as Simon and Hoppy conducted Grady firmly out of the room and out of the house.

"I can't tell you how glad I am," the Saint said as they drove northward up Fifth Avenue, "to know that you're not in cahoots with Spangler, Mike. That was the thing that bothered me most of all."

"Thanks for the bill of health," Grady responded caustically. "It's that relieved I am." He scowled. "But I can't say I go for the highhanded way you have of orderin' me about at the point of a gun!"

"Forgive me," the Saint apologized, "but I couldn't take any chances of being deprived of your company for lunch."

"I got too many things to do, Saint. No time for lunch. Just get me back to the Arena as quick as you can."

"It won't take much time," Simon smiled dreamily. "I've got a table at the Brevoort . . ."

Grady frowned: "Well—I'll see if I can make it."

They parked in front of the Arena and Simon accompanied Grady inside to his office.

The girl at the switchboard called out as they entered Mike's office: "There's been several calls from your daughter, Mr Grady, and from Mr Mullins . . ."

"Okay," Grady grunted, and picked up the stack of letters and messages piled up on his desk. "Wonder what Whitey Mullins wants," he muttered, thumbing through the sheaf. "According to this pile of call notes, he's phoned about six times."

The telephone rang. Grady lifted the receiver.

"Who? . . . Okay, put him on. . . . Hello, Whitey? . . ." Mike Grady suddenly stiffened as he listened. He paled visibly and for a few seconds listened in silence. Presently he asked: "In the Saint's apartment? What was he doing there? . . . Yes, of course. I'll be down as soon as I possibly can."

He hung up and turned to the Saint.

"Steve Nelson has been shot," he said. "In your apartment."

The Saint's whole being seemed to stand still in the same timeless stasis that affected the expansion of his ribs.

"Karl," he said slowly and bitterly. "Waiting for me in my apartment . . . Grady looked stupidly at him.

"No. . . . At least Whitey says the police don't think it was anyone layin' for you at your place. Whoever did it they think was waitin' for you on the roof of the apartment house across the street. There's a bullet hole in the window of the room where Connie found him."

"Connie?" the Saint repeated, knowing even as he said it how it must have happened.

"She was waiting for him in the car while he went up to your place to leave his things. He was going to stay with you, wasn't he?"

Simon nodded.

"Where is he?"

"Bellevue. They got the bullet out of him. Whitey says they think he's got a fifty-fifty chance." Grady's face furrowed with pain. "The poor kid. . . . He's a helluva fine boy, Saint. I've been just a damn fool, and that's a fact!"

He glared at Simon defensively.

"Listen, Mike." The Saint gripped his arm. "Whoever did it must've thought it was me. It could only have been one of Spangler's men. It was my fault that this happened."

"But why should Spangler want to do *you* in?"

"He's afraid that I'll find out what he's been up to. I started the whole thing by butting in after the Torpedo Smith fight. Now I've got to finish it. Listen—I've got to take Steve's place tomorrow night!"

Grady's eyes bugged.

"What?"

"You heard me! You've got to put me in against the Angel!" The Saint's steely fingers tightened about Grady's arm. "You've got to, Mike!"

"B-but——"

Grady stopped short and looked at him for a long moment. He stepped backwards and eyed him up and down critically. He said finally: "Well, you look big enough. And hard enough, I guess. I've heard how you can hit . . ."

"I've been working with Steve," said the Saint. "I'm in as good condition as a man ever was, Mike. And I can take Bilinski, believe me!"

"But it's ridiculous!" Grady exploded. "There's never been such a fight——"

Simon said swiftly: "Make an announcement in the ring. Tell them about my bet with Spangler. If they want their money back, they can have it. If they just want to see a fight—even if it's only the Saint——"

"*Only* the Saint!" Grady's eyes took fire. A luminous inspired glow spread over his round freckled face. "Holy mackerel! Maybe it won't be a championship fight as advertised, but with *you* in it——"

"Come on then." Simon pulled him toward the door. "Let's go—I've got to get hold of Whitey right away!"

CHAPTER FIFTEEN

THE OPENING PRELIMINARY was already under way when the Saint, with Hoppy and Patricia Holm, strode through the tag end of the crowd of street urchins who eddied about the "artists'" entrance of the Manhattan Arena.

Whitey met them in the doorway.

"I was gettin' worried," he said anxiously. "What happened to ya? The show's started."

He started them down the corridor that turned off to the dressing-room section. The Saint stopped him.

"Whitey, will you show Miss Holm to her seat? I don't think she can find her way up front from this part of the Arena."

The tempting curve of Miss Holm's red mouth drew to a pout.

"You mean I've got to spend the next hour or so in solitary refinement?"

"Well, you certainly can't spend it in my dressing room," said the Saint. "It's not exactly a ladies' boudoir."

Whitey nodded to Patricia, in visible awe of her golden-blond beauty.

"Sure, just follow me," he said. He turned to Simon. "I'll check on the Angel's hand wraps on my way back."

They disappeared around a turn from where the roar of the crowd was flowing like the muted roar of distant surf.

The Saint went on with Hoppy to his dressing room, feeling the ghostly fingers of peril once more playing their familiar cadenza along his vertebrae and up through the roots of his hair. . . . He knew, his every instinct told him, that tonight he was fighting for greater stakes than glory or dollars. Tonight would be more than a mere encounter with padded gloves. Tonight he would be fighting for his life.

A swarthy snaggle-toothed character in a dirty polo shirt was seated on a broken-down chair as they entered the dressing room. Hoppy recognized him at once.

"Mushky," he growled. "I t'ought you was in de Angel's corner."

"So I am, chum, so I am," Mr Mushky Thompson agreed affably. "I gotta take a gander when you bandage de Saint's hands."

"That's what I admire about this business," Simon remarked cheerfully. "Everyone trusts everyone else."

Hoppy fixed Mr Thompson with a baleful glare.

"Out, ya bum," he ordered.

"Now wait," Mushky protested. "It's de rules. I——"

"Oh, let him alone," said the Saint. "Whitey is watching the Angel, isn't he? It isn't exactly a unilateral proposition."

"Sure," Mr Thompson agreed with hasty anxiety. "No cause for gettin' mad, Hoppy. I'm just one of de hired hands."

Hoppy grunted and proceeded about the business of laying out the hand bandages, adhesive tape, rubber mouthpiece, collodion, ammonia, and other paraphernalia of the modern gladiator.

"You working with Karl, Mushky?" the Saint asked casually as he slipped out of his street clothes.

Thompson shook his head.

"Naw. . . . He—uh—got kicked in the face by a beer-wagon horse. Broke his jaw in two places, I hear."

Hoppy looked up at him a moment, and broke into a deep guffaw.

"Ya don't say," he yakked.

Simon slipped into his dark purple sateen trunks and began to lace his boxing shoes swiftly as Hoppy tore strips of adhesive tape into suitable knuckle strips. Mushky Thompson lounged in his chair with a cigarette dangling from a corner of his mouth until Hoppy had finished taping the Saint's hands with practiced precision, reinforcing the bones without impairing their freedom. Then Mushky got to his feet.

"Good luck," he threw over his shoulder. "You'll need it."

"T'anks," Hoppy said—and did a take after the gibe sank in.

"Come back here!" the Saint snapped, as Mr Uniatz started after the Angel's second. "Don't start anything *now,* you idiot!"

Hoppy made unintelligible grating noises through his bared teeth, his nuclear mind infected as much by the vibrant blood cry of the mob as by the taunt. Impending battle—his own or anyone else's—was apt to make Mr Uniatz emotionally unstable.

Three preliminaries and a semi-final later, the Saint lay on the rubbing table, completely relaxed, listening to ten thousand throats vibrating the walls in a massive chorus of excitement. The semi-final bout had ended in a knockout, he guessed, from the uproar. He stretched his length peacefully, his eyes closed, everything in him settled into an immeasurable stillness amid the swirling rumble of vociferation. Dimly and indistinguishably he heard the orotund bellow of the announcer introducing somebody after the roar of the crowd had died down a bit; and shortly afterwards the man who had been introduced began speaking over the audience public-address system, and he recognized Grady's unmistakable accents even though he could not make out the words.

Hoppy stumbled into the dressing room, breathless from battling the crowd en route.

"What a mob!" he wheezed, his eyes gleaming. "Grady's up dere makin' dat announcement!"

A swelling ululation rose in a gathering tidal wave of sound and broke thunderously upon their ears.

"Say," Hoppy exulted, "sounds like dey like what he told 'em, huh?" He came over to the Saint. "Boss, what does Spangler say when Grady tells him ya goin' in for Nelson?"

The Saint yawned.

"Oh, he raised a little stench about it at first, but Mike reminded him that my bet stated that Bilinski would be knocked out—it didn't say by whom. So he changed his mind. . . . By the way, did Pat get a good seat?"

"Yeah," Hoppy chuckled hoarsely. "An' guess who's she sittin' next to!"

"Are you training for a quiz program, or would you just like to tell me?"

"Inspector Foinack!"

The Saint considered him reverently for a moment, while the forth-coming possibilities of that supernal juxtaposition developed the gorgeous gamut of their emotional potential.

"Oh, my God!" Simon breathed. "I'd rather watch that than my own fight."

There was a patter of footsteps and Whitey Mullins darted into the dressing room. His face was contorted with savage glee.

"Okay," he croaked. "You're on, Saint. They're waitin' for you!" He snatched up the water bucket. "Grab the water bottle and sponge," he yelped at Hoppy, and went to the door.

The Saint swung his long legs off the table to the floor and stood up. He followed Whitey out of the door into the corridor, with Hoppy bringing up the rear.

"Brother, I only wisht it was that lousy crook, Spangler, you was smackin' around tonight," Mullins grated with vitriolic bitterness as they mounted the ramp into the Arena, "and not just that dumb ox he stole from me."

Simon sensed an excitement, a temper in the crowd that was different from the usual mass tension of the ordinary fight attendance at Grady's weekly shows. It was electric with anticipation of the unexpected, a breath-less waiting watchfulness that he felt as he mounted to the apron of the ring and slipped between the ropes amid a thunderclap of acclaim. There was a slight note of hysteria in it, he thought as he seated himself on the stool in his corner and looked about at the ocean of faces that spread on every side.

The Masked Angel hadn't appeared yet, but the Saint rather expected that. Spangler would try every trick in the bag, including the petty one of wearing down the opposition's nerves by making him wait.

He failed to spot Pat among the buzzing tide of faces at ringside, but everything beyond the glare of light centering on the ring was little more than a smoke-dimmed blur. The faces, void of all individuality, were such as one encounters sometimes in nightmare sequences, a phantasmagoria of eyes and noise—hard, critical, and skin-pricklingly theriomorphic. . . . He wondered momentarily if Steve was in good enough shape to listen to the fight from his bedside. . . . Connie had been with him nearly all day at the hospital. . . .

A roar like an approaching forest fire filled the packed coliseum with surging clamor as the Masked Angel appeared up the ramp, preceded by Doc Spangler and followed by a cohort of handlers bearing the various accessories of refreshment and revival. The incredible bulk of the Angel loomed up over the apron of the ring and squeezed between the ropes in his corner, his plates of sagging fat quivering like chartreuse jelly. Unmasked now, his ridiculous little nubbin of a head bobbed from side to side in acknowledgment of the roars of the mob, his round little cheeks and button nose more an inspiration for laughter than the fearsome horror his black mask had aroused.

Behind him, Doc Spangler leaned over his shoulder and spoke softly into an ear that was the approximate size and shape of a brussels sprout.

As the Saint watched them from beneath lowered lids, he felt once again the spectral footfalls of ghostly centipedes parading his spine, knowing that his real danger was as yet undetermined, the point of attack unknown. How it would come, in what shape or form, he wasn't quite sure. He'd covered all the possibilities, or so he thought; but whether the threat, the unknown secret weapon that the Angel must surely possess, would come from an act of the Angel himself, or from some outside agent, he wasn't quite sure. All he had was an idea. . . . He felt its shadow upon him like a ghostly mist, ambient and all-pervading. . . .

The bell clanged sharply a few times; the throbbing hum of the crowd subsided somewhat. The main-bout referee, dapper and fresh in white tennis shoes and flannels, stepped to the center of the ring and gestured the Saint and the Angel to come to him.

Simon rose, followed by Whitey and Hoppy, and came forward to face the Angel, who shambled up to the referee flanked by Spangler and Mushky Thompson. The Angel towered over them all, an utterly gross, unlovely specimen of so-called homo sapiens.

The referee droned the familiar formula: ". . . break when I say break

. . . no hitting in breaks, no rabbit or kidney punches . . . protect yourself at all times . . . shake hands, come out fighting . . ."

They touched gloves, and the Saint walked nonchalantly back to his corner. He rubbed his feet a couple of times on the resin sprinkled there while Hoppy pulled the stool out of the ring. . . . The sound of the bell seemed unreal and far away when, after what seemed an extraordinarily long time, it finally rang.

CHAPTER SIXTEEN

THE SAINT turned and moved almost casually out of his corner to meet the slowly approaching Angel. Bilinski shuffled forward, peering between forearms lifted before him, his body almost doubled over so that his elbows guarded his belly while his gloves shielded his face. No legally vulnerable square inch of his body was unprotected. He came forward steadily, inch by inch, making no attempt to lead or feint, merely coming forward with the massive low-gear irresistibility of a large tank, peering intently, cautiously—almost fearfully, Simon thought—between the bulging barriers of his ham-sized arms.

The Saint moved around him in a leisurely half-circle, every muscle, every nerve completely at ease, relaxed, and co-ordinated. He was oblivious of the crowd now, studying his problem with almost academic detachment, the latent lightning in his fists perfectly controlled. He couldn't help feeling the same guarded wonder that he knew Torpedo Smith, and for that matter all of the Angel's opponents, must have felt at the apparent impotence of the Angel's attack right up to the moment of the blow that sent them on the way to oblivion. He thought to himself: *Nothing happens the first round . . . nothing ever happens the first round.* . . . The crux of his problem, he felt sure, was what the Angel did to open his victims for the inevitable knockout later on. . . .

Bilinski, apparently growing tired of following Simon around the ring, stopped in the center and remained there, crouched, merely revolving to follow the Saint's lackadaisical circumvolutions about him.

The cash customers began to shake the stadium with the drumming of their stamping feet in the familiar demand for action. A demand, Simon thought, which was no more than fair. . . . He stepped in, threw a left that cracked like a whiplash against the Angel's fleshy forearms, and crossed with a downward-driving right that strove to crash past into the massive belly beyond. But the Angel instinctively brought his arms closer together so that the Saint's gloved fist thudded into their bone-centered barrier.

Bilinski, visibly startled by the numbing shock of the blow, even though he did catch it on his guard, flung his arms about the Saint in an octopus-like clutch, sagging slightly in order to let his overwhelming weight smother his opponent's efforts to strike again; but Simon, familiar with the old strength-sapping trick, merely relaxed with him and waited for the referee to come between them.

From her seat at ringside, Patricia Holm, her blond hair wild with excitement, her hands gripping the arms of her chair, pleaded with tense anxiety: "Watch him, Simon, watch him! Be careful!"

"He'd better watch while he can," Inspector Fernack gibed sardonically. He leaned back in his seat beside her and yelled: "All right, you Angel, shake him loose and let him have it! Give him one for me!"

The referee was still battling to break the Angel's drowning-man grip when the bell ended the round.

As he walked to his corner, the Saint noticed that there were no boos from the crowd over the inaction of that opening round. There was merely a more intense current of anticipatory excitement, as though everyone felt that they were about to witness a phenomenon of nature which, while it might be delayed somewhat, would take place as ineluctably as a predicted eclipse of the sun. . . .

The betting, Simon knew, was not on whether or not he'd be knocked out, but rather precisely when and how that cataclysmic event would occur.

Hoppy wiped nonexistent perspiration from the Saint's brow.

"Dat foist round wuz slow motion, boss," he rasped encouragingly. "Howja feel?"

The Saint smiled coolly.

"Fine. Where's Whitey?"

"He forgot de towels." Hoppy thrust the mouth of the water bottle at Simon's lips. "Take a drink?"

The Saint leaned back and turned his face away slightly as the water poured out of the uptilted bottle and slopped over his neck and chest.

"Chees, boss!" Hoppy peered at the Saint's face. "Dijja get any?"

"All I need. Wipe my face."

Hoppy reached about vaguely for a nonexistent towel, seized the Saint's dressing gown draped over the edge of the ring apron, and used it instead to mop the moisture from Simon's face and body.

"Hoppy," said the Saint in a low voice, as his faithful disciple started to fan him with the robe. "Hoppy, listen."

"Yeah, boss?"

"This is important," Simon said quickly. "Keep the cork in that water bottle—understand? Don't let anyone try to spill the water that's left in it. Do you get that, Hoppy?"

Hoppy nodded foggily.

"Yeah, b-but——"

"Hold on to that bottle!" Simon said urgently, obsessed with the nightmare problem of impressing a course of action on Mr Uniatz's reflexes beyond any possibility of confusion. "Don't let it get away from you. I want it after the fight. Put it in your pocket—or in that robe—and keep it under your arm. Don't drink out of it, whatever you do. If anyone tries to spill it or break it, grab him and hold on to him! Is that clear?"

"Sure, but I don't get it, boss. Why——"

The warning whistle blew its shrill alarm, and Simon sprang to his feet as Hoppy ducked out of the ring, taking the stool with him.

The bell clanged and the Saint moved out. . . . He could only hope that his hunch was right, that he had really penetrated the mundane secret of Doc Spangler's psycho-hypnotic technique. If he guessed wrong, there might still be catastrophic surprises in store. He was answering a gambit of whose ultimate denouement he was not at all certain.

Now the Saint opened up. He darted in with the effortless speed and cold-eyed ferocity of a jungle cat, his lithe body moving in a fierce harmony of scientific destruction, his shoulders flinging a shower of straight javelin-like blows, striving to penetrate the fortress wall of wrists, arms, and gloves that guarded the Angel's head. . . .

Bilinski began to give ground, crouching lower and lower beneath the onslaught. Suddenly the Saint changed his mode of attack, his fists winging up from beneath in a series of whiplash uppercuts. One of them managed to catch the Angel on his nominal forehead, jarring his head back momentarily. Almost simultaneously with the first blow, another crashed through the Angel's guard and left the little bulb of nose a bloody splotch.

Bilinski began to give ground faster, the first glimmer of real fear in his dull little eyes. But still he refused to retaliate; he went on catching the Saint's blows on his arms, gloves, shoulders, elbows, rolling instinctively with every one that he caught, like the battle-conditioned veteran he indisputably was. And as he felt the ropes touch his back, he leaned against them and bounded forward again, taking advantage of their spring, hurling his gross tonnage against the Saint and flinging his arms about him once again, shuffling around so that the Saint's back was to the ropes instead. Inexorably he pushed Simon backwards against the rubberized strands.

Pat was on her feet, jumping up and down.

"Get away from him, Simon!" she screamed. "Get away from him!"

"Aw, sit down!" Fernack blasted at her. He cupped his hands about his mouth and yelled: "Knock him kicking, Angel! Hit him one for me! For Fernack!"

Pat turned on him furiously.

"Yes," she shouted, "for poor feeble Fernack!" and brought a flailing hand down on the top of the detective's derby, jamming it down over his eyes.

A localized area of laughter was swallowed in a sudden earthquake as the crowd surged to its feet en masse.

The Saint was obviously in trouble. He was still against the ropes, even as Torpedo Smith had been, shaking his head as though trying to clear it, as the Angel, close up to him, pumped short deliberate blows into his body. They lacked concussive snap but were nevertheless sickening with the monstrous weight that lay behind them. The Angel seemed to be trying to shake the Saint loose to give himself room for a conclusive blow. That he would succeed seemed a matter of a very brief time. The Saint was already staggering and apparently holding on blindly.

In the Saint's corner, Hoppy Uniatz, his face tortured into a mask of pleading horror, leaned over the bottom strand of the ropes, his clenched fists pounding the canvas desperately.

"Boss!" he begged, his raucous voice screeching with the intensity of his emotion. "Boss, get away from dem ropes. Don't let him crowd ya! Boss!"

Patricia's eyes filled with frightened tears.

"Simon!" she sobbed. "Get away, get away!"

And strange things were happening to Inspector John Henry Fernack—things which, in abstract theory, he would have hooted at as fantastically impossible. Faced with the reality of his old adversary's imminent downfall, a thing which in his heart of hearts he had long ceased to believe possible, he found himself inexplicably on his feet, howling: "What's the matter, Saint? You gonna let that dumb lug do that to you? Move around, Templar, move around!"

But the Saint seemed finished. He let the referee come between him and the Angel, and staggered along the ropes, apparently helpless and ripe for the knockout blow. . . . He wondered, as he peered at the Angel with eyes that he hoped had a glazed appearance, how many more of those sickening body blows he could have taken if the referee hadn't parted them when he did. . . .

This, the Saint knew, was the final move in his play, the all-deciding feint. It would, he hoped, open the Angel's guard sufficiently to permit a blow to the jaw. It would prove something else as well. For he knew that Bilinski's experience would have warned him against such a trick—*unless he had reason to believe that the Saint's sudden torpor was not faked, but real!* For the Angel must know perfectly well that he had struck no blow that could have dazed his opponent to that extent. Nevertheless, he was opening up more and more, as if he expected the Saint to give ground—as if, indeed, he was ready for Simon to collapse about this point. The Saint doubted that the Angel actually knew how this was being achieved. He was taking Spangler's word for it, and going on past corroborative experience. . . .

The Saint slumped against the ropes, and not one person in the entire mob could have suspected the grim triumph that coursed through his every nerve as the Angel charged in for the slaughter, wide open, a bone-shattering right hurtling at the Saint's jaw.

But the blow never reached its destination.

For even as the Angel started it, Simon Templar's right hand came up from where it had been sagging near the floor, and landed, with the approximate velocity of an ack-ack shell and the same general concussive effect, flush on the Angel's froglike chin. Barrelhouse Bilinski's feet were jolted up a good three inches off the floor; and when he came down again, his eyes glassy, his arms flailing loosely, he continued all the way down—down to the canvas like a mountainous mass of boneless gelatin.

He lay there twitching slightly; and it was evident to the blindest of the now completely hysterical audience that he would continue to lie there until someone carried him away.

The Saint strolled to his neutral corner as the referee began the formality of counting out the sleeping Angel. He failed to see either Hoppy or Whitey as he leaned against the ropes, and for a moment he was puzzled. Then, through the deafening hullabaloo, he thought he heard Hoppy's bronchitic foghorn somewhere below. As the referee completed his toll and Mushky leaped into the ring to retrieve the Angel's carcass, Simon slipped through the ropes and into the midst of the raving, eddying ringside mob, looking about anxiously.

"Hoppy!" he called.

Through the unbroken pandemonium and the pleas of the newspaper reporters and cameramen converging upon him, he heard Hoppy again, this time more distinctly: "Boss, I got him! I got him!"

"Where are you?" Simon shouted.

"Under de ring! Dis way!"

The great pipe organ burst into "Hail the Conquering Hero Comes" as Simon peered beneath the apron and saw, silhouetted against the supporting joists, Mr Uniatz holding down a set of kicking arms and legs by the simple expedient of sitting on the body that sprouted them.

"He gives me an argument when I don't let him spill out de bottle," Hoppy explained in stentorian confidence. "So I do like ya tell me."

"Bring him out," said the Saint.

Several dozen spectators crowded around, seething with excitement, while the photographers, frustrated in their efforts to get the Saint back in the ring, aimed their cameras at him crouched under the apron. Their flash bulbs went off in broadsides as Hoppy wrestled with his quarry.

The blue uniforms of policemen were converging on the spot; and over the hubbub and the pealing of the organ Simon heard the brassy tones of another familiar voice approaching.

"One side, get outta the way! One side! What's going on here?" Inspector Fernack trumpeted as he fought his way through the crowd.

Hoppy finally dragged out his kicking clawing captive by the collar of its turtle-neck sweater.

"He tries to pull dis rod on me!" he said, and handed the gun to Simon. He yanked the man to his feet, as Fernack broke through the final barrier of humanity. "Stand up, youse!"

As the Saint had expected, it was Whitey Mullins.

"What the hell goes on here?" Fernack demanded; and Simon handed him the gun.

"Take this, John Henry. I've got a slug I dug out of a pawnshop doorframe that I think'll fit it. And I'll give you odds that the bullet that laid out Steve Nelson will also fit Whitey's gun."

CHAPTER SEVENTEEN

SIMON and Patricia were in Steve Nelson's hospital room next morning when Inspector Fernack arrived. Connie Grady was also there, accompanied by a subdued and sympathetic Michael. Mr Uniatz was also present, accompanied by a breakfast bottle of bourbon. It was like Old Home Week.

"I hear you're doing fine, Champ," Fernack said. "How soon is Grady going to match you with the Saint?"

"From what I heard on the radio," Nelson answered, "maybe it's a good thing I'm retiring."

Connie squeezed his hand.

"If you'd like to tell me more about this," Fernack said, with as close to a tone of respect as he had ever used in speaking to the Saint, "I'd be willing to listen. We picked up Spangler last night, by the way—he was just packing for a trip."

"Congratulations, John Henry," Simon grinned. "Never let it be said that the Police Department lets lawns grow on its feet."

Fernack grimaced.

"What I want to know," he said, "is how you figured Whitey was working with Spangler."

"Well—" the Saint began thoughtfully, "it was the way Whitey kept plugging his hatred for Spangler that first made me suspicious. Then later, when we were at Spangler's place and found Whitey apparently wounded by Karl's bullet, I noticed that the blood on his scalp had already begun to mat. He couldn't have been shot by the bullet we'd just heard fired, which he claimed. It takes a little longer than that for blood to clot. I realized then and there that he'd actually been grazed by the bullet Hoppy sent through the rear window of the car he and Karl and Slim had used when they shot up the pawnshop. Probably, when they realized I was in the house, Spangler had Karl fire into the wall to make it appear that he was the one who'd shot Whitey—thus concealing the fact that Whitey had been one of the gunmen, and prolonging his usefulness as Steve's manager."

"If he was Spangler's inside man," pondered Fernack, "Whitey must've seconded *all* of the Angel's opponents. We'll check on that."

"I've already done that. Quite a while ago. And Whitey *did* second the Angel's opponents. Every one of them. That's how the Barrel always rolled them out inside of two rounds. . . . I felt pretty sure that Whitey must've been doping the Angel's opponents, of course, if he was tied up with Spangler as I suspected. It would be easy for him to fix up his fighters' water with a few drops of something, and Spangler would know what to prescribe that wouldn't show up in case of accidents."

"Okay," Fernack agreed, "but if it was only knockout drops, what killed Torpedo Smith?"

"Why, you saw it yourself. The Angel hit him when Smith was already half asleep—and believe me, Brother Bilinski can really hit when he has lots of time. I know!"

"Darling," Patricia said, "you won't be permanently injured, will you?"

"I hope not," said the Saint.

JUDITH

FROM *Saint Errant*

THIS STORY is a sentimental piece to me because (1) it was the first short story I ever sold to a smooth-paper American magazine, (2) I got paid more for it, many times more, than I had ever received for a short story until then, and (3) this was the first sale I made after I landed in the United States in 1932, with about fifty dollars in my pocket and nothing but an unshakable faith in my own destiny to support me beyond that.

You may well ask why such an ancient manuscript should crop up so late in not even the *First,* but actually the *Second, Saint Omnibus.*

The reason turns out to be very simple.

A writer writes short stories and sells them at intervals to magazines. Presently he has enough to make a collection suitable for publishing in volume form. And if he wants to milk his work for the last golden drop, he does just that.

I went a little further. Long ago I had the idea for the title *Saint Errant,* which would be a book of short stories primarily involving dames. This story, "Judith," would be the first.

Now it is only a matter of record that fifteen years went by before that imagined collection was complete.

I wrote other stories in between, and even whole books. But *Saint Errant* did not complete itself until late in 1947. And in the *Omnibus* we are dipping into the books in the order in which they were published, without regard to the order of first publication, or even conception, of their ingredients.

I hope this explanation will satisfy the most fanatical of my self-appointed bibliographers, who have picked the hell of a subject to give themselves ulcers about.

And while we are at it, one more amplification seems to be called for. I said in the foreword to this monument that I had not tried to revise any of the stories, or bring them up to date. And a glance at this story makes me realize that that was only a half truth.

I have not changed anything between the source volumes and this one. But this story originally began in Paris, and ended with the Saint on his way to Stuttgart. When *Saint Errant* was finally being readied for the printers, that kind of movement would have invalidated a plot point for contemporary-minded readers. So I simply switched the geography across a few thousand miles of ocean.

There was nothing to it, really. Any other writer could have done the same, with a mere wave of his magic ball-point pen.

JUDITH

SIMON TEMPLAR had to admit that the photograph of himself which adorned the front page of the copy of the New York *Daily Gazette* on his knee left nothing to be desired.

Taken only a couple of years ago, at the studio of an ambitious photographer who had clearly seen the potentialities of future revenue from an authentic likeness of such a disreputable character, it brought out to perfection the rakish curve of his jaw, the careless backward curl of black hair, the mocking challenge of a gay filibuster's mouth. Even the eyes, by some trick of lighting in the original which had been miraculously preserved through the processes of reproduction, glinted back at him from under the bantering lines of eyebrow with all the vivid dangerous dance of humor that was in his own.

The story illustrated by the picture occupied two columns of the front page and was continued somewhere in the interior. One gathered from it that that elusive and distressingly picturesque outlaw, the Saint, had set the Law by the ears again with a new climax of audacities: his name and *nom de guerre* waltzed through the bald paragraphs of the narrative like a debonair will-o'-the-wisp, carrying with it a breath of buccaneering glamour, a magnificently medieval lawlessness, that shone with a strange luminance through the dull chronicles of an age of dreary news. "The Robin Hood of Modern Crime" they called him; and with that phrase the Saint himself had least fault of all to find.

At the next table on his left a fair-haired girl was struggling to explain the secret of successful Rumhattan mixing to an unsympathetic waiter. At other tables, other guests of the Windsor Hotel's Peacock Alley read their evening papers, sipped cocktails, chattered, argued, and gazed incuriously at fellow birds in that pleasantly gilded cage. Outside, but inaudible in that discreetly expensive sanctuary, flowed the common traffic of Montreal, the last outpost of Old France in the New World.

In those surroundings anyone but a Simon Templar might have been embarrassed by the knowledge that a lifelike portrait of himself, accompanied by an account of his latest misdeeds and a summary of several earlier ones, was at the disposal of any citizen who cared to buy a newspaper. The Saint was never embarrassed, except by warrants for his arrest, and in those days he was most careful to leave no legal grounds for one of those.

He folded his paper and lighted a cigarette with the comforting assurance that any casual glancer at his classic features would be far less likely to suspect him of a hideous past than to suspect the eminent politician or the debutante victim of a motor accident whose portraits, in smaller frames, had flanked his own on either side. Certainly he saw no reason to creep into a corner and hide.

At the next table the girl's gray eyes wavered in humorous despair toward him, meeting his own for an instant, which to a Simon Templar was sufficient invitation.

"Ecoute, toi!" The Saint's voice lanced through the air with a sudden quiet command, the edge of a blade so sweetly keen that it seemed to caress even while it cut, snapping the waiter's wandering eyes around like a magnet dropped within an inch of twin compass needles. "Mademoiselle desires that one mix three parts of Ron Rey with one part of sweet vermouth and a dash of angostura. After that, one will squeeze into it a very thin piece of lemon peel. It is quite simple."

The waiter nodded and moved away in a slight daze. In his philosophy, foreigners were not expected to speak his own patois better than he did himself, nor to cut short his studied obtuseness with a cool self-possession that addressed him in the familiar second person singular. In the doorway he paused to explain that at length to a fellow waiter. *"Sales Américains,"* he said, and spat. Simon Templar was not meant to hear, but the Saint's ears were abnormally sensitive.

He smiled. It would never have occurred to him to report the waiter to the management, even though he was sure they would have been grateful to be warned about such a saboteur of goodwill. To the Saint any city was an oyster for his opening, a world for conquest; anything was an adventure, even the slaying of an insolent waiter and the rescue of a damsel in distress about nothing more serious than a cocktail.

He let his cigarette smolder in absolute contentment. The Rumhattan arrived. The girl tasted it and grimaced ruefully—he decided that she had a mouth that couldn't look anything but pretty even when it tried.

"It's a good idea, but it needs co-operation," he said.

"I wish I could speak the language like you do," she said. "I'd have something to tell that waiter."

"I've spent more time in Paris than any respectable man should," said the Saint cheerfully. "I used to be the *concierge* of a home for inebriate art students in the Rue des Deux Paires de Chaussettes de M. Alexandre Dumas. We all lived on absinthe and wore velvet next the skin. It went very

well until someone discovered that half the inmates were wearing false
beards and reading Ellery Queen in secret."

The gray eyes laughed.

"But do you know your way about here?"

"Montreal is yours," said the Saint with a gesture. "What would you like?
Respectable night clubs? Disreputable saloons? Historic monuments?"

She seemed to be thinking of something else. And then she turned towards him again in a pose very like his own. The deep friendly eyes had
a queer wistfulness.

"Tell me, stranger—where do you think a girl should go on a great
occasion? Suppose she had something rather desperate to do, and if it went
wrong she mightn't be able to choose where she went any more."

The Saint's very clear blue eyes rested on her thoughtfully. He had
always been mad, always hoped to be.

"I think," he said, "I should take her out St. Lawrence Boulevard to a
quiet little restaurant I know where they make the best omelets in North
America. We should absorb vitamins and talk about life. And after that we
might know some more."

"I should like to go there," she said.

Simon flicked a twenty-dollar bill across his table and beckoned the
waiter.

The waiter counted out change laboriously from a well-filled wallet.

"Shall we?" said the Saint.

The girl gathered up her gloves and bag. Simon stood up quickly to pull
the table away from in front of her. He trod heavily on the waiter's toes,
overbalanced him backwards, and caught him again dexterously as he was
on the point of descending, like Newton's apple, on the bald head of a
customer in the next row. Somewhere in the course of the acrobatics the
well-filled wallet traveled from the waiter's pocket to the Saint's own.

"*Mille pardons,*" murmured the Saint, patting the anguished man soothingly on the shoulder, and sauntered after the girl.

There was a taxi crawling by, and they climbed in.

"I'm free till twelve, stranger," said the girl.

She pulled off her hat and leaned far back on the cushions, with one
slim silken leg stretched out to rest a toe on the folding seat in front. The
passing lights picked up her face in almost breathless perfection, and let it
sink back reluctantly into shadow.

"And then do you have to hurry home before the clock strikes, and only
leave a glass slipper for a souvenir?"

"No," she said, "I have to burgle a house."

There was an omelet. She had never dreamed of anything so delicate, wrapped in a gossamer skin, so richly red-gold inside, so different in every way from the dry coagulation of half-scrambled eggs which passes under the same name in so many places.

"There's a trick in it," she said with a sigh, when it was finished.

"Of course there is," said the Saint. "It's one of the higher mysteries of life, only to be revealed to the pure in heart after many ordeals and battles and much traveling."

She accepted a cigarette from his case, dipped it in the flame of his lighter. Across the table the gray eyes looked into his with the serene intimacy which must come with the sharing of any sensuous pleasure, even eating. She said: "I'm glad I met you, stranger. You take things very calmly, and you don't ask awkward questions."

In the course of his career the Saint had taken a good many things calmly enough, but he could not remember having heard it accounted unto him for righteousness before.

He perceived that he had fallen into the error of attaching himself too much to the viewpoint of his bereaved victims.

"The questions may come later," he said. "We burglars aren't easily startled."

She let a trail of smoke rise and disintegrate towards the ceiling.

"I'm going to talk to you, stranger," she said quietly. "A girl likes to talk; and nothing about this evening is real. We never met before and we shan't meet again. This is an interlude that doesn't count, except for remembrance."

"Is there a dragon in it?"

"There's a Robber Baron. Have you ever heard of Burt Northwade?"

Simon had. His knowledge of unlovable characters, in and out of prison, was very nearly unique.

He knew Northwade for one of the more unpleasant products of World War I, a man who had successfully conceived the notion of selling inferior bootlaces to the Allied armies for three times their cost, and had gained for himself much wealth by that patriotic service. The Northwade business, subsequently built up to almost monopolistic proportions, was still welding together the uppers of half the world; but Northwade himself had retired a couple of years ago to his native Canada and a mansion in Westmount, leaving the female part of his family to pursue its strenuous climb through the social gradings of New York.

"Yes, I've heard of Northwade. One of these monuments of other people's industry, isn't he?"

"He's also my uncle," said the girl. "I'm Judith Northwade."

Simon Templar hadn't blushed since he was eight years old. Also he considered that his remark was very nearly a compliment compared with what he would probably have said to Burt Northwade's face, had that undesirable industrialist been present.

"You have our sympathy," he said coolly.

"My father's a professor of engineering at Toronto," said the girl. "You've probably never heard of him. You couldn't have two brothers who were more different. They've always been like that. Northwade only wanted to make money. My father never wanted it. He's just a quiet, kind, completely ordinary man—almost a child outside his work. They both started at the bottom, and they both got what they wanted. Northwade made the money; my father worked his way through school, went on to Toronto University on a scholarship, and got to where he is now. The thing that came between them was my mother. Northwade wanted her, too, but she just happened to prefer Dad."

The Saint nodded.

"It wasn't Dad's fault," she said, "but Uncle Burt never forgave him. I don't think he was really jealous—maybe he wasn't really in love at all—but he'd come on something that money and success alone couldn't buy, and his vanity never got over it. Oh, he didn't say anything outright; he's always been friendly—too friendly—but Dad, who wouldn't suspect a cannibal who was weighing him, never thought anything of it. I could see. I tried to tell him, but he wouldn't believe me. He even helped Uncle Burt to make more money—he's a clever inventor, too, and during the war he designed a machine that would put tags on laces twice as quickly as the old way, or something like that. I think Uncle Burt gave him fifty dollars for it." She smiled a little. "It's beginning to sound like a detective story, isn't it?"

"It has begun," said the Saint, "but I like those stories."

She finished her glass of Château Olivier.

"It's going to sound more like that; but it's just one of those stories that are happening every day. For the last eighteen months or so Dad's been working on an infinitely variable gear for automobiles. Do you know what that means? It means that you'll just drive your car on the accelerator and brake; and whatever it's doing, up hills or down, or in traffic or anywhere, without even an automatic gear change, the engine'll always be working at its maximum efficiency—that sounds rather technical, but I'm so used to hearing Dad talk that I've got that way myself. Anyway, it's far in advance of anything that's been done in that line so far. There's a fortune in it already; but it wasn't good enough for Dad. He wanted to be sure that it was beyond any improvement. Three months ago he'd spent every penny he'd saved on his experiments. Then he went to Uncle Burt for help."

The Saint's mind moved in certain channels with the speed and precision of infinite experience. He took up his cigarette again and regarded her steadily over it.

"Northwade helped him, of course," he said.

"Uncle Burt lent him five thousand dollars. On a nominal security—purely nominal. And with a few legal documents—just as a matter of form. I expect you can guess what that means."

"I could try."

"The plans of the gear are in Uncle Burt's safe, over in Westmount—all the results of Dad's work up till now. And there's a paper with them which says that all rights in them belong to Burt Northwade—with no time limit specified. It was supposed to be until the loan was repaid, but the contract doesn't say so. Dad hasn't any mind for legal trickeries, and he signed the papers while I was away. I didn't know about it till it was too late."

"One gathers," said the Saint composedly, "that this is the house you propose to burgle."

She gazed at him without flinching, gray eyes frank and resolute, even with that strain of wistful loneliness in them.

"Listen, stranger," she said softly. "This is still the game of Let's Pretend, isn't it? Pretending that this evening is right outside the world. Because that's the only reason why I'm telling you all this. I'm going to burgle Uncle Burt's house, if I can. I'm going to try and get hold of his keys and open his safe and take those papers away, including the contract Dad signed. Dad hasn't any hope of paying back that five thousand dollars. And Uncle Burt knows it. He's practically completed arrangements to sell the gear to Ford. There's no legal way of stopping him. It's one of those cases where possession is nine points of the law. If we had that contract back, as well as the plans, Uncle Burt would never have the face to go into a court and publish the terms of it, which he'd have to do if he wanted to make any claim. Do you think I'm quite mad?"

"Only a little."

She turned the stem of her wineglass between her fingers, looking at him quietly.

"Maybe I am. But have you ever heard of the Saint?"

"The Robin Hood of Modern Crime?" murmured Simon, with only the faintest lift of an eyebrow for expression.

"I think it's the sort of thing he'd do," she said. "It's justice, even if it's against the law. I wish I could meet him. He'd understand. I think he'd say it was worth taking a chance on. You're very understanding, too, stranger. You've listened to me awfully patiently, and it's helped a lot. And now you shall talk about anything else you like, and will you please forget it all?"

Simon Templar smiled.

He poured out the last of the wine, and took up his glass. Over the rim of it his clear blue eyes raked the girl with a cavalier challenge that matched his devil-may-care smile and the mocking slant of his brows. His face was alight suddenly.

"I don't propose to forget, Judith," he said. "I am the Saint; and the safe hasn't been made that I can't open. Nor has anything else been thought of that I can't do. We'll go to Westmount together!"

"This is the place," said the girl.

Simon switched off the engine and let the car coast to a stop under the lee of the hedge. It was her car—she had been prepared for that. She had telephoned from the restaurant and it had been fueled and waiting for them at the garage.

Burt Northwade's home, an unwieldy mansion in the Napoleonic style, stood on a slight rise of ground some distance back from the road, in the center of its extensive and pleasant grounds.

Rising to sit on the door of the convertible, with one foot on the seat, Simon could see the solid rectangle of its upper part painted in dull black on a smudged gray-blue sky. He felt that he knew every corner of it as if he had lived there for years, from the descriptions she had given him and the rough plans she had drawn on the back of the menu, familiarizing him with the configurations of rooms and corridors while their coffee grew cold and neither of them cared. That had been a time of delight shared in adventure which he would always like to remember; but now it was over, and the adventure went on.

It was a night without moon or stars, and yet not utterly dark; perfect for the purpose. She saw the clean-cut lines of his face, recklessly etched in the burst of light as he kindled a cigarette.

"I still don't know why you should do this for me," she said.

"Because it's a game after my own heart," he answered. "Northwade is a bird I've had ideas of my own about for some time. And as for our present object—well, no one could have thought of a story that would have been more likely to fetch me a thousand miles to see it through."

"I feel I ought to be coming with you."

He drew smoke into his lungs, and with it the sweet smell of green leaves.

"This sort of thing is my job, and I've had more practice than you."

"But suppose Uncle Burt wakes up."

"I shall immediately hypnotize him so that he falls into a deep sleep again."

"Or suppose the servants catch you."

"I shall tie them up in bundles of three and heave them into the outer darkness."

"But suppose you *are* caught?"

He laughed.

"It'll be a sign that the end of the world is at hand. But don't worry. Even if that happens it'll cause a certain amount of commotion, and if you hear it I shall expect you to drive rapidly away and await the end in some other province. I shall tell them I came out here on roller skates. It's not your burglary any more—it's mine."

He swung his immaculately tailored legs over the side and dropped lightly to the road, and without another word he was gone, melting into the obscurity like a ghost.

He walked up the turf path beside the drive with the quick confidence of a cat. No lights showed in any of the front windows as he approached, but he made a careful circle of the house for complete certainty. His eyes adjusted themselves to the gloom with the ease of long habit, and he moved without rustling a blade of grass under his feet.

The ground floor was a rugged façade of raised arches and pilasters broken by tall gaunt windows, with a pair of carved oak doors in the middle that would have given way to nothing short of a battering-ram; but it is an axiom of housebreaking that those buildings whose fronts look most like fortresses are most likely to defend their postern gates with a card saying "No Admittance." In this case, there was an open pantry window six feet above the ground. Simon squeezed up through the aperture, and lowered himself gently over the shelves of viands on the inside.

He passed through into the kitchen. With the help of a tiny pocket flashlight he located the main switchboard and removed all the fuses, burying them in a sack of potatoes. If by any chance there should be an accident, the garrison of the house would be more handicapped by a lack of lights than he would. Then he made his way down the main hall and unbarred, unbolted, unchained, and unlocked the great oak portals. Simon Templar owed much of his freedom to a trained eye for emergency exits; and he carried on the good work by opening a pair of windows in the library before he gave a thought to the safe.

The girl had described its location accurately. It was built into one wall, behind a small bookcase which opened away from it like a door; and Simon held his flashlight on it for just three seconds before he decided that it was one of those situations in which neither a bent hairpin or a can opener would be adequate.

He slid cheerfully back into the hall and stepped soundlessly up the broad staircase. A large selection of burglarious tools was not part of his usual traveling equipment, but that shortcoming had rarely troubled him. It was another axiom of his philosophy that non-combination safes have keys, that most keys are in the possession of the owners of the safes, and, therefore, that the plodding felon who finds it necessary to pack nitroglycerin and oxyacetylene blowpipes in his overnight bag is usually deficient in strategic genius. Burt Northwade was sleeping soundly enough, with his mouth open, and a reassuring drone issuing from the region of his adenoids; but even if he had been awake it is doubtful whether he would have heard the opening of his bedroom door, or sensed one movement of the sensitive hands that lifted a bunch of keys from his dressing table and detached an even more probable one from the chain around his neck.

Simon went down the stairs again like a ghost. It was the key from the chain which turned the lock, and the heavy steel door swung back at a touch with the smooth acquiescence that even Simon Templar could never feel without a thrill. He propped his flashlight over one instep so that its light filled the interior of the safe, and went to work with quick white-gloved hands. Once he heard a board crack overhead and froze into seconds of granite immobility; but he knew that he had made no noise, and presently he went on.

The plans were dissected into a thick roll of sheets tied up with tape; the specifications were packed in a long fat envelope with "Pegasus Variable Gear" roughly scrawled on it—that, he had been told, was the name which had been provisionally given to the invention—and a short epic on legal paper was enclosed with them. There were also some letters from various automobile manufacturers.

The Saint was so busily engaged for the next ten minutes, and so absorbed in his labors, that he missed certain faint sounds which might otherwise have reached his ears. The first hint of danger came just as he had finished, in the shape of a cautious scuffle of feet on the terrace outside, and a hoarse whisper which was so unexpected that he raised his head almost incredulously.

Then his eyes dropped half instinctively to the safe which he had just closed. He saw something that he had not noticed before—a flat leaden tube which rose a bare inch from the floor and disappeared into the crack under the lowest hinge, an obvious conduit for alarm wires. The girl had told him that there were no alarms; but that was one which Northwade had probably preferred to keep secret, and it had taken the Saint off his guard.

The narrow beam of the flashlight snapped out like a silent explosion. Simon leapt through the blackness to the windows, slammed them together, and secured the catch. He was knotting a handkerchief over the lower part of his face as he crossed the room again. In the darkness his hand closed on the doorknob, turned it stealthily; at the same time his fingers stretched downwards, and could feel no key in the lock. It looked as if it might be a tight corner, a crisp and merry getaway while it lasted; but those were the moments when the Saint's brain worked at its swiftest.

He opened the door with a quick jerk and took one step into the hall. On his right, covering the retreat to the back of the house, stood an outsize butler in a nightshirt with a rolling pin clutched in one hand. On his left, barring the way to the front door, was a wiry youth in trousers and undershirt. A little way up the stairs stood Burt Northwade himself, with a candle in one hand and a young cannon of a revolver in the other. The Saint's most reckless fighting smile touched his lips under the concealing handkerchief.

"*Bon soir, messieurs,*" he murmured politely. "It appears that you were not expecting me. I am accustomed to being received in formal dress. I regret that I cannot accept you in this attire."

He stepped back rapidly through the door, closing it after him. The butler and the wiry youth took a few seconds to recover; then they made a concerted dash for the door. They burst in together, followed by Burt Northwade with the candle. The spectacle of a completely deserted library was the last thing they were expecting, and it pulled them up short with bulging eyes.

In an abruptly contrasting silence, the nightshirted butler returned to life. He tiptoed gingerly forward, and peered with a majestic air behind and under a large settee in a far corner of the room. The wiry youth, inspired by his example, made a dash to the nearest window curtains and pulled them wide apart, disclosing a large area of glass with the round goggling faces of two other servants pressed against it from the outside, like startled fish in an aquarium. Burt Northwade discreetly remained a scant yard inside the doorway with his sputtering candle held helpfully aloft.

On the top of a massive ladder of bookshelves beside the door, Simon Templar rose like a panther from his prone position and dropped downwards. He fell squarely behind Northwade, easing his fall with a hand applied to the crown of Northwade's head, which drew from the tycoon a sudden squeal of terror. The same hand pushed Northwade violently forward, and the candle which supplied the only illumination of the scene flickered and went out.

In the darkness the door banged.

"We might even get back in time to have a dance somewhere," said the Saint.

He materialized out of the gloom beside her like a wraith; and she gasped.

"Did you have to scare me?" she asked, when she had got her breath.

He chuckled. Back towards the Northwade mansion there were sounds of muffled disturbance, floating down to his ears like the music of hounds to an old fox. He slipped into the driving seat and touched the starter. The engine purred unprotestingly.

"Did something go wrong?" she asked.

"Nothing that wasn't taken care of."

The car gathered speed into the blaze of its own headlights. Simon felt for a cigarette and lighted it from the dashboard gadget.

"Did you get everything?" she asked.

"I am the miracle man who never fails, Judith," he said reproachfully. "Hadn't I explained that?"

"But that noise——"

"There seems to have been some sort of alarm that goes off when the safe is opened, which you didn't know about. Not that it mattered a lot. The ungodly were fatally slow in assembling, and if you'd seen their waist measurements you wouldn't have been surprised."

She caught his arm excitedly.

"Oh, I can't quite believe it! . . . Everything's all right now. And I've actually been on a raid with the Saint himself! Do you mind if I give way a bit?"

She reached across him to the button in the middle of the steering wheel. The horn blared a rhythmic peal of triumph and defiance into the night: "*Taaa ta-ta, taaa ta-ta, taa ta-ta!*" Like a jubilant trumpet. Simon smiled. Nothing could have fitted better into the essential rightness of everything that had happened that evening. It was true that there had been a telephone in the library, and if there was an extension upstairs there might be gendarmes already watching the road; but they would be an interesting complication that could be dealt with in its proper turn.

Then he coaxed the car around a sharp bend and saw a row of red lights spring up across the road. He dropped his hand thoughtfully to the brake.

"This wasn't here when we came by first," he said, and realized that the girl had gone tense and still.

"What do you think it is?" she whispered.

The Saint shrugged. He brought the car to a standstill with its bumper three yards from the red lights, which appeared to be attached to a long plank rigged squarely across his path—he could not see what was beyond the plank.

Then he felt a hard cold jab of metal in the side of his head, and turned quickly. He looked down the barrel of a gun in the hand of an overcoated man who stood beside the car.

"Take it easy," advised the man with grim calmness.

The Saint heard a rustle of movement beside him, and glanced around. The girl was getting out. She closed the door after her, and stood on the running board.

"This is as far as I ride, stranger," she said.

"I see," said the Saint gently.

The man with the gun jabbed again.

"Let's have those papers," he ordered.

Simon took them from his breast pocket. The girl received them, and turned on the dashboard light to squint down the roll of plans and read the inscription on the long envelope. Her golden-yellow hair stirred like a shifting halo in the slight breeze.

"Burt Northwade hasn't got a brother who's a professor at Toronto," she explained, "and I'm no relative of the family. Apart from that, most of what I told you was true. Northwade bought this invention from a young Rumanian inventor—I don't know what sort of a price he gave for it, but he bought it. Actually there's no patent on it, so the biggest value to a manufacturer is in keeping it secret till he can come out with it ahead of the others. He was going to sell it to Ford, as I told you."

"What are you going to do with it?" inquired the Saint curiously.

"We've got an unwritten offer from Henry Kaiser."

She went forward and swung back the plank with the red lights, so that the road was clear again. Then she came back. The gray eyes were as frank and friendly as before.

"We've been planning this job for a week, and we should have done the job ourselves tonight if I hadn't seen your photograph in the paper and recognized you at the Windsor. The rest of it was an inspiration. There's nothing like having the greatest expert in the profession to work for you."

"Which paper do you read?" asked the Saint.

"I saw you in *La Presse*. Why?"

"I bought an imported New York paper," said the Saint, conversationally.

She laughed quietly, a friendly ripple tinged with a trace of regret.

"I'm sorry, stranger. I liked you so much."

"I'm rather sorry too—Judith," said the Saint.

She was still for an instant. Then she leaned over and kissed him quickly on the lips.

The gun jabbed again.

"Drive on," ordered the man. "And keep driving."

"Won't you be wanting your car?" murmured the Saint.

A harsher chuckle came from the depths of the dark overcoat.

"We've got our own. I rented that one and left it at a garage for you when I had a phone call to say you were hooked. Get moving."

Simon engaged the gears, and let in the clutch. The girl jumped down from the running board. "Good-by, stranger!" she cried; and Simon raised one hand in salute, without looking back.

He drove fast. Whoever the girl was, whatever she was, he knew that he had enjoyed meeting her far more than he could ever have enjoyed meeting the real Judith Northwade, whose unfortunate motor accident had been featured, with portrait, on the front page of the New York *Daily Gazette*, alongside his own two columns. She could never have looked anything but a hag. Whereas he still thought that her imposter was very beautiful. He hated to think what she would say when she delved deeper into the duplicate envelope and dummy roll of plans which he had so rapidly prepared for her in Burt Northwade's library. But he still drove fast; because those sad things were a part of the game and it was a longish way to Willow Run.

JEANNINE

FROM *Saint Errant*

BEFORE YOU HAVE PLOUGHED very far into this episode, it is bound to become manifest even to the most obtuse of you that you are reading a sort of sequel to the one before. So I am going to take that much edge off it and admit it before you start.

But this was not anything I planned. There was a lapse of many years between the writing of the stories. The fact that the same girl turned out to be involved was almost a surprise even to me. But the story called for a character that the Saint had matched wits with before; and while I suppose it wouldn't have been too difficult to invent one, it seemed a lot simpler to dig one out of the Saint's recorded past, where the previous encounter was fully documented.

This is one of the sordid advantages of writing such an unconscionable number of stories. You don't have to keep on creating new characters indefinitely. The time comes when you only have to reach back into the half-forgotten past, pick up some personality that once flashed across your screen, and figure what might have happened to him or her (and how tediously grammatical I must be getting) since that earlier encounter.

If any aspirant authors among you want to exploit this simplified system of story-concocting, I bequeath it to you gladly with my blessing. All you have to do is to put in fifteen or more creative years, and from then on everything is on the house.

JEANNINE

WINE, *that maketh glad the heart of man*," quoted Simon Templar, holding his glass appreciatively to the light. "The Psalmist would have had things to talk about."

"It would have been a love match," said Lieutenant Wendel, like a load of gravel.

"Up to a point," Simon agreed. "But then he goes on: *And oil to make him a cheerful countenance*. Here we start asking questions. Is the prescription for internal or external application? Are we supposed to swallow the oil, or rub it on the face? . . . I am, of course, quoting the Revised Version. The King James has it *Oil to make his face to shine,* but the revisers must have had some reason for the change. Perhaps they wanted to restore some element of ambiguity in the original, dividing the plug equally between mayonnaise and Max Factor."

The detective stared at him woodenly.

"I've wondered a lot of things about you, Saint. But what a guy like you wants with that quiz stuff is beyond me."

Simon smiled.

"A man in my business can never know too much. A brigand has to be just a little ahead of the field—because the field isn't just a lot of horses trying to win a race with him, but a pack of hounds trying to run him down. Quite a lot of my phenomenal success," he said modestly, "is due to my memory for unconsidered trifles."

Wendel grunted.

They sat in a booth in Arnaud's, which Simon had chosen over the claims of such other temples of New Orleans cuisine as Antoine's or Galatoire's because the oak beams and subdued lights seemed to offer a more propitious atmosphere for a meal which he wanted to keep peaceful.

For Simon Templar was in some practical respects a devout lover of peace, and frequently tried very hard to vindicate the first person who had nicknamed him the Saint, in spite of all the legends of tumult and mayhem that had collected about that apparently incongruous sobriquet. Because a modern buccaneer in the perfect exploit would cause no commotion at all, even if this would make singularly dull reading: it is only when something goes wrong that the fireworks go off and the plot thickens with alarums and excursions, hues and cries, and all the uproar and excitement that provide such entertainment for the reader.

"Besides which," Simon continued at leisure, "I like civilized amenities with my crime—or wine. Both of them have a finer flavor for being enriched with background." He raised his glass again, passing it under his nostrils and admiring its ruby tint. "I take this wine, and to me it's much more than alcoholic grape juice. I think of the particular breed of grapes it was made from, and the dry sunny slopes where they ripened. I think of all the lore of wine-making. I think of the great names of wine, that you could chant like an anthem—Chambertin, Romanée-Conti, Richebourg, Vougeot . . . I think of great drinkers—*buveurs très illustres,* as Rabelais addresses us—of August the Strong of Saxony, who fathered three hundred and sixty-five bastards and drank himself to death on Imperial Tokay, doubtless from celebrating all their birthdays—or of the Duke of Clarence who was drowned in a butt of malmsey wine . . . Or, perhaps, I might think of pearls . . ."

Wendel suddenly stiffened into stillness.

"I was wondering how to bring pearls into it."

"Did you ever hear that wine would dissolve pearls?" asked the Saint. "If you collected these items, you'd have read about how the decadent Roman emperors, in their lush moments, would dissolve pearls in the banquet wine, just to prove that money was no object. And then there's a story about Cleopatra's big party to Caesar, when she offered him wine with her own hands, and dropped a priceless pearl in his goblet. Now if you knew——"

"What I want to know," Wendel said, "is how much you're interested in Lady Offchurch's pearls."

The Saint sighed.

"You're such a materialist," he complained. "I arrive in New Orleans an innocent and happy tourist, and I've hardly checked into a hotel when you burst in on me, flashing your badge and demanding to know what the hell I want in town. I do my best to convince you that I'm only here to soak up the atmosphere of your historic city and incidentally absorb some of your superb cooking with it. I even persuade you to have dinner with me and get this epicurean picnic off to a good start. We are just starting to relax and enjoy ourselves, with poetic excursions into history and legend, when suspicion rears its ugly head again and you practically accuse me of planning to swipe some wretched dowager's jewels."

"I'll go further than that," Wendel rasped, with the raw edges of uncertainty in his voice. "I'm wondering what made you choose this place to eat in."

"It seemed like a good idea."

"It wasn't because you expected Lady Offchurch to choose it too."

"Of course not."

"So it's just a coincidence that she happens to be here."

Simon raised unhurried eyebrows.

"Behind you, on your left," Wendel said, trap-mouthed.

The Saint drank some wine, put down his glass, and looked casually over his shoulder.

He did not need to have Lady Offchurch more specifically pointed out to him, for her picture had been in the papers not long before, and the story with it was the sort of thing that made him remember faces. The late Lord Offchurch had, until his recent demise, been the British Government's official "adviser" to a certain maharajah, and this maharajah had bestowed upon the departing widow, as a trivial token of his esteem, a necklace of matched pink pearls valued at a mere $100,000. Lady Offchurch had provided good copy on this to receptive reporters in Hollywood, where she had been suitably entertained by the English Colony on what was supposed to be her way "home." She had also expressed her concern over the fate of an Independent India, abandoned to the self-government of a mob of natives which even the most altruistic efforts of the British raj had been unable in two centuries of rule to lift above the level of a herd of cattle— except, of course, for such distinguished types as the dear maharajah.

She was a thin, bony, tight-lipped woman with a face like a well-bred horse, and Simon could construct the rest of her character without an interview. There was no need even to look at her for long; and as a matter of fact, he didn't.

What kept his head turned for quite a few seconds more than identification called for was Lady Offchurch's companion—a girl half her age, with golden hair and gray eyes and a face that must have launched a thousand clichés.

"Well?" Lieutenant Wendel's voice intruded harshly, and Simon turned back.

"Beautiful," he said.

"Yeah," Wendel said. "For a hundred grand, they should be."

"Oh, the pearls," Simon said innocently. "I didn't notice. I was talking about her daughter."

Wendel squinted past him.

"She doesn't have a daughter. I guess that's just a friend. Maybe came with her from Hollywood—she's pretty enough." His eyes snapped back to Simon with a scowl. "Now quit tryin' to head me off again. When I read this Offchurch was in town, I naturally start wondering if any big operators have checked in about the same time. I'm a lazy guy, see, and it's a lot easier to stop something happening than try to catch a crook after he's done it. . . . And the first hotel register I go through, I see your name."

"Which proves I must be up to something, because if I wasn't planning a Saint job I'd obviously use an alias."

"It wouldn't be out of line with the kind of nerve I hear you've got."

"Thank you."

"So I'm tellin' you. I'm having Lady Offchurch watched twenty-four hours a day, and if my men ever see you hanging around they'll throw you in the can. And if those pearls ever show up missing, whether anybody saw you or not, you better be ready with all the answers."

Simon Templar smiled, and it was like the kindling of a light in his keen, dark, reckless face. His blue eyes danced with an audacity that only belonged with cloaks and swords.

"Now you're really making it sound interesting."

Wendel's face reddened.

"Yeah? Well, I'm warning you."

"You're tempting me. I wish policemen wouldn't keep doing that." Simon beckoned a waiter. "Coffee—and how about some *crêpes Suzette?*"

The detective bunched his napkin on the table.

"No, thank you. Let me have my check—separately."

"But I invited you."

"I can take care of myself, Saint. I hope you can too. Just don't forget, you had your warning."

"I won't forget," said the Saint softly.

He lighted a cigarette after the police officer had gone, and thoughtfully stirred sugar into his coffee.

He was not affronted by Wendel's ungraciousness—that sort of reaction was almost conventional, and he hadn't exactly exerted himself to avoid it. But it was a pity, he thought, that so many policemen in their most earnest efforts to avert trouble were prone to throw down challenges which no self-respecting picaroon could ignore. Because it happened to be perfectly true that the Saint had entered New Orleans without a single design upon Lady Offchurch or her pearls; and if it was inept of the law to draw his attention to them, it was even more tactless to combine the reminder with what virtually amounted to a dare.

Even so (the Saint assured himself), his fundamental strength and no-bility of character might still have been able to resist the provocation if Destiny hadn't thrown in the girl with the golden hair. . . .

He didn't look at her again until Lady Offchurch passed his table, on her way to the special conveniences of the restaurant; and then he turned again and met the gray eyes squarely and timelessly.

The girl looked back at him, and her face was as smooth and translucent as the maharajah's pearls, and as brilliantly expressionless.

Then she lowered her eyes to a book of matches in front of her, and wrote inside the cover with a pencil from her bag.

The Saint's gaze left her again, and didn't even return when a passing waiter placed a match booklet somewhat ostentatiously in front of him.

He opened the cover and read:

> 27 *Bienville Apts.*
> *St Ann Street*
> *at* 10:30

Lady Offchurch was returning to her table. Simon Templar paid his check, put the matches in his pocket, and strolled out to pass the time at the Absinthe House.

This was the way things happened to him, and he couldn't fight against fate.

So after a while he was strolling down St Ann Street, until he found the Bienville. He went through an archway into a cobblestoned courtyard, and there even more than in the narrow streets of the Vieux Carré it was like dropping back into another century, where cloaks and swords had a place. Around him, like a stage setting, was a chiaroscuro of dim lights and magnolia and wrought-iron balconies that seemed to have been planned for romantic and slightly illicit assignations, and he could make no complaint about the appropriateness of his invitation.

He found an outside stairway that led up to a door beside which a lantern hung over the number 27, and she opened the door before he touched the knocker.

He couldn't help the trace of mockery in his bow as he said: "Good evening."

"Good evening," she said calmly, and walked back across the living room. The front door opened straight into it. There were glasses and bottles on a sideboard in the dining alcove across the room. As she went there she said: "What would you like to drink?"

"Brandy, I think, for this occasion," he said.

She brought it to him in a tulip glass, and he sniffed and sipped analytically.

"Robin, isn't it?" he remarked. "I remember—you had a natural taste." His eyes ran up and down her slender shape with the same candid analysis. "I guess there's only one thing you've changed. In Montreal, you were pretending to be Judith Northwade. What name are you using here?"

"Jeannine Roger. It happens to be my own."

"A good name, anyway. Does it also belong to the last man I saw you with?"

For an instant she was almost puzzled.

"Oh, him. My God, no."

"Then he isn't lurking in the next room, waiting to cut loose with a sawed-off shotgun."

"I haven't seen him for months, and I couldn't care less if it was years."

Simon tasted his brandy again, even more carefully.

"Then—are you relying on some subtle Oriental poison, straight from the pharmacopoeia of Sherlock Holmes?"

"No."

"This gets even more interesting. In Montreal——"

"In Montreal, I tried to pull a fast one on you."

"To be exact, you set me up to pull a job for you, and I was damn nearly the sucker who fell for it."

"Only instead of that you made a sucker out of me."

"And now all of a sudden I'm forgiven?"

She shrugged.

"How can I squawk? I started the double-cross, so how can I kick if it backfired? So now we're even."

Simon sat on the arm of a chair.

"This is almost fascinating," he said. "So you sent me that invitation so we could kiss again and be friends?"

A faint flush touched her cheekbones.

"When you saw me with Lady Offchurch, I knew I'd have to deal with you sooner or later. Why kid myself? So I thought I'd get it over with."

"You thought I was after the same boodle."

"If you weren't before, you would be now."

"Well, what's the proposition?"

"Why don't we really team up this time?"

Simon put a cigarette in his mouth and struck a match.

"It's a nice idea," he said. "However, you may be overlooking something. How do you see the split?"

"Fifty-fifty, of course."

"That's the trouble."

"That's how it has to be. You can't turn it down. If you can louse me up, I can do the same to you."

The Saint smiled.

"That isn't the point. You're forgetting something. Remember when you were the damsel in distress, and I was all set up to be the knight in shining armor? You had the right idea then."

"You hijacked me," she said sultrily, "like any other crook."

"But I didn't keep the spoils, like any other crook," he said imperturbably. "I found out how much Northwade had underpaid that young inventor, and I sent him the difference—anonymously. Minus, of course, my ten-per-cent commission."

She was not quite incredulous.

"I've heard stories like that about you, but I didn't believe them."

"They happen to be true. Call me crazy, but that's my racket. . . . Now in this case, it seems to me that most of the value of that necklace ought to go back to the poor bloody Indians who were sweated by the maharajah to pay for it while the British Government, as represented by Lord and Lady Offchurch, were benevolently sipping tea in the palace. So if you helped, I might let you have another ten per cent for yourself; but that's all. And you can't turn it down. Don't forget—if you can louse me up, I can do the same to you."

She sat down in another chair and looked upwards at him under lowered brows, and her gray eyes had the darkness of storm clouds.

"You certainly make it tough—stranger," she said, and her smile was thin.

"Can't I sell you a good cause, just once?"

"I think your cause stinks, but I have to buy it. You don't give me any choice. Damn you."

The Saint laughed. He crossed to her and held out his hand.

"Okay, Jeannine."

She put her cool fingers firmly in his; and he knew, he knew quite surely, that the handshake was as false as the way her eyes cleared. The certainty was so real that it was a fleeting chill inside him, and he knew that now they were committed to a duel in which no tricks could be ruled out. But his gaze matched hers for frankness and straightforwardness, and he said: "Well now, pardner, let's know what track you were on."

"I was on the Coast when she arrived. I was working out on a producer. He took me to a party that she was at. I knew I couldn't risk her in Hollywood, but I found out that New Orleans was the first place she wanted to stop over in on her way East. So right away this was my home town. I took the next plane here and got hold of this apartment, and don't ask how. Then I wired her the address and said I was sorry I'd been called away suddenly but she must look me up and let me show her the town. Then I spent my time with a guidebook finding out what to show her."

"As an inspirational worker, it's an honor to know you," Simon murmured approvingly. "Of course, you can't belong to an old Creole family, because you can't introduce her around. So what are you—an artist?"

"A writer. I'm getting material for a novel."

"Which the producer was interested in."

"Exactly."

"And how did you figure the job?"

She was silent for a few moments, her eyes turned to a corner but not looking at anything.

"I've been able to get the necklace in my hands long enough to count the pearls while I was admiring them, and take a wax impression of one of them for size. I'm having an imitation made in New York. As soon as it gets here, I've only got to make the switch."

Simon showed his respect.

"You can write scripts for me, any time," he said.

"Now tell me your angle," she responded.

"Darling, I never had one."

She stared.

"What?"

"I didn't even know La Offchurch was here, until that guy I was having dinner with pointed her out and practically dared me to steal her necklace. He just happens to be the local Gestapo."

Gun metal glinted in the gray eyes.

"Why, you chiseling . . ." Then she laughed a little. "So you do it to me again. Why do you always have to be bad news, stranger? It could have been so much fun."

"It still could be," he said impudently; but she stood up and slipped past him towards the sideboard. He strolled lazily after her and said: "By the way, when do you expect to get that imitation?"

"Maybe the day after tomorrow."

And again he felt that tenuous cold touch of disbelief, but he kept it to himself, and held out his glass for a refill.

"On account of Wendel—that's the name of the gendarme—I'd better not risk being seen with you in public." He looked across the alcove into the kitchen, and said as the idea struck him: "Tell you what—if we can't eat out together, we can still dine. I'll bring some stuff in tomorrow and start fixing. I forgot to tell you before, but I'm as good as any chef in this town."

"You just got a job," she said.

He went back to his hotel in a haze of thought. The cool drafts of skepticism which had whispered around him began to reward him with the exhilaration of walking on the thin ice which they created. He was a fool for danger, and he always would be.

This was danger, as real as a triggered guillotine. It was true that she had no choice about accepting his terms—out loud. But it wasn't in keeping with her character as he knew it to accept them finally. And she had been just a little too evasive at one point and too acquiescent at another. It didn't balance. But when the catch would show was something he could only wait for.

He went to her apartment the next afternoon, laden with the brown paper bags of marketing. She made him a drink in the kitchen while he unpacked and went to work with quick and easy efficiency.

"What are we having?"

"Oxtail." He smiled at her lift of expression. "And don't despise it. It was always destined for something rarer than soup."

He was slicing onions and carrots.

"These—browned in butter. Then we make a bed of them in a casserole, with plenty of chopped parsley and other herbs. Then, the joints packed neatly in, like the crowd at a good fire. And then, enough red wine to cover it, and let it soak for hours."

"When does it cook?"

"When you come home tonight. I'll drop in for a nightcap, and we'll watch it get started. Then it cools overnight, and tomorrow we take off the grease and finish it. . . . You'd better let me have a key, in case you're late."

"Why don't you just move in?"

He grinned.

"I guess you forgot to invite me. But I'll manage." He trimmed fat from the joints, while the frying pan hissed gently with liquescent butter. "Did the mailman deliver?"

"It didn't come today."

And once again it was like a Geiger counter clicking to the intrusion of invisible radioactivity, the way his intuition tingled deep down at her reply.

He said, pleasantly: "I hope you really do know as much about me as you indicated once."

"How do you mean?"

"I shouldn't want you to be worrying about whether I'm going to double-cross you again. I made a deal with you, and when I make deals they stay made. It's only when someone else starts dealing from the bottom that all bets are off."

"Obviously," she said, with cool indifference.

She let him take a key to the apartment when he left, and that alone told him to save himself the trouble of returning for a search while she was out. If there was anything she didn't want him to find, it would certainly not be there.

He had taken routine precautions against being followed when he went to the Bienville, but as he turned into the lobby of the Hotel Monteleone the chunky figure of Lieutenant Wendel rose from an armchair to greet him.

"Had a nice afternoon, Saint?"

"Very nice, thank you," Simon replied calmly; and the detective's face began to darken.

"I thought I warned you to stay away from Lady Offchurch."

The Saint raised his eyebrows.

"I wasn't aware that I'd been annoying her. She is at the St Charles, which is very grand and metropolitan, but the French quarter is good enough for me. I can't help it if our hotels are only a few blocks apart. Perhaps you ought to have the city enlarged."

"I'm talking about this gal Jeannine Roger. What are you cooking up with her?"

"Oxtails," said the Saint truthfully.

Lieutenant Wendel did not seem to be the type to appreciate a simple and straightforward answer. In fact, for some reason it appeared to affect him in much the same way as having his necktie flipped up under his nose. His eyes became slightly congested, and he grasped the Saint's arm with a hand that could have crumbled walnuts.

"Listen, mister," he said, with crunching self-control. "Just because I spotted you right off didn't mean I figured my job was done. When I found Lady Offchurch was going around with this Roger twist, I had her investigated too. And it comes right back from Washington that she's got a record as long as your arm. So I put a man on to watch her. And whaddaya know, first thing I hear is that you're spending time over in her apartment."

Simon Templar's stomach felt as if a cold weight had been planted in it, but not the flicker of a muscle acknowledged the sensation. As though the grip on his arm hadn't been there at all, he conveyed a cigarette to his mouth and put a light to it.

"Thanks for the tip, chum," he said gravely. "I just happened to pick her up in a restaurant, and she looked like fun. It only shows you, a guy can't be too careful. Why, she might have stolen something from me!"

The detective made a noise something like a cement mixer choking on a rock.

"What you'd better do is get it through your head that you aren't getting away with anything in this town. This is one caper that's licked before it starts. You're washed up, Saint, so get smart while you've got time."

Simon nodded.

"I'll certainly tell the girl we can't go on seeing each other. A man in my position——"

"A man in your position," Wendel said, "ought to pack his bags and be out of town tomorrow while he has the chance."

"I'll think that over," Simon said seriously. "Are you free for dinner again tonight?—we might make it a farewell feast."

He was not surprised that the offer was discourteously rejected, and went on to the bar with plenty to occupy his mind.

One question was whether Wendel would be most likely to challenge Jeannine Roger openly, as he had challenged the Saint, or whether in the slightly different circumstances he would try to expose her to Lady Offchurch, or whether he would pull out of the warning business altogether and go out for blood.

The other question was whether Jeannine knew the score already, and what was brewing in her own elusive mind.

At any rate, he had nothing to lose now by going openly to the Bienville, and he deliberately did that, after a leisured savoring of oysters Rockefeller and *gombo filé* at Antoine's, while the young officer who was following him worried over a bowl of onion soup and his expense account. The same shadow almost gave him a personal escort into the courtyard off St Ann Street, and Simon thought it only polite to turn back and wave to him as he went up the outside stairs to Number 27.

From the window, he watched the shadow confer with another shape that emerged from an obscure recess of the patio. Then after a while the shadow went away, but the established watcher sidled back into his nook and stayed.

Simon crossed the living room and peered down from a curtained window on the other side. The back overlooked an alley which was more black than dark, so that it was some time before the glimmering movement of a luminous wrist-watch dial betrayed the whereabouts of the sentinel who lurked patiently there among the garbage cans.

Simon put on the kitchen lights and inspected his casserole. He added a little more wine, lighted the oven, and put the dish in. He hummed a gentle tune to himself as he poured a drink in the dinette and settled down in the living room to wait.

The apartment was very effectively covered—so effectively that only a mouse could possibly have entered or left it unobserved. So effectively that it had all the uncomfortable earmarks of a trap. . . .

The question now was—what was the trap set for, and how did it work?

It was a quarter to midnight when the girl came in. He heard her quick feet on the stone steps outside, but he only moved to refill his glass while her key was turning in the lock. She came in like a light spring breeze that brought subtler scents than magnolia with it.

"Hullo," she said, and it seemed to him that her voice was very gay. "I hope you haven't been waiting too long."

"Just long enough. There's a bolt on the inside of the door—you'd better use it," he said, without looking up. He heard the bolt slam, after a pause of stillness, and turned with an extra glass in his other hand. "Here's your nightcap, baby. You may need it."

He thought of a foolish phrase as he looked at her—"with the wind and the rain in your hair." Of course there was no rain, and her hair was only just enough out of trim to be interesting, but she had that kind of young, excited look, with her cheeks faintly freshened by the night and her gray eyes bright and arrested. The incongruity of it hurt him, and he said brusquely: "We don't have any time to waste, so don't let's waste it."

"What's happened?"

"The joint is pinched," he said bluntly. "The Gestapo didn't stop at me—they checked on you too, since you were Lady Offchurch's mysterious pal, and they know all about you. Wendel told me. They've got both sides of the building covered. Look out the windows if you don't believe me."

"I believe you," she said slowly. "But—why?"

"Because Wendel means to catch somebody with the goods on them."

It was only an involuntary and static reaction, the whitening of her knuckles on the hand that held her purse; but it was all he needed. He said: "You had the imitation necklace today. You pulled the switch tonight. You made a deal, but you kept your fingers crossed."

"No," she said.

Now there were heavy feet stumping methodically up the stairway outside.

"You were followed every inch of the way back. They know you haven't ditched the stuff. They know it has to be here. And they know you can't get it out. What are you going to do—throw it out of a window? There's a man watching on both sides. Hide it? They may have to tear the joint to shreds, but they'll find it. They've got you cold."

"No," she said, and her face was haggard with guilt.

A fist pounded on the door.

"All right, darling," said the Saint. "You had your chance. Give me your bag."

"No."

The fist pounded again.

"You fool," he said savagely, in a voice that reached no further than her ears. "What do you think that skin we love to touch would be like after ten years in the pen?"

He took the purse from her hand and said: "Open the door." Then he went into the kitchen.

Lieutenant Wendel made his entrance with the ponderous elaboration of a man who knew that he had the last ounce of authority behind him and nothing on earth to hurry for. Certainty smoothed down the buzz-saw edges of his voice and invested him with the steam-roller impermeability of an entire government bureau on two feet.

"I'm from the Police Department, Miss Roger. I'm sure Mr Templar has told you about me. I've come to trouble you for Lady Offchurch's pearl necklace."

"I don't know what you're talking about," she said.

"Of course not." His confidence was almost paternal. "However, it hasn't gone out by the front since you came in, and I don't think it's gone out by back. We'll just make sure."

He crossed the room heavily, opened a window, and whistled.

This was the moment that Simon Templar chose to come back.

"Why, hullo, Lieutenant," he murmured genially. "What are you doing—rehearsing *Romeo and Juliet* for the Police Follies?"

Wendel waved to the night and turned back from the window.

"Ah, there you are, Mr Templar. I knew you were here, of course." His eyes fastened on the purse that swung negligently in Simon's hand. "This may save us a lot of trouble—excuse me."

He grabbed the bag away, sprung the catch, and spilled the contents clattering on the dining table.

After a few seconds the Saint said: "Would anyone mind telling me what this is all about?"

"All right," Wendel said grimly. "Where is it?"

"Where is what?"

"You know what I'm talking about. The necklace."

"The last time I saw it," Jeannine Roger said, "it was on Lady Offchurch's neck."

The detective set his jaw.

"I work regular hours, Miss Roger, and I don't want to be kept up all night. I may as well tell you that I talked to Lady Offchurch before you met her this evening. I arranged for her to give one of my men a signal if you had been suspiciously anxious to handle the necklace at any time while you were together. She gave that signal when she said good night to you. That gives me grounds to believe that while you were handling the necklace you exchanged it for a substitute. I think the original is in this apartment now, and if it is, we'll find it. Now if one of you hands it over and saves me a lot of trouble, I mightn't feel quite so tough as if I had to work for it."

"Meaning," said the Saint, "that we mightn't have to spend quite so much of our youth on the rock pile?"

"Maybe."

The Saint took his time over lighting a cigarette.

"All my life," he said, "I've been allergic to hard labor. And it's especially bad"—he glanced at the girl—"for what the radio calls those soft, white, romantic hands. In fact, I can't think of any pearls that would be worth it—particularly when you don't even get to keep the pearls. . . . So—I'm afraid there ain't going to be no poils."

"You're nuts!" Wendel exploded. "Don't you know when you're licked?"

"Not till you show me," said the Saint peaceably. "Let's examine the facts. Miss Roger handled the necklace. Tomorrow a jeweler may say that the string that Lady Offchurch still has is a phony. Well, Lady Offchurch can't possibly swear that nobody else ever touched that rope of oyster fruit. Well, the substitution might have been made anywhere, any time, by anyone—even by a chiseling maharajah. What's the only proof you could use against Jeannine? Nothing short of finding a string of genuine pink pearls in her possession. And that's something you can never do."

"No?" Wendel barked. "Well, if I have to put this whole building through a sieve, and the two of you with it——"

"You'll never find a pearl," Simon stated.

He made the statement with such relaxed confidence that a clammy hand began to caress the detective's spine, neutralizing logic with its weird massage, and poking skeletal fingers into hypersensitive nerves.

"No?" Wendel repeated, but his voice had a frightful uncertainty.

Simon picked up a bottle and modestly replenished his glass.

"The trouble with you," he said, "is that you never learned to listen. Last night at dinner, if you remember, we discoursed on various subjects, all of which I'm sure you had heard before, and yet all you could think of was that I was full of a lot of highfalutin folderol, while I was trying to tell you that in our business a man couldn't afford to not know anything. And when I told you this afternoon that Jeannine and I were cooking up oxtails, you only thought I was trying to be funny, instead of remembering among other things that oxtails are cooked in wine."

The detective lifted his head, and his nostrils dilated with sudden apperception.

"So when you came in here," said the Saint, "you'd have remembered those other silly quotes I mentioned—about Cleopatra dissolving pearls in wine for Caesar——"

"Simon—no!" The girl's voice was almost a scream.

"I'm afraid, yes," said the Saint sadly. "What Cleopatra could do, I could do better—for a face that shouldn't be used for launching ships."

Lieutenant Wendel moved at last, rather like a wounded carabao struggling from its wallow; and the sound that came from his throat was not unlike the cry that might have been wrung from the vocal cords of the same stricken animal.

He plunged into the kitchen and jerked open the oven door. After burning his fingers twice, he took pot holders to pull out the dish and spill its contents into the stoppered sink.

Simon watched him, with more exquisite pain, while he ran cold water and pawed frantically through the debris. After all, it would have been a dish fit for a queen; but all Wendel came up with was a loop of thread, about two feet long.

"How careless of the butcher," said the Saint, "to leave that in."

Lieutenant Wendel did not take the apartment apart. He would have liked to, but not for investigative reasons. For a routine search he had no heart at all. The whole picture was too completely historically founded and cohesive to give him any naïve optimism about his prospects of upsetting it.

"I hate to suggest such a thing to a respectable officer," said the Saint insinuatingly, "but maybe you shouldn't even let Lady Offchurch think that her necklace was switched. With a little tact, you might be able to convince her that you scared the criminals away and she won't be bothered any more. It may be years before she finds out, and then no one could prove that it happened here. It isn't as if you were letting us get away with anything."

"What you're getting away with should go down in history," Wendel said with burning intensity. "But I swear to God that if either of you is still in town tomorrow morning, I'm going to frame you for murder."

The door slammed behind him, and Simon smiled at the girl with rather regretful philosophy.

"Well," he said, "it was one way of giving those pearls back to the Indians. One day you'll learn to stop being so smart, Jeannine. Can I offer you a ride out of town?"

"Whichever way you're going," she said with incandescent fascination, "I hope I'll always be heading the other way."

It was too bad, Simon Templar reflected. Too bad that she had to be so beautiful and so treacherous. And too bad, among other things, that his crusade for the cultivation of more general knowledge seemed to make so few converts. If only there were not so much ignorance and superstitution in the world, both Wendel and Jeannine Roger would have known, as he did, that the story of pearls being dissolved in wine was strictly a fable, without a grain of scientific truth. . . . Nevertheless, the pearls in his pocket were very pleasant to caress as he nursed his car over the Huey Long Bridge and turned west, towards Houston.

TERESA

From *Saint Errant*

ONE MORE STORY that stems from long ago. From 1931, to be quite exact—although I didn't write it for a longish while afterwards.

This is another story in which the locale, and only that, was changed for contemporary geopolitical reasons, between the time when it was first written and published in a magazine and the time when it ended up in a book collection.

I can make no more apologies for the liberties I have taken with times and places in the reprinting of stories such as this.

The way I see it, nothing is so dated as last year—at least in fiction. Put your setting back a century, and anything goes: any apparent anachronism, any unfamiliarity, is acceptable because it is said to have occurred in an era about which the reader happily admits his ignorance. Things were different in those days—that's all. But let the period fall within the theoretical scope of his faulty memory, and the reader is at once a dissecting critic: anything that seems as if it could have happened yesterday must be submitted to the awareness of today. If a story uses a telephone, this kind of telescoping consciousness requires that it should also take cognizance of television.

This story was first written around a Corsican bandit whom I had the pleasure of meeting on his home ground in very similar circumstances to those I have used in this narrative. But they caught him eventually, although it took several regiments of the French Army to do it; and today Corsican bandits are just an old wives' tale. Mexican bandits, however, for some reason, are still exotic currency. So let the story go there. If it is considered legitimate to disguise names, why not places?

TERESA

BANDITS?" said Señor Copas. He shrugged "*Si hay siempre bandidos.* The Government will never catch them all. Here in Mexico they are a tradition of the country."

He looked again at the girl in the dark hat, appreciatively, because she was worth looking at, and he was a true Latin, and there was still romance in the heart that beat above his rounded abdomen.

He chuckled uncertainly, ignoring the other customers who were sitting in various degrees of patience behind their empty plates, and said: "But the señorita has nothing to fear. She is not going into the wilds."

"But I want to go into the wilds," she said.

Her voice was low and soft and musical, matching the quiet symmetry of her face and the repose of her hands. She was smart without exaggeration. She was Fifth Avenue with none of its brittle hardness, incongruously transported to that standstill Mexican village, and yet contriving not to seem out of place. To Señor Copas she was a miracle.

To Simon Templar she was a quickening of interest and a hint of adventure that might lead anywhere or nowhere. His eye for charm was no slower than that of Señor Copas, but there was more in it than that.

To Simon Templar, who had been called the most audacious bandit of the twentieth century, the subject was always new and fascinating. And he had an impish sense of humor which couldn't resist the thought of what the other members of the audience would have said and done if they had known that the man who was listening to their conversation about bandits was the notorious Saint himself.

"Are you more interested in the wilds or the bandits?" he asked, in Spanish as native as her own.

She turned to him with friendly brown eyes in which there was a trace of subtle mockery.

"I'm not particular."

"*No es posible,*" said Señor Copas firmly, as he dragged himself away to his kitchen.

"He doesn't seem to like the idea," said the Saint.

He was sitting beside her, at the communal table which half filled the dining room of the hotel. She broke a roll with her graceful, leisurely moving hands. He saw that her fingers were slender and tapering, delicately manicured, and one of them wore a wedding ring.

Fifth Avenue in the Fonda de la Quinta, in the shadow of the Sierra Madre, in the state of Durango in Old Mexico, which was a very different place.

"You know a lot about this country?" she asked.

"I've been here before."

"Do you know the mountains?"

"Fairly well."

"Do you know the bandits too?"

The Saint gazed at her with precarious gravity. He looked like a man who would obviously be on visiting terms with bandits. He looked rather like a bandit himself, in a debonair and reckless sort of way, with his alert tanned face and clean-cut fighting mouth and the unscrupulous gay twinkle in his blue eyes.

"Listen," he said. "Once upon a time I was walking between San Miguel and Gajo, two villages not far from here. I saw from my map that the road led around in a great horseshoe, but they told me at an inn that there was a short cut, straight across, down into the canyon and up the other side. I climbed down something like the side of a precipice for hours—the path was all great loose stones, and presently one of them turned under my foot and I took a spill and sprained my ankle. When I got to the bottom I was done in. I couldn't move another step, particularly climbing. I hadn't any food, but there was a stream running through the bottom of the canyon, so I had water. I could only hope that someone else would try that short cut and find me. . . . At the end of the third day a man did find me, and he looked like one of your bandits if anyone ever did. He did what he could for me, gave me food from his pack—bread and sausage and cheese—and then he said he would go on to San Miguel and send help for me. He could have taken everything I had, but he didn't. He was insulted when I offered to pay him. 'I am not a beggar,' he said, and I've never seen anything so haughty in my life—— 'I am El Rojo.' "

"Then why is Señor Copas so frightened?"

"They're all frightened of El Rojo."

Her finely penciled brows drew together.

"El Rojo?" she said. "Who is El Rojo?"

"The greatest bandit since Villa. They're all scared because there's a rumor that he's in the district. You ought to be scared, too. They're all offended if you aren't scared of El Rojo. . . . He really is a great character, though. I remember once the Government decided it was time that something drastic was done about him. They sent out half the Mexican army to round him up. It was the funniest thing I ever heard of, but you have to know the country to see the joke."

"They didn't catch him?"

The Saint chuckled.

"One man who knew the country could laugh at three armies."

For a little while the girl was wrapped in an unapproachable solitude of thought. Then she turned to the Saint again.

"Señor," she said, "do you think you could help me find El Rojo?"

Even south of the border, he was still a Saint errant, or perhaps a sucker for adventure. He said: "I could try."

They rode out on the dazzling stone track that winds beside the river—a track which was nothing more than the marks that centuries of solitary feet had left on the riot of tumbled boulders from which the hills rose up.

The Saint lounged in the saddle, relaxed like a *vaquero*, letting his mount pick its own way over the broken rock. His mind went back to the café where they had sat together over coffee, after lunch, and he had said to her: "Either you must be a journalist looking for an unusual interview, or you want to be kidnaped by El Rojo for publicity, or you've been reading too many romantic stories and you think you could fall in love with him."

She had only smiled in her quiet way, inscrutable in spite of its friendliness, and said: "No, senor—you are wrong in all your guesses. I am looking for my husband."

The Saint's brows slanted quizzically.

"You mean you are Senora Rojo?"

"Oh, no. I am Señora Alvarez de Quevedo. Teresa Alvarez."

Then she looked at him, quickly and clearly, as if she had made up her mind about something.

"The last time I heard of my husband, he was at the Fonda de la Quinta," she said. "That was two years ago. He wrote to me that he was going into the mountains. He liked to do things like that, to climb mountains and sleep under the stars and be a man alone, sometimes—it is curious, for he was very much a city man. . . . I never heard of him again. He said he was going to climb the Gran Seño. I remembered, when I heard the name, that I had read of El Rojo in the newspapers about that time. And it seemed to me, when I heard you speak of El Rojo, that perhaps El Rojo was the answer."

"If it was El Rojo," said the Saint quietly, "I don't think it would help you to find him now."

Her eyes were still an enigma.

"Even so," she said, "it would be something to know."

"But you've waited two years——"

"Yes," she said softly. "I have waited two years."

She had told him no more than that, and he had known that she did not wish to say any more, but it had been enough to send him off on that quixotic wild-goose chase.

He had been leading the way for two hours, but presently, where the trail broadened for a short distance, she brought her horse up beside his, and they rode knee to knee.

"I wonder why you should do this for me," she said.

He shrugged.

"Why did you ask me?"

"It was an impulse." She moved her hands puzzledly. "I don't know. I suppose you have the air of a man who is used to being asked impossible things. You look as if you would do them."

"I do," said the Saint modestly.

It was his own answer, too. She was a damsel in distress—and no damsel in distress had ever called on the Saint in vain. And she was beautiful, also, which was a very desirable asset to damsels in distress. And about her there was a mystery, which to Simon Templar was the trumpet call of adventure.

In the late afternoon, at one of the bends in the trail where it dipped to the level of the river, the Saint reined in his horse and dismounted at the water's edge.

"Are we there?" she said.

"No. But we're leaving the river."

He scooped water up in his hands and drank, and splashed it over his face. It was numbingly cold, but it steamed off his arms in the hot dry air. She knelt down and drank beside him, and then sat back on her heels and looked up at the hills that hemmed them in.

A kind of shy happiness lighted her eyes, almost uncertainly, as if it had not been there for a long time and felt itself a stranger.

"I understand now," she said. "I understand why Gaspar loved all this, in spite of what he was. If only he could have been content with it . . ."

"You were not happy?" said the Saint gently.

She looked at him.

"No, señor. I have not been happy for so long that I am afraid."

She got up quickly and put her foot in the stirrup. He helped her to mount, and swung into his own saddle. They set off across the shallow stream, the horses picking their way delicately between the boulders.

On the far side they climbed, following a trail so faint that she could not see it all, but the Saint rarely hesitated. Presently the trees were thicker, and over the skyline loomed the real summit of the hill they were climbing. The valley was swallowed up in darkness, and up there where the Saint turned his horse across the slope the brief subtropical twilight was fading.

Simon Templar lighted a cigarette as he rode, and he had barely taken the first puff of smoke into his lungs when a man stepped from behind a tree with a rifle leveled and broke the stillness of the evening with a curt: "*Manos arriba!*"

The Saint turned his head with a smile.

"You've got what you wanted," he said to Teresa Alvarez. "May I present El Rojo?"

The introduction was almost superfluous, for the red mask from which El Rojo took his name, which covered his face from the brim of his sombrero down to his stubble-bearded chin, was sufficient identification. Watching the girl, Simon saw no sign of fear as the bandit came forward. Her face was pale, but she sat straight-backed on her horse and gazed at him with an unexpected eagerness in her eyes. Simon turned back to El Rojo.

"*Qué tal, amigo?*" he murmured genially.

The bandit stared at him unresponsively.

"*Baje usted,*" he ordered gruffly. He glanced at the girl. "You too—get down."

His eyes, after that glance, remained fixed on her, even after she was down from the saddle and standing by the horse's head. The Saint wondered for the first time whether he might not have let his zest for adventure override his common sense when he deliberately led her into the stronghold of an outlawed and desperate man.

El Rojo turned back to him.

"The señorita," he said, "will tie your hands behind you."

He dragged a length of cord from his pocket and threw it across the space between them. The girl looked at it coldly.

"Go on," said the Saint. "Do what the nice gentleman tells you. It's part of the act."

He could take care of such minor details when the time came, but for the present there was a mystery with which he was more preoccupied.

When the Saint's hands had been tied, El Rojo pointed his rifle.

"The Señorita will lead the way," he said. "You will follow, and I shall direct you from behind. You would be wise not to try and run away."

He watched them file past him, and from the sounds that followed, the Saint deduced that El Rojo had taken the horses by their bridles and was towing them after him as he brought up the rear.

As they moved roughly parallel with the valley, the slope on their right became steeper and steeper until it was simply a precipice, and the rocks on their left towered bleaker and higher, and they were walking along a narrow ledge with the shadow of one cliff over them and another cliff falling away from their feet into a void of darkness. The path wound snakelike around the fissures and buttresses into which the precipice was sculptured, and presently, rounding one of those natural breastworks, they found themselves at a place where the path widened suddenly to become a natural balcony about twenty feet long and twelve feet deep—and then stopped. A natural wall of rock screened it from sight of the valley or the hills on the other side.

El Rojo followed them into the niche, leading the two horses, which he tied up to an iron ring by the mouth of a cave that opened in the rock wall at the end.

There was a dull glow of embers close by the mouth of the cave. The bandit stirred them with his foot, and threw on a couple of mesquite logs.

"Perhaps you are hungry," said El Rojo. "I have little to offer my guests, but you are welcome to what there is."

"I should like a cigarette as much as anything," said the Saint. "But I'm not a very good contortionist."

The bandit considered him.

"I could untie you, señor, if you gave me your word of honor not to attempt to escape. It is, I believe, usual in these circumstances."

His speeches had an elaborate theatricalism which came oddly out of his rough and ragged clothing.

"I'll give you my word for two hours," said the Saint, after a moment's thought. "It can be renewed if necessary."

"*Es bastante. Y usted, señorita?*"

"*Conforme.*"

"*Entonces, por dos horas.*"

El Rojo laid down his rifle and untied the Saint's hands; but Simon noticed that he picked up the gun again at once, and that he kept it always within easy reach. The Saint understood the symptom well enough not to be disturbed by it. He lighted a cigarette and stretched himself out comfortably beside the fire and beside Teresa Alvarez, while the night closed down like a purple blanket and El Rojo brought out the bread and cheese and sausage and coarse red wine which are the staple fare in the mountains.

He said presently: "I take it that you have ideas about ransom."

The bandit shrugged.

"I regret the necessity. But I am a poor man, and you must be charitable. Let us say that it was unlucky that you chose to travel this way."

"But we were looking for you," said Teresa.

El Rojo stopped with a knifeload of cheese halfway to his mouth.

"For me?"

"Yes," she said. "I wanted to see you, and this gentleman was good enough to help me. We were not unlucky. We came here on purpose."

"You pay me an unusual compliment, señorita. Could one ask what I have done to deserve such a distinguished honor?"

"I am looking for my husband," she said simply.

He sat watching her.

"*No comprendo.* It is true that I often have the pleasure of entertaining travelers in the mountains. But, alas, they never stay with me for long. Either their friends are so desolate in their absence that they bribe me to ensure their safe and speedy return—or their friends are so unresponsive that I am forced to conclude that they cannot be very desirable guests. I am incapable of believing that a gentleman who had won the heart of the señora can have belonged to the latter category."

"It is possible," she said, without bitterness. "But I knew nothing of it."

She was silent for a moment.

"It was two years ago," she said. "He came here to Durango, to La Quinta.

He was going into the mountains. No one ever heard of him again. I know that you were here then, and I wondered if you might have—entertained him. Perhaps I was foolish . . ."

El Rojo dug his knife in the cheese.

"*Por Dios!*" he said. "Is it like that that one lives in Mexico? You have lost your husband for two years, and it is not until today that you want to find him?"

"I don't want to find him," she said. "I want to know that he is dead."

She said it quietly, without any force of feeling, as if it was a thought that she had lived with for so long that it had become a commonplace part of her life. But in the very passionlessness of that matter-of-fact statement there was something that sent an electric ripple up the Saint's spine.

He had finished eating, and he was sitting smoking with his feet towards the warmth of the fire and his back leaning against the rock. On his left, Teresa Alvarez was looking straight ahead of her, as if she had been alone, and El Rojo's eyes were riveted on her through the slits in his mask, so that the Saint almost felt as if he were an eavesdropper. But he was too absorbed in the play to care about that.

"I was very young," said the girl, in that quiet and detached way that left so much emotion to be guessed at. "I was still in the convent school when I was engaged to him. I knew nothing, and I was not given any choice. I was married to him a few weeks later. Yes, these things happen. It is still the custom in the old-fashioned families. The parents choose a man they think will make their daughter a good husband, and she is expected to be guided by their wisdom."

Her face was impassive in the firelight.

"I think he was unfaithful to me on our honeymoon," she said. "I know he was unfaithful many times after that. He boasted of it. I might have forgiven that, but he boasted also that he had only married me for my dowry —and for what pleasure he could have out of me before he wanted a change. I found out that he was nothing but a shady adventurer, a gambler, a cheat, a petty swindler, a man without a shadow of honor or even common decency. But by that time I had no one to go to. . . . My father and mother died suddenly six months after we were married, and I had never had any friends of my own. It will seem strange to you—it seems strange to me, now —but I never realized that I could leave him myself. I had never been brought up to know anything of the world. So I stayed with him. For four years . . . and then he came here, and I never saw him again."

The Saint could feel the suffering and humiliation and disillusionment of those four years as vividly as if she had told the story of them day by day, and his blue eyes rested on her with a new and oddly gentle understanding.

She went on after a while: "At first I was only glad that he had gone, and that I could have some peace until he returned. He had told me that he was going away for a holiday, but one day a man from the police came to see me, and I found out that he had gone away because for once he had not been so clever as he had been before, and there was a charge against him.

"Then I hoped that the police would catch him and he would go to prison, perhaps for many years, perhaps forever. But they never found him. And I hoped that he might have fallen over a precipice in the mountains, or that he had escaped to the other end of the world, or anything that would mean he would never come back to me. I didn't mind very much what it was, so long as I never saw him again. But I was happy. And then, six months ago, I fell in love. And my happiness was finished again."

"Because you were in love?" El Rojo asked, incredulously.

"Because I was not free. This man is everything that my husband never was, and he knows everything that I have told you. He wants to marry me. Before, I never cared where my husband was, or what had happened to him, but now, you see, I must know."

El Rojo looked up toward the Saint.

"And the señor," he said, "is he the fortunate man with whom you fell in love?"

"No. He is in Mexico City. He is in the government service, and he could not leave to come with me."

"He is rich, this man?"

"Yes," she said, and her voice was no longer cold.

There was silence for a long time—for so long that the dancing firelight died down to a steady red glow.

Teresa Alvarez gazed into the dull embers, with her arms clasped around her knees, absorbed in her own thoughts, and at last she said: "But I have only been dreaming. Even in such a small territory as this, why should any-one remember one man who was here two years ago?"

El Rojo stirred himself a little.

"Was your husband," he said, "a man of middle height, with smooth black hair and greenish eyes and a thin black mustache?"

Suddenly she was still, with a stillness that seemed more violent than movement.

"Yes," she said. "He was like that."

"And his name was Alvarez?"

"Yes. Gaspar Alvarez de Quevedo."

Her voice was no more than a whisper.

The bandit drew a gust of evil-smelling smoke from his cheap cigarette.

"Such a man was a guest of mine about two years ago," he said slowly "I remember him best because of the ring, which I gave to a girl in

Matamoros, and because he was the only guest I have had here who left without my consent."

"He escaped?"

The words came from the girl's lips with a weariness that was too deep for feeling.

"He tried to," said El Rojo. "But it was very dark, and these mountains are not friendly to those who do not know them well."

He stretched out his arm, toward the black emptiness beyond the rock wall that guarded the niche where they sat.

"I buried him where he fell. It was difficult to reach him, but I could not risk his body being seen by any goatherds going up the valley. In the morning, if you like, I will point you out his grave. It is below the path we followed to come here—more than a hundred meters down. . . . The señora may go on without fear to the happiness that life has kept waiting for her."

It was very dark, but Simon could see the tears rise in the girl's eyes before she hid her face in her hands.

The morning sun was cutting hot swaths through the fading mist when El Rojo followed the Saint and Teresa along the winding ledge between cliff and cliff that led out of his eyrie high above the river. Where the slope of the mountain opened clear before them he called to them to stop, and held the bridle of the horse which the girl was to ride while she climbed into the saddle.

"I give you—*buen viaje*," he said. "You can make no mistake. Follow the side of the hill until you come to a belt of trees, and then go downwards. To find your way back here—that is another matter. But if you keep going downwards you must come to the river, and on the other side of the river is the road to La Quinta. I will meet you somewhere on that road in three days from now, at about four o'clock in the afternoon."

"I can never thank you," she said.

"You have no need to," he answered roughly. "You are going to bring me —how much did we agree?—one hundred thousand pesos, and the señor remains as my guest as a surety for our meeting. I regret that I have to be commercial, but one must live, and if your lover is rich he will not mind."

She held out her hand to the Saint.

"I shall be there to meet him in three days," she said. "And then I shall be able to thank you again."

"This was nothing," he answered with his lazy smile. "But if you ever meet any dragons I wish you'd send for me."

He kissed her fingers, and watched her ride away until the curve of the hill hid her from sight. It was true that he had done very little, but he had seen the light in her eyes before she went, and to him that was reward enough for any adventure.

He was thoughtful as he walked back along the cliff edge track towards the bandit's cave with El Rojo just behind his elbow, and when they were halfway along it he said casually: "By the way, I ought to warn you that the parole I renewed last night is just running out."

The muzzle of the bandit's rifle pressed into his chest as he turned.

"In that case, señor, you will please put up your hands. Unless, of course, you prefer to renew your parole again."

Simon raised his hands to the level of his shoulders.

"My friend," he said, "have you forgotten the Arroyo Verde?"

"*Perdone?*"

"The Arroyo Verde," said the Saint steadily. "Between San Miguel and Gajo. Where there was a man with a sprained ankle who had been there for three days without food, and who might have stayed there until he starved if a brigand with a price on his head had not stayed to help him."

"I have not the least idea what you are talking about."

"I thought not," said the Saint softly. "Because you weren't there."

He saw the bandit's hands go rigid around the gun, and the blue steel was as sharp as knife points in his eyes.

"I didn't think this brigand would have forgotten me so completely that we could spend an evening together without him recognizing me. You see, we got quite friendly down in that forsaken canyon, and when my ankle was better I paid him a visit here. That's why I was able to find my way so easily yesterday. I came to Durango because I hoped to meet him again. And yet this brigand's name was El Rojo, too. How do you explain that —Señor Alvarez?"

For a moment the bandit was silent, standing tense and still, and Simon could feel the shattering chaos whirling through the man's mind, the wild spin of instinctive stratagems and lies sinking down to the grim realization of their ultimate futility.

"And suppose I am Alvarez?" said the man at last, and his natural voice was quite different from the way he had been speaking before.

"Then you should tell me more about what you said last night—and about El Rojo. Where is he?"

"I found him here by accident, but he thought I was looking for him. We fought, and he fell over the precipice. He lies in the grave which I said was mine."

"And because you wanted to disappear, and because you loved the mountains, you thought that the best way for you to hide would be to take his place. No one had ever seen the face of El Rojo, no one ever knew who he was. You took his mask and became El Rojo."

"*Eso es.*"

Alvarez had not moved. Simon could sense the taut nerves of a man who held death in his hands and was only waiting for one word to turn the scale of his decision.

Simon Templar was also waiting for the answer to one question. He said: "And last night?"

"*A usted que más le da?*"

"The answer is in your hands," said the Saint.

His eyes were as clear and unclouded as the sky over their heads, and there was something as ageless and unchangeable as justice in the even tones of his voice.

"Perhaps in these two years you might have changed," he said. "Perhaps you were glad that you could never go back to the old life. And perhaps you told that lie to cut the last link with it, and you were glad to set your wife free for the happiness which you never gave her. If that was so, your secret will always be safe with me. But I've never seen a man like you change very much, and I wondered why all you asked about your wife's lover was whether he was rich. I wondered if it had occurred to you that if you let her believe you were dead, so that she would marry this man, you could go back to Mexico City and charge a price for your silence. And if that was so——"

"You will never tell her," said Alvarez viciously, and the rifle jerked in his hand.

The crack of the shot rattled back and forth, growing fainter and fainter, between the hills, and something like fire struck the Saint's chest. He smiled, as if something amused him.

"You're wasting your time," he said. "I took all the bullets out of the shells in your gun while you were asleep last night. But you've told me what I wanted to know. I said that the answer was in your own hands——"

Alvarez came out of the superstitious trance which had gripped him for a moment. He snatched the rifle back and then lunged with it savagely. Simon stepped to the right, and the thrust passed under his left arm. Then he swung his right fist to Alvarez's jaw. Alvarez was on the very edge of the path, and the force of the blow lifted him backwards with his arms sprawling. . . .

Simon Templar stood for some time gazing down into the abyss. His face was serene and untroubled, and he felt neither pity nor remorse. His mind went on working calmly and prosaically. There was no need for Teresa Alvarez to know. Nothing would disturb her conscience if she went on believing what she had been told the night before. And she would think well of El Rojo, who to her would always be the real El Rojo whom Simon had called his friend.

He would have to think up some story to account for El Rojo deciding to waive his claim to the hundred thousand pesos she had promised. He went thoughtfully back to collect his horse.

DAWN

From *Saint Errant*

I suppose no feat of cerebration exercises an imaginative person so much as the deathbed speech that he or she would make if he or she (and this ghastly grammar has got to stop somewhere) knew for sure that it was their (oh, goody!) positively final utterance, the crystallization of a life by which posterity would remember it, whatever else it might have lived.

"It is a far, far better thing . . ."

"My only regret is that I have but one life to give . . ."

"Kiss me, Hardy . . ."

Oh, great!

You know what you'll probably say?

"Why the hell didn't that fool dim his lights?"

Or: "The Government should have done something about it!"

A writer who has been writing for a long time may legitimately begin to feel even more apprehension about what might be his last story. And a lot more may well be expected of him. After all, his life has been built on nothing but words. His last ones should give a good account of him. They should summarize, somehow, everything he has thought and learned, every technique he has acquired.

His last story, dramatically, should be his best.

But who knows which will be his last story?

Thus we come to the last story in this book, at any rate. And it is certainly one of the latest written. And it is not the best.

But it is placed here because there is an element in it which you will have to read it to discover, which in a collection of this kind is almost impossible to top. Anyhow, I am not yet ready to try.

DAWN

SIMON TEMPLAR looked up from the frying pan in which six mountain trout were developing a crisp golden tan. Above the gentle sputter of grease, the sound of feet on the dry pine needles crackled through the cabin window.

It didn't cross his mind that the sound carried menace, for it was twilight in the Sierras, and the dusky calm stirred only with the rustlings of nature at peace.

The Saint also was at peace. In spite of everything his enemies would have said, there actually were times when peace was the main preoccupation of that fantastic freebooter; when hills and blue sky were high enough adventure, and baiting a hook was respite enough from baiting policemen or promoters. In such a mood he had jumped at the invitation to join a friend in a week of hunting and fishing in the High Sierras—a friend who had been recalled to town on urgent business almost as soon as they arrived, leaving the Saint in by no means melancholy solitude, for Simon Templar could always put up with his own company.

The footsteps came nearer with a kind of desperate urgency. Simon moved the frying pan off the flames and flowed, rather than walked, to where he could see through windows in two directions.

A man came out of the pines. He was traveling on the short side of a dead run, but straining with every gasping breath to step up his speed. He came, hatless and coatless, across the pine-carpeted clearing toward the cabin door.

He burst through it; and in spite of his relaxation the Saint felt a kind of simmer of anticipating approval. If his solitude had to be intruded on, this was the way it should happen. Unannounced. At a dead run.

The visitor slammed the door, shot the bolt, whirled around, and seemed about to fold in the middle. He saw the Saint. His jaw sagged, swung adrift on its hinges for a moment, then imitated a steel trap.

After the sharp click of his teeth, he said: "How did you get in here? Where's Dawn?"

"Dawn?" Simon echoed lazily. "If you're referring to the rosy-fingered goddess who peels away the darkness each morning, she's on the twelve-hour shift, chum. She'll be around at the regular time."

"I never dreamed you here," the man said. "Who are you?"

"You dropped a word," the Saint said. "'I never dreamed you *were* here' makes more sense."

"Nuts, brother. You're part of my dream, and I never saw you before. You don't even have a name. All the others have, complete with backgrounds. But I can't place you. Funny, I—— Look here, you're not real, are you?"

"The last time I pinched myself, I yelped."

"This is crazy," the man muttered.

He walked across the pine floor to within a couple of feet of the Saint. He was breathing easier now, and the Saint examined him impassively.

He was big, only a shade under the Saint's six feet two, with sandy hair, a square jaw, and hard brown eyes.

"May I?" he said, and pinched the Saint. He sighed. "I was afraid this was happening. When I put my arms around Dawn Winter in my dreams, she——"

"Please," the Saint broke in. "Gentlemen don't go into lurid detail after the lady has a name."

"Oh, she's only part of my dream." The stranger stared into space, and an almost tangible aura of desire formed about him. "God!" he whispered. "I really dreamed up something in her."

"We must swap reminiscences someday," the Saint said. "But at the moment the pine-scented breeze is laden with threshings in the underbrush."

"I've got to hide. Quick! Where can I get out of sight?"

The Saint waved expressively at the single room. In its four hundred square feet, one might hide a large bird if it were camouflaged as an atlas or something, but that would be about the limit.

The two bunk beds were made with hospital precision, and even a marble would have bulged under their tight covers. The deck chairs wouldn't offer sanctuary for even an undernourished mouse, the table was high and wide open beneath the rough top, and the small bookcase was made to display its contents.

"If we had time," the Saint mused, "I could candy-stripe you—if I had some red paint—and put on a barber's smock. Or—er—you say you're dreaming all this?"

"That's right."

"Then why don't you wake up—and vanish?"

The Saint's visitor unhappily gnawed his full underlip.

"I always have before, when the going got tough, but—— Oh, hell, I don't know what's going on, but I don't want to die—even in my dream. Death is so—so——"

"Permanent?"

"Mmm, I guess. Listen, would you be a pal and try to steer these guys away? They're after me."

"Why should I?"

"Yeah," the man said. "You don't owe me a damn thing, but I'm trying to help Dawn. She——"

He broke off to fish an object out of his watch pocket. This was a small chamois bag, and out of it he took something that pulsed with incredible fires. He handed it to the Saint.

"That's Dawn."

The circular fire opal blazed with living beauty—blue, green, gold, cerise,

chartreuse—and the Saint gasped with reverent wonder as he looked at the
cameo head carved on the unbelievable gem.

There is beauty to which one can put a name. There is beauty that in-
spires awe, bravery, fear, lust, greed, passion. There is beauty that softens
the savage blows of fate. There is beauty that drives to high adventure, to
violence.

That stone, and above all the face cut eternally on its incandescent surface, was beauty beyond belief. No man could look on that face and ever
know complete peace again.

She was the lily maid of Astolat, the lost loveliness that all men seek and
never find, the nameless desire that haunts the ragged edge of sleep, that
curls a lonely smile and sends vacant eyes searching far spaces.

Her face was made for—and of? the Saint asked himself—dreaming.

"Count me in, old boy."

He went outside. Through the dusky stillness the far-off unseen feet
pounded nearer.

The feet were four. The men, with mathematical logic, two. One might
be a jockey, the other a weight lifter. They tore out of the forest and confronted the Saint.

"Did you see a kind of big dopey-lookin' lug?" the jockey asked.

The Saint pointed to the other side of the clearing where the hill pitched
down.

"He went that way—in a hell of a rush."

"Thanks, pal."

They were off, hot on the imaginary trail, and the sounds of their passage
soon faded. The Saint went inside.

"They'll be back," he said. "But meanwhile we can clear up a few points.
Could you down a brace of trout? They've probably cooled enough to eat."

"What do you mean, they'll be back?"

"It's inevitable," Simon pointed out as he put coffee on, set the table, and
gathered cutlery. "They won't find you. They want to find you. So they'll
be back with questions. Since those questions will be directed at me, I'd
like to know what not to answer."

"Who are you?"

"Who are you?" the Saint countered.

"I'm—oh, blast it to hell and goddam. The guy you're looking at is Big
Bill Holbrook. But he's only something I dreamed up. I'm really Andrew
Faulks, and I'm asleep in Glendale, California."

"And I am the queen of Rumania."

"Sure, I know. You don't believe it. Who would? But since you've got
me out of a tight spot for the time being, I'd like to tell you what I've
never told anybody. But who am I telling?"

"I'm Simon Templar," said the Saint, and waited for a reaction.

"No!" Holbrook-Faulks breathed. "The Saint! What beautiful, wonderful luck. And isn't it just like a bank clerk to work the Saint into his dream?" He paused for breath. "The Robin Hood of Modern Crime, the twentieth century's brightest buccaneer, the devil with dames, the headache of cops and crooks alike. What a sixteen-cylinder dream this is."

"Your alliterative encomia," the Saint murmured, "leave me as awed as your inference. Don't you think you'd better give out with this—er—bedtime story? Before that unholy pair return with gun-lined question marks?"

The strange man rubbed his eyes in a dazed helpless way.

"I don't know where to begin," he said conventionally.

But after a while, haltingly, he tried.

Andrew Faulks, in the normal course of events, weathered the slingshots and arrows of outrageous playmates and grew up to be a man.

As men will, he fixed his heart and eyes on a girl and eventually married her. As women will, she gave birth in due course to a boy, Andy Jr, and later a girl, Alexandria.

He became a bank clerk, and went to and from home on an immutable schedule. He got an occasional raise; he was bawled out at times by the head teller; he became a company man, a white-collar worker, and developed all the political ills that white-collared flesh is heir to.

And he dreamed. Literally.

This was what Big Bill Holbrook told the Saint in the mountain cabin to which Simon had retired to await the blowing over of a rather embarrassing situation which involved items duly registered on police records.

"In the first dream, I was coming out of this hotel, see. And whammo! Bumping into her woke me—— Oh, the hell with it. Whoever was dreaming woke up, but it was me bumped into her. And I was sorry as hell, because, brother, she was something."

Some two weeks later, Big Bill said, he bumped into her again. The dream started exactly as its predecessor, progressed exactly to the point of collision.

"But I didn't awaken this time. We each apologized all over the place and somehow we were walking along together. Just as I was about to ask her to have dinner, I woke up again."

"Or Andy did," the Saint supplied.

"Yeah. Whoever. Now this is what happened. Every ten days or two weeks, I'd be back in this dream, starting out of the hotel, crashing into her, walking along, having dinner, getting to know her better each dream. Each one started exactly the same, but each one went a little further into her life. It was like reading the same book over and over, always starting back at the beginning, but getting one chapter further every time. I got so used to it that I'd say to myself, 'This is where I woke up last time,' and then after the dream had gone on a bit further I'd begin to think, 'Well, I guess this must be getting near the end of another installment,' and sure enough, about that time I'd wake up again."

The accidental encounter began to develop sinister ramifications, picked up unsavory characters, and put Big Bill Holbrook in the role of a Robin Hood.

"Or a Saint," he amended, "rescuing a beautiful dame from a bunch of lugs."

And there was, of course, the jewel.

It had a history. The fire opal, which seemed to be eternal yet living beauty, had carved upon it the likeness of Dawn's great-great-grandmother, of whom the girl was the living image.

The talented Oriental craftsman who had chiseled those features which were the essence of beauty—that wily fellow had breathed upon the cameo gem a curse.

The curse: It must not get out of the possession of the family—or else.

Death, deprivation, and a myriad other unpleasantries were predicted if the stone fell into alien hands.

The name of Seldon Appopoulis sort of slithered into the tale. This was a fat man, a lecherous fat man, a greedy fat man, who wanted—not loved—Dawn; and who wanted—and loved—the cameo opal. In some fashion that was not exactly clear to the Saint, the fat man was in a position to put a financial squeeze on her. In each succeeding dream of Andrew Faulks, Glendale bank clerk, Dawn's position became more and more untenable. In desperation she finally agreed to turn the jewel over to Appopoulis. The fat man sent for the jewel by the two henchmen whom the Saint had directed off into the Holbrook-bare woods.

"Now in this dream—this here *now* dream," Holbrook said, "I took it away from him, see? Andy Faulks went to sleep in Glendale Saturday night and—say, what day is it now?"

"Tuesday."

"Yeah, that's the way it seems to me too. And that's funny. If you're really part of this dream you'd naturally think it was Tuesday, because your time and my time would be the same. But you don't seem like part of a dream. I pinched you and—oh, nuts, I'm all mixed up."

"Let's try and be clear about this," said the Saint patiently. "You know that it's Tuesday here, but you think you're dreaming all this in Glendale on Saturday night."

"I don't know," said the other wearily. "You see, I never dreamed more than one day at a stretch before. But tonight it's been going on and on.

It's gone way past the time when I ought to have woken up. But I don't seem to be able to wake up. I've tried . . . My God, suppose I don't wake up! Suppose I never *can* wake up? Suppose I never can get back, and I have to go on and on with this, being Big Bill Holbrook——"

"You could take a trip to Glendale," Simon suggested gravely, "and try waking Faulks up."

Holbrook-Faulks stared at him with oddly unfocused eyes.

"I can't," he said huskily. "I thought of that—once. But I couldn't make myself do it. I—I'm scared . . . of what I might find. . . . Suppose——"

He broke off, his pupils dilated with the formless horror of a glimpse of something that no mind could conceive.

Simon roused him again, gently: "So you took the jewel——"

Holbrook snapped out of his reverie.

"Yeah, and I lammed out for this cabin. Dawn was supposed to meet me here. But I guess I can't control all these characters. Say," he asked suddenly, "who do you suppose I am? Faulks or Holbrook?"

"I suggest you ask your mother, old boy."

"This ain't funny. I mean, who do you *really* suppose I am? Andy Faulks is asleep and dreaming me but I've got all his memories, so am I a projection of Andy or am I me and him both? None of these other characters have any more memories than they need."

Simon wondered if the two men chasing Holbrook were his keepers; he could use a few. In fact, Simon reflected, keepers would fit into the life of Holbrook-Faulks like thread in a needle. But he sipped his brandy and urged the man to continue.

"Well, something's happened," Holbrook-Faulks said. "It never was like this before. I never could smell things before. I never could really feel them. You know how it is in a dream. But now it seems like as if you stuck a knife in me I'd bleed real blood. You don't suppose a—a reiterated dream could become reality?"

"I," said the Saint, "am a rank amateur in that department."

"Well, I was too—or Andy was, whichever of us is me—but I read everything I could get my hands on about dreams—or Andy did—and it didn't help a bit."

Most men wouldn't have heard the faint far-off stirring in the forest. But the Saint's ears, attuned by long practice to detect sound that differed from what should be there, picked up evidence of movement toward the cabin.

"Some one," he said suddenly, "and I mean one, is coming. Not your pursuers—it's from the opposite direction."

Holbrook-Faulks listened.

"I don't hear anything."

"I didn't expect you to—yet. Now that it's dark, perhaps you'd better slip outside, brother, and wait. I don't pretend to believe your yarn, but that some game is afoot is so obvious that even Sherlock Holmes could detect it. I suggest that we prepare for eventualities."

The eventuality that presently manifested itself was a girl. And it was a girl who could have been no one but Dawn Winter.

She came wearily into the cabin, disheveled, her dress torn provocatively so that sun-browned flesh showed through, her cloud of golden hair swirled in fairy patterns, her dark eyes brooding, her mouth a parted dream.

The Saint caught his breath and began to wonder whether he could really make Big Bill Holbrook wake up and vanish.

"Do you belong to the coffee and/or brandy school of thought?" he asked.

"Please." She fell carelessly into a chair, and the Saint coined a word. She was gamorous beyond belief.

"Miss Winter, pull down your dress or I'll never get this drink poured. You've turned me into an aspen. You're the most beautiful hunk of flesh I've ever seen. Have your drink and go, please."

She looked at him then, and took in the steel-cable leanness of him, the height of him, the crisp black hair, the debonair blue eyes. She smiled, and a brazen gong tolled in the Saint's head.

"Must I?" she said.

Her voice caught at the core of desire and tangled itself forever there.

"Set me some task," the Saint said uncertainly. "Name me a mountain to build, a continent to sink, a star to fetch you in the morning."

The cabin door crashed open. The spell splintered into shining shards. Holbrook-Faulks stood stony-faced against the door.

"Hello, Bill," the girl said, her eyes still on the Saint. "I came, you see."

Bill's gaze was an unwavering lance, with the Saint pinioned on its blazing tip.

"Am I gonna have trouble with you too, Saint?"

The Saint opened his mouth to answer, and stiffened as another sound reached his ears. Jockey and weight lifter were returning.

"We'll postpone any jousting over the fair lady for the moment," Simon said. "We're about to have more company."

Holbrook stared wildly around.

"Come on, Dawn. Out the window. They'll kill us."

Many times before in his checkered career the Saint had had to make decisions in a fragment of time—when a gun was leveled and a finger whitening on the trigger, when a traffic accident roared toward consummation, when a ship was sinking, when a knife flashed through candlelight. His decision now was compounded of several factors, none of which was the desire for self-preservation. The Saint rarely gave thought room to self-preservation—never when there was something more important to preserve.

He did not want this creature of tattered loveliness, this epitome of what men live for, to get out of his sight. He must therefore keep her inside the cabin. And there was no place to hide. . . .

His eyes narrowed as he looked at the two bunks. He was tearing out the mattresses before his thought was fully formed. He tossed the mattresses in a corner where shadows had retreated from the candle on the table. Then he motioned to Holbrook.

"Climb up. Make like a mattress."

He boosted the big man into the top bunk, and his hands were like striking brown snakes as he packed blankets around him and remade the bed so that it only looked untidily put together.

"Now you," he said to the girl.

She got into the lower bunk and lay flat on her back, her disturbing head in the far corner. The Saint deposited a swift kiss upon her full red lips. They were cool and soft, and the Saint was adrift for a second.

Then he covered her. He emptied a box of pine cones on the mattresses and arranged the whole to appear as a corner heap of cones.

He was busy cleaning the dishes when the pounding came on the door.

As he examined the pair, Simon Templar was struck by the fact that these men were types, such types as B pictures had imprinted upon the consciousness of the world.

The small one could be a jockey, but one with whom you could make a deal. For a consideration, he would pull a horse in the stretch or slip a Mickey into a rival rider's sarsaparilla. In the dim light that fanned out from the door, his eyes were small and ratlike, his mouth a slit of cynicism, his nose a quivering button of greed.

His heavier companion was a different but equally familiar type. This man was Butch to a T. He was large, placid, oafish, and an order taker. His not to reason why; his but to do—or cry. He'd be terribly hurt if he failed to do what he was ordered; he'd apologize, he'd curse himself.

It crossed the Saint's mind that a bank clerk such as Andrew Faulks had been described would dream such characters.

"So you lied to us," the little man snarled.

The Saint arched an eyebrow. At the same time he reached out and twisted the little man's nose, as if he were trying to unscrew it.

"When you address me, Oswald, say 'sir.' "

The little man sprang back in outraged fury. He clapped one hand to his injured proboscis, now turning a deeper purple than the night. The other hand slid under his coat.

Simon waited until he had the gun out of the holster, then leaped the intervening six feet and twisted it from the little man's hand. The Saint let the gun swing from his finger by its trigger guard.

"Take him, Mac!" grated the disarmed man.

Mac vented a kind of low growl, but did nothing but fidget as the Saint turned curious blue eyes on him. The tableau hung frozen for a long moment before the little man shattered the silence.

"Well? Ya afraid of 'im?"

"Yup," Mac said unhappily. "Criminy, Jimmy, 'f he c'n get the best uh you, well, criminy, Jimmy."

Jimmy moaned: "You mean you're gonna stand there and let just one guy take my gun away from me? Cripes, he ain't a army."

"No," Mac agreed, growing more unhappy by the second, "but he kind of seems like one, Jimmy. Didja see that jump? Criminy, Jimmy."

The Saint decided to break it up.

"Now, Oswald——"

"Didn'ja hear, Mac? Name's Jimmy."

"Oswald," the Saint said firmly, "is how I hold you in my heart. Now, Oswald, perhaps you'll pour oil on these troubled waters, before I take you limb from muscle and throw you away."

"We don't want no trouble," Jimmy said. "We want Big Bill. You got him, but we got to take him back with us."

"And who is Big Bill, and why do you want him, and why do you think I have him?"

"We know you got him," Jimmy said. "This here's Trailer Mac."

The Saint nodded at Mac.

"Charmed, I'm sure."

"Hey, Jimmy," Mac broke in, "this guy's a phony."

Jimmy blinked.

"Owls," Mac explained, "can't swim."

"What the damblasted hell has owls to do with it?" Jimmy demanded.

"He said pour owls on the something waters. So that," Mac said in triumph, "proves it."

This, the Saint thought, wanders. He restrained Jimmy from assaulting Mac, and returned to the subject.

"Why should the revelation of this gent's identity be regarded as even an intimation that I have—what was the name?—Big Bill?"

"Holbrook," Jimmy said. "Why, this is Trailer Mac. Ain't you never heard of him? He follered Loopie Louie for eighteen years and finally caught 'im in the middle of Lake Erie."

"I never heard of him," Simon said, and smiled at Mac's hurt look. "But then there are lots of people I've never heard of."

This, he thought as he said it, was hardly true. He had filed away in the indexes of his amazing memory the dossiers of almost every crook in history. He was certain that he'd have heard of such a chase if it had ever occurred.

"Anyway," Jimmy went on, "we didn't go more'n a coupla miles till Mac he says Big Bill ain't here, 'n he ain't been here, neither. Well, he come this far, 'n he didn't go no farther. So you got him. He's inside."

"The cumulative logic in that series of statements is devastating," the Saint said. "But logicians veer. History will bear me out. Aristotle was a shining example. Likewise all the boys who gave verisimilitude to idiocy by substituting syllogisms for thought processes, who evaded reality by using unsemantic verbalisms for fact-facing and, God save the mark, fact-finding."

Mac appealed to the superior intellect in his crowd.

"Whut'n hell's he talkin' about, Jimmy?"

"I mean," the Saint said, "Big Bill ain't here. Come in and case the joint."

"Whyn't cha say so?" Mac snarled, and pushed inside.

They searched nook and cranny, and Mac fingered a knothole hopefully once. They gave the bunk beds a passing glance, and were incurious about the seeming pile of pine cones in the corner. Mac boosted Jimmy up on the big central beam to peer into ceiling shadows, and they scanned the fireplace chimney.

Then they stood and looked at the Saint with resentment.

"Sump'n's fishy," Jimmy pronounced. "He's got to be here. This here"— he pointed—"is Trailer Mac."

"Maybe we better go get the boss, huh, Jimmy?"

"Yeah," Jimmy agreed. "He'll find Big Bill."

"Who," the Saint inquired, "is the boss?"

"You'll see," Jimmy promised. "He won't be scared of you. He's just down the hill in the town. Stopped off to play a game of billiards. So we'll be seein' ya, bub."

They went off into the night, and the Saint stood quite still for a moment in a little cloud of perplexity.

Never before had he been faced with a situation that was so full of holes.

He added up known data: a man who had a fabulous jewel, who claimed to be the projected dream of his alter ego; a girl of incredible beauty said to be another creation of that dream; and two characters who were after the man and/or the jewel and/or—perhaps—the girl.

Mac and Jimmy had searched the cabin. They professed to have overlooked an object the size of Big Bill Holbrook. Their proof that they had overlooked him: "This here's Trailer Mac." They assumed he would remain here while they walked four miles to the settlement and back with their boss who was said to have stopped off to shoot a game of billiards.

But would a man on the trail of that fire opal stop off to play billiards?

Would two pseudo-tough guys go away and leave their quarry unguarded?

No, the Saint decided. These were the observable facts, but they were unimportant. They masked a larger, more sinister pattern. Great forces must be underlying the surface trivia. Undeniably, the jewel was a thing to drive men to madness. It could motivate historic bloodshed. The girl, too, possessing the carven features of the gem, could drive men to—anything. But for the life of him, the Saint could not get beneath the surface pattern to what must be the real issues. He could only cling to the conviction that they had to exist, and that they must be deadly.

He turned back to the bunk beds.

"Come on out, kids," he said. "The big bad wolves have temporarily woofed away."

Fear lingered in the dark depths of Dawn Winter's eyes, making her even more hauntingly beautiful. The Saint found strange words forming on his lips, as if some other being possessed them.

He seemed to be saying: "Dawn . . . I've seen the likeness of every beauty in history or imagination. Every one of them would be a drab shadow beside you. You are so beautiful that the world would bow down and worship you—if the world knew of your existence. Yet it's impossible that the world doesn't know. If one single person looked at you, the word would go out. Cameramen would beat a path to your door, artists would dust off their palettes, agents would clamor with contracts. But somehow this hasn't happened. Why? Where, to be trite, have you been all my life?"

He couldn't define the expression which now entered her eyes. It might have been bewilderment, or worry, or fear, or an admixture.

"I—I——" She put a hand as graceful as a calla lily against her forehead. "I—don't know."

"Oh, don't let's carry this too far." It sounded more like himself again. "Where were you born, where did you go to school, who are your parents?"

She worried at him with wide, dark eyes.

"That's just the trouble. I—don't remember any childhood. I remember only my great-great-grandmother. I never saw her, of course, but she's the only family I know about."

Big Bill's facial contortions finally caught the Saint's eye. They were something to watch. His mouth worked like a corkscrew, his eyebrows did a cancan.

"I gather," said the Saint mildly, "that you are giving me the hush-hush. I'm sorry, comrade, but I'm curious. Suppose you put in your two cents."

"I told you once," Big Bill said. "I told you the truth."

"Pish," Simon said. "Also, tush."

"It's true," Big Bill insisted. "I wouldn't lie to the Saint."

The girl echoed this in a voice of awe.

"The Saint? The Robin Hood of Modern Crime, the twentieth century's brightest buccaneer, the"—she blushed—"the devil with dames."

It occurred to Simon, with a shock of remembrance, that her phrases were exactly those of Big Bill's when he learned his host's identity. And even then they had been far from new. The Saint thought of this for a moment, and rejected what it suggested. He shook his head.

"Let's consider that fire opal then, children. It's slightly fabulous, you know. Now, I don't think anybody knows more than I do about famous jools. Besides such well-known items as the Cullinan and the Hope diamonds, I am familiar with the history of almost every noteworthy bauble that was ever dug up. There's the Waters diamond, for example. No more than a half dozen persons know of its existence, its perfect golden flawless color. And the Chiang emerald, that great and beautiful stone that has been seen by only three living people, myself included. But this cameo opal is the damn warp of history. It couldn't be hidden for three generations without word of it getting out. In the course of time, I couldn't have helped hearing about it. But I didn't. . . . So it doesn't exist. But it does. I know it exists; I've held it in my hand——"

"And put it in your pocket," Big Bill said.

The Saint felt in his jacket.

"So I did." He pulled out the chamois bag with its precious contents and made as if to toss it. "Here."

Big Bill stopped him with flared hands.

"Please keep it for me, Mr Templar. Things will get rather bad around here soon. I don't want Appopoulis to get his fat hands on it."

"Soon? Surely not for a couple of hours."

Big Bill frowned.

"Things happen so quickly in dreams. This may *seem* real, but it'll still hold the screwy pattern you'd expect."

The Saint made a gesture of annoyance.

"Still sticking to your story? Well, maybe you're screwy or maybe you just think I am. But I'd rather face facts. As a matter of fact, I insist on it." He turned back to the girl. "For instance, darling, I know that you exist. I've kissed you."

Big Bill growled, glared, but did nothing as the Saint waited calmly.

Simon continued: "I have the evidence of my hands, lips, and eyes that you have all the common things in common with other women. In addition you have this incredible, unbelievable loveliness. When I look at you, I find it hard to believe that you're real. But that's only a figure of speech. My senses convince me. Yet you say you don't remember certain things that all people remember. Why?"

She repeated her gesture of confusion.

"I—don't know. I can't remember any past."

"It would be a great privilege and a rare pleasure," the Saint said gently, "to provide you with a past to remember."

Another low growl rumbled in Big Bill's chest, and the Saint waited again for developments. None came, and it struck the Saint that all the characters in this muddled melodrama had one characteristic in common— a certain cowardice in the clutch. Even Dawn Winter showed signs of fear, and nobody had yet made a move to harm her. It was only another of the preposterous paradoxes that blended into the indefinable unreality of the whole.

Simon gave it up. If he couldn't get what he thought was truth from either of these two, he could watch and wait and divine the truth. Conflict hung on the wind, and conflict drags truth out of her hiding place and casts her naked before watching eyes.

"Well, souls," he said, "what now? The unholy three will be back sometime. You could go now. There is the wide black night to wander in."

"No," Big Bill said. "Now that you're in this, give us your help, Saint. We need you."

"Just what, then," Simon asked, "are we trying to prevent, or accomplish?"

"Selden Appopoulis must not get his hands on the opal or Dawn. He wants both. He'll stop at nothing to get them."

"I believe you mentioned a curse breathed on this gewgaw by some Oriental character."

Dawn Winter's voice once more tangled itself in Simon's heart. As long as he could remember that quality—of far-off bells at dusk, of cellos on a midnight hill—time would never again pass slowly enough.

"Death shall swoop on him," she chanted, "who holds this ancient gem from its true possessor, but all manner of things shall plague him before that dark dread angel shall come to rest at his shoulder. His nights shall be sleepless with terror, and hurts shall dog his accursed steps by day. Beauty shall bring an end to the vandal."

The mood of her strange incantation, far more than the actual words, seemed to linger on the air after she had finished, so that in spite of all rationality the Saint felt spectral fingers on his spine. He shook off the spell with conscious resolution.

"It sounds very impressive," he murmured, "in a gruesome sort of way. Reminds me of one of those zombie pictures. But where, may I ask, does this place me in the scheme of dire events? I have the jewel."

"You," Big Bill Holbrook said, "will die, as I must, and as Trailer Mac and Jimmy must. They stole it from Dawn; I stole it from them."

The Saint smiled.

"Well, if that's settled, let's pass on to more entertaining subjects bordering on the carnal. Miss Winter, my car is just down the hill. If Bill is resigned to his fate, suppose we leave him and his playmates to their own fantastic devices and drift off into the night."

Her face haloed with pleasure.

"I'd like it," she said. "But I—I just can't."

"Why not? You're over three years old. Nobody is sitting on your chest."

"I can't do what I like, somehow," she said. "I can only do what I must. It's always that way."

"This," the Saint said to nobody in particular, "sounds like one of those stories that fellow Charteris might write. And what's the matter with you?" he demanded of Holbrook. "A little earlier you were eager to get rough with me because I admired the lady. Now you sit listening with disgusting indifference to my indecent proposal. I assure you it was indecent, from your viewpoint."

Big Bill grinned.

"It just occurred to me. She can't go with you. She must do what she must. She can't get out of my sight. Good old Andy," he added.

The Saint turned his eyes away and stared into space, wondering. His wandering gaze focused on a small wall mirror that reflected Dawn Winter. Her features were blurred, run together, an amorphous mass. Simon wondered what could have happened to that mirror.

He swung back to face Bill Holbrook.

"I'm afraid," he said softly, but with the iron will showing through his velvet tones, "that we must have some truth in our little séance. Like the walrus, I feel the time has come to speak of many things. From this moment, you are my prisoners. The length of your durance vile depends on you. Who are you, Miss Winter?"

The look she turned on him made his hands tingle. Hers was a face for cupping between tender palms. Dark and troubled, her eyes pleaded for understanding, for sympathy.

"I told you all I know," she pleaded. "I've tried and tried, ever since I could remember anything, to think of—well, all those things you think of at times."

Again she passed a hand across her face, as if wiping away veils.

"I don't ever remember snagging a stocking on the way to an important appointment," she said. "And I know that girls do. I never had to fight for my"—she colored—"my honor, whatever that is. And I know that girls like me have fought for this something I don't understand, by the time they've reached my age. Whatever that is," she added pensively. "I don't even know how old I am, or where I've been."

A pattern suddenly clicked into place in the Saint's brain, a pattern so monstrous, so inhuman as to arouse his destructive instincts to the point of homicidal mania. The look he turned on Big Bill Holbrook was ice and flame.

His voice was pitched at conversational level, but each word fell from his lips like a shining sword.

"Do you know," he said, "I'm beginning to get some new ideas. Not very nice ideas, chum. And if I'm guessing right about what you and your fellow scum have done to this innocent girl, you are liable to cost your insurance company money."

He moved toward Holbrook with a liquid grace that had all the co-ordination of a panther's movement—and the menace. Big Bill Holbrook leaned back from it.

"Stop acting the knight in armor," he protested. "What in hell you talking about?"

"It should have been obvious before," Simon Templar said. "Up on your feet, Holbrook."

Holbrook remained at ease.

"If you've got an explanation for all this that doesn't agree with mine, I want to know it."

The Saint paused. There was honest curiosity in the man's voice—and no fear. That cowardice which had characterized him before was replaced with what seemed an honest desire to hear the Saint's idea.

"This girl," the Saint said, "whoever she is, has breeding, grace, and beauty out of this world. She has been brought up under expensive and sheltered surroundings. You can see that in her every gesture, every expression. She was bred to great wealth, perhaps nobility, or even royalty."

Big Bill leaned forward in almost an agony of concentration. Every word of Simon Templar's might have been a twenty-dollar gold piece, the way he reached for it with every sense.

The Saint patted his jacket pocket.

"This jewel is the symbol of her position—heiress, princess, queen, or what have you. You and your unsavory companions kidnaped her, and are holding her for ransom. That would be wicked enough; but you've done worse. Somewhere in the course of your nasty little scheme, it seemed like a good idea to destroy a part of her beauty that could be dangerous to you and your precious pals. So you destroyed her mind. With drugs, I have no doubt—drugs that have dulled her mind until she has no memory. Your reasons are clear enough—it was just a sound form of insurance. And now your gang has split up, fighting over the spoils. I don't know who would have come out on top, if you hadn't happened to run into me. But I know what the end is going to be now—and you aren't going to like it. Get on your feet!"

The command was like a pistol shot, and Big Bill Holbrook jumped. Then he leaned back again and chuckled in admiration.

"Everything that's been said about you is true. There's nobody like you. That's so much better than Andy Faulks did there's no comparison. Say, that really would have been something, and look, it'd have explained why she couldn't remember who she was. Saint, I got to hand it to you. Too bad you're not in bed in Glendale."

For once of a very few times in his life, the Saint was taken aback. The words were spoken with such ease, such sincerity, that Simon's deadly purpose cooled to a feeling of confusion. While it is true that a man who is accustomed to danger, to gambling for high stakes with death as a forfeit, could simulate feelings he did not actually feel, it is seldom that a man of Big Bill Holbrook's obvious I Q can look annihilation in the face with an admiring grin.

Something was still wrong, but wrong in the same way that everything in the whole episode was wrong—wrong with that same unearthly off-key distortion that defeated logical diagnosis.

The Saint took out a cigarette and lighted it, slowly; and over the hiss of the match he heard other sounds, which resolved themselves into a blur of footsteps.

Simon glanced at his watch. Jimmy and Mac had been gone less than half an hour. It was impossible for them to be returning from the village four miles away.

What had Holbrook said? Something about everything happening faster in dreams? But that was in the same vein of nonsense. Maybe they'd met the boss at the foot of the hill.

Holbrook said: "What is it? Did you hear something?"

"Only your friends again."

Fear came once more to Holbrook and Dawn Winter. Their eyes were wide and dark with it, turning instantly toward the bunk beds.

"No," Simon said. "Not this time. We'll have this out in the open."

"But he'll kill us!" Holbrook began to babble. "It's awful, the things he'll do. You don't know him, Saint. You can't imagine, you couldn't——"

"I can imagine anything," said the Saint coldly. "I've been doing that for some time, and I'm tired of it. Now I'd prefer to know."

He crossed the room as the footsteps outside turned into knuckles at the door.

"Welcome to our study club," the Saint said.

Trailer Mac and Jimmy preceded an enormous hulk through the door and, when they saw Holbrook and Dawn, charged like lions leaping on paralyzed gazelles.

The Saint moved in a lightning blur. Two sharp cracks of fist on flesh piled Mac in one corner, Jimmy in another. They lay still.

A buttery chuckle caused the Saint to turn. He was looking into a small circular hole. A .38, he computed. He raised his eyes to twins of the barrel, but these were eyes. They lay deep in flesh that swelled in yellowish-brown rolls, flowing fatly downward to describe one of the fattest men the Saint had ever seen. They could only have belonged to a man called Selden Appopoulis.

"Mr Sydney Greenstreet, I presume?" Simon drawled.

The buttery chuckle set a sea of flesh ebbing and flowing.

"A quick action, sir, and an efficient direction of action. I compliment you, and am saddened that you must die."

The Saint shrugged. He knew that this fat man, though butter-voiced, had a heart of iridium. His eyes were the pale expressionless orbs of a killer. His mouth was thin with determination, his hand steady with purpose. But Simon had faced all those indications before.

"I hate to disappoint you, comrade," he said lightly, "but that line has a familiar ring. And yet I'm still alive."

Appopoulis appraised and dismissed the Saint, though his eyes never wavered. He spoke to Holbrook.

"The opal. Quickly!"

The butter of his voice had frozen into oleaginous icicles; and Holbrook quailed under the bite of their sharp edges.

"I haven't got it, Appopoulis. The Saint has it."

Simon was astonished at the change in the fat man. It was subtle, admittedly, but it was there nonetheless. Fear came into the pale gray eyes which had been calmly contemplating murder as a climax to unspeakable inquisitions. Fear and respect. The voice melted butter again.

"So," he said warmly. "Simon Templar, the Robin Hood of Modern Crime, the twentieth century's brightest buccaneer, the—ah—devil with dames. I had not anticipated this."

Once more it struck the Saint that the descriptive phrases were an exact repetition of Holbrook's. And once more it struck him that the quality of fear in this weird quintet was not strained. And once more he wondered about Holbrook's fantastic tale. . . .

"You are expecting maybe Little Lord Feigenbaum?" Simon asked. "Or what do you want?"

"The cameo opal, for one thing," Appopoulis said easily. "For the other, the girl."

"And what do you intend to do with them?"

"Cherish them, sir. Both of them."

His voice had encyclopedic lust and greed, and the Saint felt as if small things crawled on him.

Before he could make an answer, stirrings in their respective corners announced the return of Mac and Jimmy to another common plane of existence. Without a word they got groggily to their feet, shook their heads clear of trip hammers, and moved toward the Saint.

"Now, Mr Templar," said Appopoulis, "you have a choice. Live, and my desires are granted without violence, or die, and they are spiced with emotions at fever heat."

Mac and Jimmy had halted: one small and thunderstruck, one large and paralyzed.

"Boss," quavered Jimmy, "did youse say Templar? Da Saint?"

"The same." Simon bowed.

"Chee!" Mac breathed. "Da Saint. Da Robin Hood of Modern Crime, da——"

"Please," Simon groaned. "Another record, if you don't mind."

"Boss, we ain't got a chanct," Jimmy said.

Appopoulis turned his eyes on the little man.

"He," the boss said, "has the opal."

This news stiffened their gelatinous spines long enough to set them at the Saint in a two-directional charge.

The Saint swerved to meet it. He held Jimmy between himself and the unwavering gun of Appopoulis with one hand. With the other he wrought havoc on the features of Mac.

It was like dancing, like feathers on the breeze, the way the Saint moved. Even to himself it had the kind of exhilaration that a fighter may only experience once in a lifetime. He had a sense of power, of supernatural co-ordination, of invincibility beyond anything he had ever known. He cared nothing for the knowledge that Appopoulis was skipping around on the outskirts of the fray, trying to find an angle from which he could terminate it with a well-placed shot. Simon knew that it was no fear of killing Jimmy that stayed the fat man's finger on the trigger—it was simply the knowledge that it would have wasted a shot, that the Saint could have gone on using Jimmy as a shield, alive or dead. The Saint knew this coolly and detachedly, as if with a mind separate from his own, while he battered Mac's face into a varicolored pulp.

Then Mac's eyes glazed and he went down; and the Saint's right hand snaked hipwards for his own gun while his left flung Jimmy bodily at the paunch of Appopoulis.

And that was when the amazing, the incredible and impossible thing went wrong. For Jimmy didn't fly away from the Saint's thrust, as he should have, like a marble from a slingshot. Somehow he remained entangled with the Saint's arm, clinging to it as if bogged in some indissoluble birdlime, with a writhing tenacity that was as inescapable as a nightmare. And Simon looked down the barrel of Appopoulis's gun and saw the fat man's piggy eyes brighten with something that might have been lust. . . .

The Saint tried to throw a shot at him, but he was off balance, and the frenzied squirming of his erstwhile shield made it like trying to shoot from the back of a bucking horse. The bullet missed by a fraction of an inch, and buried itself in the wall beside the mirror. Then Appopoulis fired back.

The Saint felt a jar, and a flame roared inside his chest. Somehow, he couldn't pull the trigger any more. The gun fell from his limp fingers. His incredulous eyes looked full in the mirror and saw a neat black hole over his heart, saw it begin to spread as his life's blood gushed out.

It was strange to realize that this was it, and it had happened to him at last, as it had always been destined to happen someday, and in an instant he was going to cheat to the back of the book for the answer to the greatest mystery of all. Yet his last conscious thought was that his image was sharp and clear in the mirror. When he had seen Dawn's reflection, it had been like one seen in an agitated pool. . . .

When he opened his eyes again it was broad daylight, and the intensity of the light told him that it must have been more than twelve hours since he had been shot.

He was lying on the floor of the cabin. He felt for his heart. It was beating strongly. His hand did not come away sticky with blood.

His eyes turned hesitantly down to his shirt. There was no hole in it. He jumped to his feet, felt himself all over, examined himself in the mirror. He was as whole as he'd ever been; and he felt fine.

He looked around the cabin. The mattresses were piled in the corner under the pine cones, the bunks unmade. Otherwise there were no signs of the brawl the night before. No trace of Jimmy and Mac, or Appopoulis. No Big Bill Holbrook. No Dawn. . . .

And no hole in the wall beside the mirror where his hopeless shot at Appopoulis had buried itself.

The Saint shook his head. If it had all been a dream, he might have to seriously consider consulting a psychiatrist. Dreams reach only a certain point of vividness. What he remembered was too sharp of definition, too coherent, too consecutive. Yet if it wasn't a dream, where were the evidences of reality, the bullet hole in his chest, in the wall?

He went to the door. There should be footprints. His cabin had rated with Grand Central Station for traffic last night.

There were no footprints, other than his own.

Simon reached for a cigarette, and suddenly sniffed it suspiciously before he put it in his mouth. If some joker, either in fun or malice, had adulterated his tobacco with some more exotic herb . . . But that, too, was absurd. A jag of those dimensions would surely bequeath a hangover to match; but his head was as clear as the mountain air.

He fumbled in his pockets for a match. Instead, his questing fingers touched something solid, a shape that was oddly familiar—yet impossibly alien. The tactile sensation lasted only for an instant, before his hand recoiled as if the thing had been red hot. He was afraid, actually afraid, to take it out.

The address of Andrew Faulks was in the Glendale directory. The house was a modest two-bedroom affair on a side street near Forest Lawn Memorial Park. A wreath hung on the door. A solemn gentleman who looked like, and undoubtedly was, an undertaker opened the door. He looked like Death rubbing white hands together.

"Mr Faulks passed on last night," he said in answer to the Saint's query. Unctuous sorrow overlaid the immediate landscape.

"Wasn't it rather sudden?"

"Ah, not exactly, sir. He went to sleep last Saturday, passed into a coma, and never awakened."

"At what time," Simon asked, "did he die?"

"At ten-forty," the man replied. "It was a sad death. He was in a delirium. He kept shouting about shooting someone, and talked about a saint."

Simon had moved into the house while listening to the tale of death and found himself looking off the hallway into a well-lighted den. His keen eyes noted that while most of the shelves were gay with the lurid jackets of adventure fiction, one section was devoted to works on psychology and psychiatry.

Here were the tomes of Freud, Adler, Jung, Brill, Bergson, Krafft-Ebing, and lesser lights. A book lay open on a small reading table.

The Saint stepped inside the room to look at it. It was titled *In Darkest Schizophrenia* by William J Holbrook, Ph D.

Simon wondered what the psychic-phenomena boys would do with this one. This, he thought, would certainly give them a shot in the aura.

"Mrs Faulks is upstairs, sir," the professional mourner was saying. "Are you a friend of the family? I'll be glad to ask whether she can see you."

"I wish you'd just show her this." Simon forced one hand into a pocket. "And ask her——"

He never finished the question. Never.

There was nothing in the pocket for his hand to find. Nothing to meet his fingertips but a memory that was even then darkening and dying out along his nerves.

AFTERWORD

AND SO, *dear friends, incurable devotees, tolerant critics, good book-buyers, enthusiastic thieves—I take leave of you again.*

At the end of The First Saint Omnibus, *I left you with the firm proclamation that, come hell or high water, you could confidently*

WATCH FOR THE SIGN OF THE SAINT

HE WILL BE BACK!

I cannot give you that assurance today.

Much as I have abused you, you have been generous to me. I have been able to save a little money, in spite of the best efforts of the tax collectors. I still get royalties on all the books I have written. The Saint radio show (as of this writing) is still on the air. The Saint comic strip is syndicated to an increasing list of newspapers from New York to Los Angeles, and also from Stockholm to Singapore. I don't have to work very hard to avert starvation.

And even the court jester should have the right to retire sometime.

I have a few unfinished projects. I have a few fairly good short stories which have already appeared in magazines, accumulating in a drawer against the day when there may be enough of them to assemble in another book. I have half a dozen biographical articles of quite a different kind, which also have appeared in magazines, and I had planned to make another book of those, under the rather brilliant title Not So Saintly. *But I don't have enough of them yet, and the way things are going I don't know when I shall complete them to my satisfaction. I have had one more Saint novel in my head for a couple of years, but not a line of it written yet, although long-suffering publishers pester me for it at least once a month.*

It is good to have a few things waiting to be done, a few ideas to play with and make vague plans for. But I am very lazy, as I said, and getting around to them is another matter.

So I make no more promises. And I shall be as interested as you are to see what happens.

LESLIE CHARTERIS

Hollywood, California
18 April 1951